LEGEND LAND

NOAH BARFIELD

LEGEND LAND

WHERE LEGENDS GO TO DIE

NOAH BARFIELD

Legend Land

Editors: Donna Melillo, Adam Tillinghast, Christian Pacheco
Cover Design: Jason Kauffmann / Firelight Interactive /
firelightinteractive.com
Interior Design: Kyle Weichman

Indigo River Publishing
3 West Garden Street Ste. 352
Pensacola, FL 32502
www.indigoriverpublishing.com

Ordering Information:
Quantity sales: Special discounts are available on quantity purchases by corporations, associations, and others. For details, contact the publisher at the address above.

Orders by U.S. trade bookstores and wholesalers: Please contact the publisher at the address above.

Printed in the United States of America

Publisher's Cataloging-in-Publication Data is available upon request.

Library of Congress Control Number: 2016931445

ISBN: 978-0-9962330-7-1

First Edition

With Indigo River Publishing, you can always expect great books, strong voices, and meaningful messages. Most importantly, you'll always find…words worth reading.

To my mother, Mandy, for supporting me.
And to my father, Chase, for helping my dreams come true.

CHAPTER ONE

There comes a time in your life when you begin to wonder: to wonder about life, about death, about yourself…about everything. You wonder what fate lies for you beyond the grave, how the mechanisms of the cosmos function; you wonder on the origins of everything that is, was, or will be. Sitting on the side of the dirt road in this dark forest, where the sunshine does not penetrate and only the most desperate of the common rabble dare to wander, I wonder. I wonder what it's like to not know the answers to these questions. I feel the weight of an individual burdened with supreme knowledge, yet I cannot help but feel that there is more to discover in the universe. Some part of me still wonders if I do not know all there is to know about anything—about everything; I am currently crushing that part of me in a timely and systematic fashion. I simply cannot afford to not know everything. To be ignorant is to invite chaos into the fold, and chaos is something that cannot be tolerated. Still, I wonder if all of this knowledge is a blessing or a curse. Some creatures would say it is bliss to not know all of these things, and some might say that it is the worst kind of torture to tolerate even the slightest shred of ignorance. I stand up and put a black-gloved hand on one of the old, ancient oak trees that tower above me; these are the trees of Legend Land, or "The Black Forest." This is where legends come to die. They have been forgotten, tossed away, or otherwise disregarded in some way. There are others who come to this land seeking power by replicating the actions of past legends, hoping to gain some notoriety; they pretend to be what they are not. Occasionally a real legend, such as myself, will make it here, though this is a rare occurrence. I can remember the time when this was a place filled with legends that still had some semblance of power and dignity; now it is a world of charlatans and criminals. For instance, take the wolf that is currently devouring the girl across the road—a mere criminal, a waste of space.

I quickly walk over to the wolf, who by this point has devoured the girl whole. With one swift stroke of my blade, I slice open the creature's bulging belly and watch with a carefully neutral expression as the girl tumbles out, covered in stomach fluid. These creatures are filled with such greed that they put their own lives at risk to fulfill it. I say nothing as the girl comes to herself and looks up at me, determination and caution etched on her face. Her emotions are splayed out clearly for me to read. At this moment I could do a multitude of things, but I decide to simply wait a moment, letting her take in my appearance. A whisper of wind lifts my hair briefly off my shoulders, the sunlight filtering through the autumn leaves above nearly turning my dark locks purple. The girl stares into my dark eyes. Instantly, I feel a tug in some deeper part of me that I had long forgotten about—the unfamiliar sensation of feeling connected to an individual. I blink, clearing my mind, and the immediate feeling disappears. But the vague impression still lingers.

"Do you have some spare clothes? Preferably some not covered in wolf guts," she asks, looking down at herself and wiping her slimy hands on the grass. Generally, I endeavor to not give out charity unless it will benefit me in some way; however, I must admit to myself that this girl intrigues me. Regardless, I cannot allow myself to be distracted at such a crucial phase in my plan.

"Um…hello? Are you going to give me some clothes? Or am I going to have to beg some other stranger for some?" she asks, glaring up at me.

Does she know nothing of courtesy? I can tolerate a great many things as long as they will benefit me in some way or another, but one thing I cannot stand is rudeness. Crossing my arms across the dark material of my shirt, my cloak brushes the scuff marks on my boots, the sound of tightening leather creaking out as my hands become fists. When the girl stands, reaching her full height, average for a human female, she must raise her gaze above my chest to continue making obstinate eye contact.

"What makes you believe that you have the right to not only ask for clothes that I may or may not have, but also be utterly rude when I don't immediately comply?" She opens her mouth to interrupt me, but I raise my voice and glare at her. "I just saved your life, and you have the audacity to be rude to me? In addition, you dare to try and interrupt me? I do not tolerate disrespect, and I expect you to develop some manners quickly if you still entertain any hope of getting what you desire."

She makes a small move toward me, and I unsheathe my sword quickly and wrap one gloved hand around her throat, shoving her against a nearby tree, holding the edge of my blade to her throat. She ceases trying to move when my grip on her throat tightens. I grit my teeth as I press the edge of my blade harder into her neck, knowing if she makes another move, I will end her life. "Cease moving or I will not restrain myself."

She moves her hand toward my sword, and I quickly sheathe it, throwing her violently to the ground. I clench my fist, trembling slightly with restraint. Slowly I let out a breath, lowering my arm, unclenching my fist. She starts to scoot away, and my hand goes to my sword quickly, but both of us stop. Trying to keep my voice as calm as possible I speak, "I will make you a deal. You will apologize for your rudeness, and I will give you some clothes."

"You just put your sword to my throat and threatened me! I'm not making any deal with you! If anything, you should be the one apologizing to me!" she shouts as she stands up. "In fact," she continues, pointing a slimy finger at me, "I'm going to take your pack and whatever's in it. Then you will apologize for your rudeness to me!" She wipes her hand on a tree and pulls a dagger out of her boot.

This wench wishes to test herself against me? If I was in a more humorous mood, the mere thought of this girl wishing to challenge me would cause laughter to burst forth from me into the forest. As I am not in a humorous mood, however, I instead quickly remove my sword. With a quick flick of my wrist, I send her dagger spinning from her hand. I quickly close the distance and slam my knee into her stomach and she crumples over; I grab her by the red roots of her hair and throw her against a tree. "Apologize, now!" I growl, pointing my sword at her. She stands up slowly and spits at my feet, contempt etched in her vicious snarl. I bring my boot up and catch her in the chin, stepping forward to run my sword through her, but she quickly dives to the left. I spin quickly, following her and lunge at her, twisting in the same movement as she throws a dagger at me. I complete my spin and slam my elbow into her temple, and she crumples.

I pause, tightening my grip on my sword before putting it back in its sheath. I kneel down and take a piece of rope out of my pack, quickly moving to tie her hands and feet together; if she wishes to be disrespectful to me, then she will learn the consequences. Suddenly her eyes snap open and she spins on the ground, swinging her legs at me and flipping herself backwards away from me, slinging a dagger at me. I fall backward flat on the ground to avoid the dagger, then stand quickly as the girl launches herself at me. I knock her away with a blow from the back of my hand and slam my foot down toward her throat. Rolling to the left, she aims a kick between my legs. I dodge and grab her hair, slamming my knee into her nose, causing her to reel back.

Before she can recover, I close the distance and thrust my foot at her knee, but she moves her leg and hooks it around mine, using her free leg to kick me between my legs, using the point of her elbow to crush my throat. I drop to my knees as the pack is wrenched from my shoulders, and all I can do is shake as my body registers the pain and my mind screams for me to overcome it. I grit my teeth and stand up shakily, but the girl kicks me in the chin and I land on my back. There was no resistance from my body this time as I stand up and look around, but the girl is gone. I growl low in my throat and turn around, slamming my fist into the nearest tree, closing my eyes. It takes everything I have to not wrench this tree from the ground, but I will save my anger for the detestable wench who has stolen from me.

I open my eyes, and I can spot the trail of her moving through the forest, my ears picking up the snapping of twigs. Without a moment's hesitation, I find myself chasing after her.

As I get closer to the girl, I can hear her more clearly and I speed up. Once she's within sight, I leap toward her and tackle her, rolling as we hit the ground. I complete the roll and stand, pack in hand, feeling victorious. I kick her in the face as she tries to stand up, and she crumples to the ground again. I stomp down at her, intending to crush her skull, when she catches my boot with her hands for a brief moment before throwing my foot to the side and standing up, grabbing my sword and pulling it out of its sheath as she jumps back.

"Enough!" I roar, extending my hand. Tendrils of snarling, hissing, inky black shadow leap up from the ground behind her, pulling her back and binding her to the tree securely, more tendrils of shadow wrapping around her mouth and eyes. She still clutches my sword and I grab the hilt, wrenching it from her grasp and slamming the pommel of it into her chest before sheathing it again. I must teach her what happens when she steals from me. I squeeze my hand by my side and the tendrils of shadow squeeze her tighter, the bark of the tree groaning and cracking, the strain evident on her face. Suddenly her face goes lax and, after a moment, I relax my entire body and the tendrils of shadow disappear.

The girl drops unceremoniously to the ground, and I cross my arms across my chest. I will not be mistaken for a fool and believe another ploy or trick she has up her sleeve. I take a slow, deep breath and close my eyes for a moment, removing myself from the present. In the span of a few minutes, this girl has ruined my entire day—all because I was careless. What did it matter to me if the girl was devoured by the wolf? Nothing. It didn't matter at all. Then why? Why did I have to save her? I grit my teeth and shake my head, opening my eyes with a snarl—simply careless! I clench my fists and grind my boot into the ground. The small amount of light that is able to filter through the thick leaves of the trees is growing smaller until it fades slowly away, the creaking of my tightening leather gloves mixing with the hissing and snapping of the shadows circling my feet. I stomp my foot and they snap up at me, then slink back down under the fire in my gaze, hissing restlessly, but slinking away all the same. The girl squirms and my eyes widen slightly, unclenching my fists; she is more resilient than I thought. My body tenses, hand on my sword, as I wait for her to wake; when she does, she will have wished that she had been crushed. Her eyes flutter open and she tilts her head up at me, looking at me blearily.

"What…where am I?" she groans, rubbing her head and sitting up.

She looks at me again and I hold the hilt of my sword tighter; what game is she playing? The shadows slink into the ground and begin to creep toward her from behind when she asks, "Do you know where I am?" in a voice more polite than my ears have heard in this land of dead legends. The shadows withdraw and my hand unclenches while I look deep into her eyes and delve into her consciousness, being careful to not alert her to my mental presence inside her mind. The result is even more surprising than her survival of the shadows: her mind is completely blank—a clean slate.

That's not…it can't be possible—at least it shouldn't be possible! I delve deeper, and the girl whimpers as I push further, though her mindscape remains unchanging. This shouldn't be possible! I grit my teeth and growl in annoyance. Why is there nothing?! She cannot hide what she has done from me! She slumps over crying and gives a shriek that provokes no pity as I slither deeper into her, probing out at every opportunity. I will leave no stone unturned. This girl has stolen from and insulted me, and now she dares to think that she can hide her crimes from me! I will not be denied by this…blank nothing.

I blink away sweat, my hands trembling as I grip her hard enough to leave bruises, the shadows snapping at me insistently. Reveal yourself to me!

The shadows leap at the girl and I grab them, squeezing them until they whimper and go limp. "Do not interfere," I growl, turning my attention back to her. I resume my efforts, the shadows slinking away, spitting angrily. The deeper I must go into this nothingness, the more difficult it is to keep a hold on myself; I will not lose myself to a vacuum. Red clouds my vision and I gasp out, severing the link.

I stand up, shaking, wiping blood from my mouth, eying the girl warily. There is something in her after all; curious.

After a few moments, she stirs and sits up, looking up at me. "I'm sorry... I seemed to...I don't know...I..."

I sit down and nod. This girl represents something unique; she is broken and unknown to even herself. She can be molded in any way I desire; her fate rests in my hands. I tilt my head slightly, my eyes flashing. I will make her strong, and she will support me. She will be a pillar upon which I can build. But now, she is mere dust; she will have to be handled with care.

"It's alright," I say soothingly. She looks down at the ground and I break the silence. "Do you remember anything?"

"No," she says, softly shaking her head. "I feel like something was in my head...but the last thing I remember is waking up and seeing you."

"It seems you have a case of amnesia," I say and she frowns; she will never trust me if I can't convince her that I know what is wrong with her and present a solution to that problem. "I don't know how long it will last, but these things normally take time; I get the feeling this has happened to you before but you may not know it."

"How did I get here?" she asks again looking at me.

Without hesitation, I say, "I honestly have no idea." She frowns again. "I found you here, passed out, covered in slime. I looked around the surrounding area and found the dead body of a wolf, split open along the stomach." She says nothing, and I hold up one of her daggers. "I also found this," setting it in front of her as her eyes widen.

"I don't remember that," she says, picking up the dagger and turning it slowly. "Did I kill it? Am I a killer?"

"I don't presume to know anything about your past," I say; she can know nothing of what I know. Considering her behavior, this shouldn't be too difficult to conceal; the problem will be having her use her skills without triggering any memories of her past—if there are any memories to trigger. "However, what I do know is that you can make a future for yourself, independent of your past. Even if you were a killer, you don't remember and can't be held responsible." I tap the dagger with a finger and she blinks. "What you do now determines who you will become."

"How will I even remember who I am though? What if this happens again?" Her hand tightens around the dagger; I tilt her chin up slowly so that I'm looking into her eyes. I resist the urge to grab her throat, my fingers tensing slightly; old habits. The girl before me is not the same one as before; I must keep that in mind going forward.

I force calm into my voice, "I can make it to where you retain your memories from this encounter on, but I cannot guarantee success."

She ponders it for a moment then nods. "Alright, do it."

I slowly move my hands to hold her head, and I squeeze, my fingers digging into her skull. "Are you sure? You lose nothing if you do not wish to; it will be an extremely painful process," I warn; I must convince her that I only have her wellbeing in mind.

"I'm sure," she says firmly, hands tightening into fists. "If I don't do this now, then I will be losing everything I would have gained if I had gone through with it. I stand to lose my future, an entire life time. I have no idea how long I've been this way but...I...I can't continue on not being able to remember yesterday." Her eyes look into me and in them I see something I thought I would never see again. I shake my head slightly; no, that is past. Now I must do what is necessary to make the past present again. She has resolve; it will help her overcome the pain. Most likely.

I force my way into her mind roughly. Despite that, she gives no resistance, and I faintly register her pain; a mere indulgence I partake in for the annoyance she caused earlier. My more human traits cannot all be suppressed I suppose. I delve deeper, my probe becoming a drill as it bores down into her mind, past the layer she remembers; I am not interested in those few paltry minutes of remembrance. I clamp down forcefully on any memories that try to suppress themselves as I dig deeper; no part of her will deny me from this point on. She is mine, and I will do as I see fit; do not dare hide from me! Though she starts to shake in my hands, I continue to go deeper into her mind, relying on her resolve to hold her together. She may be able to hide things from herself, willingly or not, but no amount of subconscious shall hide anything from me; there will be no more secrets.

Something bars my way and I grit my teeth, forcing myself against it until my ears register her screams. Her hand shoots out to grab my arm, her skin touching the barest sliver of my exposed skin. I gasp, roaring into her; not this! My eyes widen briefly before I screw them shut, snarling, shoving past the barrier and then down and planting an anchor. I yank myself away, gasping, my eyes flying open to behold like fresh lenses to an old world. Her eyes are a brilliant green hue. Like emeralds, they sparkle and shine; it can only be the late noon sun that makes them look orange for a fraction of a second. Determination lives within her once again—determination that I will use.

"Thank you," she says and then seems to notice the state of her clothes. "Do you have any spare clothes?"

I stand up slowly and remove my pack, taking out a spare outfit that matches mine and tossing it to the ground. She looks up at me and I cross my arms; she clears her throat, but I don't move.

"Would you turn around?" she asks. I remain steadfast and she takes the clothes, standing up. "Please?"

"It does nothing for me to watch you undress," I say. "But if it makes you feel any better, I'll turn around; make it quick." I turn around and take this moment to think about my next move. I will have to be considerate if I wish to retain her trust, and I must keep our previous dispute hidden. If she even senses that what I have said is not true, then I will have to once again adjust my plans. They have already changed to suit this course of action, and it would be more than a minor inconvenience if they had to undergo another transformation.

The wind shakes off a few of the bright, dying leaves as the shadows begin to creep toward me. I clench a fist, but they continue to creep forward. I do not care whether they disapprove or not of my actions—I will do as I please. I grit my teeth and they condense into a thin tendril and snake toward me; I do not tolerate disobedience! You are merely a means to an end to achieve my desires, do not forget your place! I growl low in my throat, and the tendril grows smaller still, but continues to slither toward me. I step forward and twist my heel on the tendril, feeling a burst of pain in my head, but I grind my heel down harder. I will not allow myself to slip—not now—not when I am so close. I stomp hard and the tendril disappears with a shriek, and I collapse to my hands and knees, breathing hard as my vision blurs. Why is this happening now? I grip the grass as my vision goes dark; I cannot allow myself to be weak in front of this girl! I shake my head and gnash my teeth, and my vision returns for a moment before I collapse.

I'm high above the ground, and I look around, trying to get my bearings. I am sure that I remain in Legend Land, which is better than the alternative. I look down at my hands, my eyes widening slightly—I have no hands. I try to inspect myself, but I cannot see any of my own body. I close my eyes, knowing I must return to the girl and continue with my plan. At this crucial stage, I cannot afford to be taken away on the fancy and whims of some immortal entity; I am not at the beck and call of any being.

"Who is doing this to me?" I call, but the only answer I receive is silence. I open my eyes and look around. "Who is doing this to me?" I repeat, raising my voice; but still no reply. "Show yourself!" I roar. I wait for a moment; nothing. A sudden buzzing is the only warning I have before I feel myself slammed downward, and I collide with the ground, the impact sending ripples of pain through my body, my limbs stiffening. I have no body, yet I interact with the world as if I do—an irritating situation. I growl, wresting control of my numb limbs from the pain; I will not be held helpless like some mere insect. I roll and swing my hand through the air, grabbing hold of an invisible something. I feel the distinct shape of fingers inside my crushing grip, and I wrap my other hand around the supposed wrist of whatever is causing the wind to howl at a bitter velocity.

"Do not toy with me," I growl. "I will not allow any entity to interfere with my plans." The wind intensifies, but I will not relinquish my hold; any being that believes it can stand in my way will pay the price for its undesired meddlesomeness. "I will not stop! I will never stop! Neither you nor anyone else will ever make me stop!" A blast of energy wrenches my hands from that invisible arm, sending me flying and careening through the air. A large tree sees to my abrupt stop, and I slide to the ground . The pain is real enough, but I cannot shake the feeling of this not being my body.

"Godkiller," a voice whispers. I leap to my feet, but my legs give out nearly immediately, my back spasming, wracking my body with pain-induced convulsions. I tear at the grass and dirt, desperately trying to direct outward some of my pain, but to no avail. A brief distraction from the pain is afforded to me when I notice that the ground is unmarred by my frantic tearings; I latch onto this distraction, willing the pain into the background. It slowly subsides, ebbing momentarily out of focus like the tide, allowing me to rise, placing my invisible hand on the tree. I cast my gaze around for the source of the whispering voice, but I am only met with a whisper of wind.

A small tinkle of laughter interrupts, and I whirl toward the direction of the sound. But only the rasping laughter of leaves scratching against one another greets me. I stand and stretch out one hand that I cannot see, but no shadows slither up from the ground. I clench my fist, eyes burning, gnashing my teeth as I redouble my efforts, but to the same result. I roar and slam my fist into the tree; is there no escape from this place? I grind my heel into the dirt deeper in time with my mounting frustration; I must have answers, or at least escape.

"Godkiller."

I whirl around, determined to find the source of this mockery. "Who is there?" I point my finger at the air in front of me. "Show yourself!" I demand again, and a small splash of laughter serves only to infuriate me even further.

"Godkiller," the voice says tauntingly and I growl, clenching my fists. The shadows below me quiver slightly, their snapping and hissing beginning to rise and join the ringing in my ears. If this thing wishes to test me, then it will receive the full extent of my powers.

"Enough!" A much deeper voice roars, and I feel an immense pressure on my skull. I grab my head, trying to stop it from being split into innumerable fragments. "You should not have done this!

To interfere—" The voice breaks off suddenly, but the pressure only mounts.

"You will pay for this!" I roar, arching my back. "When I find you, you will understand the foolishness of your actions! You will know the pain of my ultimate success!" My jaw snaps closed and I squint my eyes shut, trying to block out the pain. All pain is surmountable, all I must...all I must do... is....

Consciousness happens abruptly, and I feel a hand on my throat. I grab the hand and twist it, twisting my hips and rolling. I open my eyes, and I'm sitting atop the girl, her dagger at my neck. I slowly let go of her hand and she takes the dagger away from my throat, looking at me cautiously as I stand up. I must maintain trust between her and myself, and I cannot do that if I am passing out and set upon by unknown entities. There are certain risks I can no longer allow myself to take or be taken. I slowly grind my heel into the ground as the wind picks up; carelessness will no longer be tolerated.

"What happened?" she asks. I don't respond, and she takes a step closer. "Why did you faint? Why did you attack me?"

"Your hand was on my throat," I say, and she looks away.

"I was checking your pulse," she says.

Maybe I won't have to regain as much of her trust as I initially thought.

"Where I come from, it is unwise to fall asleep around others; the ones who survive learn to be on constant alert, even in their sleep. That's how I survived," She crosses her arms and I take a step forward; her jaw clenches and I stop. "I didn't mean you any harm; I am sorry." I dip my head in her direction. Rarely do I ever apologize, and when I do, it is never wise to spurn it. The sound of her slipping her dagger in her boot reaches my ears and I straighten up, my shoulders tense; she must accept the apology.

As much as I am willing to invest in this girl, I will not sacrifice my honor; not for her, nor anyone else.

"It's alright," she says walking over to a tree. "I just feel…I feel like there's something inside me trying to get out; and if I let myself slip, it might just escape." I walk over to her and put my hand on her shoulder gently.

"I know how you feel," I say softly, and I feel her relax underneath my hand. I quickly remove my hand and take a step back, turning away.

"I do have one last question," she says. "Actually, I have a lot of questions." If she does not get her thoughts in order, I shall have to do that for her; that would not be pleasant.

"Ask one," I say turning around.

"What's your name?" she asks.

I take a deep breath—my name? I tap my foot once and then answer.

"Mister E," I say, twisting it around slightly in my mouth to see how it tastes. Her mouth twitches slightly. "Do you find that amusing?" I ask, a thinly laced edge creeping into my voice.

"No," she says, shaking her head, her bright red locks swaying, and I clench my fists; the shadows begin to creep toward her but I let out a breath slowly, relaxing, and they retreat. One tendril stays behind; I glare at it, and it retreats quickly. I will tolerate no more infighting today.

"Good," I say, scooping up my pack and tossing it to her; she catches it and slings it over her shoulder. "I have one stop to make, and then I will take you to the nearest village," I put my hand on a tree and I curl my fingers; I was hoping to be alone for this particular visit, but it should serve as an opportunity to test the girl.

"I heard you muttering something while you were unconscious," she says, walking after me. "You kept saying 'Godkiller'; what does that mean?"

I stand still for a moment, feeling pressure inside of me begin to build, and I clench my fists, forcing myself to start walking, my legs moving stiffly, my entire body tense. "That is two questions," I say through clenched teeth, and I speed up, walking quicker into the forest.

CHAPTER TWO

I slip out of the clothes covered in guts and who knows what else, dressing myself in the proffered clothes. I sneak a glance back at the man who gave them to me, looking him over quickly. That man in black, with eyes even darker than his hair, like two shards of obsidian—I shake my head, quickly slipping on the boots. I don't remember a thing, yet I seem to know clearly what something like obsidian is; if I don't remember anything, how can I still speak? Why don't I have the mind of a baby? Why do I know what a baby is when I don't know my own name? Why is this happening to me? Who am I? What is all of this? What...*no, you're panicking. Stop it. Just...just stop it. You're going to spiral, and you can't do that; just take a deep breath.* I take a deep breath in through my nose, tying the laces on my boots, clearing my mind. There, that's better. I have to try to do this rationally, or I'll panic and spiral again. What *do* I know? I know a lot of things about common things, just not about myself. I know what a tree is, but not my name. I know how to speak and think like an adult, but I don't know what my favorite color is. I know what color is, but I don't know where I'm from. I don't know anything about myself! Do I have family? Where am I from? *Stop it!* My breath shudders in and out; I wipe my eyes, patting my boots. I can't help but panic, trying to remember what I know or don't know; it feels like my mind is blank, a clean slate. But deep down, there's...

there's...*something*, there's something there. In the farthest reaches of my mind, deep down inside, *I know*. I just...I just...

Stop! You're hyperventilating; don't do that. Hyperventilating; I know what hyperventilating is! I focus on my breathing and think. Hyperventilating: the act of hyperventilation; to breathe at an abnormally rapid rate. I blink; I know that to a dot.

There's a thump behind me, and I turn quickly; he collapsed, that slender man in black. I look at him, sprawled out on the ground; he's defenseless. I look down at the dagger he had given me, turning it over slowly. He said it was mine; this was...this *is* my dagger. This is a link to who I was...was I a killer? I run my finger along the edge of the blade, transfixed by the sharp gleam it has to it; have I killed? Has this dagger taken a life before? How many have I killed? One? Two? Ten? Dozens? I drop the dagger, hands trembling; I can't be a killer! I...can I? *It doesn't matter if you were a killer*; get a grip on yourself. He treated me with kindness, and I should do the same. I turn him onto his back and look at his face; even unconscious he looks serious, focused, determined.

Without realizing what I'm doing, I put my hand to his neck and nod; he's alive. I stop, looking down at my hand; I did that without thinking. How many times have I done that before? Why would I need to automatically check for a pulse? How many...how many times have I needed to confirm that there was none? I look between his face and my dagger, keeping my hand on his throat, his pulse beating steadily against my fingers. What would the old me have done in this situation? I take a deep breath, trying to reach for that place inside of me, the place that just knows. The old me would have...she would have...I don't know! I huff, grabbing my dagger looking at the man; he's a mystery, that's for sure. Everything is a mystery to me right now, unless it's something I already know, which isn't a lot, except for a lot of things. I groan, putting my hand to my head; this is hard. Trying to grasp the situation just makes my head pound like my brain is trying to escape. I'm probably dehydrated; that part of me that just seems to know tells me I'm well aware of what dehydration feels like.

"Godkiller," the man whispers in a soft croak. I scamper back over to him, putting my hand on his throat; his pulse has sped up slightly, but he's still unconscious. "Godkiller," he whispers again, beginning to repeat himself; he talks in his sleep? Is he asleep? I move my hand up to peel back his eyelid but stop; that might be rude. After all, I just met him. *He wasn't going to turn around for you—you can't be sure what his definition of rude is.* Well my definition of rude would include peeling back the eyelid of a man I've only just met, thank you very much. I begin to move my hand back down—no, I'll just keep watch so that nothing happens. The wind blows softly over me, and I look around; it sure is peaceful out here. I think I'd like to live in a place like this; some part of my mind rebels at the thought of settling down, but I shake my head. *Oh hush, you don't know what you want, you don't even know who you are.*

I feel his pulse quicken underneath my fingertips and suddenly he's on top of me, pinning one hand in a painfully tight grip my other hand nearly a blur, my dagger suddenly at his throat. My dagger at his throat? How did I react so quickly? He opens his eyes and lets go of my hand, standing up. I do the same, looking at him cautiously; he did me a kindness, and I returned the favor. Now he's done me an unkindness; should I return that favor as well? What would I do if I knew who I was? Maybe the best thing to do is just let him explain himself, then I can decide what I want to do.

"What happened?" I ask, but when he doesn't respond I pause; maybe I should just leave him alone. No, he attacked me, I have a right to know why; I'm still a person, even if I don't remember ever being one. "Why did you faint? Why did you attack me?"

"Your hand was on my throat," he says, and I look away. I had done that without thinking; had I provoked him? I gave him the chance to explain himself, I should explain myself; he did just attack me without provocation. I shouldn't give him provocation; he's interesting. Maybe a little too dangerous for me though. *You like it though.*

"I was checking your pulse," I reply. He seems satisfied with my response, and I feel a small amount of relief inside; why do I feel relief? What part of me decides that I should feel relieved by his satisfaction? I'd like to trade that in for some memories please.

"Where I come from, it is unwise to fall asleep around others; the ones who survive learn to be on constant alert, even in their sleep. That's how I survived," he says.

I fold my arms across my chest; that's an explanation I guess, sort of. He still attacked me for no reason. *What are you going to do about it?* Nothing, for now. He steps forward, and I feel my jaw clench without my consent. If my body keeps responding without me telling it to, how can I expect to learn who I am now?! My body keeps thinking it's somebody else, but I don't remember who that person is.

"I didn't mean you any harm; I am sorry," he says, then he dips his head at me.

If he apologizes, I should forgive him. That's the proper thing to do, or at least that's what my mind thinks. *Shut up, you don't even remember my favorite color, you don't get to make decisions.* I frown; now I'm arguing with myself. *That's nothing new, deary.* It is to me! *Well I'm sure it's going to get irritating quite soon; god knows it already has for one of us.* Oh, his head is still dipped; he probably wants me to accept his apology. Alright, fine; he may have attacked me without provocation, but he also saved me without any as well. I bend to return the slight bow and notice a small groove in one of the boots I'm wearing; I slip my dagger in it and stand up. That's handy; thank you past self.

"It's alright," I say and he stands up straight. I walk over to a tree, looking up; he attacked me, but I put the dagger to his throat. I didn't think about it; I didn't tell my body to do it; it just did. Some part of me reacted to the situation. I put my hands on the tree; I don't know how, but my body knows what to do, even if my mind isn't entirely sure of what I should do. "I just feel…I feel like there's something inside me trying to get out, and if I let myself slip, it might just escape."

That part of me down inside, the part that reacts…I don't know what it'll do if I let it loose. I'm not sure I could, and I know I don't want to, but…do I even have a choice in the matter? This body feels familiar but so strange at the same time, filled with different responses and actions than I want it to make, but what do I want? What do I really want anyway? Want is built up over a lifetime of needs, cravings, and desires inspired from experience, recalled by memory—memory which I do not have; what do I even want? *You know what you want.* No I don't! If I did, I wouldn't be thinking these thoughts right now, and I probably wouldn't be arguing with myself about it! *Whatever you say.* I feel a hand on my shoulder and momentarily tense, my hands clenching at the tree.

"I know how you feel," he says softly from behind me. Even through his glove, I can feel the heat of his hand, soaking into me; I let myself relax under his touch. Human touch—it feels...nice; I wish he wasn't wearing his gloves. No! He is a *stranger*. No. He quickly removes his hand, and I feel a little grateful, but a large part of me mourns the loss. Hush—you don't know what you want, because I don't know what I want. *Nobody knows what they really want; the world is just broken like that.* Maybe I'm just broken. I peel a piece of bark off, turning around; I have to focus. I look at him and study his face; it's so serious, so focused. It's like he's staring a hole into me, and I couldn't possibly hide from him; it's all I can do to suppress a shudder. *You know you don't want to hide from those eyes.* That is *not* helpful or even remotely related to the situation. I still don't even know his name! I blink; his name. I don't know my name, nor his; I can change part of that at least.

"I do have one last question," I say. "Actually, I have a lot of questions." I probably have millions of questions; maybe not millions, but thousands. Hundreds. Okay, maybe just dozens.

"Ask one," he says. He sure does like telling me what to do; I don't know how I feel about that. *You don't like it.* I said I don't know how I feel about it, and I mean it...but it is a little rude.

"What's your name?" He pauses; if I knew my name, I wouldn't want to tell a complete stranger either. Then again, maybe if I knew my name I'd scream it to the heavens. *Heavens?* I'd tell a lot of people. Probably. *Maybe you would, maybe.* I'd dance about it; do I know how to dance?

"Mister E," He answers, and I suppress a smile, the corner of my mouth twitching. That's a very...interesting name. *It's hilarious and ridiculous.* No, it's just interesting. *Ridiculous.* It's interesting! I swallow hard; I wonder if my name is that ridiculous. *See? It's a hilarious name.* I mean, interesting. I wonder if my name is that interesting. "Do you find that amusing?" I hear the edge in his voice. *I'd be touchy too if I had a ridiculous name like that.* At least he *has* a name!

"No," I say, shaking my head; I shouldn't find it funny. It's rude to laugh at people's names in front of them. *Of course, just do it behind their back, that's so much more polite.* It is! *There's obviously much you still have yet to learn about the world.* You don't have to be so snide about it.

"Good," he says, scooping up his pack and tossing it to me. I catch it without meaning to and sling it over my shoulder without thinking about it. He tells me that he has one stop to make and then he'll take me to the nearest village. I blink; what? One stop? He threw me his pack? Does he think I'm going with him? *You want to.* I *just* met him. I cannot stress that point to myself enough; I just met the man. He saved me, then passed out, then attacked me; he's not predictable. Right now, I need something predictable; I'm probably unstable. *It's very likely, yes. And he's dangerous.* That has *nothing* to do with my decision. *It has a lot to do with it; he's dangerous and dark and mysterious. And you want to know why.* I do not. *Do to.* Do not. *Do to.* Notnotnotnotnot. I nod to myself; there, that should do it. Though I do suppose I could keep him company, maybe he can tell me where I might be able to get help with my memory. *And he's dark and mysterious.* That's not why! *Don't forget dangerous.* I sigh; I have to get my thoughts in order soon. I'm not sure I can live with these constant annoying remarks in my head. *Rude.*

"I heard you muttering something while you were unconscious," I say, walking after him; I guess I'll go with him after all. Just for this one thing though. *Uh huh, okay, you tell yourself that.* Just this one thing. "You kept saying 'Godkiller'; what does that mean?" He stops, his body tensing up; did I cross a line? It seems like a more personal topic than his name, at least.

"That is two questions," he says, continuing to walk. I suppose I deserved that. I speed up to catch up with him. Just this one stop, then the nearest village.

CHAPTER
THREE

The girl crouches next to me behind some brush as I pull out my sword; I can feel that strong presence near the cabin, which is unfortunately very familiar. I begin to stand when the girl speaks up.

"What is this place?" she whispers, and I stop, dropping back down into a crouch.

"It is a witch's cabin," I whisper.

Her eyes widen, "A witch?!"

I clamp a hand over her mouth and force her onto her back.

"Keep your voice low," I hiss softly. "I will not be killed because of you, do you understand me?" She nods and I let go of her. She sits up and resumes her crouch, pulling out her dagger. I frown and stand up; something is...off. I reach out with one hand and grab at the air, small tendrils of shadow snaking down my arm and across the air; I wrench my hand back and the tendrils dig into the air, then retreat back up my arm quickly. The air shimmers for a moment, and then a new scene is revealed to me as I peel away the illusion.

Several trees have been blown away; the cabin lies in broken, shredded pieces of wood; and the ground is scorched in several places. A young man lies on the ground, surrounded by moving corpses, but I quickly look past him and focus on my objective—the witch. She hovers over a small, injured, cowering dog, her hands glowing with bright green light.

"You will no longer control me!" She shrieks, her greasy black hair flying about in the howling wind, her green, warted face contorted in rage. I sweep my hand through the air, and several tendrils of shadow shoot out from the forest, wrapping around the witch, pulling her to the ground. Her attention turns to me, and her eyes narrow; green light begins to glow around her, and I grit my teeth, clenching my fist, forcing her dark bonds to stay. The light grows brighter, and I strain, arm trembling—not now, not this time. You are *mine*. You will not stand in my way; my desire reaches its culmination today. There is no warning when an explosion of green light fills the air, ripping the shadows to shreds, throwing me backward. I roll and stand up, looking to the girl.

"Keep those corpses off me," I snarl. She stands up; she shows no fear or hesitation about going into battle—this is good. I shake my head, turning back to the witch. Focus. I will not distract myself now, no matter how interesting of a case she may be.

"What about him?" she asks, pointing to the young man.

"Leave him," I retort, running at the witch.

"We can't just abandon him like this!" she shouts at me.

I will not debate this with a human! She has no scope of the time that has been invested into the events that have led to this very moment; that man is not even worth my consideration. My only concern now is that witch; I have no time for others. I roll underneath a bolt of green energy, slashing at her feet. She leaps into the air to avoid my attacks and rises higher, hurling bolts of green energy at me. I dash out of the way, taking a quick step backward, the shadows coiling underneath me like a spring. I go flying through the air, the wind whipping my hair, bolts of energy crackling near my face, and the smell of burnt ozone filling my nostrils. I close my eyes, spreading my arms, letting the sun warm my face. The thrill of combat, the pumping adrenaline, the blood roaring in my ears—this is peace. I open my eyes as I land behind the witch, clenching my fist. Shadows swirl up toward her, quickly wrapping around her feet and slamming her into the ground. She shrieks loudly, struggling against her bondage, my steps measured and slow as I near her.

"Kill...that witch," I hear a voice from behind me, deep but pained. "Kill that—"

I wave my hand sharply, several soft thuds and soft hisses abruptly stopping the sentence; no distractions. I kneel next to the witch and she freezes, her breaths short and shallow, eyes wide, darting about; there will be no escape, witch. I softly caress the side of her poisonously green cheek, moving a strand of matted black hair from her forehead.

"You know what I desire," I whisper into her ear. "I know that you are the only one who has knowledge of its whereabouts. Tell me where it is."

"I have no idea what you're talking about," she hisses, writhing in her bonds. I slam my fist on the ground, and the tendrils squeeze her tighter, constricting her slowly. I bring my face close to hers, her skin turning a noxious shade of blue, growling low in my throat.

"Do not lie!" I hiss back with vehemence, boring into her with my eyes. I grab her throat and squeeze, the material of my gloves creaking audibly, her eyes bugging out of her head as her system is further deprived of oxygen. "You know where it is. You will tell me where it is!" I release her throat, my blade slowly drawing closer. I will get the information I desire, one way or another.

"I was that dog's indentured servant for longer than I can remember," she gasps. "That pain is far worse than any you could inflict upon me." She cackles madly, arching her back within the shadows.

"We will see," I spit, sheathing my sword as I stand, extending my hands over her. I can feel the hunger of the shadows holding her— their desire for a meal, a respite from the blood drought I imposed on them. I will see to their satisfaction.

I circle my hands above her, the shadows moving in bands across her form; I will keep my eyes open. I want to see this. They slowly snake their way up her form; she twists her neck and head, trying to keep the shadows from covering her face. Her efforts are in vain. As my hands raise slightly, the shadows wrap around her head like dark strips of linen. My hands snap into fists, and I grit my teeth, my eyes rolling back in my head as her screams assault me. I will tear this information from your diseased skull, witch. My mind is bombarded with bits of random imagery, scraps of information; her screams boring into me like the constant whine of a drill. I gnash my teeth, dropping to my knees beside her, holding the bands of shadow in a death grip. Silence! Oh god how I want silence! I shake my head, squeezing the shadows tighter. Relinquish what I want, witch, then give me blessed silence! Her mind fights me, throwing her pains at me; that pain is not mine!

"Mister E!"

I cannot lose focus now! I redouble my efforts, pushing back against her memories; she knows nothing of true pain. I feel her resistance fading, her shrieks growing fainter.

"Mister E!"

Through blurred vision, I look behind me to see the girl fending off zombies in an increasingly desperate manner, trying to drag the young man with her at the same time. I turn my attention back to the witch; I am so close! If I continue to push...

The girl's cries pierce my wall of concentration. No, not her! She will survive; I must focus.

Again her pleas for help slam into me like the fiery wreckage of a train gone out of control; why? Oh god why must this happen now?! I slam my palms onto the witch's body, her screams growing louder, green light glowing beneath the bands of shadow. Damn this connection! I remove trembling hands from the witch's body, tilting my head up with a sigh. I will find you again witch, I swear it.

Slowly I stand, turning to the moving corpses swarming the girl, still trying to drag that injured young man away. With measured steps I cover the distance, unsheathing my sword along the way. I spin one of the corpses to me and, with a barely detectible movement, decapitate the putrid thing. I grip another by the throat, hurling it towards another, my sword dispatching two more with a single stroke. I sheath my blade, leaping into the tangle of corpses. She escaped! The witch eluded me again! Blood coats my cloak. I let her escape; the information is gone. My plan is set back once more! I roar, gore spattering my face. *Gone!*

I stand, trembling, the decimated remains of corpses surrounding me, grass drenched in blood, my gore-soaked form nearly indistinguishable from one of my undead victims. I turn to the girl, and she takes a step back. I saved her worthless life—I can take it as well. Before she can blink, I wrench the injured man away from her, tossing him amongst the re-dead; let him cease and rot. She starts indignantly toward me, but I stop her movements with a hand at her throat, shoving her backwards.

"I told you to leave him," I growl, pointing a blood spattered finger at her.

"I couldn't leave him to die! He had nothing to do with your fight!" She steps up to my finger, glaring at me.

I slowly lower my hand, my arms stiff at my sides; I cannot allow myself to move now, for what I might do.

"You can't just let innocent people die," she retorts.

"There are always casualties," I reply coldly, and she takes a step back, scowling. "You do not get to decide who lives and who dies. You cost me a chance I have waited countless years for; I will not tolerate your sympathy. He was here before us, and unconscious; he should have died! The weak will perish, and on them the strong will build a platform upon which they can stand; that is the way of this world. The weak serve no purpose here and will only be trampled. Sympathy is a weakness which will only get you killed. Are you one of the weak?"

She glares up, taking a step toward me; she does not know when to back down. "Sympathy is not a weakness," she growls.

"It nearly got you killed!" I shouldn't even argue with this girl.

"It also saved my life!" She retorts. I remain silent and she continues, pointing her finger at me; I crush the desire to snap it like a twig. "Having sympathy does not make you weak, it makes you human. If sympathy didn't exist, I wouldn't be able to retain memories, and an innocent man would be dead."

I hold her gaze; she mistakes sympathy for usefulness. Objects are useful. People are useful. She has the potential to be useful, though that will never be if she does not trust me. I have found that witch in the past, and I will do so again; never have I encountered a creature like this girl. She will come to trust me in time, and in time she will become invaluable; for that prospect, I must quell my anger. In my peripheral vision, I watch the shadows slink down the trees and into the ground; I cannot deny them a meal much longer. I lower my voice, nodding my head at her; I cannot always acquiesce to this girl, but time will soon render that option unnecessary. And time is something I have plenty of.

"You cannot save everyone," I say softly, taking a step forward. She takes a step backward, and I raise both my hands slightly in a subtle sign of placation. "You do not yet know who you are, and saving someone else will not give you sudden insight into your past or your very being. No one can blame you for being human, but only by spending time with yourself and with someone who can provide links to the past can you know more about yourself. You cannot help anyone if you are not willing to help yourself."

There is still fire burning in her eyes, but I know she feels my point; I do not want to douse those flames. Fire can easily be kindled in any random individual, but it is far more rare for that fire to remain in the face of adversity. I will keep that fire in her, and she will use it for me. She will question everyone save me, and she will use that fire, risking life and limb for the pursuit of my goals. I must carefully choose my next words, or all of that could be lost.

"The fact that you want to save someone says something about yourself that I could never teach you."

Her head lifts up, acceptance and satisfaction registering side-by-side with that fire. Admitting your own faults is normally guaranteed to grant forgiveness; the admission itself need not be true, they must simply believe it is.

"I am willing to help you find out more about yourself. When I journeyed into your mind, I was able to receive bits and pieces—a jumble of fragments from your mind. It's not complete, and I'm not sure it will ever be, but I am working through them. If you are willing, I will share what I can with you. I have already gleaned something, though it is small; if you wish, I will tell you."

She looks at me cautiously, then cautiously hopeful; she will want to know. That same trait in her that will not allow her to back down will never allow her not to know.

She tilts her head down, hiding her eyes from me; she must accept the offer. She gives a quick nod as I thought she would.

"As I said, it is small, but I was able to discover your name. And, if you are willing to remain with me as a student, I will hopefully be able to discover even more about you, Scarlett."

Her eyes widen and she steps back; I can practically hear her heart hammering in her chest as her breathing comes in short, quick gasps. I can feel the gears turning in her head, the emotions slamming into her; fear, uncertainty, distrust, but prominently among them: hope. Hope that I am telling the truth, hope that this is just the beginning of knowledge about herself, and hope that one day she will be lucky enough to know herself as well as the common beggar does.

I look her directly in the eyes; sometimes liars believe their own lies so they can tell them better; I have no need for such methods. People will see what they want to see, and all I have to do is make sure that I can match their mental image—an easy enough task, though a grain of truth is always an ideal place to build from. A single truth is all that she needs for her to believe me; in this case, even a name, as long as it is the truth, will suffice. Whatever comes after, true or not, she will readily accept as long as she knows there is a grain of truth for her to cling to.

She takes a half step forward but then stops; she wants to trust me—to accept what I have said—but she cannot quite bring herself to do it. The last thing I need on my hands in addition to her sympathy is a trusting, compassionate idiot; I would much rather have her cautious, that way I can be sure that her trust will not be gained easily by others, and she will not be used against me in the future. I take a full step forward, and this time she doesn't back away. I complete the motion she could not, bridging the gap between us; behind her back, the shadows wriggle, creeping toward us. I put my hands on Scarlett's shoulders and they stop, retreating back; this girl will be my student, I am sure of it.

"I know it's not much, but it's a start; you have to start somewhere. Now that we—" I must create a sense of connection with her, and constantly reinforce it "—know your name, we can begin the journey to finding more about your past and who you were. You have to remember that who you were is not as important as who you are," Creating a signification on the present allows present loyalties and actions to later be weighed over whatever I allow her to discover from her past. "To do so requires a certain amount of faith; I have faith in your abilities and have shown that. Just earlier I put my life in your hands," I take my hands off her shoulders, taking a small step away from her.

"I have risked life and limb to protect you, Scarlett. I have shown a certain amount of faith, loyalty, and devotion to you. I will help you, but I expect the same in return," I turn her around so she can look at the young man, looking battered and defeated even in his unconscious state. The sun has begun to set, casting long shadows on the clearing, nearly hiding the young man in a blanket of darkness. Scarlett watches, unmoving as the shadows extend, darkening the trees to a more evil characteristic and now hiding the young man completely from her sight, forgotten under the shadows, amid the corpses.

"You cannot save everyone, Scarlett, but I am giving you a chance to save yourself."

She turns, looking up at me, biting her lip. She stands on the precipice of a decision that will change the rest of her life; but with no facts to help make the correct decision, she will solely have to rely on her feelings. Fortunately, like the things many people take for absolute fact, feelings can be manipulated.

"You wish to help people, Scarlett?" I look into her eyes, her green irises sparkling brightly even in the impending night. It is difficult to communicate need and weakness where none exist, but I am quite resourceful. "Help me." Making a person feel needed and valuable is paramount when gaining the trust of an individual; creating weakness within myself makes her feel responsible for me. The lengths I will go to in order to ensure my plans are met sometimes astounds even myself. "I desperately need a student to help me—someone I can pass my knowledge and skills onto. I cannot do everything myself," Whatever needs to be said I will say, and whatever needs to be done

I will do. Neither morality nor the truth will impede the progress of my plan. "And maybe we can help others too." I will not go out of my way to help someone who has done nothing to deserve it, nor will I instill that desire in a student of mine. But even an appeal to what will surely be a temporary sense of sympathy can gain trust.

Scarlett nods, stepping back and dipping her head slightly lower. "Alright," she says quietly; I gesture for her to begin walking, and she doesn't hesitate in doing so. She walks, entirely upright, her head up high, shoulders square, not looking back once. The shadows snake toward her, and I stomp my foot, growling low; they stop hissing and retreat slowly. I allow myself, for once, to feel content, even if but for a brief moment. I let out a long breath of air and clear my mind. Closing my eyes, I feel the stillness around me save the steps of Scarlett. Carnage may lay behind me, but only possibility lies ahead. There is a certain peace in that.

CHAPTER FOUR

I stare down at the floor; I can't believe it—my name! I know my name. I know something about who I was, who I can be now. The first piece has dropped into place, and I—I don't know how I feel. I shake my head, tears dropping onto the floor, creating small, dark spots. Scarlett. My name is Scarlett. I am Scarlett. The person I am and will forever be from now on is Scarlett. With the tears comes something more; the whirlwind hits me. My shoulders slump and I sob, holding my face in my hands; my name is Scarlett. I smile, looking up at the ceiling, falling back onto the bed.

My name is Scarlett! I stand up, wiping the tears from my eyes, and I move my arms and legs a little. I began shaking my head back and forth, whipping my hair about as I squirm in place. *You are a horrible dancer.* I laugh, tears dripping onto the floor; my name is Scarlett! *What happened to the heavens?* I wiggle my arms and scoot my feet back a little, then shake my arms over my head. *You're being entirely irrational at this point.* I shake my head, not caring; I know a little of who I was, and that's enough. I collapse backward onto the bed, breathing heavily, my eyes red and swollen, my jaw aching from smiling so wide, but I feel good. I feel so good; my heart hammers life into my limbs, and I feel that I can enjoy that life. *You didn't enjoy yourself earlier? Not even*—I shut that part out. I feel protests in that part of me that seems to know, but I completely disregard it;

not now. I look around the room; other than the bed, it's completely empty and bare.

Mister E had taken me to his house immediately after we fought the witch—well, after he fought the witch. I close my eyes, gripping the sheets hard; he fought the witch, but I fought too. They weren't alive, but I didn't show any fear or hesitation; I just acted. I acted and reacted, killing as if it were second nature. They weren't really alive though, so was it really killing? Can I use that to justify my actions? I ended life; even if it was perverted, sick life, I ended it. I turn over on the bed, looking at the wall. I don't know which is more disturbing though—the fact that Mister E showed a complete disregard for innocent life, or that I'm now staying at his house for the foreseeable future. He wanted me to let that man die, to be ripped apart by those things, and some part of me...some part of me wanted to let him die too. I didn't though; I tried to save him, but I couldn't defend him. I caused that witch to get away, and he had to help me save that man; I caused that witch to get away.

I twist in my bed, looking up at the ceiling again, conflicted; why? Why am I conflicted? Because I couldn't do what he asked and he's still housing me, training me? Or because I ended up abandoning that man? I abandoned him to the dark—just left him there. It was easy to do; it was scary how easy it was. The thing that bothers me...I sit up, unable to find sleep…the thing that bothers me was how much I enjoyed it all. The thrill of combat, the killing-that-wasn't-killing, the conflicting emotions then the resolution, the anger and adrenaline...I enjoyed it. No, I didn't just enjoy it. I loved it. I put my head in my hands looking at the ground trembling, tugging at my hair. My name is Scarlett, and I enjoy killing.

CHAPTER FIVE

"Arms up!" Scarlett's arms tremble from the impact as I bring down the wooden blade, aiming for her head; her own wooden blade intercepts, her body doing all it can to just stop my own blow. I kick at her legs and she dances back, breaking the bladelock. I follow up with a savage swing at her torso, and she stops the blow with a vertical block. The force of the blow makes her slide back several inches, her muscles quivering. Most likely she will not be dealing with foes that possess a particular finesse when it comes to sword fighting, or a mastery of any sort of weapon. She will either be dealing with conniving low lives who would not resort to such brazen force in the first place, or opponents significantly stronger than herself; I am currently teaching her how to deal with the latter.

"You will not be physically stronger than your opponent!" I reach forward, grabbing her arm and pulling her toward me; if this training stick was a real blade, I would surely be about to pierce her. I had debated on training her with real weapons, though now I realize that would have been a mistake. Scarlett twists in my grip, blocking my blow and jamming her elbow into my stomach. I take the force of the impact and simply pull her closer, trapping her blade arm between our bodies and holding her tightly with one hand, putting my blade to her neck. "Now you are dead," I smack her in the throat and push her away; she stumbles, gasping for breath, mouth opening and closing like a fish that suddenly found itself on dry land. "Don't turn your back on an opponent unless they are about to meet their end."

Finding her breath, Scarlett stands up straight and rubs her throat, glaring at me, but remains silent. She can learn; that's good.

"We go again," I say and take several steps back, assuming a reckless, unguarded stance; it is much more difficult for me to fight in such a sloppy manner than I originally thought it would be. Scarlett doesn't complain, wearily settling back into her stance. I swing wildly at her head, cringing inwardly at having to use a sword more as a club than anything else. She ducks underneath the swing, quickly making her way behind me, slicing my ankles in the process. She smacks me in the back, and I drop my practice blade, signaling her victory. She walks into my view with a self-satisfied smirk, and I pick the blade back up; she learns quickly. A tentacle of shadow appears out of the ground, plucking her blade from her hand and giving it to me; I toss both of them aside next to the water and towels. She turns around and sees me fall into a fighting stance.

"Now we fight without weapons?" She asks, settling into a different fighting stance, one designed more for speed than strength.

"Everything is a weapon," I reply, charging at her. She ducks under a wide swing and gets in close, using her smaller size as an advantage to jab me several times in the ribs before dancing back out of reach. I spin around, and she dodges an uppercut, sidestepping as I make a jab at her head. As she does, I open my hand, grabbing her hair and pulling her back in, slamming my fist into her jaw. While she is reeling, I bring her closer, throwing my knee against her stomach. I throw her to the ground, wrapping my hands around her throat, pinning her down with my weight.

"Fight, Scarlett! Fight!" I snarl.

She brings her knee up, jerking it into my side until my body is forced to roll away. She barely is able to roll away before I stomp at her head. I barely give her time to catch her breath before swinging at her again. She ducks underneath a left hook, and I aim a savage kick at her ankle, sending her toppling. I pin her arms behind her back, planting one knee on her chest, my free hand sliding slowly across her throat; dead. I let go of her, and she stands up slowly, nursing her jaw, a bruise starting to form.

"Your opponents will never fight fair, and neither should you," I will drill the same lessons into her however many times it takes before she learns them. I walk over to the towels, tossing one to her and filling a small cup with water from the bucket, handing it to her. I sit down in the dirt and she joins me, sipping the water slowly, nursing her injured jaw, thinking over the lessons. When it comes to combat, Scarlett commonly learns these lessons quickly, though there is still so much to teach. I would prefer to have taught her more before the first snow comes in, but that is drawing ever closer, and I am not yet comfortable at the thought of training in such undesirable conditions.

"How did you get all of this?" She says, gesturing to everything in front of us. I take a moment to look at it all before responding. Rolling fields are laid out before us, long blades of dry grass swaying in the breeze, a lonely tree dotting the ocean of brown here and there. Beyond the fields lies the forest, an impenetrable darkness blanketing the tall, gnarled trees and thick canopy of leaves even in the bright sunlight. To my left is the large house I currently call home; dark stone walls are offset by lighter wood paneling, stained glass windows above. The roof is a combination of a classic shingled roof and medieval castle fusion, with several small turrets dotting the low-slanting roof. A single large oak door makes up the only entrance visible from the outside; wrought iron gates and a high fence surround the house itself. From the house to the edge of the forest is all my property; it is useful for impressing guests, when they are the type of guests that need impressing.

Scarlett rubs her hands together while I form a response, her breath frosting in the air; what vulnerable creatures humans are. A sharp gust of wind snaps through the air, and Scarlett draws closer to me. After a moment, I pick up my cloak from the bench, wrapping it around her shivering form; she is no good to me sick and bed-ridden.

"A great many different people owe me favors," I finally say. Next to the house is a large dirt patch, with straw training dummies recently installed; a small shed lies next to the dirt patch, housing the newly acquired equipment I have been using to train Scarlett. She looks at me, waiting for more; the girl is never satisfied, always looking for more. I would be willing to set limits on her curiosity and desire, but right now it is more important that it be encouraged. With humans, curiosity is initially strong, then commonly withers and dies away; it would be best to entertain her curiosity for as long as possible.

"There is a very wealthy man who, despite his enormous character flaws, holds a large amount of sway over many of the upper class residents in the Kingdom. Another man had the pleasure of being with his wife, and this nobleman found out and wanted him dead. Powerful allies should always be endeavored to be acquired, so I offered to kill the man. Upon tracking him down, however, I discovered he was head of a rather extensive underground crime syndicate."

"So if you killed the head of the syndicate, you would make just as powerful an enemy if you had disobeyed the nobleman," Scarlett said.

I nodded; while I initially was interested in her for her fighting skills, her intelligence has its uses as well—the main one being that I am not burdened with talking to a simpleton. It is a nice enough respite as I deal with the ignorant common folk on a regular basis.

"Perhaps even more powerful, since the head of this crime syndicate was able to get into the nobleman's house undetected," I point out; she must be aware of these situations, for her decision making and problem solving skills will undoubtedly be tested in her service to me.

"What did you do?" she asks inquisitively.

I turn to Scarlett, dipping my cup into the water bucket and taking a slow sip; she is hanging onto my every word and some small part of me feels…satisfaction at that. "What do you think I did?" If you truly wish to improve a student, never stop testing or challenging them; a student is like a muscle. If you train it hard often, with brief respites in between, it will work efficiently and harder as time goes on. If you let it go and don't train it, it will get slack and inefficient.

"I think you sided with the nobleman," she says after some thought, taking another drink of water. "There are more criminals in the Kingdom—more gangs and syndicates that you could gain favor with—but only a small noble class. If you lose your standing with them, it would be much more difficult to gain it back."

I nod slowly, letting her think over her answer for a moment before speaking. "What would you have done?"

She answers without hesitation. "I would have sided with the criminal; if the nobleman isn't good enough to keep his wife, she shouldn't be with him. The better man shouldn't be punished just because he was better."

Having a student that can see both sides of the story and yet retain her own opinion has its merits. I pat Scarlett on the shoulder, standing up, and she quickly follows suit.

"What did you do though?" she asks.

I pause on my walk to the house, turning back to look at her. "There's always a third option," I reply. "In this case, that happened to be killing a man of similar size so brutally that he couldn't be recognized, and assuring the nobleman it was the crime lord, then helping the head of the crime syndicate set up his network in a different section of the Kingdom."

"Gaining you favor over both parties," she says, sounding impressed, as she should be.

I nod, walking back into the house.

"Why do I even need to know this?" Scarlett glares down at the book, gripping her hair in frustration. "I can't see how *any* of this will help me!"

I stand in front of her while she sits in a wooden chair behind a small desk, trying to absorb the information from one of the many books in my possession. I breathe in deeply, the smell of ink and old paper and bound books that must be treated with care curling into my brain pleasantly; the library is my favorite room in this otherwise useless house. There is peace in it. A fireplace remains unlit; instead, windows provide all the illumination required while hundreds of volumes remain tucked away in ascending spirals, leaving no portion of the walls visible.

"You cannot best every enemy with force," I reply. She opens her mouth, but I continue. "Or with pleasant aesthetics." Her mouth closes again, and I put my hands on the small desk. "Some situations will call for a more intellectual or strategic approach; that is why you need to know this."

"You say people are such simple creatures, but I'm having to learn a lot of things that aren't very simple to deal with them." Scarlett says, slamming the book shut. "I'm smarter than any person you've met, or you wouldn't have taken me on as your student, even if you do feel pity for me. I don't see why I need to learn this if I'm already more intelligent than my enemies."

My hands slowly curl into fists and I lean back, folding my arms across my chest, carefully controlling my breathing. To suggest that I feel pity for such an insolent girl is something I've never been accused of; the shadows wriggle, crawling across the floor, oozing down across the books like a creeping curtain of darkness. A book falls off its place on a shelf and lands with a loud thud on the hard tile floor. I grit my teeth and the shadows whirl, placing the book back on the shelf and retreating before Scarlett can notice them as she turns around. Her eyes search, investigating every space and crevice before turning back to me.

"It's that arrogance that will allow an enemy less intelligent than you to end your life."

"It's not really arrogance if it's true though," she says with a smirk.

I grab the desk and shove it out of the way, putting a hand on her throat, leaning her back on the rear two legs of the chair.

"This is not a game!" I growl. I let her go and she tumbles back, the chair creaking as she stands silently, setting the chair up and moving the desk back with rigid, jerking movements, her jaw clenched. She stands next to her desk and I incline my head, but she remains standing. "Sit!" I command.

She plops herself down onto the chair, haughtily flipping a strand of her long red hair out of her face.

"I chose you because I see that you have the *potential* to be very intelligent and gifted," I say, turning my back on her and removing several volumes from the shelves behind me. "You are not, by far, the most intelligent person I have ever met; you don't even make it on the scale, student. If I am to take you with me about in the world, though, you must make it to the top position on that scale. How can you hope to possibly comprehend what is required to get your memories back if you can't even understand basic mathematics? In addition," I place the books on the desk and it groans under the weight, dust flying into the air, "if you are to be my student, you will not be solely dealing with humans."

Her eyes widen and I lean back, my eyes hard and cold now. "If you are to deal with people, as such simple creatures as they are, you must elevate yourself above them so that you cannot even call yourself 'human' any longer. You must be a god among mortals," I flip open one of the books to the beginning and put my hand on her head, forcing it closer to the book. "How can you hope to fight gods and kill gods if you yourself are not one?" I jerk her head down and let go, striding to the double wooden doors and opening one.

"To fight gods—to kill gods—must I become a Godkiller?" she asks.

I pause, a sharp intake of breath chilling the roots of my teeth. "You do not yet understand what a Godkiller is," I say slowly, one foot out the door now. "Godkiller. And if your training goes as planned, you will never have to." I exit quickly, slamming the door behind me.

I watch the door slam shut behind him, glaring at the book in front of me. Some part of me longs to know what a Godkiller is; it lurks right there in front of me, yet remains hidden. The part of me that just knows keeps trying to tell me, but I can't...I can't catch it. I shake my head and try to focus on the content of the book: *I think and therefore I am.* You never suffered amnesia, teacher! Everything anyone ever is or was is in their memories; and without that, I'm nothing. I try to throw myself into these things, but they just remind me how much I don't belong here. Mister E tells me that who I was is not as important as who I am now, but who I was continues to dictate my reactions! My body reacts when I don't want it to; and it won't when I do want it to. Who I was is just as important as who I am now, in this moment.

I feel like a ghost inhabiting a body that hasn't accepted me. People's lives are shaped by their experiences recalled by memory, but I have no memories to recall. How can I ever have a life? How do I know who I am? Who am I? I excel in combat, acting and reacting without thought; but as soon as I try to think about it, about how to improve myself when fighting, I slip out of it. It's as if my body doesn't want me to change; it is stuck in its old ways. *Sometimes old, time-proven ways are best.* Well they're not much use if I can't remember them; and if I can't remember them, then it's not really me. Everything I will do must be in accordance with who I am now. If make a mistake, that mistake is exploited, and then I'm dead. How do I get better if some part of me won't let me improve myself? How can I simply rely on muscle memory?

I glare at the book, slamming it shut. I thought maybe throwing myself into studying would allow me to find something that would require me to think to excel, but I can't at excel at the material at all! Not only does my mind not know what to do, but my body has no action to take either. I glare at the book, the question running through my head: *what is the answer to the conundrum that plagues Tervusius?* This is the latest in Mister E's tests to see if I am truly worth his time; even after I have proved my worth and willingness, he still isn't fully convinced I should be his student. But why should he though? I always slip up eventually in combat, and I have the most difficult time grasping any material he places in front of me.

I stand up, pacing, gripping my hair, some part of me restraining my hands, taking care not to tear any out. *It would be awful if you were to go bald from a bad habit.* Finally we agree on something. *Baby steps, baby steps.*

Knowledge is built over what we have learned in a lifetime, but I don't remember my lifetime. For all I know I could never have existed before that day when Mister E met me. I think and therefore I am? I shake my head, slamming my palm on my desk; I think, though I'm not convinced I exist. How do I know I exist if I can't remember anything? I only have a few weeks of memory; that does not bespeak existence. I remember, and therefore I am. If that were the rule then I do not exist; I turn to look at one of the tall bookshelves. *Fortunately for you that is not the case.* What does it matter what I do if I do not exist? My actions will carry no weight; someone who does not remember who she is cannot accomplish anything that others will remember. *That's not true.* Prove me wrong. Nothing? That's what I thought.

I sit down, leaning my head against the bookshelf, looking up. Why does this happen to me? *A person of greatness is never built over an easy life.* I don't want to be great though; I just want to know who I am. *You are destined to be great—that cannot be helped.* I don't want to be great! *It still can't be helped.* I cradle my head in my hands, breathing deeply. Why do I have to be put through hell to be great? Why can't I just tell the powers that be that I have no interest in being great? I just want...I just want to be me. *But who are you?* I look up, rubbing my eyes; I don't know. I don't know who I am, but I know who I am not—I am not a great person. I'm not even a remarkable person! *You are great…you just refuse to admit it.* I can't even answer a stupid question!

For a moment there is silence, though I can practically hear the gears turning in the back of my head. My body makes up for the lack of action happening in my mind—trembling, my shoulders tense, my spine rigid but bending. *Then give up.* I snort; thanks for the pep talk. *If you can't even answer the question, give up if you're that weak…if you don't want to know. That's why you can't remember; you really don't want to know. You don't want to know the answer to the question, so you don't. You don't want to know what will happen if you actually apply yourself, so you don't.* I shake my head, my hair flying about. That's not true. *It is true.* It's not! *Then prove it.* Fine. I stand up, anger welling up in me. I yank books from the shelves, setting them down beside me and piling more onto the desk, plopping down in my chair and angrily flipping the book open to the first page; I'll show you.

CHAPTER SIX

Striding down the hall quickly, I make my way to my room and slam the thick wooden door behind me, sliding several deadbolts in and jamming a bar between the frame. Breathing heavily, I pace my room, hands clenching and unclenching, growling and gnashing my teeth like some caged animal. I growl and spin, glaring at the stone wall that my fist easily makes a dent in; if it crumbles so easily under my fist, how will it ever hold against a siege? I roar, slinging my dresser across the room, kicking my bed over and ripping the wooden frame apart. I live in an indefensible house with an infuriating student, and I'm no closer to achieving my goals than I was before! I had finally tracked down that witch Impres, *again*, after so many long years of searching. I had come within mere inches of finding the last piece of the puzzle!

I throw a piece of my broken headboard at the door, and it shudders under the impact as I fume. Instead, I found a student who does not appreciate my teaching! I've wasted my time saving that girl, trying to train her when it's pointless; she'll never make it in this world, much less alongside me! I drop to my knees, ripping at my mattress; why can't she just *listen* to me?! I look at the mirror on my wall, my eyes orange, hair wild, and my clothing disheveled—such an animal. I spit in disdain, leaping at the mirror, slamming my fists against it, glass piercing my skin. I clench my fists, blood seeping around the shards of glass, and slam my fists into the ground. I should have just left her in the forest! I grab the remains of the mirror and fling it across the room; then I follow it across the room, my impaled hands wrapping around the thin metal frame. I slam it on the ground, against the bed frame, against the walls; she should just listen to me! If she would have just listened, she would still be alive!

Something wraps around my throat and wrenches me off my feet, dragging me across the debris-strewn floor, my feet kicking and lashing out, my hands trying to pry the thing off of me. I hold both my hands out, but the thing tightens around my neck and I realize the tendrils of shadow are not obeying me. I dig my nails into the thing around my neck, and there is a hissing behind me, the room growing darker. I grit my teeth, scrambling to stand up, fighting the tendrils around my neck; rebellion will not be tolerated. I reach down for my sword as my airways are blocked by the pressure on my neck, but the tendrils wrap around my belt, yanking it off my waist and slinging it across the room. I growl, leaping forward, but the tendrils strain, snapping taut like a leash on an animal, dragging me down to the ground again. My fingernails dig into the cracks between the stones on the floor; the tendrils snap like reins, jerking me back, and blood sprays from my fingers as my nails are forcibly ripped off.

"How *dare* you!" My lungs scream for air, telling me I shouldn't be talking, but I refuse to listen. "You do not rebel, you obey!" I give up on the tendril around my neck, my fingers tugging at the tendrils wrapping around my legs. My blood soaks into the dark, serpentine phantasms and they writhe, hissing in pleasure. "Take…my life…" I growl, squeezing my hands, blood oozing out onto the shadows; my bindings loosen, and I suck in a deep breath. "If you take my life, you take my pain." I wrench the tendrils off me, and they hiss, snapping back and lashing out at me. I leap over one, using my momentum to vault over another before a thick tendril slams into my stomach, wrapping around my midriff and squeezing. I beat my fists against the tendril in rage as spit and blood flies out of my mouth; no! I can't go, not now! I can…I can still change Scarlett! She can still be saved!

I lean over, my ribs straining, and I sink my teeth into the tendril, yanking upward. The tendril rips with a tearing, screeching sound, slinging me toward a wall. I land hard, sliding among the broken glass and wood, thudding against the wall. I reach out, and my hand closes around something small and solid—Scarlett's dagger—taken to be given back after her training. I unsheathe the dagger, rolling out of the way as a tendril shoots toward me. I stab the dagger in and hold on with both hands as the tendril retreats back quickly. I plant my feet on the wall, yanking the dagger toward me as the tendril disappears into the wall, rending a large gash in the shadows. I drop to the ground, rolling backward and slashing at a tendril as it lunges at me. A sharp pain shoots up through my side and I double over, another tendril slamming into me from behind, pinning me to the wall. It wraps around the dagger to yank it away, and I twist the dagger, slicing through the tendril, dropping to the ground. Turning, I wrap one hand around the tendril, plunging the dagger into it over and over again, forcing it to the ground, slicing and hacking at it. The only sound filling my ears are the high, shrill shrieks of the shadows before there is silence. Breathing heavily, I stand up slowly, stumbling over to one of the lanterns that, while crushed and battered, is still lit. I sit down, leaning against the wall, clenching Scarlett's dagger tightly.

I hold the lantern up higher, gritting my teeth as my arm obstinately protests against being used at all. My mirror is on one of the walls, fully repaired; my blood can be seen on it, and I growl, looking at the words: *Learn from your mistakes Godkiller*. I sling the lantern at the mirror and it cracks, several pieces falling out as the lantern rolls along the floor, light flickering weakly.

"I will never forget them," I growl; the shadows must still be listening. They never leave me; they never can—they are necessary. Though if I let my guard down...if I forget my path, they will turn on me like savage dogs. If I stoop to becoming an animal, I invite the same; I despise my safeguards. I look down at the dagger, which is immaculately clean, and I wish there was proof of my victory; however, my bruised and battered body is proof enough of my defeat.

These shadows so easily disobey me; they afford me no quarter. I would only put my life in the tendrils as cruel as my own hands. By the same token, I would never trust someone like me with my own life. I squeeze the dagger tight; I have no choice. They are necessary. I need them to complete my mission. I weakly make my way over to where the remains of my bed lay, below my mirror, and I lay down on what remains of my mattress, stabbing the dagger deep into the wood of what used to be my bed frame. I lay on my back, looking up at the ceiling; I close my eyes and breathe out slowly. I feel a small tendril slowly sweep across my cheek, and I pick up the lantern, slinging it across the room violently, ridding the room of any light. I open my eyes to the same darkness that lay behind them and clench my fists; this is where I belong—amidst allies and enemies, where one is indistinguishable from the other—the grey in the darkness.

I reach back and wrench Scarlett's dagger free, turning it over, invisible in the shadows; a knife in the night, unseen before it is too late. My eyes flick to where I know the door is, and I throw the knife at it, the dagger embedding itself into the wood. No knife will stab me in the back.

CHAPTER SEVEN

Darkness swirls around me, coating everything—soaking up my memories, creating a new space…a new slate, stained with blood. I reach out blindly into the darkness, coming into contact with nothing; I whimper, looking around quickly, trying to find something not covered in darkness.

"Why are you doing this?" I whisper, stumbling forward, putting a hand out to catch myself, but I don't fall. Something solid wraps around my waist, pulling me gently back to a standing position. "I did everything you said." A sharp laugh, like a knife cutting through my heart, slices through the air causing me to cringe.

"Indeed you did," the voice slithers out of the darkness, chilling me to my soul. Something caresses my cheek softly, and I shudder, cringing away. What feels like a tendril wraps firmly around my head, stroking my cheek again, and I hold still, trembling. "What a pretty young face you have, boy," Something sharp digs into my cheek, and I tense, fighting the pain as it clamps down on my cheek. "Barely a teenager and still so very youthful."

Hot blood wells up, trickling down my face, and I hear a low hiss of pleasure from all around me, echoing. I cover my ears, trying to crouch down, but something holds me up.

"Ah ah…it isn't polite to try and get away from company, boy."

"I have a name," I retort angrily, and a loud growl slams into me, knocking the air out of my lungs.

"No, you do not," the voice hisses, and I feel more tendrils sliding over my body, slithering under my clothes and attaching to my skin with sharp pricks of pain. "You are an unnamed thing, abandoned by the cosmos, a disgrace to your family…which is where I come in."

The voice is right next to my ear, but I keep myself still, fighting the urge to move away as something wet and slimy slowly licks the blood off my cheek. Out of the corner of my eye, trying to penetrate through the darkness around me, I spot what looks like a large, disembodied red mouth. I shiver, biting my lip, squeezing my hands into fists; don't move, don't move. Don't move.

"Your father is disappointed with you, boy."

My eyes widen and I struggle, jerking at the tendrils. "Don't tell him! Please don't tell him what I did!" I squirm and the tendrils tighten around me, digging deeper into my flesh. I try to escape, but they force me down, tugging at my skin, my hair, my clothes before going still, slowly coiling around me like a large serpent, incorporeal muscles flexing.

"What? Tell him you tried to run away? Tell him you disobeyed a direct order? Tell him you couldn't finish her off?" The voice was hissing, slithering inside my ears, worming its way into my brain.

"I couldn't…I can't—I can't do that to her. Please, *please* don't tell him!" I fight against the coils, working my way upright, kneeling, looking up into the darkness, begging.

"He'll find out eventually; you can't hide her forever, you know. How long will it take before you crack and tell him? A week? A month?"

"I won't ever tell him!" I shout, and the thing chuckles, which is worse than its voice.

"Good; you do have *some* backbone at least. I was worried you were completely spineless. But that doesn't change the fact that he'll find out."

My lower lip trembles and I take a deep breath, blinking quickly and tilting my head back, trying to put some force into my quivering voice.

"Then…then make me stronger," I gasp out. For a moment, there is only silence, so I continue. "If he's going to find out and I can't stop it, then I need to be able to stop him." The tendrils immediately uncoil from around me and I rub my wrists, looking around, trying to see something in all of this.

"Very interesting proposition," the voice says slowly, and I lick my lips, heart hammering; I only have one option here. "You must do whatever I say, and it won't be easy. If you want to be strong enough, you will have to become a Godkiller."

My breath hitches, but I gulp, nodding my head, leaning forward. "Anything. I'll do anything, whatever it takes. My father summoned you so you could manage me; he won't think anything of·it when you start training me." I wait, and there's a small cough, like blades smacking against each other, and I wince.

"I *do* quite despise being the family guard dog…being treated like an *animal*. I hate it!"

I wince, needles digging into my brain as the voice grows more agitated.

"At least you can think on your feet," the voice mutters and the darkness starts to fade.

I fall down several feet and land on a hard stone surface, sharp rocks and pebbles digging into my skin; I pick myself up slowly, wiping dust off my face. I look behind me and see Simiel, asleep on her small cot, and relief floods through me; thank heavens she's safe. Even in this dank cave, I can smell her familiar scent, so comforting to me…wildflowers. Her small form lies huddled on the cot, dark hair falling about her cheeks, tiny eyelids hiding orange eyes that just occasionally will flash the brightest green; all of this is for her. I look out the cave entrance and see the forest outside, dark and foreboding as ever. How did we get here?

"I suppose introductions are in order since we've yet to officially meet."

I turn around; and from the shadows toward the back of the cave, a tall, dark figure slowly steps out, as if detaching itself from the shadows. The only visible feature is a large, bright red smile on the figure's face. He extends a hand to me, "You will call me Mutovinatum,"

I swallow hard, taking a hesitant half-step forward, then close the distance, my hand jutting out of my body quickly, my arm stiff. This is for Simiel; this is all for her.

"I've been told I don't have a name," I reply, and Mutovinatum chuckles, nodding.

"Indeed, you do not." He takes my hand in his own, and a chill makes its way down my spine. For the first time, I notice dark suction marks on my arms, and Mutovinatum seems to notice my awareness. "Let me take care of that." A long cloak of darkness extends, wrapping up my arm and retreating slowly, sending shivers throughout my body, but leaving my skin clean, devoid of any marks, including the scar from…the accident. "Now let's take a look at that wonderful sister of yours that you couldn't bring yourself to—"

"Don't touch her!" The words are out of my mouth before I can even think about what I should have done; and my hand is out, trying to grab at Mutovinatum.

I stumble, slipping right through him; and then a cold, dark hand closes around my throat, slamming me into the cave wall. The sound echoes throughout the cave, bits of rock shaking loose from the ceiling and pain explodes up my back, my vision swimming briefly before that red grin comes into view again.

"You do not tell me what to do, boy." The red mouth is still a large grin, with sharp white teeth barely visible behind the splattered on red lips, the cold grip tightening around my throat. I struggle, grabbing at the arm, but my hands go through it, my feet not even reaching Mutovinatum's body, no matter how much I kick.

"Don't…touch her," I gasp out, glancing over at Simiel, sleeping soundly before looking back at that dark mask of a face, devoid of any features save the ghastly mouth.

"You have a bit of fight in you," Mutovinatum hisses, his mouth so close to my face I can smell the rotten stench of his breath. "I like that. But you don't understand; I can do whatever I want—to you or your sister."

He drops me, and my knees buckle as I collapse to the ground, gasping for breath, my lungs screaming for air and greedily gulping it in. I look up at him, fighting the urge to retch, and I double over, keeping my mouth firmly shut, swallowing the bile creeping up in my throat.

"There's a good boy," Mutovinatum snides as he pats my head. I look up at him, unclenching and clenching my jaw.

"I don't care what you do to me; so do whatever you want because I honestly, truly don't care. From the day I was born I was told I was nothing; I was told I would never amount to anything—that I was useless. So maybe I believe it," I groan, standing up, shaking, yet keeping one arm wrapped around my stomach, still somewhat bent over as pain is lacing intricately up and down my back.

I set my eyes on that red mouth, swallowing hard, steeling my soul. I was told in the past that sometimes people have to do unpleasant things to get what they want, even if what they want is the right thing; I will need a soul of steel to do that for her. After all, I'm only doing this for her; I couldn't...I couldn't do what was right, and now I have to protect her from my own weakness. I have to become strong. I straighten up, wincing and cringing, but forcing my spine straight, tilting my chin up.

"Maybe I believe I'm worthless—a wretched spawn abandoned by the cosmos. I know that she," pointing to Simiel, not for once taking my eyes off those large, red lips, "is valued and strong; she has potential and can make it in this world. But not if my family is around. They would kill their own as soon as they would kill anything else. So I'll do whatever it takes to get strong, because nothing will ever happen to her while I breathe, and I want to make damn sure of that. If you really want to, give me hell, Mutovinatum." I push my messy dark hair out of my orange eyes, trying to square my shoulders against the aching pain.

"Very well, boy," Mutovinatum says softly, nodding the dark outline of his head. "I'll leave your sister alone, but I'll take it out on you. You're going to die time and time again before you get strong enough to save anyone; and maybe by that time, you won't even want to. I'll indulge you though."

He leans forward, but I can't move away; my back is against the wall so I stand my ground, eyes burning fiercely with determination.

I'll die a thousand deaths if that's what it takes.

"I love a fun little game now and then. Just remember," he clicks the talon-like fingers of his dark form against the cave wall to enunciate each word, "I know your weak spot now; I can get to you whenever I want. I can make you scream without laying a finger on you. No matter how strong you think you are, your sympathy makes you weak."

I look at Simiel; she will make me be strong, no matter how weak he thinks I am. My sympathy and my love for her will make me strong; she will be my soul of steel.

"You'll learn to love the fire and brimstone. There's a saying we demons have," Mutovinatum's mouth begins to open wider slowly, wide enough to fit my head in. "Through the fires of hell are wills of iron forged."

The mouth grows wider, and I look into that cavernous maw of darkness, sweat dripping down my forehead—not the darkness again. I don't think I can go in again; I start to tremble, and Mutovinatum chuckles deep from within, somewhere where his soul probably should be.

"I've spent an eternity in the fire, boy. Now it's your turn."

That maw comes closer, slowly engulfing me as I let out a scream, but that too is swallowed by this demon and his gruesome red mouth.

"Welcome to hell, boy."

Roaring, I leap up, shadows whirling around me, grabbing pieces of debris and slinging them around the room as I rush forward, mouth disfigured in a snarl.

"You do not own me! I will show you hell!" I leap forward and slam into the wall, crumpling to the ground. My mind swims through a fog, blearily realizing where I am, and I slowly sit up, my muscles groaning and protesting. Even after so long, my body remains stubborn and resistant to my will. I look down at my hands, completely healed as I knew they would be; after they rebelled, the shadows have at least gone back to doing their job. A shadow slithers over to the door, yanking Scarlett's dagger from it and slinging it across the room as I stand up, slowly removing the bar from the door frame, unbolting all the locks and pushing the heavy door open. My mind is still having difficulty creating the distinction from past and present; and for a moment, the smell of wildflowers pervades the air before my mind settles on the present, wafting the scent away.

I pause for a moment, turning back to look at the destruction in my room, focusing on Scarlett's dagger. I begin to close the door, then stop, quickly grabbing the dagger, closing and locking the door behind me, and sliding the dagger into my belt. I make my way slowly through the large house, silent as the beginning of time and emptier still. I've spent decades in this house; and for all intents and purposes, it lacks the qualities of home. I have never had the need for a home, with all of its furnishings and other associations; though now with a student, I cannot help but wonder if she would be more receptive in a more comfortable environment. I make it to the double doors of the library, pausing for a moment before I enter.

I open the doors and lock them behind me. Scarlett sits at the desk, appearing to be reading in the pale morning light, a lantern lit next to her. Several books devoid of any dust sit in a neat pile next to her desk, and several more, still dusty, sit in a pile on the opposite side. She doesn't show any sign of having heard me enter the room, and I make my way to her desk, knowing at a glance what the book is that she seems to be studying. A soft snore sends a puff of dust up from the book; and for a moment, I don't disturb her; she commonly never quits. Never does she rest, stubbornly pushing herself to her limits until the task is complete. I reach a gloved hand out to her; in the low light, her red hair nearly looks black. And for a moment, I can detect a whiff of wildflowers in this dusty old room. The similarities between the two—no… I snatch my hand back quickly, shaking my head. No.

"Answer me the conundrum that plagues Tervusius," I say loudly, pulling the book away from her. Her head slips down and hits the desk; and, after a moment, she lifts her head up. Dark bags weigh down the skin under her eyes, the veins red and apparent in her tired eyes which only look orange for a moment. Her mouth opens slowly, her voice scratchy and dry as she makes a response, peeling a strand of hair from her tongue. "What was the conundrum that plagued

Tervusius?" I repeat, now that she is at least conscious; she will not always have the luxury of being well rested when facing a problem.

"Tervusius's conundrum was—"

"No! I said *answer* it!" I correct her, and her mouth closes, her brow knitting. She glares up at me, standing up quickly, knocking her desk over in the process.

"I can't!" she shouts, tugging at her hair, pacing. "I've tried and I've tried, but I can't! I must have gone through half of the books in here, but I can't answer the question!" She turns to me, her eyes wide and wild, her fingers twitching at her sides. "It's an impossible question that can't be answered; I tried all night to answer it, but I couldn't do it! Congratulations, you proved yourself right; maybe I can't make it." She looks down angrily, folding her arms, her hair hiding her face.

"Why can't you answer the question?" My voice is deadly calm, low, and nearly as quiet as the flame fluttering in the lantern.

"Because it…" her voice drops, and her face lights up in realization as she moves her hair out of her face. "Because it can't be answered." She looks at me, eyes wide, taking a step forward, confident of what she is saying now. "It can't be answered!"

"Tervusius committed suicide once he realized that," I say, affirming her answer as the correct one. It took her long enough to figure that out, but she was, at the very least, able to; some of the brightest minds I've come across haven't been able to accomplish that much. They refuse to accept that there is no solution to the problem, though Scarlett came to the conclusion after only a night. "I would say you fared better than him." That will continue to be the case, so long as she gains a hold on her temper, though now I know at least that she has enough potential to continue her training.

"You gave me an unanswerable question," she says quietly, taking another step forward. "I stayed up all night working on this blasted thing, and you let me think that there was an answer to it!"

"I never told you that it had an answer, or didn't have one." I respond.

"To hell with you and your training! If this is how you're going to train me, then I want no part in it!"

"Get some rest." I may not always allow her the luxury of rest, but success should be rewarded.

She stops walking toward me, her shoulders high and tense before slumping down, her breath coming out in one long sigh. Turning around, she keeps her head hung, walking away from me, every muscle and fiber of her being communicating defeat; she is merely pouting. She makes it to her flipped desk, pausing for a moment before turning back toward me.

"You shouldn't torture me like that," she says through clenched teeth; while her body communicates defeat, her eyes still maintain a fiery and defiant look in them. If this would have been all it took to break her, I would not have wanted to keep her around at all.

"Torture is subjective," I reply.

She growls, lunging at me; she must learn control, even when she is in a bitter mood. I sidestep and she skids to a stop, spinning around and swinging wide; I casually block it, taking a step back. She swings again, flowing around my block into a quick jab, spinning to my side and aiming an elbow at my ribs. I bend back out of reach of the jab, grabbing her elbow and shoulder, sweeping her legs out from under her. She tries to spin out of my hold, but I follow her, pinning her face down on the ground, putting my knee in the small of her back. She is slow and sluggish when tired. I force her down as she squirms, swinging her legs and writhing, trying to get some small advantage over me.

"You see, this is not only torturous, but boring as well." I get off of her, and shadows wrap around her, keeping her several inches off the ground, binding around her until only her head is visible. She opens her mouth and coils of shadow wrap around her mouth as well, the only sound being her heavy breathing through her nose. I walk out of the library, a bound Scarlett trailing behind me until I reach her room. I open the door and the shadows set her down on her bed. "I told you to get some rest, student; I expect my orders to be followed." The shadows uncoil around her, disappearing from the room quickly as I shut and lock the door, just as she slams against the heavy wooden frame. She pounds at it for several seconds before I make it out of earshot, walking out of the house. It is for her own good, though her reactions toward it did not make for a pleasant morning for either of us. I clench my fists, speeding away from the house; her sour attitude seems to have rubbed off on me. Happiness and work are not related, and one should not affect the other. Work still must be done, and whether I am in a pleasant mood or not should hold no sway over it. The shadows hiss and snap, following close behind me as the landscape turns to a blur; that, of course, doesn't mean that I have to be kind to others whilst I work. The shadows still hunger for a meal, after all.

CHAPTER EIGHT

I pound at the door, screaming. "Let me out! Let me out!" I pause, catching my breath and pressing my ear to the door; he's not out there. He left me here! He just got angry and threw me in my room like a child! *Don't you like it though?* No, I don't! *Not even a little?* Not even a little. I kick the door then swear, hopping around, clutching my foot; even through the boot that hurt! I glare at the bed as if it this was all somehow its fault. *You can blame what you want, including an inanimate object, but you know the blame lies only with you.* That's not true! I tried for hours upon hours to find an answer to that question, when in reality there was no answer; I understand the lesson behind that, but I still can't stand it! He tricked me! *And you reacted to his baiting and got angry; you lost your temper with him.* But instead of explaining it to me, he just remained smug about it, letting me get angrier and angrier. He didn't try and teach me a lesson; it was just another test. He was testing me, poking at me like I'm some experiment; I am *not* a lab rat! I will not be used like one! *Perhaps his entire test was to see how well you could maintain your control.* That doesn't make what he did right. *What are you going to do about it?* I...I'll...I'll do *something* I can tell you that. *But what?*

I huff, lightly kicking at the floor, looking around my room. I've filled it out a little since I got here; I was able to get some clothes, a mirror, a pack, and some little metal hair clips. Hair clips; I'm a genius after all. *You keep telling yourself that deary.* Give me my moment! I walk over to the dresser and pull out a few hair clips. I get on my knees, looking at the lock; it's a large, sturdy thing, but the inner workings look easy enough. I break the hair clips into a few pieces, ripping at my shirt to tie the pieces together. Putting them in the lock, I stop; I don't know how to pick a lock. *Of course you don't.* Hey! I thought of the idea! *Close your eyes.* No. *Just do it.* I sigh and close my eyes, frowning. *Reach deep down inside of you, to that place you don't like to visit, that place you're scared of.* I shake my head, clearing the voice; I can do this on my own. *Just trying to help.*

I slowly reach down to that place inside me that just seems to know, grabbing for it. It eludes my grasp, moving around out of my reach; why must I fight so hard, even against myself? I grit my teeth; just hold still! I reach for it again and it once again moves away, eluding my grasp. I take a deep breath, relaxing myself; I need to know how to pick this lock. What I need to know is how to pick this lock, and I'm sure the old me knew how to do that. If I don't fight myself, if I don't force it...all I need to know is how to pick the lock, okay? That's all, then we can go back to fighting. I feel a small sense of acknowledgment and I nod to myself; okay, I can do this.

I slowly immerse myself in that place, letting it wash over me. In a rush sensations, feelings, images, and thoughts all slam against me, trying to pry their way into my mind. I try to hold on, gritting my teeth, letting them slam into me; they crack into my head, swirling around, all vying for attention. I yank back; it's too much! They depart with a spurned snap, and I gasp, my eyes flickering open. An echo remains inside my head, like I almost knew everything for a moment. I reach back inside, but the place remains stubbornly out of reach. I continue to try for some time, but it refuses to cooperate. Fine, be that way; I was able to get what I wanted anyway. I turn my attention back to the lock and deftly move my hands; and after a moment the lock clicks—I did it! *Congratulations, you successfully moved one step closer to having the complete skill set of a criminal.* I stand up, slipping the small pieces of metal into my pocket, stepping out the door. *Aren't you forgetting something?* I stop and turn, my eyes settling on the pack, then the reflection of my ripped up shirt in the mirror. I step back into my room, changing; I don't want anyone getting the wrong idea about me. *Or the right idea.* That was uncalled for! *You just have one of those faces.* I angrily stuff my pack full of clothes and quickly make my way out of the house. I look both ways down the road, but they look like they both lead to nowhere. *You want to go right.* I decide with finality to go left. *Alright, but don't start complaining when things go south.* Left is actually in the east. *You know what I mean!* It feels good to have the upper hand for a change; perhaps leaving really is for the best.

CHAPTER NINE

Compared to the bright sun outside, the bar is dark and grimy, filled with the seedy scum of the earth that make up Legend Land—the things that I hardly consider worth my time. Yet these very same scum are the reason I am here; the shadows wriggle around, pleased to be in such a dark place after so long in the light, and I share their sentiment. A few of the characters turn to look at me with bloodshot, heavy eyes that openly display the malice contained in the heart of the individual. I return each and every look, slowly and calmly, before they all look away, going about their business once more. All it would take is one cross word from any of one these pieces of filth—just one. I walk up to the counter, leaning forward and putting a small golden piece on the counter; until such time as they dare utter such a thing, I must control myself. It's gone within the blink of an eye, and the bartender is standing in front of me, swirling out a dirty mug with a dirty rag using his meaty, dirty hands; the place is a pigsty. He grunts at me in acknowledgment, covered in bristly hairs, with large tusks curving out of his mouth.

"I have an interest in finding a group of eight individuals: one tall, the other seven stout and bearded." I keep my voice calm and even, low enough that only the bartender can hear it over the din of the bar. A low life such as this bartender will not require more than the base methods of persuasion, though due to this morning I am not in a patient mood.

"We have a lot of people like that," he grumbles, his gravelly voice sounding like rocks tumbling against each other, barely audible over the sound of tankards hitting the tables and fat lips being smacked together.

"These individuals are particularly known for the contacts they keep," I reply, sliding two more gold pieces across. "I merely have a few questions pertaining to one of them." Once again the coins disappear as quickly as they appeared, the boar making a show of cleaning his glass as he thought it over, his brutish brow turning itself into a frown. Looking into his shiny black, piggish eyes, I can practically see the steam coming from his small mind as it works itself over. I put another coin on the table and he takes it, though he doesn't say a thing. He's debating whether it would be best to comply with my wishes, simply remain quiet, or betray me; it would be best for him if he chose the first option. My arm tenses below the counter, hand closing around the hilt of my sword; I will have what I desire, one way or another. The boar puts his glass and rag beneath the counter, swinging his bulk out from behind it, shooting hard glances at the few patrons that sit at the counter.

Gesturing to me, he leads me to a slim door, so dark and stained that it nearly blends in with the darkness. He opens the door, walking away; if I am to find that witch Impres, and complete my mission, I must enter. I live in the darkness; it knows me as intimately as I know it. I have nothing to fear inside.

"Have a seat, mystery man," a cloaked figure speaks in a soft voice that, despite its attempts to sound menacing, still has a bit of a tinkling air to it. I remain standing, positioning the proffered chair directly in front of me. The room is dark, a single candle on a small round table providing the only illumination. The only figure visible is the cloaked one that currently remains sitting in front of me. The small shoulders of the figure shrug, and I see a small outline scurry in darkness that, even to eyes used to such low levels of light, is difficult to penetrate. "What can I do you for, hmm?"

I keep one hand on my sword, keeping close to the door, not taking my sight directly off the figure; the darkness and I know each other, but I do not mistake knowledge for trust. It would harbor my enemies as readily as it would harbor me or my allies.

"I'm looking for a contact of yours," I reply calmly, and the figure chuckles, coming deep from the chest and reverberating throughout the room.

"All contact information is privy; that's how we operate."

I take a step forward, and something flashes in the darkness. A heavy throwing knife embeds itself into the wood next to me, leaving a small cut on my cheek.

"My companions are miners by trade, so they're quite used to the dark. They're quick learners of whatever you set them to, though; I would suggest not angering them…or threatening me, for that matter, as they owe me their lives."

"I have no intention of going after any of your clients, and this will not come back on you. I am willing to pay for the information," I reply, putting one hand on the heavy knife and silently pulling it out of the wood.

"As I've said, all of our information is privy; that's how we keep business going. If that's all you wanted, you can see yourself out; if you had a job for us, then—"

Mid-sentence, I throw the knife at the candle, the blade hitting the flame and extinguishing it, then trapping the cloak of the person to the wall. I spin, shooting my leg out and catching one of the short, stocky mercenaries in the face with my foot, bringing my leg down and grinding his face into the ground. I unsheathe my sword in the same motion, smacking another with the flat of my blade, sending him spinning. A tendril reaches behind me, hoisting another would-be assailant in the air, slinging him against the wall. I dance back as a large ax tries to cleave me in half, and I grab the long handle, ripping it away like taking a toy from a child. I backhand the stout man, sending him careening away. I drop into a crouch as another launches himself at me, screeching; I stand up just as he passes, grabbing one thick leg and swinging him into the last two mercenaries. With a quick step, I am in front of their darkness-enshrouded leader, the tip of my sword pricking the throat lightly.

"You can tell your men to light some candles and we can talk properly, face to face, or I can cut your throat now; and while you lay bleeding out on the floor, I will brutally kill every one of your men. Then," I press the point of my blade in deeper, though there is no resistance, "I will go through the documents I know you keep and find out where the last known location the contact I want found was seen."

"Light it up," the leader grudgingly growls, and there is only a brief moment of scurrying before the room fills with flickering candle light, the room bright enough for me to make the others now.

I move a hand toward the leader, and the men rustle behind me, but I simply pluck the knife pinning the leader's cloak to the wall and set it on one of the small round tables.

"I should have known it would be you," the leader says, throwing back the hood of the cloak. A tall, thin woman, garbed in tight-fitting dark cloth and a loose cloak folds her thin arms across her chest. What exposed skin that can be seen is white as the impending snow outside, almost sparkling in the candlelight. Her long, wavy hair is dark as ebony, partially hiding one of her bright blue eyes and high cheekbones. Her cheeks are red as blood, lending an air of life to what would otherwise appear to be a pristine corpse.

"We have indeed met on better terms before, Lesva," I reply, and she shakes her head, dark curls swinging. I have seen her beauty enchant humans time and time again; I have seen it throw nations into chaos and fell kingdoms, and she is well aware of her power. Though in the past she has made an attempt, her charms have yet to completely fell me; a stab to her personal pride, I am sure.

"I remember *vividly*," she says, a playful smirk appearing on her lips, nearly as red as the blood that courses right beneath the surface of her skin. "You didn't have to attack my men though."

I look at the seven other mercenaries in the room, bruises beginning to form as they glare at me, hands on weapons. They are nearly identical, each being short and squat, with thick legs, burly hairy arms, and wide chests. They cover themselves in chainmail armor, holding knives, axes, and clubs. Long grey manes of hair extend from beneath metal caps; their faces scarred and lined, their shiny black eyes hard from experience, their round noses twitching and thin mouths turned down in distaste. They each have a long grey beard tucked into their belts and would proudly boast to anyone who would listen about their heritage. Lesva taught them pride when she should have attempted to quell their natural unruly and stubborn nature.

"They made the first move, and you made the second," I reply, sheathing my sword and taking several steps back. "You could have just given me what I want."

"You know that's not how I operate, E," Lesva says with a smirk.

I fold my arms, and her expression hardens.

"I'm still not going to give you what you seek," she replies firmly.

I clench my hands, gloves creaking slightly as the shadows wriggle; I spared her life and the life of her men, but she will not give me a simple piece of information. That is typical of her, but I will not indulge any more whims today. I will leave with what I desire, or I will leave bloody.

"You don't want to deny me, Lesva," I reply calmly, unclenching my fists; she is observant when she wants to be. I should never have told her to cultivate her naturally observant nature.

"I remember what happens when I do," she replies, shrugging off her cloak, revealing slender, bare shoulders. One of the men is by her side in a moment, taking her cloak and neatly folding it up, setting it down almost reverently. "So it isn't really a threat, dear." She pats my cheek, walking past and opening the door a crack. I spin around, grabbing her wrist and wrenching her backwards, the door clicking shut at the same time that I unsheathe my sword, thrusting it at her heart. A thin dagger blocks my own blade in an instant, but I flick my wrist and my blade changes direction, the tip catching the cross guard of the dagger, spinning it out of her grasp, keeping my sharp tip at her wrist.

"You have ten seconds," I growl. I already indulged Scarlett and paid that pig outside instead of forcing my way in; I am through holding my temper in check.

The shadows slide down the door in eager anticipation, and I only barely stop myself from releasing them.

"You're not going to do it," she replies, locking her eyes onto mine, holding up one hand to stay her men, their knuckles white on their weapons.

"Six seconds."

"I hardly think that you can bring yourself to kill me."

Her voice doesn't quiver, but her muscles are tense beneath her skin—that much I can feel through my sword. My muscles tense, my wrist just begins to flick when her eyes widen and she blurts out, "I don't even know who you're looking for!" I stop myself in the middle of my micro-motion, pulling my sword away without leaving a scratch.

"Impres," I reply coolly, and she swears, kicking one of the small chairs across the room angrily. The shadows slink across the floor, oozing past my feet.

"Gods man! It was hard enough to lock her away the first time for you! You nearly—"

"This time I have no interest in locking her away," I growl, cutting her off. "That was because I owed Niclaus," I walk over to one of the walls and the shadows follow, searching over it; a small click seems to echo throughout the room and a panel slides open, revealing a cabinet of files. "This time she has the last piece of the puzzle—the final ingredient. I must have it. I need it, and I won't let anyone or anything stand in my way."

"It's an impossible task, what you're trying to do. What you think you will find with Impres—it can't be done. It doesn't even exist." she says from behind me.

"That is why I must create it," I reply.

She continues talking as I search through the files, but I pay no attention; I have put too much time and effort to stop now. Finally I pull out the one I desire, leafing through it. After a moment, I throw it on the table in disgust, glaring at Lesva.

"What are you playing at, Lesva?" I growl, and she folds her arms across her chest, stepping toward her men who make a protective circle around her.

"I don't know what you mean," she says, her voice even and flat.

"Her location isn't in here!"

"Of course not! It's to prevent people like you from just taking what they want. My business is built on privacy, and that is why I'm so successful. Only I know the location of each meeting and how to contact them."

"I will rip that information from your mind," I snap, taking a step forward and the dwarves bare their weapons to me, knuckles whitening as they clench their hands tighter; they would die for her. The shadows wriggle across the floor like serpents, circling my feet; they beg for a meal, their hunger only growing with my mounting frustration.

"We both know you don't have that kind of time," she retorts, opening the door.

I sheathe my sword, clenching down on my anger. I will gain nothing from killing her or her men; as much as I would enjoy doing so, it would be a mere waste. The shadows begin circling the cabinet, twisting up along its faces until it nearly blends into the darkness. Slowly the shadows sink back into the floor, the cabinet disappearing along with them.

"Since your memory is so great, you shouldn't need those." I growl, slamming the door behind me.

Why the hell didn't I pack any water?! It's been a few hours since I broke out of the house, and I still haven't come across a single person. *You should have gone right.* I haven't had water in nearly twenty-four hours; that can't be at all healthy. And it's freezing outside! *That's winter for you, but maybe that little cottage up there has water.* What cottage? *That one.* My eyes travel up from my trudging feet, looking up of their own accord, settling on a small cottage. It rests on a grassy knoll by the side of the road, with wooden walls dotted with colorful pebbles and small glass mosaics, having a simple, shingled roof above the low walls. It has a small fence around it and what looks to be a flower garden in the front, a tangle of vines growing up the side; well, it's...cute.

I will my feet to move faster, and they meet me halfway, speeding up to a quick walk. I finally get to the cabin and stop, my hand poised, ready to knock. *What are you waiting for? Aren't you thirsty?* I'm about to knock on some stranger's door and ask for water with no weapons or money; I'm not sure this is the smartest idea. *You agreed to live and train with a man you've only known for a few weeks.* I nod, knocking; point made. For a moment nothing happens, then there's a large crash and a loud thud. Maybe this wasn't a good idea; I begin to back away slowly when the door swings open.

A young man blinks at me, his eyes wide and brown. His shaggy brown hair sticks out in almost every imaginable direction. I take in his loose white shirt and ripped, worn shorts; he dresses a little... casually. *Obviously you woke him up.* It's far too late in the day for him to have still been asleep. He rubs his eyes, unsuccessfully trying to stifle a yawn. You win. *Doesn't he look familiar to you?* My eyes widen and I take a step back, nearly falling off the steps to his door; he's the man from before, at the cabin! He reaches out to steady me as I regain my footing, still eyeing me cautiously. I—I thought he had died in the aftermath, or surely he would have died from his injuries! Seeing the man that I left behind for dead in front of me, alive and well—it fills me with a mix of emotions. *Just get it out of your system quickly so that you can get some water in your system.* For once, I might listen to myself.

I'm ashamed that I left him there in the first place but relieved that he's alive. The small part of me deep down sees his life as a failure because I wasn't responsible for saving him, but I pay no attention to that; it doesn't get a say in the matter. He doesn't seem to recognize me; *of course not, he was unconscious!* Ultimately, though, I can't change the past; I should be grateful he's alive and I don't have his blood on my hands. He stands there silently looking at me, and I take a step forward, offering him a tired smile; god I am tired. I know I should feel guilty about imposing on him again, but I haven't slept in what feels like an entire day, and my throat feels like it's going to start cracking if it gets any drier.

"Hi." Good, start out simple; if I keep it simple, he might never know that I left him for dead. *How could he know that, you dolt?* My teacher manipulates shadows; I have *no* idea what anyone could be capable of. *He was unconscious!* Still. I offer him a cold hand to shake. "I'm Scarlett." I feel a swell of pride in my chest at being able to greet someone and offer my name. He shakes my hand, his eyes looking at me curiously.

"Wilhelm," he says, his voice offering further proof that he obviously just woke up. "You're not going to fall again, are you?"

He couldn't have been rude, could he? Maybe if he was completely rude I wouldn't feel so bad about having left him, but he's considerate. *You just can't win, can you?*

"I don't think so," I say, feeling my cheeks start to heat up. "But I've been walking for a while and—" I cough, my dry throat heaving and convulsing, craving water. "—and I forgot to pack any water." I show him my pack full of nothing but changes of clothes; I don't expect him to just take my word for it, after all. "I was wondering if—" I dissolve into a coughing fit again, and he ushers me inside; stop being so nice! He motions for me to sit down on the couch and disappears into a separate room.

The room has a small, used leather couch and a table next to it with an unlit gas lamp. A large trunk sits directly in front of the couch, and an old reclining chair rests next to the wall, close to the door. A small brick fireplace hosts several logs, but they remain unlit like the gas lamp; the room is unnaturally warm. I hear the tinkling of glasses behind me; that must be the kitchen. *No, he just keeps drinking glasses in his bedroom all the time.* Some people might! *That was sarcasm.*

Wilhelm comes back with a glass of water and a plate of food; I didn't even ask for food. If I eat his food, I would never be able to forgive myself; my stomach rumbles, and I sigh. A life of guilt it is. He hands me the water and I take it gratefully, smiling at him then quickly gulping the contents down. I look at the plate of food and my stomach rumbles again; I wasn't even hungry until he put food in front of me. He laughs, standing up again after having just sat down in the reclining chair, taking my empty glass before I could protest.

He certainly is a gentleman; bet you like that. I actually do. *Of course.* This isn't exactly easy on me!

"I had a feeling you would be hungry," he says, going back to the kitchen again. I look to the food once more; it's very colorful, but I haven't the faintest idea what it is. *It could be poisonous.* I doubt he would poison me. *You never know.* I would deserve it though. *Agreed.* He comes back with the glass and a utensil, handing me both. I take a long drink from the glass, then set it down on the table. He doesn't say anything, just lifts the glass up and sets a knit coaster down underneath, setting the glass back down. He looks from me to the food; I know I should probably eat, but it's just so...well...colorful. Despite my new hunger, it still looks like a tropical bird from one of Mister E's books.

"I know it looks like a rainbow decided to vomit on the plate—" I laugh at his comment, and he smiles; he's good at breaking the tension. *Are you wondering what else he's good at?* Shut it. "But it's actually very good; I ended up fixing too much last night. I was expecting company, but—but they never showed. I suppose that works out well for you," he says, leaning back in his chair. I look at the food once again and take the utensil, stabbing a piece of something blue, slowly bringing it to my mouth. Suddenly my hand speeds up, and it's in my mouth. I chew and my eyes roll up slightly as I let out an involuntary moan, taste exploding into my mouth. I see him looking at me with his wide eyes, and I quickly chew and swallow so I can speak.

"It's...I...it's..." I struggle for the words to describe the sensations it brings to my taste buds, making them dance and croon for more, but I can't quite find them. *Just tell him you like it.* His expression falls slightly before he gives a small smile, standing and reaching for the plate. *First you leave him for dead, and then you make him think that you don't like his cooking.* Not helping!

"You don't have to eat it if you don't like it," he says, extending his hand to take the plate.

"No!" I shout, perhaps a little too harshly, jerking the plate away from him, nearly spilling it on his floor. He stops and I take another bite, subsequently trying to talk around said bite. "No, I mean...it's...I like it." I mumble around the food. He steps back, his eyes lighting up.

"Okay then," he says smiling. I feel my chest heat up, and I quickly look at the rainbow food, taking another bite.

You are such a mess. I can't believe you don't feel guilty over this. I do feel guilty he's just...good at making me feel good. *Oh really? That's not what I meant!*

"That's all there is, unfortunately, but I have a well out back so there's plenty of water. There should be a canteen or two lying around in the kitchen; just help yourself," he says, thankfully interrupting my thoughts as he walks toward the kitchen and then takes a left, disappearing down a hallway.

Hearing a door close, I quickly devour the food, appeasing the monster that had been growling in my stomach. Leaning back, I let out a content sigh and take a sip from the glass. *What will you do now?* I look around the cottage slowly, with its wooden walls and floors, fireplace, and worn furniture; it feels homey. I don't know what I'm going to do now, but I like it here. *Do you think he'll just let you stay?* I bite my lip; maybe. *You left him for dead!* What happens when he finds out?! I just...won't tell him. *What will happen when Mister E returns to find you gone?* I grip the glass harder; I don't want to think about him. *Well you have to! He'll come after you and you know it!* I look around the room again and sigh; staying here any longer will put Wilhelm in danger. *You can't say here, you know it.* I already left him for dead once and abandoned him; I won't put him deliberately in danger again. I stand up and go to the kitchen, rooting around for a canteen. It takes a few minutes of opening drawers filled with items I assume are used to prepare food, though some look like they belong on a torturer's rack. *Maybe he tortures people after he drugs their food—you never know. Perhaps he really is a horrible person who deserved to be left for dead.* Ha, I should be so lucky. I shake my head, using the pump in the kitchen to fill up the canteen. I take a swig then fill it back up, closing the lid. I turn to see Wilhelm leaning in the doorway, watching me with those wide eyes, an amused expression on his face.

"The capital is a walk an hour or two that way," he says pointing in the direction I had been walking.

I nod, brushing past him. I knew left was the correct path! I feel a quick tap on my shoulder and turn to him; I can't stay any longer.

"Would you like to talk?"

I look at the door; I really can't stay any longer. *But you want to.* I can't though. *No, you can't.* I really shouldn't. *Nope, really shouldn't.* I might as well at least stay to apologize about being so imposing. *No that's not*—Shut it. I nod, and he moves over to the couch, sitting down on one end, and motioning for me to sit on the other. Due to the size of the couch we're not that far away, but he keeps as much distance as he can between us; I wonder if he does it for my benefit.

"I don't really do this much," I say, picking at my pants; what exactly am I supposed to talk about? What's expected of me? I can't talk about my past; I don't have much of a past. I could lie, but that just feels...wrong, to lie to him. *Do you know what the solution to this problem is? Get out of his house; just get out.* Or I could just not mention the part about leaving him for dead. *I give up.*

"What? Go into a strange man's house, eat his food, drink his water, and then talk to him instead of making a run for it as quickly as you can?" he says with a smirk.

"No, I actually do that all the time," I say, He laughs in response, causing me to smile. "I just don't talk much."

"Why not?" he asks, leaning forward curiously; I don't get the feeling he's trying to be intrusive at all. He just wants to know; it's almost a childish curiosity.

"I'm currently living with my teacher ,and he's...not an open man. It doesn't leave very much room for just conversation." I'm not sure what I would talk about with him anyway; I don't really know much about him—or anything, for that matter.

"Here's your opportunity for some old-fashioned conversation," he says.

I nod, swallowing hard; what am I supposed to say? Isn't there a rule or protocol for these sorts of things?

"Would it be easier if I started?"

I nod quickly. "Yeah," I blurt out.

He leans back, propping his feet up on the chest; he still hasn't changed out of his sleepwear.

"Since you're heading to the capital, and from your state it looks like you were in a hurry, it seems you were running away from something. I'm guessing your teacher?" he keeps his voice calm and kind; it sounds very nice to my ears.

Careful, he's using psychology. Yes, but he's being *nice* about it. *You can smile while you run someone through with a blade—doesn't mean it's not murder.*

"I didn't actually know the capital was that way," I say.

His eyebrows go high, his expression almost comical; it makes me comfortable, in a way. I feel the tension beginning to uncoil from me, and I'm able to look up from my twisting hands to his eyes occasionally. *You are a terrible person. You leave a man for dead, then you eat his food and want to talk to him about your problems.* He offered! Besides Mister E trains me and gives me material to learn, but he hasn't taught me much in the way of social interaction; I honestly don't think he knows enough to teach. This is really a learning experience.

"You must not be from around here," he says.

"I..uh..don't actually know where I'm from," I stammer. *Why are you being honest with this man? You hardly know him; you shouldn't even be here still.* I hardly know Mister E either, and so far Wilhelm hasn't attacked me; point Wilhelm. *You're putting him in more danger just by staying. If you care about him, why are you still here?* I can't answer that question, but somewhere inside it just feels...right. His expression shifts to worry and sympathy.

"I'm sorry," he says, holding up his hands slightly. "I didn't mean to—"

"It's okay," I interrupt, maintaining eye contact with him; eye contact is good, right? "I'm still figuring things out."

He looks at me for a moment, his great big eyes taking me in. They don't judge or try to pierce me—try to figure out who I am or bore holes into me. They just see me, taking me for who I am. I open my mouth then close it, heart hammering; what do I do now? What do I do? I don't know who I am—how do I tell him that? How do I tell him when I don't know? I don't know, I just don't know. *Calm down! Your panicking is infuriating!* I take a deep breath; right, calm down. Breathe, just breathe; I take another deep breath, my eyes focusing on Wilhelm's again. I want to tell him, I really do, but how much can I involve him in this? None of this is his problem, but I can't...I can't keep everything to myself, bottled up inside. I open my mouth, and it begins to run of its own accord. I tell him everything, and it spills out of me from deep inside, rushing out in a jumble of words that I don't really hear but never seem to end. His expression doesn't change throughout the entire thing, remaining calm. I finish and my mouth snaps shut, my chest heaving, my heart hammering; at least I managed to somehow avoid telling him I abandoned him, injured and alone, in a forest. Although if Mister E finds out what I've done now, Wilhelm will die for certain; I've involved him more than I should have. *You think?* Oh god, this was so selfish of me! I should never have said a thing! *You just couldn't keep things bottled up, could you?* I stand up, giving him a quick excuse, taking a step toward the door. I feel his hand grip mine, and I turn quickly, his eyes casting their sympathetic gaze up from the couch.

"Stay," he says, his voice soft and more of a question, despite his firm grip on my wrist. He blinks and quickly removes his hand, running it through his messy hair. He seems to realize how messy it is and tries to flatten it, but it just sticks up; I laugh, using it as a way to release my panic. As much as I should, I can't keep it all in; I'll explode. This panic, this worry, this fear—they will eat me alive if I don't let it out. He laughs too, and we soon dissolve into a laughing fit, our laughter echoing around the room. I collapse onto the couch, no longer able to breathe, tears at my eyes.

I suck in a deep breath, sitting up, shaking my head; he makes me do the weirdest things. *He isn't making you do anything; you just can't help but be awkward and weird around him for whatever reason.* That is a possibility, I admit. More than anything, he makes me feel good, makes me feel listened to; he makes me feel...safe.

I look at him, his eyes sparkling and smiling; I don't want him to die. I can't...no, I won't let him die. Mister E saved my life, but this man has saved me in a way that means so much more; a life of misery and worry isn't worth living. I won't let harm come to him; I will protect him no matter what because he saved me. I don't remember ever feeling this way about anyone, but I never want to forget it. The rush, the safety—I don't want to ever lose this.

"I'm sorry," I say, and he shakes his head, his hair swaying. "It was all very sudden for me to just—"

"Don't apologize," he interjects. "It sounded like you needed to get that off your chest; I'm glad I was here to listen to it. Though," he looks down at me, brow knitting slightly, "it sounds like you have something you need to resolve with your teacher. Right now the relationship is built on fear; and not only is that unhealthy, but it makes for an extremely short and unstable relationship. A healthy one must be built on respect."

I suppress a snort, turning it into a cough; the idea of Mister E respecting anyone is difficult to picture at best.

"You need to explain to him that you want to be his student, but that you're not afraid of him—that you want him to respect you. Fear seems to be a prominent emotion in you whether you know it or not." He stands up, holding his hand out.

He's still using psychology on you; that's manipulative. It's kind, not that you would understand.

"Which is only natural," he continues. "We're only human, after all. You shouldn't ever let your fear stop you from doing something that you want."

I put my hand in his, and his warm hand closes around mine, pulling me up. He lets go, and I leave my hand there for a moment before moving it to my side as he grabs my pack and hands it to me. I slip it on, and he moves around me, opening the door; I guess it's time for me to leave. I'm not sure if I want to go back though; I want to stay. I stop just outside his door and he smiles at me, his eyes sparkling in the sunlight.

"Feel free to stop by any time you're thirsty or hungry or... anything. Just feel free to stop by," he says with a laugh, running his hand through his hair.

I nod and smile, and the door closes behind me.

I'm not sure if I want to go back; I'm not sure if I even can now. If I go back, the chances of Mister E discovering Wilhelm are that much higher. *If you don't go back, and you stay, those chances increase exponentially.* I can protect Wilhelm, I know I can. *Do you honestly believe that? If you betray him now, he will destroy both you and Wilhelm without a second thought.* We could leave, go into hiding. *You don't hide from someone like Mister E, and Wilhelm would slow you down, if he would even go with you. You just met; trust wouldn't be at its highest between you two.* We could make it. *Even if you could, you would forget all about Wilhelm and that feeling that you hold so dear. You have to return to Mister E if you want to retain any memories.* I sigh, turning to the left, my steps slow and heavy; I have to go back. Once Mister E has taught me all he can—once I find out how to retain memories by myself—I will leave him. Until I am strong enough to defend Wilhelm, I will rely on Mister E. I must ensure that it is only a temporary solution; I cannot stay with him forever.

It's nearly afternoon when I make it to the glen. Here the crisp winter wind is kept out. Instead, a small warm breeze is whispering through; the seasons do not change here. Soft bright green blades of grass sparkle with perpetual dew, the sun shining brightly down on them warms the soil. Little critters scurry throughout the thick bushes that lay on the fringe of the glen, and large red berries litter the ground. Small, willowy trees sway in the breeze, the gentle rocking and creaking of wood lulls the birds to sleep better than their own lullabies. I look to the bottom of a small pond, the water clear enough I can see the bright fish found nowhere else in Legend Land; the shadows cast by objects on land do not hit the bottom, as the pond is deceptively deep.

"What can I help you with today, Mister E?"

I turn around and dip my head at a middle-aged woman, humbly dressed with her greying hair tied back behind her head. Her smile is pleasant enough, but her eyes are wary and cautious.

"I'm here to see Jack, Mrs. Helvare," I reply courteously; she deserves only my utmost respect; and no matter what prior events may be, she will get it. She sighs, letting me into her small, quaint cabin.

"We moved out here to avoid people after the…incident," she says, her voice hard and disapproving.

I nod, the shadows gently closing the door behind me. They would not dare disobey me here; the consequences, regardless of the repercussions upon myself, would be severe.

"We just celebrated his seventeenth birthday, you know; you might want to make mention of that."

"Thank you," I say in a low voice as we make our way into a small, dark bedroom. The only furniture is a single bed, and shutters are drawn over the lone window in the room; the darkness suits me just fine.

Mrs. Helvare sets a chair down in the room, and I sit as she walks over to the bed, gently whispering with all the care of a loving mother, "You have a visitor, Jack." There's a rustle in the sheets, and she helps a small figure sit up.

"Light please," a hoarse voice croaks softly. Mrs. Helvare pulls a small candle from inside her dress, lighting it with a match. The person before me is small and slight, only the size of a child of nine or ten. Long, messy white hair tangles in a beard of the same color. His eyes are milky white and filmy, his skin pale and wrinkled, sagging off of his thin frame. His head turns to look at his mother, and she cringes slightly, quickly covering it up by kissing his forehead and leaving the room in a hurry.

For a moment, we sit in silence as he studies me, and I wait patiently; I have been able to rely on Jack in the past. I will not wait an eternity, though he will get to it before then, because he doesn't have an eternity to wait; the subject of mortality is often enough on his mind.

"I disgust her," he says in that same hoarse voice, the kind that belongs to a dying man—one who is old and has lived his life.

"She tells me you recently celebrated your seventeenth birthday,"

I say, removing a small box from my cloak, setting it gently on the bed. "Happy birthday, Jack Helvare."

"She didn't have to tell you it was my birthday, did she? You knew already."

I nod and assume he sees the small motion because one thin, veiny claw of a hand wraps around the box, trembling hands try to unwrap it. Several small tendrils take the box from him, unwrapping it with care and precision, setting it back down on his lap. He fumbles with it and then finally manages to get it open. A small bean and note fall onto his lap; his face sets, and he stares at the bean for several minutes. "What does the note say?"

"Make the climb, Jack," I reply softly, and he looks at me, his brows knitting as he decides whether he wants to be angry or not.

"I know you want something, and I don't need to make the climb to give you an answer. I don't think I could anyway," he says, looking down at his hands. "I'm so old, so old. Ever since I made that climb... what was it, seven? Seven years ago, my body stopped growing, but I began aging rapidly. All for the 'gift' of sight," He says bitterly, small frame trembling. "I've had my life stolen from me and now I'm going to die soon; I can feel it. I haven't been out of this bed in weeks."

"Death isn't so bad," I reply, and he snorts, dissolving into a coughing fit.

After a minute, he straightens back up, sucking in a rattling breath. "Not to someone so experienced, no. I've never done it before though; it's a frightening concept. This will be the only time I die," He looks up at the ceiling, sucking in sharply. "Oblivion."

I get up, walking over to his bed, and pick up the bean. His eyes lock onto it, and his breathing slows down even further.

"Despite it all, you loved the climb, didn't you? You loved seeing the world for what it really was when you got to the top, despite everything that happened afterward. When you got to the top, you could look into the light of the world. You survived, and you saw. You loved it, didn't you Jack?"

Slowly, he nods, transfixed.

"Then do yourself a favor and do it again."

"I—I can't." His shoulders slump, his voice broken and defeated. "I can barely move; I can't make the climb."

I stand up straight, grabbing his thin hand tightly in my gloved one, knowing that my next words will seal his fate; I must do this. I have to—there is no other way; I can't let personal feelings get in the way. Though I will be damned if I don't make this the best experience of Jack Helvare's life—I owe him that much at least.

"Let me carry you,"

I come outside of the room, Jack clutching the bean in his hands, his small body curled up in my arms. His mother runs to me, but Jack looks at her and she stops.

"Mom, I have to do this." He shows her the bean, and she pulls in a breath, anger and worry forming on her face.

"No—no! You can't do it again! I won't let you. Not after what it did to you the last time! I can't lose you, Jack!" She takes a step forward, but Jack holds up his hand wearily, his voice tired when he speaks.

"Mother, I'm dying. You know it; my body is dying, and I can't even walk. This life isn't meant for me any longer." Her mouth opens but he continues, drawing on reserves of strength to continue talking. "I know what it did to me last time, and I'm counting on it to do the same; I want to die up there, among the giants and gods, looking down at the world. I could never be a giant or a god or anything but human, but I can die pretending to be."

"Oh Jack," she sniffs, wiping a tear from her face, hiccupping and caressing his old, gnarled face. "My baby boy," she whispers, turning away and retreating into the house.

We walk to the pond in silence; this is a last resort. It is necessary. I do this not because I want to, but because I must. Separating a mother from her child is one of the worst evils in this world; in the worst situations, the worst evils must sometimes become necessary. He drops the bean in; and, for a moment, nothing happens. Then the water gleams brightly, bubbling and steaming ferociously. In a torrent of bright and wild lights, a large green beanstalk shoots up, towering higher than any tree in this world—or any world for that matter. It pierces the clouds high above, ascending into the heavens. I look down at Jack, this small boy that the world decided to make a man, weighing nothing in my arms; he looks up at me and nods, determination on his face. With one hand, I hold him tightly; and with the other, I begin to climb.

The ascent is at an easy pace, but I make steady progress up, stopping every once in a while to adjust my grip on Jack. As we near the clouds, I use the shadows to hold me to the beanstalk, taking my cloak off and wrapping it around Jack; I want him to be as comfortable as possible on his last journey.

"It's about to get very cold, and very hard to breathe," I warn, but he just nods again, teeth chattering, his eyes fixed heavenward. I once more begin my ascent, the shadows slinking away; I could use them to climb this in a fraction of the time, making it thousands of times easier. But some things just shouldn't be made easy. I won't disgrace Jack by making this quick and easy; it was hell for him when he did it, and I won't dishonor that memory.

The air begins to get thinner, the temperature dropping; I can detect these things, but they don't affect me. I check on Jack, but he urges me to keep going, and so I do. As we pass through the clouds, moisture clings to us, and I hold Jack closer, bundled in my cloak.

All at once, everything shimmers—golden palaces appear before us, gardens and fountains resting on the clouds. In the far off distance, a large castle for the giants looms over these palaces and temples, but that's not why we're here; I don't have the necessary ingredients to make that part of my journey yet. I am here for, and because of, Jack; that is the only reason at this moment.

I step off the beanstalk onto the clouds, setting Jack down and turning him, letting him see the light of the world. Some call it truth, others hope or fantasy; it is all and none of those things. It directly affects each and every person in Legend Land, and they are joined to it in an intimate way that they are not knowledgeable of. It is not divine, nor has it ever been. When the last legend dies, the light will go out; but for now, it remains shining—not as bright and brilliant as it used to be, but it still possesses enough power to either blind or drive insane most mortals who look at it, and even some of the gods themselves.

It is bright, brighter than all the stars in the sky, its light shining up, nearly blinding even to me. Indescribably unique, though separate feeling wells up within both of us; only one looking at the light of the world, as it truly is, could feel this emotion. That is how it always is, and there is never quite a feeling like it. An addiction—a drive builds within you until the only thing you wish to do is stare in awe and wonder at the light; the light of the world is more beautiful and dangerous than anything else in Legend Land.

I turn to Jack, his eyes slowly clearing to a soft, light hazel. They sparkle with the light of the world reflected in them, his mouth open in wonder, joy etched into every line on his face.

"I—I never thought I'd see this again," he whispers reverently, silent tears streaming down his face. I wrap one arm around his shoulders, holding him tightly to my solid frame; I won't have a gust of wind blow him away. "Thank you, thank you so much." He says, looking up at me, and once again his face is that of a young boy, the age he was when he made the first climb. Curtains of blonde hair frame his reacquired youth, a light dusting of freckles on his plump, rosy face. He looks down at his chubby, youthful hands—hands that he hasn't seen in nearly a decade. I turn his head gently back to the light; I want the thing that he loves most to be the last thing he sees. "I'm near the end now, aren't I?"

"Yes," I reply softly.

He nods, wiggling his fingers.

After a moment of silence, I speak up. "Jack," his expression is unreadable, save the happiness in his smile and the sparkle in his eyes. "I need you to do something for me." His smile doesn't fade, and he nods. "I need you to find someone for me."

He is the only mortal I know who was ever able to look at the light of the world and not only live, but also remain sane—at a price of course; there is always a price with these things. Every gift has a curse trailing silently behind; and by the time you hear the whisper of it, it's already too late.

"Who?"

"Impres," I reply.

He clasps his hands together tightly, his smile falling slightly, but he nods, looking into the light of the world. When he does so, he sees something I could never hope to see—nor would I ever want to. He sees the truth, and the truth is not for everyone.

"She's with someone named Merecil," he replies in a soft, faraway voice. "I can't find them, but I know where the person who can is." He starts to turn away from the light. "Sorry."

"That's more than I had when I first came here," I say, pulling him close again, and turning his head to look at the light. "Look at it until the end."

He nods, his eyes going wide and bright, a happy grin on his face as tears streak down. A sob of joy wracks his entire body, switching between a cry and a loud, joyous laugh.

"When you look at the world, you see more than just the truth; you see everything and everyone you could ever have loved. That is the best way to leave this world; you are very fortunate." I remain quiet after this, holding him to me.

Gradually, his body grows stiff and cold—the slow, final rattle escaping his lips. I look at him, his eyes still wide and sparkling, still smiling. I wish to leave him sitting on the edge of the clouds, looking at the world, with the giants and the gods, but I must return his body to his mother. He remains in spirit and will forever remain with the light of the world.

"You're one of them now," I say softly, standing up slowly and looking into the light. Slowly, tendrils appear out of my arms, extending toward the light. They shriek and hiss, burning and writhing in pain, but I make them continue; there is no other option here. I pierce the light of the world, slowly writing six small words into the light; they will appear in everyone's mind now. I collect Jack's body and walk back over to the beanstalk, beginning to descend. As soon as I make it below the clouds, the thought that I had written into the light of the world hits me, as I knew it would, just like everyone else. *Jack Helvare: He made the climb.*

I return before the sun begins to set; good, I still have time. I put my pack in my room and stand outside, looking out; he really does own a beautiful piece of property. *Think that when he dies you'll get it?* He doesn't seem like the type of person to die. *You're right, he doesn't; he'll just live forever.* Was that sarcasm? *Of course it was; everyone must die eventually.*

I move to the storage shed and pull one of the practice blades out, giving it a twirl. I return to the dirt patch and take a few practice swings at the air. I cringe at how pathetically slow they are, and I work my limbs, warming them up. I swing the sword again and it slices through the air faster, but not fast enough.

I stop, looking at the wooden blade; why can't I get through this? Wilhelm says that fear is a prominent emotion in me, and I should never let fear hold me back; but if I am afraid, I don't feel it. Why would I be afraid of fighting? It's the one thing I seem to be good at. *Could it be you're afraid of fighting because you're worried that you might find out who you were before? Or that you'll start to really enjoy the killing?* I look at the blade; I do enjoy killing. I found that out at the cabin; I enjoy ending life.

I twirl the blade, looking slowly around the dirt patch; I enjoy bringing about the ending to someone's story. The blade twirls faster, and I duck under an imaginary swing from an opponent, slicing at his ankles, then rising up and slicing him across the neck as he falls. I like killing. I turn and parry a different blow, not meeting him in a bladelock but making sure his blade glances off of mine so I can slide mine up quickly, piercing him through the neck. I spin out of the way, grabbing the extended wrist of the foe who thrust his weapon at me, twisting it and chopping the limb off at his shoulder at the same time, then slicing his throat before he can recover.

I look at the imaginary corpses around me, and a knot forms in my stomach; I didn't even think about it. I thought about killing, how much I enjoy it, and my body acted. I know it should feel wrong, perverse; I shouldn't enjoy doing it, but I do. I swing my sword angrily, and it slices through the air so quick that I can barely see it; I like the killing! I enjoy the adrenaline in combat—the freedom it gives me, the clarity. I hate that I love it, that I feel the most alive when I am causing death. I turn and slice an imaginary foe across the chest, watching him sink to his knees and then drop dead to the ground; I never feel more alive than when I'm killing. *You see the irony there right?* I nod, parrying a heavy slash, flicking the point of my blade across my imaginary attacker's bicep, then sliding it up his arm, slashing him across the neck. I dance backward out of reach of another foe, twirling my blade, feinting right then stabbing left, running him through the heart.

I stop, breathing heavily, sweat beginning to give my skin a sheen. Will I have to think of the joy I gain from killing just to be able to defend myself? Is that the only way around the fear? I shake my head; as long as I don't let myself get overcome by it, it doesn't matter. It works, and that's all that *does* matter. As long as I don't lose myself in it, I should be fine; I can't stop myself from feeling enjoyment when I kill, no matter how sick it makes me feel, but I can at least not lose myself in it. Several more imaginary opponents appear, and I begin battling against them, twisting and turning to avoid attacks. I parry when necessary, slicing and sometimes hacking, dropping foe after foe; I like killing. A couple more drop dead to the ground and I go faster, my hair flying around me; I enjoy killing. I feel my mouth twist into a mixture between a snarl and a smile, nearly losing myself in the thrill of combat; I *love* killing.

I feel the swish of air hit my hair; I turn and block the strike, sliding my blade up Mister E's towards his neck. He twists his wrist, and my blade misses his neck as he moves out of the way quicker than any human should. The point of my blade embeds itself into the ground; but before I can wrench it free, I feel the point of his blade against my neck. I sigh softly and tilt my head in defeat; I feel him remove the blade and I turn to him, taking a deep breath, remembering Wilhelm's words. A relationship needs to be built on respect; I have to respect him, and he has to respect me. *At least, until you've learned all you can.*

It is evening, the sun beginning to set by the time I make it back to my house. My breath frosts in the air, though the cold doesn't touch me; it hasn't for some time, and it wouldn't dare start now. Blood red shafts of sunlight clutch at the ground, unwilling to leave the world behind, unaware that they will return the next day; the shadows hiss, eager for darkness to return to the world once more. My ears prick up, detecting the sound of heavy breathing coming from the training patch. I make my way over and fold my arms across my chest, watching the scene before me.

Scarlett holds a practice blade, spinning and twirling, dodging strikes from imaginary foes. Brutally, she dismembers one and then knees another, decapitating him. She works herself into a frenzy, twisting and ducking, slicing and running. Sweat drips down her skin, taught against her muscles, hair flying about like wild flames, sword dancing and hacking whenever it was needed. I admit it is a majestic sight; she could be great, when she thought no one was watching. She puts herself into a place where nothing but the task at hand enters her mind, and she executes it with great efficiency and precision; when others are around, her emotions invariably get the best of her.

I silently pick up a practice blade, swinging it at her back. She spins around, blocking the strike and sliding her blade up against mine, slicing at my neck. I twirl my wrist, her blade missing my neck and skimming the air before the point of her blade is embedded into the ground; I put my practice blade at her neck and she stops, tilting her head in defeat, yanking the sword savagely out of the ground. She sits herself down against the shed, scooping a cup of water out of the water bucket, breathing heavily and flipping a piece of sweaty hair out of her eyes. She's lucky the water didn't freeze—and even more lucky that she didn't freeze in her thin training garb. I will have to get her heavier clothes if she is to be out in the cold. I wait a moment before joining her, cooling my throat with a cup of water.

"You got out," I said simply, and she nods in reply. I take my gloves off slowly, looking at my pale, scarred hands. Experienced hands. "You stayed." She nods again, and I feel a small twinge of contentment. I have the urge to crush it, but I don't; I should be proud of her, as my student. "You will not get the option to leave again."

"I know," she says, her voice low and firm. She turns to me, her bright green eyes glowing in the setting sun.

I look deep into them, and I know I could swallow her up with my darkness if I wanted to. It would be easy enough; just reach out and let the shadows envelop her. She would struggle, for a moment, then there would be eternal stillness; I find it is always good to remind yourself that you have the power in the situation. Should you forget, you can be defeated by a weaker opponent, which is more than disgraceful; it warrants suicide, for such a pathetic creature shouldn't exist. All things considered, I doubt Scarlett would warrant such action; and now that she has proven her worth and I see her potential, I'm not sure I could bring myself to eliminate such a valuable resource.

"I'm not scared of you, you know."

I raise an eyebrow, slipping my gloves back on; this wasn't what I was expecting, in all honesty.

She continues, "I suppose some part of me is; you're powerful, and you could crush me. It would be as easy as killing an annoying pest, and I don't think you would lose much sleep over it, either. Knowing how you treat me, I don't pretend to think that you care about me. I know you don't care about me as a person, as someone with thoughts and feelings; you care about me as an object, something to help you achieve your goals. I don't mind that though because right now that will help me achieve my goals." Her eyes narrow, her knuckles white from keeping a death grip on the cup. "But I don't want you to trick me anymore; you can prepare me for when the world will try, the same way you can prepare me for when the world tries to kill me. As your student, I need to be able to trust you, or else I won't be able to learn from you. I should have to be weary of the rest of the world, but not you." She extends her free hand, muscles tense beneath her cooling sheen of sweat.

The shadows creep toward her, and I nod calmly, taking her hand in mine and giving it a firm shake. The shadows disappear quietly again, and I can feel their approval, though it is dwarfed by their hunger, denied for so long. I can put it off no longer, or I risk them becoming a threat.

"Very well," I reply, standing up, sipping from my cup. "You will find material laid out to study when you enter the library; I have an errand to run, and I expect you to be finished upon my return." She looks disappointed, but she moves toward the house nonetheless. "Afterward, weather permitting, we will spar." Her eyes brighten and she quickly makes her way into the house, shutting the door behind her. It is as easy to deal with her as a child. I turn to the forest as the sun finally sets; I look at the house again, knowing Scarlett is inside, studying. The shadows slink out of the ground, whimpering for attention; I am well aware of your plight. Hold yourself still a moment longer, and you will be satisfied. I growl, throwing my cup into the air, tendrils of shadow shooting out and piercing it, shredding it to fine sawdust.

I press my back against the door, breathing heavily; study before he returns, right. This is another test to see if I can do what he says; always with his tests. I quickly head to my room, tossing my clothes from my pack onto the floor then rushing to the library, sliding the books off my desk and into my pack. I rush to the front door and crack it open, then wait several minutes, controlling my breathing as best I can; he shouldn't be back for several hours. That means if I run, I can get to Wilhelm's house in an hour, study there, still have time to talk, and make it back in time. I nod; it can work.

Why are you going back so soon? Why are you taking such a big risk for a man you just met? I shake my head; you wouldn't understand.

Mister E will think that he has me tight under his leash, but I won't let him control me completely. He thinks he's using me, but I am using him just as much and he either doesn't know or doesn't care, which works well with me. I know our relationship is now supposed to be built upon respect, but I'll acknowledge that when he makes the first move toward mutual respect. When that happens, I will trust him. *You may be waiting a long time*. I grin, heading out the door; that's the idea.

CHAPTER TEN

The city of Descra is one of the more noxious, filthy holes that criminals find haven in when officials hunt after them; knowing the Kingdom intimately, that is saying something. Makeup heavy enough to be on a clown hides the faces of women too ashamed to admit they are on the street, and tattoos and brands mark where loyalties lie. The filth and film on the gas lamp covers hardly give any light, though I don't mind; I relax my body, moving my shoulders and neck to relieve some of the tension. Something catches the low light, which is bound to draw attention quickly. I'm the first one to the object, which is a pendant worn by one of the women; her clothes are dirty but try to pass themselves off as nice, her hair done quickly and carelessly. She makes a face that these low-life scum probably find alluring, in their base and animalistic sort of way. I step close to her, pushing her into a dark alley and against one of the rough, crumbling walls that pass themselves off for buildings in Descra.

"Oh you're rough," she purrs, her voice full of phlegm and smoke. I rip the pendant off her neck, wrapping one hand around her throat and holding it up to her close.

"The woman I am looking for sells these pendants here. Where is she?" I growl, tightening my grasp on her throat; I am in no mood to pamper these individuals with niceties that they do not deserve. I am here to feed the shadows, but I will do my best to get work done as well; I cannot waste a second in the pursuit of my mission.

Her mouth opens but no sound escapes. I loosen my grip slightly, and she sucks in a quick breath—and in that same breath gives me the information I desire. I let her go and she slumps to the ground in the waste-covered, filthy alley; there is no difference between the trash that litters the streets and her. I will not feed the shadows garbage; they nearly rebel at the thought. I throw the pendant down and stride out. My gait and countenance afford me the luxury of making my way to my destination uninterrupted, though shadows in my head hiss for a meal to satisfy their hunger, and I am almost willing to comply, though this spot is too public. I spot the woman I am looking for; she is covered in the same makeup as the street women, though she differentiates herself with fine silks and a bright red shawl around her shoulders as she advertises her cart of trinkets and pendants to potential customers.

I make my way up to the cart, and she smiles at me, her teeth yellow and crooked. Her voice is even huskier than the last woman's as what passes for words in Descra spill from her mouth.

"Looking for a treat for a young lady?" she asks with a thick city accent, showing off one of her pendants. Seeing my expression harden, she pulls out a more masculine necklace. "Perhaps for a young gentleman?" She gives me a wink and I step closer, leaning in to her ear, the scent of cheap perfume and smoke heavy on her.

"I am looking for Impres; I know she came by here. If you lie to me, I will rip out your tongue and make you write where she is in your own blood. Do you understand me?" It was only a rumor of Impres, and one overheard by a drunkard at that, but I have already been denied again and again in my search; I will not be denied now, no matter how thin the chance may be. The shadows being in the state they are, I could not risk following a serious lead, though this time I will not bother myself with such pleasantries as being kind, especially when the hissing of the shadows only grows louder. I detect that she nods quickly, and I lower my voice to a growl, the shadows slithering around her feet behind her cart; patience. "I expect you to tell me where she is now, or I will tear you apart piece by tiny piece."

The shadows slowly slither up her legs, sliding back down, leaving thin cuts on her legs. She shivers, trying to flinch away, but more tendrils wind their way around her waist and legs, keeping her in place. "I don't care what these people think, because I can and will kill them as well; no one will come to your aid, even if they care enough to do so. After I make an example of one or two brave souls, the rest will suddenly turn deaf and blind to your plight; you are all alone."

Tears start to run down her cheeks, ruining her makeup, though it's an improvement to me.

"Tell me where she is," I hiss.

"I don't know," she whispers, her lips quivering. She looks up at me, her eyes wide and scared. "Please, please just let me—"

In one smooth movement, I grab her and whirl her into a dark alley, stepping into the darkness, letting it surround me, blocking out the rest of the world. She scoots herself back on the ground as I walk closer. The shadows hiss in pleasure, snapping at her heels.

"I'll give you one more chance to tell me where she is," I slowly pull my gloves off, putting them in one pocket of my cloak, opening my mouth. I breathe in, and the shadows breathe out. The shadows slither around her, and my eyelids flutter, my hand splaying and they stop, hissing; they need a meal. For your sake, wench, I hope you have the information I seek; I will not leave Descra with the shadows unsated.

"I don't know where she is," she blubbers, her back against the wall. Her nails dig into the bricks, and she presses herself closer to the wall. Each step I take toward her, the shadows hiss even louder. "I was just told by a man to expect her, I swear. That's all I know!"

I crouch down next to her, cupping her cheek; I haven't allowed myself to feel someone's skin for so long. A real shame it's the skin of an impending corpse—though she proved more useful than I thought she would; a genuine piece of information was far more than I was expecting.

"Do you know where that man is?" My voice is deceptively soft and polite, and she sniffles, shaking. I will give her some small kindness before she is devoured, though I doubt she appreciates it.

"I—I—I—" Her eyes go wide, her mouth agape as I stroke her dirty, painted face with one thumb.

"No, of course you don't," I growl, the shadows snapping at her, drawing blood from a few shallow cuts. They hiss so loud I cannot hear my own thoughts; feast then! If only to quiet your incessant demands! They screech with glee, shooting into the woman, piercing holes in her. Several tendrils slide down her throat, choking off her screams. Her eyes remain locked on mine, pleading, begging as the shadows burrow deeper, worming around inside of her. "Don't play with your food," I snap and the shadows roar, lunging at me. I grab a tendril, snapping at my face and I squeeze it until it screams, splitting my skull. Through the haze of pain I growl, "I give you a meal, but I will not wait forever. Be glad for what you get and do not push your luck." I release the tendril and it slinks away, joining its brethren, now quickly snapping at and devouring the woman.

After a few moments, they slither away, crooning in contentment, leaving the mangled, hollow corpse of their victim—my victim. I slip my gloves on once more, turning my back on the grisly scene; merely another unfortunate victim of the city of Descra.

"Was your errand productive?" Scarlett raises her head from her books as she asks the question. I keep the doors to the library open, and she carefully puts the books back in their places, leaving a sheaf of papers on her desk. "Those are yours to read over, by the way," she says, walking to me.

"It could have been more so," I reply, making my way to the training patch. The moon shines overhead while I pick up a training blade and toss it to Scarlett as she walks out; she catches it, deftly spinning it. The wind is mercifully still, as Scarlett is not dressed for winter weather, and the temperature has already dropped lower than I am comfortable with exposing her to. She drops into a fighting stance, and I stand up straight, keeping my blade loose at my side. I will not be playing a role in this fight, but rather fighting as myself. Scarlett must know that for all her prowess in combat, she is no match for me; the student will eventually become the master, but that is not for a long time to come. She must be kept in her own place, lest I lose a student to her own poor judgment.

Scarlett slowly circles me, her eyes drinking in my form under the bright moonlight; I remain still, like an object to be studied. She's at my blind spot now; not behind me, striking where it would be obvious, but in that slight area that escapes even my superior peripheral vision. I easily hear her coming, turning and batting aside her blade with my own, sliding forward and elbowing her in the neck. She stumbles back and I dance forward, slicing at her neck and chest with the tip of my blade quickly, knocking her feet out from underneath her with a sweep of my leg. She looks up at me, gasping for breath; I pull her up, taking her blade from her loose grasp and tossing mine aside as well.

"That...that was quick," she says once she has caught her breath.

"It was designed to be," I reply, snapping my fingers and her eyes focus on me. "Listen well student, for this is how you will learn; I will beat you time and time again until you learn the lessons I wish to impart upon you. First," I hold up one finger. "If you can even hold your own against me, then you can best nearly anyone else you will come across as my student. Second," I grab one of the blades, putting it in her hand. "There are more senses than just your sight, and they all function in battle. The sound of a whistling blade, the smell of steel, the taste of blood in the air, the feel of slippery skin underneath you as you battle for supremacy with your opponent—they all play an important role in combat; and if you can master detection in these senses, then you will just as easily avoid being detected yourself. You are too loud when attacking; you must be quieter. Move your blade so quickly that the enemy has neither the chance to see or hear it; and by the time they recognize the threat, they will already feel the cold bite of your blade. If you can make yourself disappear in the heat of battle, you will have the advantage."

Scarlett looks down hard at her blade, swinging it through the air a few times. I continue, holding up a third finger. "Going to my blind spot was a good move; it wasn't as obvious as going behind my back, and not as many enemies will expect it. Just don't do it too often, or it will be countered."

She lifts her head up, her eyes bright; as long as you hide an obvious compliment within constructive criticism, most people will focus on the former. When I speak, she listens, and she absorbs knowledge at a ravenous pace, ever eager to test and push her abilities. She enjoys the thrill of combat and will be a competent student and ally, or a dangerous enemy.

"Again?" I raise my sword up. Scarlett nods, grinning as she settles back into her stance, eagerly rotating her blade in the air. Come, student, let us see how well you take to my lessons.

"Again."

CHAPTER
ELEVEN

Shadows shoot out from the ground, winding through the muggy early summer air, impaling themselves into the trees and nearly hitting Scarlett in the process. Bright green leaves in their prime flutter down, tendrils of shadow piercing them in their journey to Scarlett.

"Concentrate!" She rolls underneath several more and flips backward, slicing at one that rapidly changed direction in midair. I stand at the opposite end of the clearing, my hands spread out before me, directing the shadows as one force, then as independent assailants. I must take advantage of the season and increase the intensity of her training. She grew rusty in combat as winter progressed to the point of being unable to leave the house, and spring was spent reviewing everything already taught. I cannot allow myself to be lax on her; that will only get her killed. "Do not fall into the same pattern!"

A tendril wraps around her waist as she flips through the air again to dodge, slinging her against the tree and wrenching the dagger from her grasp. She struggles, writhing against the tree, tugging at her bonds. I yank my hand and the shadows hesitate, then slither away, though not as willingly as I would have liked. Winter was spent in hibernation for all of us, and I had to completely focus on Scarlett in spring. They grow ever more restless with each passing day, just like Scarlett. She drops to the ground, rolling and grabbing her knife, sheathing it as she stands. I walk to her and look down at her, folding my arms; she looks back up at me, her eyes determined. Still stubborn, even after training; I wouldn't have my student any weaker of will, not even after these last few weeks of intensive training. "Tell me what you did wrong."

"I wasn't born with eyes in the back of my head," she grumbles, turning away and kicking at the dirt.

I grab her shoulder and whirl her around; I will not spoil her. Life is not easy, and my training will not be either. "This training is intended to keep you *alive!* I will not have my student dying simply because I was too hard on her!" I take a deep breath, squeezing her shoulder until she winces, then relax my grip. "I know some knowledge has sunk into your head, so use it. An attitude does not help either of us and gets us nowhere. Shake it off and answer my question."

She folds her arms and leans on one leg, scrunching her eyebrows slightly. "I stayed in the air too long," she says, forcing the words out from behind clenched teeth. I nod for her to go on, and she sighs, rolling her eyes. "Remaining in the air leaves you vulnerable and should only be done for immensely short periods of time when there is no other option available. You are waiting in the air; and unless you can grow wings, you have little maneuverability." She looks at me again, every word dripping with her sardonic attitude. "Was that suitable, teacher?"

I growl, unclenching my hand and letting the tension dissolve out of my shoulders; she is correct, but her attitude nearly nullifies that. I nod and she turns her back, stomping away. I move one finger slightly, and a tendril slithers out of the ground, wrapping around one of her ankles and slinging her into the air. I did not say that training was finished. She grabs a low-lying branch, swinging herself onto it and scuttling backward as a curtain of darkness chops at where she had just been. Another thin curtain slices down at her like a guillotine, and she flips backwards, slipping down the tree. Tendrils of shadow spiral down after her, hissing and snapping and she executes a backwards roll, unsheathing her dagger in the process and slicing at a tendril that encroaches too far into her personal space. A tendril slams into her from the side, and she quickly slices it off before it can wrap around her, rolling and thudding into a tree.

Picking herself up, she slices another tendril, running and diving under another one, coming up and slicing at me, going for the source. Good—take out the leader, and the others will fall. I duck back and she slices at me again, this time with intent; I grab her wrist and she aims an elbow at my temple. I duck back, twisting her wrist behind her back, kicking her legs out from underneath her, taking the dagger, and pressing it to the back of her neck. I will tolerate many things; but when she begins making serious attempts at my life, I draw the line. Perhaps I didn't evaluate her as thoroughly as I thought; perhaps she is not yet ready for intensive training. I cannot rush her training, but I cannot wait around for her to decide to commit herself. Summer has begun, and with it, rumors of Impres have become more numerous; her activity has been increasing. I cannot wait on Scarlett forever.

"Go to the house and cool off," I growl, shoving her away and throwing the dagger next to her.

I slam the door to Wilhelm's house shut behind me, throwing my pack onto the couch. "I hate that man!" I shout. I can't believe the way he treats me, even after I have proven myself to him more than once—even after I continue to pass his tests. *He is pushing you this hard because he cares.* There is such a thing as being pushed too far! *You will never know your limits if he doesn't.*

"Glad to see you too," Wilhelm says, cleaning a glass and then putting it away, coming over to me. He wraps his arms around me from behind, pulling me close. He kisses my neck gently and I sigh, leaning back more against him; his body heat melts the tension in my muscles, and I relax against him. "Now tell me what happened." He lets go, sitting on the couch.

I lay down, setting the back of my head in his lap, looking up at him as he strokes my hair. *This happens far too often between you two; it's disgusting.* It calms me when he strokes my hair! I have a difficult time opening up as it is, he knows that. *That's not the part I was talking about.* I blush, closing my eyes; oh shut up.

"With all of the intense training I've been doing recently, I haven't had as much time to see you," I say, focusing on his pulse through his fingers. "Which annoys me, so I get angry at Mister E. I hate not being able to just be around you, and I know I shouldn't take that out on him. These past seasons have shown me that he does care about me in his own way, even if he doesn't know it; I know he's just trying to keep me alive. He just has such an attitude about everything, and he doesn't help the situation!" I open my eyes to see Wilhelm's large brown ones looking down at me, a small smile playing at the edge of his lips.

"You still haven't told him about us, have you?"

I sit up, shaking my head. "I have no intention of ever doing that," I say firmly; I will not let Mister E come into contact with Wilhelm. *That's probably for the best; love triangles are always needlessly dramatic.* That's not what I meant! If Mister E ever met Wilhelm and he knew about my relationship with him, he would kill him without a second thought; he doesn't want me having any distractions. Even if he didn't know about my relationship with Wilhelm, he would undoubtedly recognize him from the witch's cabin and kill him just to tie up loose ends. I'm not yet strong enough to defeat him; he proved that today. *You got reckless.* I know. I blink and notice Wilhelm is still looking at me, waiting patiently; I do this far more than I like to admit. His eyes are wide, and I have to look away. "You're doing the thing!" I look at him and his eyes seem even wider, shining in the light. "Stop!" I yell playfully. He scoots closer, blinking his big eyes at me, and I laugh despite myself, smacking him lightly on the nose.

"Ow," he complains, rubbing his nose. "I don't see what the big deal is; sure you make him sound scary, but I'm sure he's not that bad. And I'm a likeable guy."

I shake my head; if anything, I tone it down for Wilhelm when I vent. I'm not sure he could handle it if I told him the entire truth about Mister E. Sometimes, it even chills me; those nights the nightmares are the worst.

"I just know what he would say though," I say, sucking a breath, lowering my voice as much as possible. "'Emotional attachments are a weakness; any emotion that cannot be used in the heat of battle should be avoided.'" I say, quoting Mister E. Wilhelm bursts out laughing. "And then he'd kill you," I add. Wilhelm laughs louder, pretending to die, collapsing on top of me. *You are making far too light of this situation.* I grunt, trying to push him off me, but he doesn't budge; he's put on a little weight recently it seems. I need to make light of this situation; everything in my life is already so serious, so intense. It's all life or death; I just need one little part that's fun, that's not stressful. Being around Wilhelm, I know he will listen to me, I know I'm safe. *You're safe around Mister E.* Maybe from other people; but if I make a big enough mistake, I become an expendable liability—an acceptable loss. That will never be an issue with Wilhelm. So, yes, I will make light of everything while I'm around him, because I want to, and I *need* to.

"Get off," I groan, but he doesn't move or make a sound. I jab him in the ribs and he sits up quickly, covering his ribs.

"Rule breaker!" he shouts playfully. "We have explicitly discussed that tickling is *not* allowed!"

I lightly jab him in the ribs a couple more times, wiggling my fingertips up and down his sides. He scoots away, swatting my hands until I stop, grinning evilly.

"Alright, you made your point," he says rubbing his ribs gingerly. "Listen, you need to show a gesture; give him a sign that you're working hard, that you're committing to him. That way he'll lay off on you a little. If he doesn't think that his training is actually working, he'll only make your training more and more difficult," he says.

His training is effective, but he doesn't know my limits so he just keeps pushing; eventually, he will break me. *To be fair, you don't know your limits either. If you never discover them, then you won't know how far you can push; you will overextend yourself. Then you're dead.*

"I know this is difficult on you; you just want to quit and run away. I understand the feeling," He takes my hands in his, kissing me gently. "I have faith in you."

"How can you even be sure this will work?" I ask, and he laughs.

"Trust me," he says while my eyes search over his face; after a moment I nod.

Wilhelm typically knows what he's talking about; while I know my teacher, Wilhelm knows people in general. *This time you trust your life to his advice though.* I trust him. *With your life?* I do, I really, truly do. *Sounds like you're trying to convince yourself.*

"Find him and show him that training you has paid off, and ask him for more; he should let up a little if he knows what he's doing is actually working. Do you know where he's going to be tonight?"

I think for a moment then nod; I've already been through his papers several times. His books, his meetings—I know them all; one of the perks of being his student. I have to make myself valuable to him in more ways than one; if I ever get put into a precarious situation, knowing valuable information will make him want to protect me all the more.

"I have a pretty good idea of where he's going to be."

CHAPTER TWELVE

The man in front of me shifts nervously, twisting one of the many rings on his fingers as I sit down in front of him, the shadows hissing behind me. In this situation, their hunger will play to my advantage; I simply must keep them from devouring him.

"I have spent more years than you can fathom searching for Impres," I say coolly. The man nods hurriedly, lighting another lamp. The shadows hiss angrily, smacking it aside, the flame sputtering weakly before going out. With every interrogation, a different approach must be taken based upon the initial evaluation of the subject. "If you have something to say, then say it," I say, leaning back in the chair.

The man jumps at the sound of my voice, turning his transfixed gaze from the recently put out lamp to me. I can tell his small, watery eyes are trying to pick me out from the rest of the darkness in the room.

"Y-yes, w-well, you see—"

"Do you have information or not?" I grow tired of dealing with people who simply wish to waste my time; I have spent far too much of that already following useless leads. While the increased amount of rumors and leads pertaining to Impres surely shows an increase in her activity, there are far more useless leads and baseless rumors than anything of actual import or significance. Combined with the recent behavior of Scarlett, my temper is not at its most forgivable position. Fortunately for me, this particular breed of informant responds well to the tactics I am most likely to use at this point.

"I know the man who does," his words tumble out of him all at once in a single gasp; I lean forward, the wood creaking beneath me, the hissing of the shadows growing louder.

"No less than sixty-eight people have said those exact same words in front of me, and none of them were right." That figure is just the number of individuals who have claimed that same thing; the number of leads I have followed up with personally is, irritatingly, far higher. The hissing of the shadows echoes around the small room, the man jumping and twitching in front of me. The smell of his profuse sweating invades my nostrils, and I lean back. "None of those lying wretches remain alive to this day. If I am disappointed, I will kill you too. If you leave now, you will have wasted my time, and I will kill you anyway. I am a busy man, and you are nothing but a meager, pathetic rat. Now you may tell me your information."

The man gulps, telling me the location of where I can find the informant in a hurried, breathy tone—a successful interrogation. The man he divulged to me is a newcomer to the information business, so I have yet to pay him a visit; I will rectify that error. I nod, standing up, the shadows snapping at his feet under the table.

"Stay here; I'll be back when I discover whether your lead is true or not." I open the door, closing it behind me. I'm in a room almost as dark as the one that I just met in; I lock the door behind me and take a deep breath. Dealing with the common rabble on such a regular basis is beginning to take its toll on me.

"You get annoyed too easily when dealing with the layman," I turn to look at Lesva as she sips from a small metal cup, her henchmen only a short distance away.

"If you had to deal with these people, you would understand," I retort, brushing past her, catching her smirk out of the corner of my eye. She chuckles, setting the cup down and following me out the door, her henchmen trailing behind her.

"I deal with these people every day," she says. "They are my bread and butter." She puts a hand on my shoulder, squeezing it gently. I whirl around, hand on my sword; I am not in the mood for her antics. She takes her hand off, holding her hands up and taking a step back.

"Just listen, okay?" I take a deep breath, slowly relaxing my hand and barely inclining my head; it's enough for Lesva. "I understand you've been chasing Impres for... a while now, and you're getting frustrated. That's perfectly understandable."

I tap my finger against my hilt impatiently; I have a lead to discover. It is most likely another wild goose chase, but I must pursue everything, no matter how thin or weak it is.

"But you can't treat my contacts like that. The only reason I told you about that man was because I already checked him out; I know how much this all means to you. I did what I did because I respect you, but I expect respect in return," her bright blue eyes harden to small shards of ice and she steps closer, poking me in the chest. "Do not threaten another one of my contacts again, or it will be the last time you do."

I grab her finger, slowly lowering it. "You associate with what I view as trash, and that is difficult for me to overcome." My voice gets softer, releasing my hold on Lesva's hand. "I know Impres betrayed you," I brush a large scar crossing from her left eyebrow, across her nose, down to her upper lip, recently healed over; it is the only blemish on her skin. She flinches away, but I hold her in place; I understand her position, and I can even...empathize, with it. "But do not pretend that you do this for me; you are ravenous in your desire for revenge." She smacks my hand away, her henchmen stalking forward. She stops them with an upturned hand, turning her attention back to me.

"This 'trash' I associate with—they are *people*. I look out for them; I help them; I care for them. When I care about someone, I do everything in my power to help them; *that* is why I'm helping you." The challenge in her eyes is reflected by the calm in mine.

"The only reason I am doing any of this is because I care about someone, as difficult as it may be to imagine."

"You do it because you can't let go," she replies.

My hand tightens into a fist, but I take it off my sword. Lesva is an important asset; and now that Impres has spurned her, she will be even more valuable in her assistance to me. Hide as she might beyond self-righteousness, she cannot hide her true feelings from me.

"You have your excuses," I turn my back on her, opening the door to the setting summer sun. "I have mine."

Once again I find myself in the wretched city of Descra. I growl in disgust, stomping on a passing rat and grinding my heel into the loose stones of the road; I despise this city. Full of vermin and trash, low-life scum, and harlots; Descra is chaos, and I abhor chaos. I take a firm step forward, steeling myself for the scum of the city, then another. I walk down the streets with my back straight; I will not let my anger distract me. I must find this contact and then find Impres. I recognize what this chase is doing to me—has been doing to me for years—but I will not let it stop me. I will become whatever I need to become to complete my mission—an interrogator, a friend, an enemy, a murderer. I am not interested in honor or morality; the end will always justify the means. I will douse my hands in blood and wash them clean time and time again; I will live in the grey within the darkness. Once I find Impress, I will rip the information I desire from her mind, and then I will kill her. With that, I can complete the last phase of my mission, and this will all be over; I will be at peace.

The sun has set before I finally make it to the building Lesva's contact told me about; I take a deep breath, looking at the dark grey, dirty, stained building. Two large, cloaked figures stand outside the small front door; I keep my hand off my sword, walking up to them. I stay at the bottom of the steps that lead up to the building; they are the kind of people that like to feel larger than others—overcompensation. They look down at me and one opens his mouth, staying at the top of the stairs. This is a completely new contact; and while I am not in a forgiving or kind mood, I do not want to immediately provoke hostile action from a valuable resource.

"Are you lost, friend?" His low voice rumbles out; a partaker of Styx. It's marketed, passed off as an "enhancement," providing a boost of energy and strength. There is, of course, a price; there is always a price, just sometimes you must simply dig to find it. Personally, I can't stand the thought of using it, with all of the degrading effects on the body I have discovered it causes; these two won't put up much of a fight then, considering that. They most likely aren't even aware of the negative effects; if they do not let me pass, they soon will be.

"I'm actually here to meet Ruphreus," I keep my voice on the more pleasant side of neutral, forcing a smile; I can wait a few seconds, but any longer and I will tear these two apart. They bend their heads together, conversing in coarse, growling whispers. The shadows sneak up the walls, spreading out like thin cracks in the walls. Just as the shadows begin to peel themselves off the walls, the two men resume their initial positions, the one who had spoken before speaking again.

"You can meet Ruphreus for a price," he rumbles, holding out one large, deformed hand crisscrossed with thick white scars; they don't deal in elegance. That suits me fine—I'm tired of doing the same anyway. This city is said to bring out the worst in all of us, and it doesn't understand quiet, polite dealings and elegant gifts and exchanges. For that, I am unwilling to pay these two neanderthals.

"Unless the price is your blood, I am unwilling to pay," I reply, keeping my voice level but polite, all things considered. The silent one cracks his knuckles, and the more talkative one folds his arms across his large chest.

"Then we seem to have a problem, friend." They both step in front of the door, arms folded; they could be twins—deformed, abominable, wretched twins. I slowly make my way up the steps, my footfalls echoing throughout the relatively abandoned area; I'll have to remember the deserted nature of this part of Descra if I am ever forced to return. I hope that is never required, ever again. Upon making it to the top, they tilt their heads up to continue looking at me. The shadows yank them backwards slamming them against the crumbling stone banisters that flank the steps. The shadows tighten around the two men, the banisters cracking against their weight; small veins of shadow wriggle in front of their faces, hissing.

"Gentlemen, my associates here are far less patient than I am, and far hungrier. I'm going to go in now," I put my hand on the doorknob, raising an eyebrow. "Any objections?"

They both shake their heads and I nod, smiling politely, "Good." I twist the old doorknob, entering the building; the old wooden door doesn't muffle their high-pitched screams. I need the shadows compliant, not rebellious; I will allow them to gorge themselves here, and they will be perfect servants. Or they will never eat again. I raise an eyebrow, walking through the old, creaky building; perhaps this city does bring out the worst in us.

I hear shouting from down below, and I search the first floor until I find a set of old wooden steps, descending into a dimly lit room.

"No! I cannot accept substandard guards! Do you know how many people would like to do this majestic body harm?! A great deal, *that* is how many! The competition hates newcomers, especially *successful* newcomers. If one of my guards cannot complete such a simple task as frisking a guest, then—"

The steps creak underneath my feet as I descend slowly, putting weight into each step. The room is lit by several low-burning oil lamps, cobwebs, and dust coating everything. Several old, plush chairs and a couch with an obnoxious flower print make up the only available furniture in the room. A small man with heavy glasses looks at me with wide, magnified eyes. He has sleek, blonde hair that lies plastered over one lens of his glasses. He is standing, wearing a dark, distastefully shabby suit that was obviously tailored for his small form, though patches of it are worn and ripped in several places. Several large men are in the room with him, cloaked and standing in the spaces of shadow left by the sparse light. I grab one of the chairs and sit myself down in it, leaning back, clasping my hands on my chest.

"It's rude to remain standing in front of a guest." I say calmly. One tendril pulls another chair up behind the man, knocking him behind the knees, making him plop into the chair; the tendril giving an amused hiss. As I predicted; when they are full, they are far more compliant. Perhaps I will take to feeding them regularly; Descra is useful for little else. He coughs as a cloud of dust puffs up; once the air clears, he turns to one of the guards.

"Who is this man that dares to just walk in?" He hisses. A tendril of shadow snakes out, tapping him in the cheek and he turns back to me with a start; even after having just been sated, the shadows are gluttons, always eager for their next meal. I'm unsure as to whether I'll indulge them, His information is directly tied to his life. Depending on how useful his information is, his life may or may not serve a purpose as food.

"It is also rude to talk about your guest like he's not there." This contact has the potential to be the last step needed to find Impres, though I will not allow him to be rude to me. It will be nearly everything anything required to complete my mission, but I will not be a push-over. "The proper thing would be to introduce yourself." He's a mere child, really; the outcome of my search, after all this time, could be dictated by this small young man. How the cosmos likes to torture me, though it's almost amusing—almost. The young man clears his throat, adjusting his glasses.

"Well, ehem, yes. Yes, yes, okay. My name is Ruphreus Erique." He puts on a small smile, lifting up the corners of his thin, smug lips.

As he is a newcomer, the name means nothing to me, and my body language shows it. I am not impressed, Ruphreus, and first impressions are very important. When dealing with me, they could be your last.

"My name is Mister E," I say. He snorts, trying to hide it with a cough. My eyes harden, and the shadows pierce the walls, turning into small claws and dragging themselves slowly down the walls, creating a screeching sound. I stop after Ruphreus winces; I will not put up with a brat. "I'm not going to poke around the matter, Ruphreus; I was directed to you by a contact who told me you could locate the witch Impres for me. Is this true?"

He looks uncomfortable, squirming in his seat. "I can locate many people, as I am in the information business, but—"

"Ruphreus," I lean forward, the shadows sending the stool crashing into splinters against one of the large wooden support beams in the back of the room. This compliance, this willingness from such stubborn entities, it is a nice change; perhaps I will return to Descra. It is starting to grow on me. "Do not play games with me; it would be best for both you and your business if you just answer my questions directly and give me what I want."

He frowns, huffing himself up, pushing his glasses up on his nose. "I do not just give away my information!"

I narrow my eyes disapprovingly; he will give me whatever I wish, at the exact moment that I wish it. However, as a potential future informant, I will foster this relationship, for now.

"I am willing to pay for it," I reply calmly, and he leans back, calming himself. I'm positive his blood would cover up these obnoxious pieces of furniture nicely, but I need my information before I do anything drastic.

"Impres is a very impressive and powerful woman; it is not wise to cross her," he says, his eyes glinting.

He expects me to pay a very large sum for his information. The shadows snake out of the darkness, petting his hair slowly, caressing his face gently. Those same shadows trickle over his body, slithering down and toward one of the support beams, wrapping around it; a loud crack resonates throughout the room, the tendril ripping the support beam apart. The shadows slither back over to Ruphreus, petting his head and he trembles slightly; as always, the shadows merely pray for a meal. Though their gluttony knows no bounds, they are, at least, predictable in it; I can easily use that.

"It is not wise to cross me either," I retort.

He adjusts his glasses, taking a deep, shaky breath. He must give me true information; I cannot risk him not giving me that information or lying to me.

"Ruphreus, if I am pursuing Impres, then there are two possibilities. Either I am stupid, or I am more powerful than her. Do I seem like a stupid man, Ruphreus?"

He shakes his head quickly; he wouldn't dare lie to me in this situation, even if he did fear for his life.

"Then I must be more powerful than Impres; you do not want me as your enemy. I assume Impres has threatened you, which is why you remain loyal."

He nods slowly, sweat trickling down his temple.

"I assure you—I have no intention of double-crossing you or killing you." At this moment, I am telling the truth; he could very well do something that would annoy me to the point of his demise; for now, though, I mean what I say. The truth is, after all, designed to be bent and viewed in whatever light necessary.

"I suppose a deal could be—" At that moment, a guard comes down, making eye contact with Ruphreus. "What is it?" he asks in an exasperated tone.

I tense, my hands squeezing the arms of the chair; I do not appreciate an interruption when so close to my goal.

"I found this girl sneaking around inside; Brolus and Tevron are dead outside." He hoists a girl, bound and gagged, into sight. Anger wells up within me, and I stand up so quick the chair flips backward, tendrils of shadow cracking several support beams and shooting into the floor.

"Scarlett!" I shout without thinking. Why did she have to be here, now?

"You know this girl?!" Ruphreus stands up quickly, backpedalling into the arms of one of his guards. "She was here to kill me, wasn't she?! You're working with her!" I turn to him, but he shouts out, "Kill them!"

The guards rush at me, several more coming down the stairs. I try to keep Ruphreus in my field of vision, but the guards block me, swinging their weapons; I'm going to lose him! Tendrils of shadow pierce the guard holding Scarlett, the tendrils wrapping around her and throwing her out of the way. I unsheathe my sword, slicing one guard across the neck, ducking under the club of another, stabbing him in the gut and slicing him open as I move past him. I must take these men out. I cannot risk being chased through the city of Descra, as a mob will grow from just a few angered individuals.

I spin, decapitating one who tries to tackle me. I stab another through the chest, pushing him into two more who come rushing at me. I take a step forward, kicking one of the stumbling guards between the legs, backhanding him into the wall and elbowing the other, thrusting at one more who rushes at me, spearing him in the eye. I push forward, the tip of my blade poking through the back of his head, and I wrench my sword out, slicing the remaining two guards quickly across the throat. I turn, swinging my sword at Scarlett, cutting her bonds and gag off. I look around the room, but Ruphreus is nowhere to be found. I swear, slamming my palm against the wall; I let him escape! Shadows pierce the pieces of furniture, whirling around, smacking into walls, crushing support beams and legs of furniture. I slam my fist into the wall, breathing heavily. So close and now...now so very far; I cannot pursue him, I must deal with Scarlett. It has been made clear that she is as much my priority as anything else; I took on her responsibility, so I must be responsible for her. Right afterward, however, I will hunt this man down to the ends of the earth if I have to.

"Explain yourself," I growl, flicking the blood off my sword and sheathing it, folding my arms. I inhale deeply through my nostrils, the blood on the floor beginning to pool at my feet. The shadows cautiously inch toward the dismembered corpses in the room; gorge yourselves until you burst for all I care. Scarlett rubs her wrists and arms, working her jaw up and down. "Now!"

She looks at me, holding her hands up at an attempt to placate; I do not need placation, I need answers; I need to know why she... why she cost me Impres.

"I came looking for you," she says, looking toward the stairs leading up. The shadows reach for cellar door, pulling it closed and barring it shut. She sighs, taking a small step back. "You've been leaving more and more often, and I am just wondering if that means you are planning on allowing me to go out on my own missions."

I nod, taking a deep breath; she didn't know what I was doing.

She continues, "I appreciate all the training you've done with me, but I really feel like I need to start getting out on my own now, trying to find out more about my past. You've helped me with that, but I think it would be best if you started to let me go out on my own missions. Your training has taught me so much—and I know I have far more to learn—but I feel that sheltered training can only get me so far."

I clench my fists slowly; she cost me my chance. I will find Ruphreus, but now it is uncertain as to whether I can get the information I require out of him, or at the very least, verify it's validity.

"Impress holds the key to something I have spent many long years searching for, something of the utmost importance to me. Everything else pales in comparison to this mission. I have been chasing Impres for longer than most of these people in this god-forsaken land can remember, and tonight I was nearing the end of that chase. You cost me that chance," I step back, the cellar doors opening. I turn my back on her, the shadows pulling one of the chairs to me. I sit down in it, covering my face with one of my hands, sighing. "Get out of my sight," I say in a low voice, running a hand through my hair.

"Mister E, I—" Tendrils wrap around one of the plush chairs, slinging it against the wall violently, a loud hiss splitting the air.

"Go!" I roar. I sigh, leaning back in the chair, closing my eyes. "Just...just go, Scarlett." I don't open my eyes until the sound of her footsteps have disappeared, her presence weak enough that I can barely sense it. I lean forward, clasping my hands together in front of me, squeezing hard enough for my bones to begin to bend. The shadows slither up, hissing in my ear, slithering over my back and neck. They wanted me to keep Scarlett around, and I did. And now she has cost me everything.

"I don't need you to try and comfort me," I snap, smacking one tendril away, and the rest ooze back into the darkness, hissing angrily. I sigh, giving my hair a sharp tug and close my eyes again. "Scarlett, why did you have to blunder in here? I cannot get rid of you; that's not even a possibility. We've been through too much; too much time, effort, and energy has been put into you to just dispose of you and let it all go to waste." I have her life in my hands, and so many options have been crossed out; I know this won't be an easy decision, but nothing with Scarlett is ever easy.

I cannot stop Impres, but she has cost me so much already. I pursue her without thought to my network, myself, or even Scarlett. Here I am, telling myself I cannot let Scarlett die, yet...if it meant catching Impres, I would sacrifice her, similarities be damned. No, she's not similar at all; that is in the past. That is my goal; Scarlett is a useful tool, nothing more. Then why? Why am I so conflicted over this?! I growl, picking up one of the chairs and throwing it against the wall; that wretched witch will be the ruin of me! Yet I can't stop chasing her, not now; that is no more of an option than killing Scarlett. They are both viable options though, one directly contradicting the other; which do I choose? I throw myself onto the couch, looking up at the ceiling. I clench my fists, rigidly moving my arms and crossing them over my chest; I cannot decide what to do here. I growl low, slowly closing my eyes and letting out a breath; I need help. As much as I would prefer to do this all on my own, I cannot. With my contacts, with Scarlett, I cannot consider myself alone. In fact, I would never have gotten this far without others; loathe as I am to admit it, sometimes I must ask for help.

I let my body begin to relax, going deep into my mind; she always knows what to do. I hate drawing her out; it hurts somewhere where my soul used to be, but I can't avoid it. Sometimes the cosmos just chooses to point out how fallible I can be. A pleasant smell tickles my nostrils—wildflowers.

I open my eyes, and I'm nearly blinded by the dazzling sun; I give my eyes a moment to adjust, scanning my surroundings. White and lavender wildflowers sway in the cool breeze, carrying their scent into the air. The sun is high overhead, but the breeze keeps the temperature pleasant, even in my multi-layered, dark garb.

"You always do things in such a systematic fashion."

I tense up, my breath hitching, my heart briefly stopping as my chest momentarily constricts. That voice…it breaks me every time. I turn around, my eyes softening. Her long, raven-black hair only looks red for a moment; it flows down her back and frames those sparkling orange eyes of hers that occasionally flash green; they seem to look right into the heart of me every time. Her thin, white dress pools around her as she sits down, and she pats the ground next to her.

"Come and sit—it's rude to remain standing around company."

I make my way over to her, sitting down, and she makes a disapproving noise, slapping me on the shoulder gently.

"You always wear these clothes about; you'll catch your death from heat if you stay bundled up like this all the time."

I remain still as she removes my cloak, boots, socks and gloves. She pulls my gloves off one finger at a time, and I resist the urge to shudder as her warm skin touches mine; she feels so real. I can almost let myself believe she is real; I can just lose myself in this fantasy—her warm skin, her tinkling laughter, the soft grass, and wildflowers. I shake my head and she raises an eyebrow.

"What's on your mind? Let your sister help you out here," she smiles and takes one of my hands in her two small ones, running her thin fingers over the scars.

"I have a problem," I say, realizing I sound a little breathless. I breathe in quickly through my nostrils, trying to let the air clear my head. "I need your help, Simiel."

"Of course you do; that's why I'm here. I comfort you in your times of hurt and help you in your times of need; I have always done that and always will, E. What else are sisters for?" She grins, scooting back and hugging her knees, peering at me over the top of them. "You're riddled with character flaws and holes; you're like cheese that a mouse got into. I bet the ladies find it pretty alluring, eh?" She nudges me with her elbow and I sigh, looking her in the eyes. This is a last resort, calling up her memory, though it reminds me of my mission, as though I could ever forget.

"This is serious, Simiel," I say, putting some measure of force into my voice. My mind will distract me with pleasantries; that is the nature of my mind, despite my attempts to change it.

"Very well," she sighs, propping herself up and setting her hands in her lap. "What are your problems?"

It would be so much easier if she could just know what my problem was and then tell me her suggestion; as it is, I have to talk to her. My mind likes to torture me with the past, no matter how much I vow to change it.

"My student ruined the final stage of tracking down Impres, but she didn't do it willingly. I can't kill her because I'm too invested, and I'm unsure of how I should proceed. In addition, in pursuing Impres for so long, I have unwittingly let my network begin to crumble, yet I can no more stop chasing Impres than I could kill Scarlett at this point. Impres could hold the key to—to everything. However, stopping my chase for Impres and killing Scarlett are still both inherently viable options. Honestly, I just—" She grabs my head, pushing me to her chest, slowly stroking my hair. Her hands—they feel so real; I let my eyelids flutter closed, letting out a long breath.

"You like to come up with toughies, don't you?" she says with a small laugh. "But, you getting your brains from me, I can figure it out. Now," she slowly pulls me away, her eyes serious, brow knitted slightly; I remember the face well. She holds up one finger. "As for your student, you need to give her time. You haven't been with her for very long, but she shows potential—so of course you can't kill her. You're attached, whether you like it or not. I know how you are with attachment, and how you haven't let yourself feel anything resembling it for a long time. But that needs to change. You need to remember what it's like to feel attached to someone, to feel dependent on someone. To feel vulnerable. Just give her a chance to prove herself."

"What if she doesn't?"

"Not everyone is going to leave or disappoint you, E," she says softly. She shakes her head and holds up a second finger. "For your second problem, you have to consider something. How long have you been setting up your information network?"

She knows the answer to the question but wants to hear me say it; it was always part of her process. You could never rush her into anything or slow her down; I always humored her.

"I've been developing it ever since I began my mission," I reply and she nods, satisfied.

"And how long have you been chasing Impres?"

"Not nearly as long," I reply and she nods, a self-satisfied smirk on her face.

"There's your answer," she says.

I stand up, putting my other articles of clothing back on. "You're…you're going?"

I can't bring myself to look at her face; it's the same face she made in the house. I promised her I would be back before anything happened. I slip one of my gloves on, keeping my back to her.

"Yes, I have to be going now. Thank you for your help; I know I can always rely on you, Simiel." My mind is screaming at me to go now, hammering my thoughts. I feel her touch on my shoulder.

"Please just…stay a bit longer. You rarely ever visit me anymore."

I gently remove her hand from my shoulder without looking at her, closing my eyes. "I have to be in the real world now, Simiel, but I'll come back. I promise." The last gust of wind sounds like a soft sigh, blowing across my face.

CHAPTER THIRTEEN

I stand outside of the dirty building in the dirtiest city in the Kingdom; I journeyed to Descra to try and aide Mister E, but I ended up costing him his final lead. I turn and smack my palm against the wall, a loud slap filling the air. I can't believe that I let this happen! I tried to show that my training had paid off, that I was making progress, and I botched it all up. *You took one step forward and two-thousand steps back.* I had to make up some story about wanting to go out on my own missions to hide the fact that I completely screwed up in an attempt to help him; if I hadn't, he may very well have killed me. I saw the look in his eyes and it was raw, unfiltered anger—the kind that's coursing through my veins right now. Even worse—worse than that vehement rage I saw—was the crushing disappointment. *You need to change your scale.*

I turn on my heel, glaring out at the dark, dirty city; I have to make this right. I stride down the streets, holding my head high, uncaring if I draw any attention. I *want* to draw attention; Ruphreus Erique is my target. I walk down the street until I come to my destination. People go in and out on a constant basis, the noise from inside spilling out onto the street. I join the flow of people going in and soon find myself in a large, noisy, crowded bar. *Why is it always a bar?* Bars are where people with loose mouths gather; and if they're not loose beforehand, they will be by the time I'm finished with them. People are shouting, laughing, drinking, and dancing; loud percussionists are banging away on a stage, their sound carrying throughout the bar. I slowly scan the joint; there's no one in particular that draws my gaze. I turn my attention to the bar counter; time to test my people skills. I find an open seat at the counter and order whatever the house draft is; waiting for the bartender to bring my drink, I fish out a coin and place it on the table. *Where did you even get money?* Some people just have too much of it. *Full-blown criminal, here we come.*

"I'm looking for someone," I say, but he doesn't pay any attention to me. *Can you blame him? In that outfit?* Just shut it; I am not in the mood. I clear my throat, but he continues servicing other custumers, not giving me the slightest amount of attention. I quickly drain my drink, grimacing as it burns its way down my throat like a snake trailing venom as it goes. Immediately the bartender appears, filling up my drink. I speak up before he disappears again, raising my voice over the noise of the bar. "I'm looking for someone!" He looks at me hard for a moment then shrugs, showing me a toothy smile.

"A lot of people come in and out of here every day," he says, taking the coin I hand him. "It's hard to keep track of them all. Sorry."

Before he can leave, I place another coin on the counter, not taking a sip of my drink. He looks at me warily then takes the coin, staying in front of me.

"My memory, of course, is not as good as it used to be."

"How about a new question then? Where would I go if I wanted to disappear?" Sometimes subtlety is a great way to get things done, but straight up bribery is also a good way to go. Besides, I am not in a mood to wait; I want results, now. I must find Ruphreus Erique before the sun rises; by then, he could be long gone. He remains silent and I sigh, sliding a few more coins across the counter. He collects them from underneath his rag as he sweeps it over the perfectly clean counter; apparently his memory isn't the only thing that's broken. If he doesn't answer my questions soon, he'll be lucky if that's the only thing that's broken by the time I leave.

"Hezmer over there," he says, nodding at a corner then quickly slipping away to deal with some restless customers. I turn to where he had nodded, seeing a dark figure in a large coat and hat sitting in a corner booth, completely alone, a drink on the table but untouched. I make my way over to the opposite side of the booth and lean in, the figure shifting slightly.

"I hear you're the person to go to if you want to disappear," I say, and he leans forward, hissing.

"Shhh!" he hisses, looking around quickly, the coat and hat hiding his features from view. "Keep your voice down!"

I look around, making sure we're in the same bar; seeing that we are, I frown. The noise from the bar is more than loud enough to cover the sound of my voice. I really don't have the time to be picky though, but I also don't have time to wait around; I lower my voice, leaning in closer.

"Are you or aren't you?" I ask impatiently and he looks around, checking for spies or god knows what else. He nods quickly and I sit; good. Finally, there's some progress. "I'm looking for a man named Ruphreus Erique; he would have come by not too long ago, looking to disappear quick." The man leans back, shaking his head.

"I—I don't k-know who you're t-talking about," he stammers.

I lean forward; I have to find Ruphreus before he disappears completely. I'll use whatever means I have to. *Perhaps you aren't as different from your teacher as you once thought.*

"You're lying," I growl. "I know he was here; tell me where he went." He shakes his head again, and I clench my hands; fine, alternative methods it is. I grab the man and yank him to his feet, dragging him out of the bar before he can make a scene. I toss him onto the street and his hat flies off, his coat spilling open under the street lights. He's a small portly man with beady eyes, a bald top shiny with sweat and a thick neck. A mustache adorns his upper lip like a thin caterpillar, sweat dripping down one of his four chins; I'm not impressed.

"Please!" he pleads.

I jump off the steps leading up to the bar, and he scrabbles backward; he looks like a cross between a pig and a crab when he does that. It's very disturbing. If he's going to act like a lying animal though, I'll treat him like one. I walk to him and grab him by his collar, straining to lift him up. I manage to do so, the strain turning my voice hoarse.

"I will do whatever it takes to find this man," I say, struggling to hold up his bulk. "You do not want to stand in my way." His beady eyes blink rapidly, looking into mine; he will find no quarter in them. He nods quickly and I drop him, my arms crying out in relief; even if he hadn't nodded, I would have had to drop him.

"He s-said that he wanted t-to have some f-fun before he disappeared. I s-saw him head down an alley t-that way not t-too long ago; you can p-p-probably still catch him," he stutters; I pat his sweaty cheek and smile.

"That wasn't so hard now, was it?" I move past him, racing down the street to where Hezmer had directed. Mister E is the only link I have to my past; I enjoy my life with Wilhelm, but late at night when I have to return to Mister E's home, I can barely get any sleep thinking about my past life. The nightmares, broken pieces and fragments, torture any sleep I get; the nights where I acknowledge Mister E's cold brutality, they're even worse. I still don't really know who I am or who I was; I can't let Mister E just dismiss me. There is still so much more I have to learn, both about myself and so I can protect Wilhelm from anyone who would threaten him, including Mister E himself. I round the alley and stop, the scene before me stopping me in my tracks.

Ruphreus holds his hand to a woman with heavy make-up, using a knife to cut off her dress. It falls off her shoulders, and he forces himself on her, removing his hand and replacing it with the blade of the knife. She starts to scream, but he works the knife into her mouth, cutting and slicing at her lips and tongue as he forces himself on her. *Move. You have to do something. Move!* My legs refuse to obey, remaining rooted in place, my eyes wide. He grunts and groans, dragging the knife down her mouth, stopping at her neck. He trails the tip of the knife down her neck then works it down her exposed chest, carving into her, swearing and spitting at her. He's just taking his anger out on her; she's just an object to him.

I begin to tremble, willing myself to move; god I have to move and do something. It's not her fault that he's angry; he's taking his anger out on her. She didn't have a say in it; she didn't know what he was going to do. A choked scream bubbles up from her throat, blood gurgling after her mouth.

My foot jerks forward, and I rush at him, screaming. He turns, the metal of the knife flashing as I tackle him around the waist. He lands on the concrete, the knife skittering out of his hand, his head slamming on the concrete. I enjoy killing; I enjoy killing; I enjoy killing. I repeat this over and over to myself as he struggles beneath me while I try to pin him. I'll kill this man; I'll kill him! He will pay for this! He throws me off of him, stumbling backwards and falling down again. I roll and grab the knife, stalking closer.

"Please," he says, holding up his hands, standing up, trembling. "I just want to disappear; I swear you'll never see me again. Just let me go, please." He looks at me with pleading eyes; my eyes flick to the woman he attacked. Her insides spill out of her torso, her eyes wide, what remains of her tongue lolling out of the carved hole in the side of her face. Blood spurts from her mouth, a shallow breath rattling out; she's still alive.

"You didn't even have the courage to kill her?" I take a step forward, and he takes a step back.

"Please, I'm sorry. Just don't kill me, please!" His eyes are wide and panicked, tears forming at the corners of his eyes; pathetic wretch.

"I'm not going to kill you," I say, keeping the image of that woman in my head; I'm going to need it to do what's about to happen. "After all, you didn't kill her." his eyes widen and he turns around, racing for the exit to the alley. I race after him, tackling him around the ankles; he lets out a yelp as he goes down, trying to scramble away. I slice at his legs and arms as he flounders around, leaving thin cuts. I wrench his tie off his neck, wrapping it tightly around his mouth, hoisting him back up; I have to do this. He brutalized that woman and didn't kill her; I have to do the same. She *deserves* justice. I shove him onto his knees, making him look at the woman.

"Look at what you did to her!" I shout, shoving his head closer. He tries to close his eyes, but I hold the knife to his cheek and he whimpers, tears streaming down his face. *Look!* He keeps his eyes open as I cut apart pieces of his suit, binding his wrists and ankles together behind him. I walk over to the woman, kneeling next to her. Tears leak out of her eyes as she draws another weak breath; I swallow down vomit, blinking back tears. I stroke her bloody, matted hair and croon to her softly. I press the knife against her chest directly over her heart and shove it in, twisting quickly; she jerks and then goes still. I remove the knife and keep my eyes on the woman, my voice hoarse and choked.

"Courage isn't simply attacking someone with a knife," I say, standing up and walking over to Ruphreus, glaring down at him with wet eyes. "It's making sure you finish the job once you start. You lack courage, Ruphreus Erique," I lean down, my mouth close to his ear, my voice a cold hiss. This man deserves no pity, no quarter; if I didn't have to deliver him to Mister E to apologize, I would kill him on the spot. I understand now, how Mister E can act with such cold, unfeeling brutality; I know my teacher now. "I, however, do not lack courage."

He jerks away, tears running down his face. He flops onto his belly, trying to wriggle away like a worm. Pathetic trash! I savagely kick him in the side and he groans, curling up. You deserve far worse than this! I slam my boot into his side again, and he cries out as much as he can behind the gag. I wrench him up by his hair, letting go and he remains kneeling, looking up at me with pleading eyes. My eyes show him no kindness and he whimpers, the knife gleaming wickedly in the low light, blood dripping off the point. I like killing; I enjoy killing; I love killing. My teacher enforces my killing instinct; he told me my sympathy is a weakness. Perhaps he was right; I cannot allow myself to feel sympathy for this...this trash. Ruphreus whimpers again, trying to plead with me through the gag. My knuckles turn white as I squeeze the knife handle harder, my jaw locking. I don't know if I like the process that leads up to death. The torture, the slow last rattling breaths sucked in around cold steel; I don't know if I'll enjoy it. *There's only one way to find out.* I nod, taking a step closer, touching the knife to his cheek; there's only one way to find out.

My eyes snap open as the cellar doors bang open. I sit straight up, unsheathing my sword in the same motion that carries me to my feet, the shadows crawling up the walls, waiting to ensnare the intruder. A body flies down the steps, bouncing occasionally before crashing into the stone wall. The body groans, trying to writhe itself into a seating position. I take a step forward when my eyes detect a quick blur of movement, only seeing a flash of bright red before a voice hits my ears.

"I told you to hold still!" Scarlett kicks the body hard, dragging and throwing him onto the last remaining chair in the room. I look at the body, then at Scarlett. My eyes take in the tatters of clothing that barely cover the body, bruises and cuts making it hard to distinguish any discerning features, then the bloody knife in her hand. Scarlett cuts the gag out of the puffy, bloody mouth and the person coughs, hacking up blood.

"Please," a hoarse voice croaks out, and I raise an eyebrow; Ruphreus Erique. I sheathe my sword, looking from the mumbling, pleading Ruphreus to Scarlett who is glaring down at him. Perhaps Simiel's advice was more sound than I thought; no! No, it was my advice to myself; I have to remain grounded. Focus on the task at hand; she has redeemed herself, think of nothing else.

"You will not speak unless spoken to," Scarlett hisses, raising her hand; Ruphreus flinches but remains silent. She took her anger out on Ruphreus; now she must learn the cold, calculated ways of torture. Mere rage will not always extract information; sometimes it takes a slow blade, rather than a mercifully quick one. That's what I'm ultimately here for; I must teach her. If she watches, she will learn.

"Ruphreus, where is Impres?" I take a step forward, getting down on my knees so I'm at his level; the little things matter. I tilt my head; he will not respond well to more pain.

"She's in Malor!" he shouts, his eyes wide and wild. "Just please… please don't do anything else! I promise I'll tell you whatever you want on anyone else! Just—"

I stand up, ripping apart pieces of fabric off the furniture, blindfolding and gagging him, stuffing small bits into his ears. The shadows move to help, and I dismiss them with a flick of the wrist; this is a personal matter. I turn to Scarlett, meeting her angry gaze; she's barely holding herself back.

"You brought me Ruphreus Erique," I say, more of a statement than a question. Scarlett nods stiffly, looking at Ruphreus, then at me. "You took your anger out on him."

"He deserved it," she spits, her hand tightening on her dagger. "That pathetic low-life should be a corpse rotting in the gutter right now." That anger, I understand it. My expression softens; she realized her mistake, and more than corrected it. She made my decision for me.

"Tell me what happened," I say, siting down, leaving a space for Scarlett on the couch.

"What about him?" she glares at Ruphreus.

I strip him down to his undergarments, binding him to the chair, and binding the chair to one of the remaining support beams with the remains of his suit.

"He doesn't seem to be going anywhere," I reply, and she lets out a shaky breath, sitting next to me. Scarlett looks down at her hands, twirling the dagger slowly, blood dripping onto her legs with each rotation of the blade.

"I found him in an alley," she says, clenching the dagger, her jaw locking and unlocking; an alley, where one commonly finds rats and scum such as him. "He was...he..." she looks at me, her eyes hard and filled with anger. "What he did to that woman...he didn't even kill her, just...brutalized her. I had to put her out of her misery," she turns her gaze to Ruphreus, breathing heavily. "He deserves to die a wretched death," I nod; I understand her anger. Now, I shall show Scarlett that I understand and teach her how to exact her revenge.

"Do you know what the difference between justice and revenge is?" I ask, standing up.

"Revenge is for personal reasons," she stands as well, glaring at Ruphreus while she speaks. "Justice is doing what is right."

"What if you do the right thing by exacting revenge?" I make my way over to Ruphreus, standing behind him.

"Then it becomes justice," Scarlett says firmly.

"No. Then justice and revenge become one and the same," I remove the pieces of fabric from his ears, leaning next to him. "Thank you for the information Ruphreus," I whisper softly, running the leather of my gloves across his blood-stained, sweaty skin, untying the gag from his mouth. He tries to speak, but I yank him back by his hair, the chair creaking. "You will not make a noise."

I beckon Scarlett closer, and she walks forward with heavy, stiff steps; I will unleash her upon this man, in all her vehemence and fury. I will funnel it into small, condensed actions that will last her for years to come; for now, we will begin with the torture of Ruphreus Erique.

"You tried to kill me and my student."

He whimpers, and I smack him hard across the face, motioning for Scarlett to do the same. She raises her hand and Ruphreus cringes, but she doesn't bring it down. My eyes narrow, and Ruphreus looks up at her; her hand comes down, a loud smack resonating through the room. He whimpers again and I motion to Scarlett, who smacks him again; this time, he remains quiet. "Don't worry, Ruphreus, what follows will merely be a learning exercise."

I come to stand by Scarlett, taking her dagger from her hand.

"Do you want to make this man suffer for what he did?" She nods, jaw locked. "Then you can have no sympathy for him. Can you do this?" Again she nods, clenching and unclenching her hands. "Pay careful attention student; learn from this, and you will have your justice."

"Please!" Ruphreus cries out.

"I told you not to make a sound!" I snarl, coming at him quickly. I grip his cheeks with one hand, placing the dagger against his lips. "One more noise and I will cut your tongue out and sew your lips shut. Do you understand me?" He nods quickly, tears and snot streaming down his hiccuping face. I step out of the way, handing Scarlett the dagger. "Cut him."

She takes the dagger, putting the tip on his arm. She pauses, looking down at the blade trembling against his skin. I cover her trembling hand with mine, steadying the dagger, moving it down slowly, leaving a thin cut behind. "Aggravate the wound with dust."

She picks up a pinch of dust, sprinkling it into his wound. He cries, and she backhands him across the face before I give the signal.

"Quiet wretch!" she spits. I move behind Scarlett, placing my hands on her tense shoulders.

"That anger, all of it, can be used. Channel that anger into each cut you make; do not make deep ones or fatal ones. Leave hundreds—leave thousands of cuts—and with each one, let go. Brutalize him with the impending thought of when the next cut will be; torture him until he spills every secret he has. With each cut let go, until you cut without feeling. When you are calm, when you have ripped every useful piece of information out of this filth, then you can let him die. His life is in your hands, and you must make it hell. Torture him; with every cut, let go of a little more of your anger. Then you will have your justice."

She trembles underneath my hands, looking Ruphreus directly in the eyes. I lean in closer to her ear, watching her expression; it is cruel, unyielding, unsympathetic, unpitying. It is a contorted mask of hate, her eyes afire, locked onto the tear-laden ones of Ruphreus Erique. My voice is a low whisper, slithering into her; I always saw this potential in her, from the very moment we met. This is what I have been training her for.

"Cut him again."

CHAPTER FOURTEEN

"Where are we going?" Scarlett buckles up her pack, slinging it over her shoulder as I do the same.

"We're going to Malor," I reply. Ruphreus said I would find Impres in Malor; it's time I investigated that lead.

"I've never heard of a place called Malor," she says, following me out the door. "It's not in any of the books I've read, nor have I heard of it from anyone."

"The Kingdom, which is the empire we are in now, is fairly isolationist. Distant lands are talked about in hushed tones and fairy tales; of course the Kingdom is but one of the many powers in Legend Land. There are few books in the Kingdom about other lands, but I own many of them; however, there are some books in my collection that are not found in my public library. It's also where Ruphreus said I could find Impres," I say. Her face hardens at the mention of his name, and she looks down at the ground; she still hasn't gotten over it.

Taking a life quickly, with a quick swipe of the sword, is easy enough; it doesn't require much thought. Torture, especially torture until death, takes methodical, systematic planning; you must think of each action and plan your next one. The first time is a memorable experience, and can be difficult to get over; I have confidence in my student, however. I know she will not only overcome this, but she will grow stronger for it.

"It's a large metropolis in Visland." She remains looking at the ground so I continue; eventually her curiosity will push unwanted thoughts from her mind. I know she can overcome anything she sets her mind to, but right now I cannot have her distracted; perhaps I can take her mind off of it. "Visland is a country that lies across an ocean from the Kingdom; its environment is more diverse than the Kingdom's, containing deserts, large metropolises and lush jungles teeming with life. Unlike the Kingdom, it is split into four parts: Malor, Temprara, Ismar, and Ismar Minor—the latter of which seceded from the former. We will be staying in Malor until we find Impres,"

Scarlett continues to look at the ground, seemingly attempting to stare it into submission.

"There is a temple in Temprara where monks train in the art of understanding the mind and the memories attached to it." Scarlett looks up quickly and I continue, looking straight ahead. "After Impres is dealt with, we will make a journey there and see what can be done about your amnesia."

I trained at this particular temple for some time and am well acquainted with its current leader; they understand the importance of secrets, even when those secrets are about memory. Some things should not be remembered, and some I cannot afford Scarlett to remember.

"If you knew about this temple and how it could help me, why didn't you tell me before?" she looks at me; we've been through too much for her to accuse me of betraying her, but nations fall because of such simple oversights.

"Imagine I took you there immediately and you regained all your memories, discovering you were a prostitute from Descra," I look at her and adjust my pack. "Would you have been able to handle that?"

She shakes her head, sighing. "I suppose I hadn't thought of that."

"It is my job to think of the things you do not, student, and let you know of them. It is my responsibility to make you stronger—to prepare you for the journeys to come. Sometimes I will hide things from you—not because I do not believe you to be strong enough—but because some things must simply be given time. As your teacher, I must always have your best interests at heart."

At the beginning of this, when I rescued her from that wolf, I would not have meant a word of any of it; now I...I can't be sure. I was told I must relearn attachment; perhaps there is value in it. She looks up at the sky, her long hair falling down her back, the shadows of the trees turning it darker than any shade of red.

"Sometimes I think that maybe it would be best if I didn't find out about my past. I have a life now, but what if I find out I have a family?" She shakes her head, closing her eyes and looking straight ahead again, opening them. Her bright green irises sparkle in the sunlight, flashing orange. I shake my head, staring straight ahead; a trick of the end-of-summer sun. "I don't know if I could choose between what I have now and what I had then," she continues, and I remain silent for a moment.

Would she choose me? I scoff at myself, quickening my pace; I need not even think such thoughts. There will be no choosing. She will never discover anything that will jeopardize her role as my student; if we visit the temple, I will see to it that nothing that would jeopardize her role even remains.

"Whatever your past life, you have a place here in the present. If you have to choose, I know you will make the right decision." I put a hand on her shoulder and she looks at it, nodding.

We make it to the port, and I make my way to the very end of all the vessels. A young man leans against a post, his wide straw hat casting a shadow over his face; he never sleeps when he's expecting company. Out of the corner of my eye, I see Scarlett look cautiously at the man, eyeing his torn overalls and dirty shirt, his bare feet, and his scarred, tan skin. She knows better than to openly judge someone around me; despite his appearance, he can be quite perceptive. An offended party is one that is difficult to manage.

"You keep lookin' at me like that, you might make me blush, darlin'." He has a slight accent which he never was able to get rid of;

more than one fight has broken out over it. Tilting his hat up, he looks at Scarlett with bluish green eyes, the same color as the sea.

Scarlett looks him back in the eye, and they hold each other's gaze for a moment before he steps forward, extending his hand out. "Name's Tomrius," he says. I step in front of Scarlett, shaking his hand; he still hasn't learned to take his eyes off any woman that comes by.

"I know," I reply and he grins, stepping back, hooking his thumbs in the straps of his overalls.

"After that last bit of business went sideways, I never expected to see you back at my port," he spits on the wooden dock, looking back to me. "Figured you cared more about your reputation."

"Your port?" I say, looking around dubiously.

"I'm the only one who can navigate over to Visland; and unless that changes, business stays good."

"You're right," I say, stepping up to him. He has to crane his head back to look me in the eye when I get this close. "Though I expect this trip to go better than the last one. Clear?"

He smiles wide, revealing four missing teeth; I still remember the men who knocked them out. Tomrius had it coming, but I can't have a client damaged in such a way and let the offenders escape alive.

"Crystal clear boss," he says, stepping away and turning toward the open ocean, cupping his hands and hollering, "Finn!" A small boat slowly sails to the dock, and Tomrius secures it to the dock. A man slightly older than Tomrius steps out of the boat, spitting into the water. He's dressed slightly better than Tomrius, his dark, curly hair nearly covering his dirty, grimy face.

"These two are going to sail us to a different country in *that?*" Scarlett looks dubiously at the two young men and their small boat. The small waves rock it much more than the other vessels, and the sails have several different colored patches in them. She takes a few steps away and I join her, her voice lowering to a whisper. "How am I supposed to trust them to get us across an ocean in that?"

"When he was a boy, Tomrius got shipwrecked on an island with a boat full of children and a few guardians; only Tomrius and Finn survived. They escaped the island by using that very same ship, and they refuse to sail anything else. More than a few sailors who have attempted the trip to Visland end up at the bottom of the ocean," I keep my voice a low whisper. "There's a reason his eyes are the color of the sea; there's no safer place on the open ocean than on the boat of Tomrius and Finn."

"It just looks unsafe," she says; rarely whenever I've proven a case as definitive as this one does she still question me. I cast my gaze over her, noticing the way her body shies away from the water, the way she eyes it warily; I suppose I never did teach her to swim.

"If anything else, they run a very successful import/export business; when a foreign land is the stuff of wild legends and rumors, the objects procured from it take on a mythical air and are thus, very expensive. I once saw Finn sell a two-piece plate from Visland for enough money to build half a fleet. Let their results speak for themselves."

I grow quiet as Finn approaches, keeping his eyes on me while Tomrius sulks by the boat, shooting a glance at Scarlett every once in a while, but she keeps her wary gaze on the small waves crashing against the dock.

"We won't sail you to Visland," Finn's voice is more refined, and he holds himself up straighter; he thinks he's been in the world long enough to earn it.

"Both of you agreed on that?" I look past him to Tomrius. Finn steps into my line of vision again, clasping his hands behind his back.

"That we did," he says, dipping his head in a shallow nod. "We appreciate the business you've provided to us up until this point; but after our last order of business, I'm afraid we can no longer give you transport."

I nod slowly, pondering. "I see. We seem to have reached an impasse; I must get to Visland, and you two are the only ones I want to get me there."

"I'm very sorry about the inconvenience sir," he says coldly. I lean in close to him, my breath on his ear, my voice a low whisper.

"I do not want to threaten you, Finn; truth be told, I like both you and Tomrius. Tomrius has a very likeable personality, and you have a keen business sense about you. Which is why," I put one hand on one of his shoulders, squeezing firmly, "it is so difficult for me to believe that you are making such a very stupid and poor business decision. If you turn me away here, your business will be finished, and you and Tomrius will be penniless, living on the streets. Is that what you want?" The veins in his neck bulge, right eyelid twitching as he does his best to control his breathing.

"I will never do business with you again after what happened last time. What you did to those people, it was...it was sickening."

"What I did to those thugs saved both of your lives!" I hiss. "If it weren't for me, you both would be dead! You owe me, Finn."

"We won't sail you," he growls, glaring at me out of the corner of his eye.

"You mean you won't sail me," I retort, looking past him at Tomrius. "You can barely sail a ship; you're kept around because you're his friend and you manage the company. What do you think will happen when he learns you won't sail me because of when I saved both of your lives? He will turn you out; and when I begin managing the company, he will never let you back in. You are dispensable—replaceable." I squeeze his shoulder tightly and his face goes livid, the color draining from his face.

"You—"

"What will it be, Finn?"

"I...I..." He looks behind him at Tomrius and sighs, shrugging off my hand. "How do you sleep at night, extorting others for your own selfish needs?"

"Because the end justifies the means." I hoist my pack back onto my back. "Also, you started it." I move past Finn, flashing a rare smile at Tomrius; he won't respond to anything but a positive, careless attitude. Fortunately, that lies within the scope of my abilities, though it feels foreign. "We sail!"

Scarlett stretches on her cot, opening her eyes and sitting up all at once. Silently she picks herself off the deck and joins me by the helm of the boat. The sun is just beginning to rise, the first rays of yellow and orange sunlight beginning to light up the grey landscape. Grey ocean, grey clouds, grey horizon—such uniformness does need some color, even I can see that.

"Are we close?" I nod and she leans on the helm, the wind picking up slightly. "I'll be glad to get off this boat," she grumbles.

"I guessed as much," I reply, the ocean spraying my face. "You're obviously not enjoying being out at sea."

"Can you blame me? We're on a boat that could probably break if a strong wind blew through. If this thing breaks apart, I'm going to be stranded with no way of reaching land, heading toward unfamiliar surroundings. Puts me on edge." She leans forward, glaring at the ocean, the conceived source of all her current problems.

I have traveled to Visland in the past, and I will undoubtedly need to bring Scarlett with me again. She needs to get over this fear of the ocean; the only thing to fear from the ocean are those that patrol it in their ships

"Let's go for a swim," I say, shedding my cloak. I fold it neatly in a small square before removing my other items of clothing, save my undergarments. I raise an eyebrow at her wide eyes and she turns, stripping down to the same state of undress. I extend a scarred hand to her, putting one foot on the edge of the boat. She takes my hand, looking down at the calm stillness of the blue/grey water. I turn and motion to Tomrius, making his usual rounds on the boat; he nods, moving things about the boat until we come to a relative standstill. I pull Scarlett closer to the edge of the boat, and her hand clenches mine tightly, sweat on her palms.

Without warning, I leap off the boat, pulling her with me. We hit the cold water; and despite my usual numbness, a shock hits my system, my limbs briefly stiffening. The rising sun is barely visible at our depth, the small waves slowly rocking us back and forth. Scarlett scrabbles over me once she regains control of her limbs, trying to push herself up onto me. I wrap an arm around her firmly and she squirms, kicking and flailing, trying to break loose. I kick powerfully with my legs, using my free hand to pull us to the surface. We break above the waves with a gasp, Scarlett sucking in air, trying to whirl and turn around, but I keep her firmly in place.

"Ohmygodohmygodohmygodohm—"

I cut her off, keeping us above the edge of the water. "*I will not let you go,*" I say firmly, my grip tightening on her. Her wide, frightened eyes look into mine, and she weakly tries to break way.

"I don't, I can't, I—"

"Stop panicking and look ahead of you," I command, my voice carrying over the sound of the rocking and creaking of the boat and our heavy breathing. I can see the tension in her as she forces herself to calm down, looking ahead; she wants to trust me, but she doesn't know how to trust herself in this unfamiliar environment. The sea water has turned her red hair dark, plastering it to her face and shoulders; she never learned to swim. I will teach Scarlett, at least.

The sun lights the water up to a brilliant bluish green, sparkling across the top as a small school of fish swims across. On the horizon, the fog slowly parts and tall buildings can be seen, the light shining through various windows, silhouetting other large structures. A soft breeze blows Scarlett's hair, the spray from the ocean caused by waves crashing against the shoreline hits the rising sun, a small, faint rainbow arching across our current field of vision. I slowly swim back to the boat, pulling myself up, gently lifting Scarlett up behind me with the shadows. Tomrius brings each of us a towel, and I wrap both around Scarlett. Her eyes remain locked on the horizon, wide, her breathing slow and deep, calm. She stands up slowly, extending a hand out to the rainbow. She stays like that, wide-eyed and mystified until we make it to shore. I dry myself off with one of the towels, slipping back into my clothes. I drop Scarlett's clothes next to her and she starts, looking up at me.

"It's...it's..." I place a hand on top of her head, running strands of her hair through my fingers.

"Do not try to fit words to an indescribable thing," I advise. She turns her attention back to the rocking waves and the nearly risen sun. "Get dressed"

She fits her clothes back on as we sail along the shore until I point a dock out to Tomrius who nods, changing our course. We make it into the dock unnoticed, far enough away from the city that besides the squawking of the birds and the soft crashing of the waves, it's relatively quiet. I make my way off the boat, Scarlett following. I turn to Tomrius, standing on the edge of his boat, looking down at the dock enviously. "I don't care what you do while we're gone; but when we get back, this boat better be here, ready to sail." His expression brightens and he shows me his toothy smile, snapping a sloppy solute.

CHAPTER FIFTEEN

Malor is loud, even this early in the morning. Trash litters the streets, the buildings looming over so far that they nearly block out the sun, casting the streets in a perpetual shade. Residents more sewer rat than human scurry back and forth, conducting their business. Further in, street vendors shout their wares, which can be heard echoing between the buildings. In many ways, it is like Descra; but in many ways, it is far, far more.

"This place is disgusting," Scarlett says, looking around in disgust.

"That depends on who you ask," I say, keeping close to the center of the streets; Scarlett staying at my side. "Some consider Malor the crown jewel of Visland; a sprawling urban metropolis, a testament to the willpower and ingenuity of the human race. Every inhabitant of Malor is a proud one and would willingly bleed and die for this city, no matter their differences in race or status. They are united by their pride, and so they survive everything that is thrown at them. Whatever else Malor is, it is necessary. Take a look around."

Scarlett slowly inspects the area, my eyes following hers. A well-dressed man argues with one of the peddlers on the street, and the former throws the first punch. Soon they scrabble on the street, a small crowd forming, chanting for a fight. In the crowd, a man slips a woman a small monetary note and they quickly leave the fight, only to be stopped by a haggard, knife-wielding man. The crowd parts, the well-dressed man going on about his day, his hands bloody; the crowd notices the man with the knife and quickly descends on him.

"It's lawless," Scarlett mutters in disgust.

"It is representative of their nature," I say, watching the crowd overwhelm the man with the knife, smearing the street with his blood. "To deny their nature is to deny themselves, and humans prefer to indulge rather than deny themselves. Malor is a city of indulgence." The crowd turns from the beaten corpse of the man toward us, eying us hungrily. I meet each of their eyes, my hand openly on my sword; after a moment, the crowd disperses, shuffling in different directions.

"Where are we supposed to find Impres?" she asks. I remain silent for a moment, scanning the area; I remember it being quite close to the dock. I spot the object of my desire, making my way toward a long building, low to the ground. The windows are grimy, but the sounds of raucous laughter and clanking, even this early in the morning, can still be heard. I open the door quietly, slipping in unnoticed amongst the din inside, Scarlett trailing behind me.

"The man on the left manages the rooms," I whisper, nodding at a thin, elderly man, cautiously eying patrons from behind a small desk. I hand Scarlett a few pieces of coin. "One room; go book it." I hand her my pack without waiting for a response, making my way through the crowd, sitting down at the long counter.

The bartender, and owner, immediately notices me, quickly making her way over to me. Her floral print dress is stretched over her round form, and her hair is piled precariously high atop her head, but she greets me with a large, friendly smile.

"Mister E!" she says warmly, pulling me nearly across the counter with her large hands, planting a wet kiss on each of my cheeks. I can feel the stick of her obnoxiously red lipstick, but I don't make a move to wipe it off; that would only offend her. One should always avoid angering or offending the owner of a bar, at all costs.

"Rosbi," I reply with a courteous smile.

"It's been far too long, little Merce is nearly grown! It's getting so quiet Hugh and I decided to have another," she says with a smile.

"Congratulations," I dip my head at her and she beams with pride. "I could hardly tell."

"You are such a liar, Mister E! It's a filthy habit I tell you," She says wagging a thick finger at me.

"I speak only the truth, madam," I reply, keeping my expression polite; every contact, every informant is different. Some simply care about the business, others care about making the business, and the clients, family; Rosbi falls into the latter category.

"Oh E you flatter me," she says with a blush, turning to the rack of alcohol behind her. "What can I get you?"

"That's not necessary, Rosbi," I say, and she waves her hand at me.

"Nonsense! If I remember correctly, you enjoyed," she pulls a dusty bottle off of the bottom shelf, hidden away from the light, filling a clean glass halfway, "this particular poison. Don't worry, it's on the house. Now where is that pretty little number I saw you walk in with?"

"My student is booking us a room and taking care of our things," I say, leaving the glass untouched.

"Why Mister E, you charmer! I never thought you would involve yourself with a student, and a *lady* at that! Why I—"

I occupy myself with the glass of alcohol, knocking back its contents in one swallow, the burning sensation in my throat distracting me mercifully from the rest of her sentence; sometimes I truly regret my inability to get drunk.

"I'm actually in Malor on business," I say after she finishes her ramble. She nods, wiping the counter.

"I see," she says, sliding a piece of paper across the counter and I scan it, slipping it into a pocket. "I'm really very sorry—it was the best I could come up with. I hope it will help you somehow."

"I'm sure I can find a way to make this work. Thank you Rosbi," I say, going to stand up.

"Won't you come by for dinner? Hugh is cooking a wonderful broth that is just lovely," she looks at me hopefully, and I apologetically shake my head; I will not be over at her house for dinner unless it is an emergency.

"My business here is time sensitive; the rooms here are merely a last resort. I'm sorry, but I don't think I'll be able to; Tomrius and Finn sailed me here though—perhaps they might be interested."

She refills my glass, stopping up the bottle and putting it back in its place. "Ah, alright. Well, there's one for the road." I stand, downing the glass in one go again, reaching in a pocket, my fingers wrapping around a small purse of money.

"Do you know what gender the baby is?" While the technology doesn't exist in Legend Land, I am never one to doubt a mother's intuition.

"I have a strong feeling it's going to be a girl, but Hugh and I haven't settled on any names," she says, wiping down the counter again.

"Might I make a suggestion?" She nods, and I pull out the purse of money, covering it with my hands. "I'm particularly fond of the name 'Scarlett'."

"Scarlett," she says, rolling it around in her mouth. "I like it."

I give her another courteous smile, placing the small purse of money on the counter, pushing it toward her.

"Oh Mister E—I—we couldn't."

"Please—I insist," I say, pushing the purse toward her as she tries to push it away. "Think of it as a congratulatory gift for you and Hugh—something to help when the new baby comes."

She frowns but takes the money. I dismiss her thanks with a small nod, turning my back on the counter.

I scan the room for Scarlett and spot her, avoiding eye contact with others by the stairs. I make my way over to her and gently push her in the direction of the door; it's time to go.

"Did you find out where Impres is?" she whispers as a brawl breaks out in front of us. We skirt it, making our way to the exit.

"I have another lead," I reply, stepping in front of her and pushing the door open. "I want to make sure it will be the last."

--·—⟨⟩⟨⟩—·--

I wait on the roof of one of the taller buildings, Scarlett squatting next to me.

"Who is this woman?" she whispers, and I keep my voice low as I reply.

"She's a local vigilante; I wouldn't take notice of her if she hadn't grown so popular with the people. They like the spirit she represents—a stronger Malor."

"And she's supposed to know where Impres is?" Scarlett sounds skeptical, a feeling I cannot help but share. Rosbi has never given me a reason to doubt her in the past, but this mission is critical.

"As a vigilante, she should have intimate knowledge of the city. If Impres is hiding in Malor, she will know where."

There's a small blur of movement below, and I put my hand on my sword, then slowly remove it. I cannot have a repeat of what happened with Ruphreus Erique. "Make your way down; if she tries to escape, cut her off at the entrance of the alley."

I jump off the rooftop, the shadows gathering underneath me to soften my landing. I roll and stand, the shadows reluctantly dissipating; it was a long journey to Malor, and they have grown hungry once more.

"You're not from around here," the woman says, her voice low.

"Vioda, I presume."

She nods, turning around. She seeks to distinguish herself from others by her red leather coat and dark boots—by her firm, unyielding manner; she does not want to be confused with a commoner. Despite her dark skin allowing her to easily blend into the dim light of the alley, her desire to be known and recognized is easy to see and can be easily used.

"You know where Impres is," I state, finding myself hoping that it is true.

"Why would I tell you if I did?"

"I am a man of resources; helping me would be beneficial to you." I say. She laughs a harsh, barking sound, shaking her head; it would not be wise to spurn such an offer, vigilante.

"I don't want your money or your help," she spits, standing up straighter. "It's outsiders like you who come in and think they can simply buy their way into and out of everything without consequence that destroy this city. People like you and your corruption are the disease of this city, crippling it; I seek only to make it stronger." She unsheathes two small swords from her side, and I still my hand as it goes for my own blade; I do not want her as an enemy. Not only can she lead me to Impres; but as an ally, she can be my voice to the people in Malor.

"How do you plan on making it stronger without the help and resources of others?"

She points one of her blades at me, eyes dark. "By attacking the disease at its source!" she shouts, lunging at me. I duck underneath one high swipe of her blade, sliding my foot against her ankle, throwing her off balance in her aggressive attack. I grab her arm, moving the second blade away from me as I slide behind her, pushing her away and sending her sprawling forward.

"Fighting a war alone against those with resources and connections is a fool's errand."

She turns to me, whipping her blades at me. I step back, the tips whistling barely an inch from my face. I feel brick against me from behind, and the shadows slowly gather behind me. No, not this one! I grind my heel into the ground and they slowly retreat, hissing angrily; this one is not an option.

"To take down powerful enemies, you need powerful allies."

"What makes you believe that you're powerful enough to be of any use as my ally?" she snarls, though she doesn't make a move toward me. Over her shoulder, I see Scarlett standing at the other end of the alley, daggers at the ready; I subtly shake my head and she sheathes them, albeit reluctantly.

"Allow me to prove it to you," I say, turning my attention back to Vioda. "Direct me to one of your enemies, and I will prove that I am a capable and powerful ally." She eyes me suspiciously, hands tense on her swords; I will make myself necessary to her cause. When she relies on me, then she cannot dare refuse me, and Impres will be mine.

"How do I know you won't betray me?"

"I could ask you the same question," I respond. She doesn't move her hands, either in an act of agreeance or aggression; she will accept the deal. If she doesn't, she is a fool; and I will not associate with fools.

"Fine," she hisses, jamming her swords back into their sheathes. She steps forward, finger at my throat. "But if you try anything, I will cut you to pieces."

With a small gesture of the hand, I halt the rising shadows; *depending on her enemy, you may yet have your meal. Have patience.* Reluctantly they slink away, snapping at my ankles as they leave. I clamp down on my mounting frustration; I am constantly babysitting the whims of children. I calmly look her in the eye, brushing her finger away. "You can try."

"I don't like her," Scarlett whispers, and I raise an eyebrow. "It's just a feeling I have, but I don't like that woman. We shouldn't trust her," she whispers, glaring at Vioda's back.

"I don't trust anyone, Scarlett," I reply, keeping my voice low. "What do you believe our options to be?" Scarlett must be constantly thinking—not only of the different options available, but of ones that can be created.

"We could torture her for the information; I'm fond of that option," Scarlett says bitterly, glaring at Vioda's back.

"Then we have made her a martyr and will have an entire city against us. Do not let your personal feelings or suspicions cloud your judgment; what other options are there?"

She frowns, stuffing her hands in her pockets. "We could have tailed her to see if she was going to Impres. We can enlist the aid of the enemy that we're going to kill; we could turn the city against her so that she's desperate for help." I raise an eyebrow; that last one had actual promise.

"And does any one of those end up with her not only leading us to Impres, but also as a future ally?"

She shakes her head, looking at me then glaring back at Vioda. "No, but some people are better as corpses than allies."

I remain silent; she has a point. Ever since her torture of Ruphreus Erique, she has been willing to resort to more brutal or violent methods to achieve the desired outcome; I must temper and direct that anger if she is to become a potent weapon. I must teach her self-discipline.

"This is your destination," Vioda stops, gesturing to a towering building, sleek grey surfaces dotted with large windowed offices. "The headquarters of a merchant conglomerate from Ismar who crushes our local merchants by any means necessary; their business brutality is nearly unrivaled in Malor. Their founder simply goes by 'Corval.' Take him out, and we have a deal."

"What are its security measures?" I ask, looking at the building across the street; no guards at the front entrance at least.

"No one who goes in uninvited ever comes out," she says by way of answer.

I despise going in blind.

"How do we know this isn't a trap?" Scarlett demands, stepping in front of me.

"This doesn't concern you," Vioda says dismissively.

"Like hell it doesn't!" Scarlett snaps, stepping towards Vioda. I grab her by the shoulder, yanking her to me.

"You will stay here," I instruct her in a low voice, my grip on her shoulders loosening. "Keep an eye on her; and if she tries anything, subdue her. We still need to be able to question her should she try and betray us. Scarlett," she nods, fingering the hilt of her dagger, "I'm counting on you." She places her hand on my chest, pushing me to the building gently.

"You don't need to worry about me; just kill Corval so we can get this over with and get out of this damn city." I turn my back on her, eying the tall building; I share her sentiment exactly.

—·—⊂⊃≷⊂⊃—·—

I avoid the front entrance, going into the alley located on the side of the building; a frontal assault would be the most time-consuming direction to take, and I do not want to be here longer than necessary. I make it to the back alley behind their headquarters; two men are out back. One wears a simple blue jumpsuit with the words "Ismar Trading Co." sewn onto the left side of his chest. The other is a man in a surprisingly nice suit, being beaten by the first man. The employee looks up, standing straight, kicking the whimpering man.

"You lost, pal?" he growls, wiping the blood off of his hands on his jumpsuit.

"No, I'm actually here to see Mr. Corval." I say, taking a step forward.

He chuckles, shaking his large head. "Nobody sees Mr. Corval unless they have an appointment. You got an appointment?" He looks me up and down with a contemptuous smirk; obviously not the dress of those who commonly frequent such an establishment.

"I don't need an appointment," I say calmly, taking another step closer.

"No appointment, no entry. Now I suggest you leave before things get ugly." He cracks his knuckles; such paltry attempts at intimidation in the city, it's embarrassing.

Before he can blink, I am directly in front of him, my lips so close that my breath moves the hairs on his ear. "I suggest you stand aside," I hiss, keeping my hand off my sword; I don't need to raise an alarm if it can be avoided. With such a low-level employee, other methods can be used. "Unless you wish for me to tell the board of your trea-sonous actions." A multinational corporation cannot be headed by one man—it doesn't make any business sense; there is always a board.

"Y-you're from the board?" He stutters, stumbling backwards; as I thought.

"No, I'm the one that the board sends whenever they discover that one of their people is stealing from the company." If the headquarters are in Malor, someone must be stealing from someone; it is the city of indulgence, after all.

"Mr. Corval is?"

I nod, and his face pales.

"What is your name?" I slowly step toward him, clasping my hands behind my back.

"Ergar, sir." He says, trying to keep his eyes on me as I circle him; manners, good. A healthy dose of fear can solve many social faults.

"Do you have a family, Ergar?" I place one hand on the back of his neck, the cool leather of my gloves becoming slick with his sweat; I will have to get a new pair after this is over.

"A wife and two boys, sir," he says. "Please don't—"

"Do you love your family, Ergar?" I cut him off. He nods quickly, neck fat jiggling. "Some drastic...corrections are about to take place here; you do not want to be here when they happen, do you?" He shakes his head just as quickly, and I can nearly hear the rocks rattle. "Give me your key, then go home to your family, Ergar. Tell them how much you love them and stay there until tomorrow. Do not talk to anyone until you reach your home, and do not leave it under any circumstances. Do you understand me?" He nods again, his hands fumbling as I let go of his neck, finally pulling out a small key, handing it to me without making eye contact. "Thank you Ergar; the board appreciates your cooperation."

I watch him scurry out of the alley and only insert the key into the door when I no longer hear his footsteps.

"You're not really with the board."

I look over my shoulder and see the man in the nice suit gingerly making his way to his feet. He winces as he coughs, wiping blood from his mouth; he can take a beating.

"They fired you, didn't they?" The hard expression on his face is answer enough. "I'm not here to take down the company; I'm just after Corval."

"He deserves what's coming to him, the slime," the man growls, gingerly holding his hand to his ribs. "I was running half that company for him, and he fired me just for doing a little digging into our profit reductions, the stealing swine."

"When Mr. Corval is removed from his position, there will be a power vacuum. Nature abhors a vacuum," I make eye contact with him, emphasizing each word. "That position will need to be filled; and in the scramble, who would think twice about someone replacing Mr. Corval who had previously ran half the business in Malor?" Having the head of a multinational corporation in my pocket would certainly put me in an interesting position of power.

"What do you want in return?"

I turn my attention back to the door, turning the key in the lock. "I don't have any interest in running your company, nor will I interfere in your business matters. I just want you to remember who put you in your position of power when you are at the top."

I slip inside into a dimly lit hallway without anyone around to notice. I put my hand on the wall, closing my eyes; Corval, a man of power, would be at the top. The shadows slowly extend from my hand, crawling up the wall, oozing into the cracks; they will verify.

"Excuse me?"

My eyes snap open, the shadows quickly disappearing. I turn my attention to the new arrival: a small, mousy woman carrying a large stack of files.

"Can I help you with something?" she leans back, quickly using one hand to adjust her glasses before again using it to support the weight of the files.

"Yes actually," I say, taking a few small steps forward. "Ergar let me in, but I admit I'm a little lost." I give her an exasperated smile.

"Ergar let you in?" she says skeptically, raising a thin eyebrow. I carefully close the distance between us, nodding.

"Yes he did. You see," I put a hand on her arm, her eyes snapping to the source of physical contact, "I'm with the Corrections Department from the board. I'm here to investigate a few, probably innocent, discrepancies with Mr. Corval's account."

Her eyes narrow, clutching the files tighter. "Oh I *highly* doubt they're innocent," she says, handing me her stack of files. She digs in one pocket of her jacket, placing a key on top of the files that nearly cover my face. "You go down this hallway, make a right, then another, and take the stairs to the top; there's the key to his office. He always has me manage all of his affairs and files rather than do anything himself. I didn't see you here, and you didn't see me."

"Of course not, madam," I incline my head as much as I can without upsetting the files.

I watch her walk quickly to the back door; and once it closes softly behind her, I drop the files. It is indeed quite fortunate that Corval is in such low regard with his employees. I follow her directions, looking up at the seemingly endless flights of stairs. The shadows grip onto the rails, wrapping around my waist, quickly climbing past several stories. They stop, their hold beginning to loosen; I grip them hard and they snap at me. "Corval will have to be eliminated; behave and you will have a meal to tide you over until we return to the Kingdom." They hiss quietly amongst themselves, then begin climbing; I do not enjoy having to barter with and convince these shadows to do my bidding. I cannot fight them; they are a part of me, and I will not win. There must be a better solution; I will devote myself to that later. The shadows deposit me at the top floor. At the end of the hallway is a large, expensive wooden door, shining brightly as if just polished. I make my way to the end of the hall, putting the key into the lock and the door clicks, swinging open.

"Jo-Ri, I told you not to disturb me until you finished with those files," the man looks up, his watery dark eyes narrowing. "Who the hell are you?"

I can understand now the comparisons between him and swine; his large, portly body is tightly tucked between a large leather chair and a solid oak desk, his many chins and neck rolls covering the knot of his obnoxiously yellow tie. His shiny dome glistens with sweat from being confined all day in an unflattering suit, his meaty hands nearly swallowing the gold-tipped fountain pen he clutches.

"Greetings, Mr. Corval. My name is Mister E." I close the door behind me.

"What kind of hippy name is that? I'm calling security!" He pulls a small rope attached to a stand next to his chair, and I hear the faint ringing of bells far below in the building. After a few moments, nothing happens; he yanks on the rope again, but no one comes. "The hell...?"

"The board also sends you its regards." I take a few steps forward and he throws his pen down.

"You're not with the board! Our books are impeccable!"

I smile coldly, shaking my head; this rude pig will suffer dearly. I cannot even get enraged at his pathetic attempts at insults or infirm power grasps; he simply disgusts me.

"I'm not here for the company, Mr. Corval, I'm here for you. Ergar let me in, and Jo-Ri was kind enough to give me the files that point to you being the one who has been stealing from the company. The board has sent me to correct this...oversight." I walk around to the large window behind his chair, looking out over the grey, smog-covered city of Malor; continuing this charade concerning the board makes Corval squirm, enjoyably so.

"What is it you want? I can give you money, women, power—anything! You name it!" he says nervously, standing behind me.

"Lovely view you have of this cesspool of a city," I remark neutrally, savagely breaking the glass with one kick, grabbing Corval by his necktie in the same motion and throwing him out the new hole. His high-pitched screams are rapidly cut off when the shadows wrap around him, jerking him back up to his office. He stammers unintelligibly, and I wave my hand dismissively at the shadows. "He's all yours."

They croon happily, dropping him again before wrenching him back up. They caress his sweaty face, drinking in his fear that emanates in palpable waves. After torturing him for a few more moments, their hunger grows and they quickly begin snapping and biting him, wriggling inside. I turn quickly as the door bursts open, unsheathing my sword and blocking two small knives thrown at me.

"Remarkably quick reflexes," a voice says from the dark hallway. I extend my hand, but the shadows are still feasting on Corval.

"Finish him quickly!" I growl, blocking another knife. I leap over the desk and slide underneath a crossbow bolt. A blur of red dashes past me, two shining blades slicing at me rapidly. I leap backward, glaring at Vioda.

"Surprised?" she smirks, sliding out of the way of my heavy, two-handed chop at her.

"Where is Scarlett?" I growl; I gave her a chance to be an ally. I offered her a hand in peace and she only bit me; I will obliterate her.

"Taken care of," she says, showing her sharp teeth with a grin.

I roar, leaping at her, slicing at her neck. She steps backward and I roll, blocking a strike aimed at my head, forcing upward, knocking her backwards. I swing at her torso; if she dared hurt Scarlett I will tear her apart! I will not have her come to harm! She blocks with one blade, the other whistling toward me. I step back and she only manages to leave a stinging scratch on my thigh. I block a high attack, disengaging my sword as she swings her second sword at my feet; I roll between the two blades, quickly bringing my hand up. These shadows will tear you apart! She chuckles, her boot slamming into my face, sending me careening onto my back; where are they?! My arms tremble as I try to push myself off the ground, my vision blurring; Corval is no longer at the window.

"What?" she laughs, boot catching me in the side, sprawling me on my back, my sword skittering across the floor.

"Your powers will not aide you."

The low light from the gas lamps catches on her swords and my eyes follow a single drop of clear liquid drop onto the floor; poison. I growl, pushing myself up onto unsteady legs, swaying; no mere mortal poison can best me! I take a step forward and collapse onto one knee, vision swimming. She sheathes her blades, backhanding me across the face. I lay face down, blood welling in my mouth at the same pace as my rage; she will not even live to regret this.

"There are three stages to this particular poison. The first is physical incapacitation," she says, holding up one finger.

I focus on her blurring outline, shaking my head; no. This is not how it will end—this *human* will not get the best of me! I roar, my fury burning through my veins in place of the poison, lending strength to my rapidly failing limbs. I rush at her, tackling Vioda around the waist, hailing her face with blows. She grabs one wrist, slamming her knee into my side, rolling onto me. Her elbow crushes my nose, blood spurting across my lips. She staggers off, spitting on me, smirking at my inability to respond.

"Like I was saying, the first stage—which should be complete now—is physical incapacitation. The second, which you should be feeling right about now," she says, holding up a second finger, "is immense physical pain."

My legs convulse, pain blossoming from one of my thighs, then quickly searing through both my legs. Fiery needles of white hot pain burn through my system; I screw my eyes shut, trying to move away from the pain, but my body refuses to respond. Let me tear it out! Through the red haze rapidly clouding my sight, I growl at Vioda.

"You..." My dry lips try to form more, but my tongue feels too swollen to move. She bends down close, cupping her ear right above my lips.

"What was that?"

I try to bite her ear, but a wave of pain hammers my skull, splitting my focus with a torrent of screeching sound in my ears.

"Y-you!" I gurgle out, spikes of torment causing my back to convulse in bone-grinding spasms.

"Is that all?" she shrugs, standing up. The convulsions subside and my head slumps to the side, blood dripping onto the wood floor.

"The third stage," she begins, getting down so I can see her contemptuous smile, her gloating gaze. "Impres said was a surprise."

My mouth snaps open, blood sputtering out as I roar, my throat being scraped raw, my vocal cords vibrating to the point of nearly snapping. Impres—that wretched witch! I will hunt her to the end of the cosmos and rip her tongue out of her skull! My rage brings about another set of convulsive spasms, leaving me gasping for breath, twitching on the sweat-covered floor.

"In here, boys!" I make out the blurry outlines of boots, a new smell joining the stench of sweat and drying blood; oil. "You are part of the disease; you always will be, and everyone like you. You must be purged from this city; now you will know the fever parasites like you cause this city." I hear the scratch of flint on steel; and before consciousness slips away, heat blossoms not only inside, but surrounding me as well.

CHAPTER SIXTEEN

My eyes snap open, and all my senses scream for sole attention.

"It's me!" Scarlett says hurriedly, putting her hands on my shoulders and keeping me down as I growl and writhe. Taking a deep breath, I slowly unclench my hands, my muscles loosening. A sharp pain shoots through my body and I close my eyes, clenching my jaw. "You were poisoned," Scarlett says in a soft voice, putting a damp cloth on my forehead, and the relative cool of the cloth allows me to realize how hot my skin is. I'm running a fever. I groan and open my eyes, looking around the room; the light is soft and muted, most of the room dark and pleasantly cool.

"Where…are we?" I manage to get out, my tongue feeling dry and swollen.

"You've been out for nine days. I managed to find Tomrius and Finn; we're on their boat. They helped with your injuries. You were running a really high fever and got a few nasty burns before I got you out. She…she got the drop on me; I'm sorry."

She looks past me, and I try to turn, but my muscles snap taught and I go rigid, arching my back, jaw locking. Scarlett pushes me gently back onto the bed, wetting the cloth again. I haven't experienced a condition like this since I was a boy, and all because of mere poison! Impres is the one responsible behind this; I am put in this condition because I continued my search for her. I gasp, letting out a long, steady breath as my back touches the bed once again.

"I've been tracking Vioda once I convinced Tomrius and Finn to agree to protect you. I'm going out tonight to find her and make her undo what she did to you."

"I...I don't need their protection," I growl, making an effort to sit up and extend my arm; the shadows do nothing. I fall back, laying down again, my arm still extended up; obey! I growl, clenching my hand into a fist, digging my nails into my skin; my arm begins to lower of its own accord, my body not having the strength to even keep it up. I listen intently for even the hiss of the shadows, but I hear nothing. I try to raise my arm up, but it refuses to even move; the most I can do is close my eyes in frustration.

"You need them protecting you because right now you can't protect yourself," she says, keeping her hand on the bandages covering my chest. "I understand you don't like having to rely on anyone else, but you're just going to have to deal with it."

This poison has made me too weak! I groan, trying to move even a finger; my right index finger twitches, but that's the most I can do.

"I'm going to head out now. I put you here because I couldn't stop that woman; I'm going to make this right, I swear it. Try and get some rest."

She looks down at me with what almost seems to be pity; I screw my eyes shut, managing to turn my head away. I don't need anyone's pity. I hear the door close and I growl; unable to move, unable to use my powers. I can do nothing; useless. No, not useless; I manage to shake my head, taking a deep breath. I may not be able to move and the shadows will not obey me now, but that will change with time; right now my mind is affected by the poison just as much as my body. I must at least clear my mind of the poison; my body will fight off this wretched poison in due time, but I truly am useless if I do not have my mind. Closing my eyes, I lean back into the pillow, burrowing deep into my mind. The familiar scent of wildflowers curls into my nostrils as I escape into my mind.

I open my eyes, but there is still only darkness around me. I look around and notice a point of light that begins to slowly grow brighter. I become aware of the air rushing past my face, tugging at my hair and clothes; I am falling. I reach out, willing the shadows to slow or stop my descent, but they do nothing; I realize my arm did not move either. My limbs refuse to move as I plummet towards the light, which grows larger and larger beneath me. I grit my teeth and will the shadows to come to me, to blanket me and to protect me, but they remain stubbornly still and silent. I gnash my teeth, glaring at the light. I can make out a single tree and green grass beneath me. This is my mind; I have control here.

I manage to clench my hands, and I jerk to a halt, like something had just caught me around the midriff. I close my eyes and let out a long sigh, and suddenly I'm falling again. I land with a heavy thud on the grass, a single wave of pain punching my chest and spreading out in small shock waves throughout my entire body. I groan, blinking away dirt and grass, trying to move my arms. They refuse to cooperate and remain limp at my sides.

"You have a habit of thinking you are concentrating, when in all actuality your mind is in so many directions you can't pay attention to them all."

I manage to tilt my head slightly backward, and Simiel is standing above me with her hands on her hips, looking down at me.

"It's a toxic form of self-deception," she says, walking away and returning with a wooden wheelchair. She bends down and puts one of my arms around her shoulders, standing up; I do my best to use my legs and support myself, but all I can manage is to twitch at the ankles. Useless.

"You're right—you are useless like this," she says, setting me in the wheelchair. I open my mouth and she shakes her head, getting behind me and pushing the wheelchair. "You came here because you want my help; my help comes at the price of your silence until I say otherwise."

I take a deep breath through my nose, and her scent of lemons, honey, and wildflowers tingles in my brain. It's all so real, so vivid—a construct of my mind mimicking a past reality. A toxic form of self-deception. I jerk my head up and down once, which is as close to nodding as I can get.

"Good. I know you're trying to rationalize everything that's happened to you."

It's how we both are; I got it from you.

"You rationalize and deceive yourself on a regular basis, you know, and this is what you get for it. You think you're invincible; you overextend yourself, you're arrogant in your presumptions of your own prowess. Now here you are defeated by poison,"

I have not been defeated! This is a mere setback, a momentary halt before I recover.

"You won't be able to rid the poison from your body, but you can rid it from your mind; you should know that. You came to me because you need help." She stops pushing, and a small leather bag appears a few yards away. "You only ever come to me when you need help, did you know that? You never visit me because you just want to see me, only when you need help. Of course, I can help you, easily, but you have to be willing to help yourself. Part of the reason your body is paralyzed is because your mind is as well; you are, at least partially, unwilling to help yourself. A simple visualization challenge should enable you to, at least partially, overcome this mental block of yours."

She tips me out of the wheelchair, and I land sprawled out on the ground. I bite my tongue hard, blood spilling into my mouth; she is not real. I must keep that distinction, especially with this cursed poison coursing through my veins. It threatens to blur the distinction between reality and fantasy in my mind. With Scarlett around, it is difficult enough to maintain a firm grasp on what is real; this poison threatens to completely destroy that conception. My mind attempts to ensnare me with the startling realistic and vivid nature of this place; a toxic self-deception.

I manage to turn my head to look up at Simiel, and my vision swims; red hair dances in front of my eyes, and green eyes look down at me as she crosses her arms. I blink, taking in her raven black hair and orange eyes; I must rid this poison from my mind soon. I must fight against this induced paralysis; slowly I turn my head to look at the bag, every stiff muscle in my neck fighting my will.

"All you have to do is grab the bag," she says.

Trembling, I demand movement from my arms and slowly, unwillingly, they comply, moving at an agonizing pace out in front of me. My hands clench the grass, and I try to pull myself forward, but the grass just shreds under my grip. I swear loudly, tearing out the grass on purpose now, and I feel a foot on my back.

"I did not say you could speak," Simiel reprimands. "Focus."

I growl, digging my fingers into the ground and sharply tugging, my elbows jerking and locking. I do it quick enough, however, that it throws Simiel off balance as I scrape forward a few inches.

"I did not say you could stand, yet you do it," I grit out; I cannot allow myself to believe she is actually here. If I let my mind trap me here, then I will never finish my mission, and I will let fantasy become reality.

"You agreed to my terms."

"I'm negotiating," I growl, pulling myself forward a few more inches. I slowly unhook my fingers from the earth, flexing them and extending my arms forward. They tremble and then drop to the earth; I anchor my fingers back in and pull myself forward, jerking and shaking for eight inches of distance. After making it two more feet in this manner, my arms refuse to move any longer. My head collapses to the ground, sweat dripping onto the grass; my clothes stick to me from the amount of perspiration coming off my body. My breathing is labored and burns my lungs, as if I'm inhaling a cloud of acid; my arms are stiff, unresponsive, and numb.

I growl, blinking the stingy, salty sweat out of my eyes; I must keep going! I cannot allow this poison to affect my mind any longer! I jerk my chin and it causes my head to spin, sending shocks and twangs of pain up my neck, but I'm able to look forward. The bag is still over two yards away, and my body is unwilling to obey my commands any more. No matter how trained something may be, it will not willingly continue to subject itself to torture. Even my body, trained over centuries of grueling trials, refuses to cooperate when it has reached its limit. I breathe in the dirt and the sharp scent of grass, my eyes following a small ladybug who is skittering over the blades of grass quickly, trying to escape this giant creature who so rudely interrupted its peaceful environment. I blink, screwing my eyes shut; I must overcome this poison! I must reach that bag!

I try to turn my head but am unable; my body truly refuses to move. My muscles will not obey; and for the first time in my memory, I am abandoned by even myself. I tremble, sweat dripping off me; no, I have been abandoned before. Though I have allies, I was on my own long before I began building my network; I shall be again. I was not weak before; I was abandoned, and my body still obeyed. It will move; it must move! I growl, biting at the grass, trying to jerk my head, but I do not move. Why will I not move?! I smell the scent of lemons and honey now instead of grass, the thin material of Simiel's dress entering my vision.

"You were unable to reach the bag," she says, not sounding disappointed in the least. She takes my sweaty, hot head in her hands, setting it on her lap so I can look up at her and she down at me. Absentmindedly she strokes my hair, moving it away from my forehead. "That's okay. You are not as alone as you might think; I am here for you. Sometimes you can't beat everything that's thrown against you," I try to shake my head, but she holds it in place, her hand cool against my feverish face.

"I will...I will not be defeated...by this poison," I manage to gasp out, my lungs burning with each exhalation of air, speaking with my swollen tongue only worsening the pain.

"You came to me for help," she says, looking down at me, bending closer. "You did not specify what you needed help with. I act in the way that I think will best assist you, and you are desperately needing a lesson in perspective and humility."

I open my mouth, but she puts her hand to it, and I can't bring myself to bite her, no matter how unreal she is.

"You were poisoned because you continued to pursue Impres. You seek to fulfill the mission at whatever cost, and now that has put you in the most compromising position you have been in for centuries.

You lack the strength to beat this poison and must hope that your powers are strong enough to keep you alive, because your body has all but succumbed to the poison."

"My powers...have deserted me," I growl, calling out to the shadows. They, like before, do not heed my wishes and remain out of reach. I close my eyes and clench my jaw, trembling.

"Rather than getting angry about it, think about why the shadows do not answer you!"

My eyes snap open to see Simiel looking down at me sharply, her eyes narrow. Her orange irises glow and dance almost like flames, burning me; being this close to her burns me. It will kill me if I let it. No, none of this is real; it's all in my head!

"Perhaps it is not to spite you, as you like to think, but rather because they fight for you. If you have spent so many years training them to obey you, to look out for you, to fight for you, maybe they are simply following their training. They are fighting the poison for you as we speak and are the only thing keeping you alive; they don't have the energy to do anything else. If you continue to be angry at them, to insult them, and to think vehement thoughts at them, they may abandon you. You cannot afford for anything else to abandon you now when you are so short on allies."

"I...have plenty of allies, I...do not need...more." Every word, every breath is agony, but I cannot simply be talked at.

"No you do not! Stop fooling yourself, because that's the only person you're fooling. You may not be alone, but every moment you have spent pursuing Impres has been a moment you lose an ally. When you make a powerful enemy, former allies must reevaluate their stance. The only true good you have done was for Scarlett and Jack, and both of those were self-serving."

"A conception...of good and evil is...outdated," I breathe, sucking in a rattling gulp of air. "People always act...act in their own interests. It is...only because...others view actions in a favorable or...unfavorable light…that actions are good or...evil." My mouth refuses to open anymore, and I breathe in and out heavily through my nostrils, the rank smell of sweat and anger choking me as it travels down my throat.

"I wasn't speaking about good and evil; I was talking about your selfishness! You pursue Impres out of selfish reasons—"

"That is not true!" I strain to sit up, but am unable; my reasons for pursuing Impres are for the mission, and that mission is the most unselfish undertaking of my entire life.

"Your reasons stopped being unselfish and noble once you let anger enter the situation," she retorts, her eyes flashing green. "You act in accordance to your selfishness, and it will be your downfall. Scarlett is the only one who has remained loyal to you, and your selfish pursuit of Impres may drive her away."

"I cannot stop...pursuing...Impres," I gasp, my chest feeling like it is caving in, my lungs aching for air.

"You will lose all your allies, anyone who you hoped to one day call 'friend' if you continue."

My head lolls to the side, trying to focus on the blades of grass as unconsciousness tries to wrest control from me.

"I...have...no friends; I came to...Legend Land with...no...friends. Friends are...unnecessary." My eyes no longer wish to remain open, closing despite my urging against it.

"If you aren't going to listen, then you shouldn't have come to me," Simiel says. "I can't help you if you don't want to be helped. Know this though: if you don't change your ways soon, you will find yourself truly alone in a world of enemies."

CHAPTER SEVENTEEN

I close the door behind me, Tomrius and Finn both standing up at once. Tomrius had been easy to convince, Finn not so; whatever Mister E had said to him really hit him hard. Tomrius steps forward but Finn speaks first, his voice harsh and firm. *You certainly seem to attract firm men.* Now is *not* the time; now is the *worst* time possible.

"We want you off our ship," he says. I open my mouth to speak but he cuts me off. "We've kept you both secretly hidden, and now I want him off our boat."

Tomrius has remained quiet so far, and I turn to him. "And you?" My body is stiff, my voice an accusation; I won't abandon Mister E, and I'm not about to let these two kick us off their ship. I'll kill them if I have to. *Seems like Mister E is rubbing off on you.* This is *my* fault; if I hadn't let Vioda get the drop on me, none of this would have happened. *True, true.*

"I uh...I mean, um..."

"We are not keeping either you or him on our boat," Finn says firmly. I put my hand on my dagger, taking a step forward.

"You're going to turn away an injured man?" I retort. He scowls, turning me away from Tomrius.

"That so-called 'man' is a *monster,*" he growls. *He's got you there.* He's not a monster! Despite some of his actions, he's kept me safe, and he's trying to help me regain my memories. He always protects me, and he's given me more chances than I probably deserve. Now, he's nearing death because of *me*.

"That *monster*," I growl back, smacking away his hand, "is the kind of monster that takes on a corporation that is crushing this city; the kind of monster who knows what evil is, and fights it every day. That monster gives money to expecting families." *You were eavesdropping?* I need to know what my teacher is doing, as much as he needs to know what I'm doing; how can we trust each other if we don't? *You said you couldn't trust him, or he you.* Things...they change. "He risks his life for mine and forgives my mistakes; he takes care of those who take care of him. There are true monsters in this world, and I believe that if you have to become a monster to defeat them, then you must do it. People don't become monsters out of choice! This *world* of monsters," I gesture to Malor behind me, the so-called "city of indulgence"; more like the city of sin, "has forced him to become a monster in his own right, because he fights monsters every day. And if—" I look down, my knuckles white on the handle of my dagger, blinking away tears; I can't let them see me cry. I can't let anyone see me...I have to fix my mistake; I can't be balling my eyes out now, there isn't time. "If that man dies in there, the real monster is you." I meet his eyes again, poking him in the chest. His jaw locks, hands slowly curling into fists; throw the first punch, I dare you. Try and hit me, try and push your anger on me; there isn't room for any more rage here, but I'd like to see you try, Finn.

"We'll look after 'im," Tomrius says quietly, putting a hand on Finn's shoulder. "C'mon." His voice remains soft, but firm, pulling Finn away.

I turn my back on them, unsheathing my dagger as I go; my intentions will be clear. Halfway to the end of the dock I break into a run, the blood roaring in my head; I will find Vioda, and I will make this right. I will do whatever it takes to take her down, even if I have to burn this whole goddamned city to the ground. I clench my dagger harder, running faster into Malor; I enter the city of sin.

--·—⟨∞⟩—·--

I stand outside of a dingy apartment building, looking it up and down; a garbage heap, only containing trash. After investigating Vioda's whereabouts for over a week, the information all points to her being here; fitting. I desperately wish that I wasn't here right now; I would love to be back in the Kingdom, in the cottage with Wilhelm's arms wrapped around me. I quickly shake my head, spinning my dagger; no, I can't think of Wilhelm when I do this. I push the entrance open and walk through the dirty hallways, the paint peeling off the walls, the thin carpet ripped up in places. A rat scurries by my feet but I don't pay attention. Someone slumped in the hallway lunges forward and catches the squirming rat, retreating backwards; trash and rats, wow, some diversity here.

I cautiously set one foot on the rickety metal stairs leading up, not bothering to put my hand on the guardrail; I wouldn't trust it to support a falling rat. *You just called yourself fat you know.* Unless you have something useful to say, don't speak. The stairs creak and groan underneath me, dirt falling over the sides with each step up I take. After six flights of stairs I arrive at the top, breathing easy; stair climbing is nothing compared to Mister E's training. I walk past nine doors and stop at the tenth looking at the apartment number; room 70-J.

I bend down in front of it and pull out two small pieces of metal, fitting them in one of the locks. I hear footsteps running and I turn, casting a watchful eye down the hallway. A small boy looks at me, one eye hidden by long, lanky hair. He just looks at me for a moment then resumes running down the hallway, thudding down the stairs. The clanging of the shaking stairs is more than enough sound to cover the soft click of the lock as I unlock it. I move onto the next one and unlock it before the child makes it to the bottom. The door opens with an obnoxious creak; I'm not trying to hide from her anyway. I want to make her pay for what she did; but if I can get the jump on her like she did with me, the irony would make it all the more sweet. I remove my dagger and smack the thin chain that holds the door closed with the pommel. It breaks with a soft snap, and I quickly open and close the door to prevent any prolonged squealing.

I creep softly through the small, dingy apartment, floorboards squeaking under me seemingly at random. I come to the bedroom and search it, but I find no one. I search quietly through the rest of the apartment, but it's empty. I swear, smacking one of the wooden counters and it creaks dangerously under my palm; I should just tear her apartment apart. *Oh yeah that'll show her. Poison my teacher? I'll break your dirty couch.* What did I say about talking?! I make my way back to the bedroom, opening the closet, only to find it empty. My ears perk up to the sound of a rustling doorknob.

I quickly step into the closet, sliding the door closed, peeking out through the cracks in the shutters. The rustling stops and the door slowly creaks open. I squeeze my eyes shut briefly, swearing under my breath; the chain! I grip my dagger harder as light footsteps avoid the creaky floorboards; notice the broken chain please. Come try and find me, try and kill me; I enjoy killing, but I'll enjoy killing her all the more. She enters the bedroom and stops, red coat falling to her ankles, her black boots causing small puffs of dust to rise up. She turns her back to the closet, running a hand over the bed. This woman poisoned my teacher, tried to have both of us killed; I start trembling, putting a hand on the closet door. I'll make her spill her guts to me, and then I'll spill her guts; I'm not going to wait for her to come to me. Tonight, I hunt!

I sling the closet door open, leaping out at her, slicing at her throat. She turns quickly and unsheathes one sword, blocking my strike and unsheathing her other. I duck under her slice, sweeping her legs out from under her. She lands on her back, rolling as I slice my dagger at her. She reaches into one of her boots, throwing two small knives at me as she stands. I slide over the bed to avoid them and they thud into the mattress. I roll across the floor, two daggers thudding into the wood behind me. I hear her steps crashing through the apartment and I race after her, leaping at her as she nears the door. She turns, blocking with one sword and slicing at me with the other. I block one blade with my dagger and reach my hand up, grabbing her wrist to stop her from splitting my skull open with her other sword; you will not stop me tonight. You got the drop on me before, took me by surprise; you cannot beat me in a fair fight. The most dangerous man in the world has trained me to kill, and you, wretched woman, tried to burn him alive; you will not kill me.

"You?!" her eyes widen, arms trembling against mine, pressing down harder, trying to inch her sword closer to my head. She jerks her knee at me, but I just take it; I will not give in. Her blade screeches against mine as she tries to slide it up, but I turn my wrist slightly, stopping the motion; amateur.

"Yeah, me." I savagely kick her in the knee, my aim precise. Her leg bends awkwardly, and I push her back. She stumbles backward into the wall, and I get in close before she can use her swords, jabbing her in the throat. She gasps for breath, weakly swinging a sword at me. I grab her wrist and twist it, snapping it with my forearm; she's still out of breath, so she doesn't scream when her wrist breaks. I wrench her remaining sword from her hand, swiping my foot at her ankle when she stumbles forward. She sprawls on the ground and I kick her sword out of reach, leveling the other at her. I take a deep breath, the tip of her sword trembling, sweat trickling down her temple; with every cut, let go. I flick my wrist and the tip leaves a small scratch on her cheek; she gasps, unbroken hand flying to her face and I flick my wrist again, leaving two more scratches on the back of that hand.

"What do...you...want?" she grits out through the pain; oh, I bet that hurts, doesn't it? Maybe I'll put a little poison on that, clear it all up.

"What do *I* want?" I push the tip of her sword against her neck and she leans back, the tip following. "I want to torture you, slowly and methodically, until you cave. I want you to suffer the way you made my teacher suffer, and I want to do like you did to me, and make you feel like a fool. What I want, Vioda," I pause whenever she's bent almost completely backward, her unbroken wrist supporting her entire weight, "is for you to suffer."

I quickly remove the sword from her throat at the same time I stomp forward, crushing her hand underneath my boot. She cries out, weakly trying to pull away. "Fortunately for you, I need the antidote to the poison."

She looks up at me trembling; I trail the tip of the sword up her cheek, resting it a fraction of an inch away from her left eye; I'll leave her with her other, so she can see what I do to her if she doesn't give me what I want. I will not let Mister E die because I lack strength to do what is necessary; I will not give this woman my sympathy. She is…undeserving.

"There…is no antidote," she growls from behind clenched teeth. I press the tip of her sword into her cheek, knuckles white.

"Liar," I snarl. There has to be an antidote; there *must* be! I can't have come here for nothing! She smirks with contempt, chuckling softly.

"Impres gave me a poison; she said nothing about an antidote."

"You are *lying!*" I press the tip of her sword harder against her cheek, drawing blood; she has to be lying! I can't go back to Mister E empty-handed, not after everything he's done; I can't fail him.

"There is no antidote," she says, enunciating each word.

"Liar!" I shout, flicking the sword across her cheek, but she doesn't flinch. I shake my head; she can't be telling the truth. This can't all be for nothing! She lifts her hand suddenly underneath my foot, sweeping her legs across the floor, knocking my other foot out from underneath me. I swipe at her feet as she leaps over me, rushing to the door.

"Now!" she shouts. I roll quickly to my feet as the door bursts open, several men and women rushing in, armed with everything from knives to bats. *It seems the entire apartment complex has come for you; perhaps she was telling the truth.* No talking! *You should stay focused; look, here comes one now.*

A large man rushes at me, and I duck underneath his wide swing, slicing him across the neck, pushing his corpse against the others swarming in, but they keep coming. I run into Vioda's bedroom, slamming the door closed and locking it. It won't hold for long; everything is so thin in these apartments. I look at the wall and take a deep breath; I have to get out of here. If I can disappear, I can return later. *So you're going to run?* I'm going to *retreat*, there's a difference. *One is spelled differently, yeah.* I shake my head and run at the wall, slamming my shoulder against it. It tears apart easily, and I crash into an empty bedroom. I wince, noting a thin piece of metal tearing a deep gash in one of my arms. *You can't run through a wall without some consequences.* I rip off a piece of shirt with my teeth, tying it around the wound; I have to get out of here and hide. I can't risk them following me back to Tomrius and Finn's boat.

The door to Vioda's room bursts open and they look at the hole in the wall for a moment. *No, don't chase the wounded lady, look at the hole in the wall; simpletons.* I move quickly, tossing the door open and hurriedly unlocking the door to the hallway, letting it hang open behind me. One man already in the hallway turns to me, swinging a bat. I slide under his legs, coming up and slicing. He howls and I stab him in the neck, kicking him forward. I run down the stairs, the stairs clanging and shaking as I race down them. I hear the others running down the hallway and I speed up; I have to make it down before they get on the stairs. *Why?* I run into the lobby of the apartments as the first steps begin to clang. The stairs creak and groan as more people thud down them, shaking and swaying ominously. I back away as the stairs collapse, pulling ceiling and people alike down with it in a clang of metal and screams. *Oh, that's why.*

I rush out of the building unnoticed amidst the screams and confusion, people flocking from the streets to see the damage. I duck out of the crowd into an alley, leaning my head against the building behind me, breathing heavily. Blood trickles down my arm and it throbs painfully each time I breathe; that was a waste. *You think?* I shake my head looking down, clenching my hand around my dagger; there is no antidote. I sheath my dagger and slam my fist against my thigh angrily; there is no antidote! I swear loudly, kicking a trash can, sending its contents spilling over; I wasted my time! I failed; I shake my head, slamming my fist into my thigh again. I failed! I was supposed to get the antidote. I told Mister E I would get the antidote, and I failed; Mister E could die because of me. *What's your problem with that? If he dies, you no longer have to be his student; you can be with Wilhelm with no worries.* What happens to my memory then? If Mister E dies, do I lose my memory? I can't go back to not remembering—I can't! *What are you going to do then? You're in no condition to fight, not with that arm, and Vioda's going to be long gone by now; she knows this city, she can disappear quicker than anyone can hope to find her. What will you do now?* I look up, wind howling through the alley, a few drops of rain falling around me. All of a sudden the clouds break open, a torrent of rain pouring down; perfect. I sigh, gripping my hair; I have to return empty-handed and explain my failure. *Since when do you care what he thinks?* Since he helped me! I *owe* him; I won't leave him, not like this. Now that he's incapacitated, possibly crippled, it's up to me to look after him, to manage his network. I have to start taking care of things now, and the first order of business will be to get out of this hellhole, this cursed city of sin.

I slowly peel one eyelid back, cracking the other one open; my mouth feels like it's been sewn shut, dry and unused on the inside. My body feels swollen and sluggish, and I can barely manage to look around the room. A sudden gust of wind hammers against the door, and a small portion of that wind blows into the room sending cool air dancing across my hot skin, cutting underneath my bandages like thin, icy blades. The sweat covering me almost seems to freeze against my skin, and I am able to move only slightly, adjusting myself so that the breeze does not chill me. The rustling of the sheets attracts attention and a figure stands up, coming over to the bed and lighting a dim lamp. Long, raven-black hair curtains her pale face, her orange eyes like a fire: warm and comforting. She smiles at me, whispering something in my ear but I can't hear it; I manage to open my mouth, sending pops of pain from my jaw up to the top of my skull.

"Simiel?" I gasp out; I'm supposed to be awake. This is supposed to be reality. Her mouth moves, and this time I can hear what she says, though her voice is drastically different than what I remember.

"I'm sorry."

I blink and see Scarlett, her red hair plastered to her face with rain, her green eyes angry and distressed, worry etching lines into her face. Blood drips down her arm from underneath a bandage; she pulls up a chair and gently sits down, wincing.

"Scarlett," I try to sit up, only succeeding in shifting my shoulders slightly; Scarlett helps me sit up, offering me a cup of water. I let the bottom part of my jaw drop open and tilt my head back; Scarlett pours the water in my mouth with her uninjured arm. My throat struggles to perform the swallowing motion, and half the water splutters back out, covering my neck and chest as the rest slowly slides down. My eyes feel like they wish to close again, my body tired from that much movement; I refuse to give in. "What happened?"

She looks away, hiding her face in the darkness as rain and wind slams against the door constantly now.

"I went after Vioda," she says softly. "I went after her to try and get the antidote to get rid of the poison. It's my fault you're this way; if I...if I had kept better watch... I had to get rid of the poison," she says, her jaw clenching and unclenching as she brings her face back into the light, pushing hair out of her eyes. "With that poison in you, making you weak, paralyzing you, I have to protect you because no one else can. But I'm not sure I can protect you all the time," she shakes her head, slowly making a fist and hitting her thigh. "I found Vioda and...and I demanded for her to hand over the antidote. She said..." Scarlett screws her eyes shut, shaking her head. Letting out a shaky breath she opens her eyes, glaring at the floor. "She said there was no antidote; I didn't believe her. I fought her and discovered there really is no antidote, but I couldn't...I couldn't just let her get away with what she did to you. So I kept fighting her and...she defeated me. I had to run away just to save my life."

She clenches both her hands, wincing and looking down at the ground; her hair hangs in front of her face, water dripping off several strands steadily. "I am so *weak*." She wanted to protect me, to avenge me. I know what it is like to want to avenge someone and to be unable to. I suck in a deep breath and straighten up, grabbing Scarlett by the shoulder, squeezing it hard. She looks at me and I look back at her, my eyes hard and focused.

"Do not blame yourself for your defeat," I growl, the poison threatening to deliver me into unconsciousness. "You tried to avenge me, and that is enough. That woman defeated me." My head begins to droop and I growl, sitting up straight once more; she must hear what I have to say. "You cannot blame yourself for not being able to defeat her. I will overcome this poison; something as mortal and earthly as poison will not defeat me, I assure you. In the meantime, you will have to act as my body in the world. This is my fault; the blame for this all rests solely on my shoulders. My search for Impres, and my refusal to back down, caused this to happen. I have let my network crumble in the pursuit of Impres; that must be changed, and you will be the one to do it. I can no longer pursue her in my condition, and I will not put you in that position; we must focus on my network. After I am well enough, I will continue training you and take you to the temple to regain your memories. I promise you that."

My arm drops from her shoulder and my head droops as I slump down, the poison finally overcoming my will. Scarlett sniffs, pulling her chair closer to me.

"When I screwed up in Descra, I thought that was it; I was afraid you would abandon me. I didn't, I *couldn't* go back to the way I was before. When I brought Ruphreus back to you, you accepted my return without question, and you helped me get *justice*. Ever since I then, I've been unsure of who I am; am I a merciless killer? Who am I to torture someone so coldly, so *exactly?*"

I will my arm to move but my body simply ignores my command. Forcing myself to concentrate, I slowly open my bare hand and Scarlett looks at it, her green eyes the darkest black in the low light; they are like looking in a mirror.

She continues, "But I told myself he deserved it; that to fight monsters we have to become them. Some of your actions, some of your words, made me doubt that; I didn't use to think that way, and I started not to again. I thought that, maybe, we could be better than the monsters we fight; I know I was wrong. You compromised with Vioda, gave her a peaceful solution, and she poisoned you. I fought her with all my anger, and she gained the upper hand again; I fought her as an angry human. I should have fought her as a cold monster."

Her head hangs down, her jaw locked, hands clenched into fists. I look at her, her eyes dark and depthless, her hair black in the shadow, body bloody; I can feel her soul slipping away. My fingertips burn as I try to reach out to her, my arm trembling. I will not let her lose herself! I reach out in a sudden movement, clasping one of her hands in mine. She looks up, on the precipice of a fatal decision.

"You... are not a monster, Scarlett. Do not lose yourself to this; do not become cold, unfeeling. If your anger makes you human, fight with your anger; do not be...consumed by this. Do not lose your soul." My grip tightens on her hand, my expression hard. "I am a monster, a killer of gods; do not sink to my level, Scarlett. As my student, I train you to become better than I could ever be." My vision begins to blur, my grip becoming loose, my hand slipping from hers; I am on the brink of death, my mind slipping. I lose nothing by confessing or lying here.

"I will be by your side," Scarlett says, leaning forward in the chair, gripping my limp hand in her warm ones. "And while you are recovering from this poison, I will take my turn as the monster."

CHAPTER EIGHTEEN

I open my eyes slowly, stretching my arms out and managing to sit myself up, pulling the wheelchair closer to my bed. Using my arms, I shift myself toward it, propping it against the wall so it won't move while I swing myself into the wheelchair, resting my head against the wall with a sigh. This poison has been in my veins long enough that I have had to get used to this morning ritual; however, with the time that has passed, I have slowly regained more control over my body. I have control over the upper half of my body once more, though from the waist down I still cannot will my limbs to move. My powers continue to fight the poison and refuse to heed any of my other commands. I take a deep breath, rolling myself to the door; I twist the knob and pull the door open, wheeling myself into the hallway.

Making my way to the kitchen, I find a plate waiting for me at the low wooden table. I look at the rice, beans, and strawberry salad that are to be my breakfast; I haven't cooked since the trip to Malor. After a few tries, Scarlett mastered several dishes, so it has not been as unpleasant as it could have been. I bring myself as close to the table as I can, carefully balancing rice on a spoon; I take a bite and crunch down on a few pieces of uncooked rice; this is not one of those dishes. I cannot afford to complain however; loathe as I am to admit it, I am unable to even cook for myself in this condition.

While I eat, I glance out the window; the onset of spring has finally thawed the ice and snow from winter. The previous autumn and winter were spent recovering as best I could and helping Scarlett get used to acting out in the world as my surrogate. In truth, she did not find herself out much during the fall; after the poison did not kill me, I expected to make a complete recovery at any moment. After each passing morning revealed that was not the case, I had to begin allowing Scarlett out. At the same time, she still has more to learn, so I have been training her as well. Under the stress and pressure, she has held up remarkably well. I shake my head, finishing my meal, pumping the handle next to the wash basin, rinsing the plate, and putting it on the counter. In my current condition, I have been unable to train Scarlett in combat, though she maintains her own training in a way that I still personally oversee.

Wheeling myself down the largely empty halls, I stop in front of the library doors, banging loudly. This is something I have had to get used to as well; the library doors are heavy wooden doors that swing on hinges. However, I cannot manage to open them myself; fortunately Scarlett is in the library often enough. She continues to spend ever more time in there as she rebuilds my network. I dislike having to wait for assistance however, being unable to even open a simple door for myself. After I fully recover from the poison, I plan on installing doorknobs on every door in the house, and perhaps replace the heavy wood with a lighter material. Scarlett opens the door and steps back, closing it behind me. She has several desks and tables covered in open books and loose paper, ink and quills; she has been busy. Papers are tacked up on boards hung on the shelves, strings connecting names, dates, and places; most of our time is spent in the library, Scarlett more so than me. With my disability, she has thrown herself into her new role with an admirable amount of determination, and her willpower has only grown through this particular trial of hers. I turn my attention to the large filing cabinets that all but surround my desk, piled high with papers; rebuilding my network requires an extensive log system, however I do most of the work on that front. My hands clench around the wheels of my chair, my arms stiffly moving me across the floor; reduced to the role of secretary. I must do whatever I possibly can to help rebuild my network, but some tasks burn me with their menial lowliness. This is, however, still my network, so I must do what I can, no matter how humiliating I find it.

"I completed the essay on appeals to human emotion at around four in the morning," Scarlett says, sitting down and bending over one of the books, pointing to one of the large stacks of paper on my desk. "Also, Zabolir caved yesterday; it didn't get nearly as messy as I thought it would. Most of the men he had hired were mercenaries and gave up rather quickly, some even offered me their services. This should serve as a warning to any of the others who think they can abandon us now though."

She talks about the ordeal casually; taking on this new level of responsibility has forced her to become more sure of herself—carry herself in a different manner. It has been good for her, that much I can see, and fortunately the missions serve as an extension on her combat training, though recently those methods have become less and less necessary.

"Good," I wheel over to one of the shelves, removing a book from the highest shelf I can reach. "I'll look over the papers while you're gone."

Scarlett folds her arms but says nothing while I leaf through the book and place it next to her.

"In that book is lore on an item I wish to acquire."

Scarlett picks up the book and skims through the first few pages, looking up at me in disbelief.

"A giant?" she frowns, looking back at the book. "You want me to go after a giant?"

"I want you to retrieve the spear from Skrymsli," I say as she leafs through more of the book.

"It says that the spear is actually Skrymsli's left leg," she frowns, looking up at me. "If that's true, then it's a part of him and it won't be easy to get."

"I'd prefer it if he'd not die," I reply, taking the book and putting it back on the shelf. "It might create more trouble than I'm prepared to handle at the moment, but I won't be furious if he suffers an accident.

I need that spear," I look at Scarlett, my eyes dead serious. "Acquire that spear for me, by whatever means necessary."

"I understand," she says standing up. "I have a few questions before I go."

I nod and she grabs the book about Skrymsli back from the shelf, carrying it with her as she exits the library; I commonly debrief her to whatever extent she desires. I cannot have her going into a situation unprepared or uninformed. I follow her to her room where she puts the book in her bag. "Why is the spear so important?"

"It's made out of a rare metal called orichalcum," I explain as she begins packing her bag. "A long time ago in Visland, Ismar used to be one country. An island off the coast of Ismar, however, was found to be rich in orichalcum, and the country was divided on how it should be used. Orichalcum is a nearly indestructible material capable of canceling out magic and other powers, including mine; it is also rumored to be able to kill spirits. One part of Ismar wished to mine orichalcum and use it to create weapons; the other wished to let the large store of orichalcum remain, believing it to be too dangerous a substance."

"Then why is it so rare? If there's an island full of it, why go after the spear?" Scarlett hooks several daggers on her belt, slipping throwing knives into each boot.

"Because the island was sunk in a night," I reply.

She looks up, raising an eyebrow. "How do you sink an entire island in a night when you can't use any powers to do it?" she asks, slinging the pack over her shoulder.

"You start a war," I say, looking away from Scarlett. "It was a bloody, ferocious war designed to resolve the Ismar Conflict once and for all. It ended in the sinking of the island and Ismar Minor seceding from Ismar Major."

"I still don't see how a war between nations could sink an island," she says shaking her head.

"It wasn't a war between nations," I say as she folds her arms across her chest; she should know all the information pertaining to the subject before she heads out. "Both sides of the conflict, Ismar

Minor and Major, prayed for an end to the conflict. Above the clouds, their prayers were so loud that they woke up the sleeping giant Skrymsli. Angry at being woken, Skrymsli went down to the island and slaughtered nearly everyone that inhabited the island and sunk it into the sea. Horrified at the amount of carnage and death caused by a dispute over the orichalcum, Ismar Minor seceded."

"How did the spear end up in his leg?"

She's genuinely curious now, a good trait to have in a student, and one I have cultivated throughout her training. I turn my back on her, wheeling to the door of her room. "I tried to kill Skrymsli," I say, clenching my hands.

The giant still deserves to die, but I can't send Scarlett there to kill him. If Oberon got wind that I sent Scarlett to specifically kill one of his subjects, even a giant...the result would be a tedious affair, at the very least. However, if she goes there for the spear, she will have to fight Skrymsli for it; giants cling to even the most trivial of things. She will kill him in the process, and I will have the spear. If Oberon accuses either me or Scarlett of assassination, I will have the Council on my side. Scarlett hasn't said anything for several seconds, but I pause before exiting her room.

"You can find Skrymsli by going to Mersa Helvare's house; you know the place. Skrymsli will be up the beanstalk above the clouds in his castle; you'll know it by the pikes with heads on them in front of the main gate. If it comes to you fighting him, giants can almost instantly regenerate limbs. However, they cannot regenerate something which has been pierced by orichalcum. That means once you remove the spear, his leg will grow back." I consider whether she needs to know anything else, but decide against it. I have still been unable to find Impres—to find that last ingredient. I have to move on without it and simply hope for the best. I cannot stop; but after the devastation caused by my chase, I can no longer search for her. I must let her slip through my fingers and forgo the missing piece. The chances of success are still high; but in my current condition, I can no longer afford to wait.

"If you have any other questions before you leave, I'll be in the library since you left the door open." She doesn't say anything, so I wheel myself out.

I set the last paper of Scarlett's essay down and sigh, pinching the bridge of my nose. This is what my days have been reduced to: grading papers. I look down at those papers, organized so neatly and I snarl, slinging them off the desk. Useless! This poison has beaten me, and I am powerless to do anything but hope I will eventually overcome it. I wheel over and am able to reach far enough down to begin plucking papers from the floor. There is no use getting angry over a situation that only time will change, but I no longer have the luxury of infinity. Setting the stack back on the desk, I wheel out of the library, heading to my gym.

While my training was normally done outside, I constructed the gym for pure exercise reasons; I cannot let myself slip, even with my disability. I move the chair to the wall and reach down, placing clasps on the wheels of the chair so I can lift myself up and out of it without the chair slipping away. I crawl the short distance to a device I specially altered to help stay in shape while in this condition. I strap my ankles and legs securely to a metal bar and begin to turn a crank next to the bar. The bar and crank both begin to rise until my head no longer touches the ground. Crossing my arms across my chest, one hand on each shoulder, I sit up. Unable to move my legs, I have to rely completely on my abdomen, as I repeat the motion again.

I originally used this device, before I modified it, to hang people upside down as a form of torture. The memory of their screams helps in its own way; any discomfort my exercising causes is nothing compared to the pain I inflicted upon them. That is its own small comfort to my protesting muscles. I pause, breathing heavily, and I manage to remove my sweaty shirt and cloak, resuming my exercise. My abdominal muscles cry out with each repetition, my throat dry from breathing through my mouth. Once my hands no longer clasp onto my shoulders due to the vast amount of sweat, I stop; the air rattling in and out of my lungs in quick gasps echoes in the otherwise unoccupied room. My entire body trembles as I crank myself back down and undo the straps on my legs.

Flipping myself over, I push my shirt and cloak away, reaching back and strapping my legs back to the bar. After, I reach behind me and crank my legs up slightly off the floor; I place my hands underneath me and begin to do pushups. As long as my legs remain secured, it's easy enough to do. I let my breathing resume a regular pace with the easy exercise, the motions beginning to come naturally; up, then down. Down, then up. I do this over and over again until my chest starts to feel like it's going to collapse on itself, the strain of my weight and breathing at the same time nearly too much; anything becomes difficult over time.

I slowly lower myself to the floor, sweat dripping off the ends of my hair. Taking a deep breath I grimace, turning and ignoring the spike of pain in my already sore stomach, I lower and unstrap my legs. Turning myself around, I grab my gloves from one of the pockets in my cloak, slipping them on. With one hand, I grasp the bar firmly; and in the other, I crank myself up. Putting my other hand on the bar, I suck in a deep breath. It's just the same motions as before; up, then down. Down, then up.

Over and over again.

Repetition builds muscle memory; moving a sword in the direction the same way over and over again, day after day, can be more effective than training in complicated forms. When you're attacked and must execute a complicated form, your brain must remember the steps in conjunction with your muscles while they execute the steps. Training a simple move over and over will allow you to take your mind out of the immediate battle while your body takes over, using that one move, and you will have a strategy to defeat your opponent, which will be more than he will have. You can build a form from that simple move, but it starts with simplicity; it begins with repetition. Even if I pass out while doing this, there's a chance my muscles will continue doing the exercise, until my energy is depleted. I hang my head, sweat dripping on my lips as I gasp out, my single hand struggling to maintain its hold on the bar while I lower myself down.

As my feet touch the floor, my hand lets go and I collapse, a pool of sweat building underneath me; I might actually drown if I lay face down in it. I let my face remain in the puddle for a moment before I weakly shake my head, grabbing my clothes and dragging myself to my wheelchair. I grasp at the handles and pull myself up, my torso trembling as my arms jerk me up, hitching twice. I collapse into the chair and muster the energy to put my clothes on, resting my head against the wall with a sigh, closing my eyes.

Even if I regain the ability to use my legs, how will I know? Not having used my legs for some time now, they might be too weak for me to walk. How will I know if I can use them if I can't tell the difference in strength? This question enters my thoughts as I lay awake at night, unable to sleep because I cannot not feel my legs. How will I know I can feel and use my legs again when I beat this poison? Opening my eyes, I look down at my legs and slam my fist down onto my right thigh; no feeling. At least if I do this often enough, maybe I'll know when I have beaten the poison.

I wheel myself to the bathroom and lock the clamps around my wheels next to the shower; since my return from Malor, I've had these clamps installed in nearly every room. Before I get out of the chair, I begin to work the pump next to the shower; it will build up the pressure so that I can clean the sweat from my body. After I'm confident the pressure is high enough, I lift myself out of the wheelchair and onto a marble bench in the shower; I turn the shower on and cold water sprays over my body. It chills my body, goosebumps raising all over my skin; my teeth unwittingly begin to chatter as I grab the soap.

The soap business in the Kingdom was especially competitive when it first began; I found the provider with the best quality of it and began backing them. They provided me with free soap whenever I wished. Sometimes I would kill for them, if necessary; the soap business is a ruthless one. Shivering, I scrub all over my skin and then let it all wash off. The cold water begins to send pins and needles from the base of my neck all the way to my waist, so cold now that it begins to hurt. I turn the water off and grab a towel from a nearby rack, wrapping myself in it as I shiver and shake. Being cold is something I recently had to rediscover, since my powers had deserted me to fight the poison still coursing through my veins.

Wrapping the towel around my waist, I get back in my wheelchair, wheeling myself to my room. I wheel myself over to the chair in the corner where I had set out a change of clothes the night before. I take the towel off, causing a breeze to wash over me; I only feel half of it. I lift up one leg with one hand, shifting and tugging until my pants are on. It's easier to slip my shirt on, though I don't bother with a cloak; I towel my hair dry and fold the towel up neatly, placing it on the bed as I get a pre-folded change of clothes off the floor of my closet, setting them on the chair for tomorrow. I put the towel back on the rack in the bathroom and wheel back to my bedroom, clamping the wheels of my chair down and swinging myself into bed. I close my eyes, letting out a long breath; Scarlett should be back by tomorrow. She normally completes missions within a day. I let all my muscles uncoil and relax, my head sinking into the pillow.

I look at the beanstalk growing from the ground in Mersa Helvare's yard; the thing is huge. *You've said that about more than just a beanstalk.* Shut it. I look up and see the thing twisting up into the heavens; I whistle, shaking my head. I have to climb this thing? Then fight a giant? I've done some crazy things since becoming Mister E's body in the world, but giant-fighting is going to be a first, even for me. I grab the beanstalk and begin climbing up, looking at Mersa's house as I do; there's really no reason for me to let her know I'm here. All she would do is say I'm trespassing, and then I would have to convince her otherwise; that's just how people are. No, it's better to just do this while she's inside so that she never knows I'm here; Mister E would approve. My limbs settle into the motion of climbing, my body taking over; climbing was never an extensive portion of my training, but maybe I used to climb a lot. It certainly seems like it, my hands and feet easily finding obscure or hard to reach holds. With my body taking care of the climbing, my mind is free to think.

This mission is obviously personal for Mister E; the giant the spear is stuck in sunk his home. He didn't explicitly say it, but I know he was from that island Skrymsli sunk. Having his home sunk as a child, killing nearly all of his people, would explain why he's the way he is, but I don't understand how he got orichalcum off the island with him. Or how he was able to make a spear out of it; how did he even find Skrymsli in the first place? More importantly, how am I going to get the spear out of his leg? If he, a giant, can't get it out of his leg, how I supposed to do it? *You could ask the giant.* I frown, speeding up; I'm pretty sure that if he knew how to remove the spear, then he would have done so by now. *Do you have any better ideas?* No, but I know this is possible; Mister E wouldn't give me an impossible task. *He gave you one without an answer.* That it didn't have an answer was the *answer*; he's taught me there will always be a solution to the problem, it just may not be obvious. There's always a third option.

I stop, breathing heavily; I'm going to have to slow down. I look up and swear; I'm not even halfway! I shake my head and reach my hand up, beginning climbing at a slower pace; it's not as if I can stop to rest.

I pull myself up above the clouds and roll onto my back, gasping for air. Finally! I let out a groan, trying to turn over, but the stitch in my side adamantly refuses; okay, no moving yet, got it. I remain lying down, panting; well that wasn't so hard. *You thought you were going to die.* My training prepares me for even the worst situations; I wouldn't have died. *Right, because your training would have stopped you from plummeting down several hundred or thousand feet and colliding with the ground, and it surely would have prevented your death.* Your sarcasm is obnoxious. *My sarcasm is art.* I steel myself, rolling onto my stomach and gritting my teeth, pushing myself up, all my muscles protesting fiercely. I look at the beanstalk and swear loudly, groaning; after I do this I'm going to have to climb *back* down!

I look around the clouds; gleaming palaces and castles lie dotted around, golden fountains spewing a thick gold liquid. I feel like the clouds shouldn't be able to support my weight; each step they give slightly, and I feel like my feet will just push through them. Then they push back up, letting me continue walking. I stop, noticing for the first time a bright white light that seems to shine on everything. I turn to the light and gasp, my eyes going wide. My mind is washed clean by the light, my mouth hanging open; reason deserts me. Any coherent thought that tries to form is immediately obliterated, and a sense of deep pleasure bubbles up into my chest. Suddenly the light disappears and I blink, the outline of a hand against the light, covering my eyes.

"Mortals shouldn't look at the light for too long," a voice says behind me. "It tends to turn their little mortal minds to mush." I turn around, the light at my back and the hand removes itself. A tall spindly old man looks at me, a kind smile on his face. He has a long beak of a nose, a frail, pointy chin, and intelligent, sharp eyes. All that remains of his hair are a few thin white wisps covering his head; he's dressed in a suit that hangs off of him slightly.

"I—I..." I can't seem to form a coherent sentence and he smiles, nodding understandingly.

"That's a common reaction after seeing the light of the world," he says. I resist the urge to turn around, doing my best to remain focused on him.

"What exactly is it?"

He frowns, looking past me at the light then shaking his head. "No one really knows what it is or what its purpose is. When people look at it, different things happen for each person. Mortals tend to either die or go insane if they look at the light of the world for too long. Even gods can't stare at it for too long or we go a bit...looney."

"What do you mean 'looney'?"

"You ever heard of Kronos? You know, the guy who went crazy and ate his kids?"

I nod and he continues, walking away from the light. I follow behind him, my neck itching to move, my head desiring to turn so I can look at the light again. I've never felt such a feeling of satisfaction and pleasure as I did when I looked that the light. *You should definitely not tell Wilhelm that.*

"He used to like to sit outside of his throne and look at the light of the world all day; gave him a pleasant buzz. And we all know how that turned out," he moves his finger in a spiral near his temple, looking back at me, widening his eyes behind his rectangular glasses; they look too young for him. "So, like I said, looney."

I nod, stopping. "Thank you for saving me back there."

He stops too, nodding back. "No problem, sweetheart."

I inwardly cringe at the name but smile on the outside. "I'm actually here looking for Skrymsli," I say; I would rather not go door to door looking for a giant. "Would you happen to know where he lives?"

His smiles drops, his eyes narrowing, his entire expression turning suddenly serious. "Everyone knows where Skrymsli lives," he says, not even bothering to hide his disdain. "You just go to the end of the houses to the right and turn left; you'll know his residence when you see it. A word of advice," he grabs my wrist, having a surprisingly strong grip for an old man. "Don't let your guard down for even a second around Skrymsli; it may be the last thing you do."

I nod and he lets go of my wrist; with everyone warning me about Skrymsli, I'm not so sure that I will be able to do this the nice way. *That hasn't bothered you in the past.* I don't have a problem killing humans, or just creatures around my size; a giant is another thing entirely. I'd rather not have to fight one if I can help it. *Coward.* That makes me smart, not cowardly. *Whatever helps you sleep at night.*

I follow the old man's instructions and turn the corner at the end of the row of houses. A large dark castle looms before me; portions of it are falling off, and two of the turrets have crumbled. An empty moat surrounds it, a drawbridge made of rotten wood barely holding itself up over the moat. As I place my foot on the bridge, it groans loudly. I quickly take my foot off, looking down in the moat; it's filled with spikes, where decaying corpses and severed heads are stuck on. I look back at the castle, vines crawling up the sides; Skrymsli lives in a dump. *It's a castle!* Still a dump. I put my foot on the drawbridge again and gingerly begin walking across. The drawbridge groans and creaks, having an alarming amount of give to the wood. I scamper across the end, letting out a breath I didn't know I had been holding once I land on solid ground. I walk up to the large doors that tower above my head and see two doorknockers—one high above, and the other slightly above my head. I reach up and heave the knocker back, letting it tap against the door; a loud boom echoes around, making my hair fly back. The door opens by itself and I slip through; it slams shut behind me, leaving me alone.

"Hello?" I keep my hand on my dagger, my footsteps silent on the thick, moth-eaten carpet. My voice echoes throughout the large empty halls eerily, coming back almost as a haunting wail. *Perhaps he isn't home.* I don't think I could be that lucky. I wander through the seemingly endless maze of halls until I see the large outline of flickering flames. Running toward them, I skid to a halt, looking into the large room.

On the right is a large fireplace capable of fitting a normal-sized castle, and at the end of the hall is a large chair with animal skins thrown over. The man on the chair starts, sniffing. His green shirt is riddled with food stains and strains to cover his large belly. He has large, hairy arms and a face that looks like it was smacked by a large hammer. His nose is long and flat, his lips curling upward in a snarl, several snaggle teeth jutting out from his mouth. His one eyebrow stretches across his entire forehead like a giant hairy snake, curved downward. His eyes are small for such a large head, beady and black. He has a long mane of grey hair with pieces of food and nature stuck in it, the knotted, curly mess falling nearly to his waist. He's missing his left leg from the knee down; instead, a comparatively small spear sticks out from his knee. Spotting me, he reaches under a large white goose and pulls out a golden egg, which his hand covers easily, throwing it at me. As it whistles through the air, I realize it's nearly as large as me, and I roll out of the way. It crashes into the wall and I turn, seeing a pile of dented or crushed golden eggs; this seems to be a regular thing he does.

"Leave, mortal!" He roars, his voice booming loudly throughout the hall at such a volume that it makes my ears ring. I stretch my jaw, my ears popping; his voice is like a clap of thunder right next to your skull.

"I'm here to help," I shout and he winces, raising his hands up. He moves his hair behind his ears, massaging them; his ears are nearly half the size of his head! I cringe, realizing how my loud my voice must have sounded; I guess I don't need to shout. "Sorry," I apologize in a normal voice; I am still trying to avoid combat with a giant as much as possible.

"Leave!" he roars again, grabbing another golden egg. *Perhaps it is merely the pitch of human voices that hurts his ears.* Well if things have to get messy, I'll make sure to shout at him.

"Wait!" I cry out and he winces. "Just hear me out!"

He throws the golden egg at me anyway and I dodge it, holding my hands up.

"I'm just here for the spear."

His hand pauses underneath the goose and he slowly removes it, eggless.

"What do you want with the spear?" he growls, looking at me shrewdly. "Are you going to kill me if you remove it?"

Because I would tell you if I was going to. Studying the material Mister E had given me on my journey to Mersa Helvare's house had led me to believe giants were typically clever; he seems to be slipping in his old age.

"No," I say shaking my head. "I just want the spear."

He looks me over then grabs a stick, propping himself up on it. He walks over to me, each step sending a shudder through the ground, the vibrations rattling the teeth in my skull. Once he comes closer, I realize how tall he is, his knee several feet above my head; I look up and realize that the "stick" he's leaning on is actually a large tree. He looks down at me, breathing heavily.

"The spear was cursed by the one who put it there," he growls. "The one who put it there was mortal at the time, and so it can only be removed by a mortal." He bends his right knee awkwardly until the spear is within my reach. "If you wish me no harm, then remove the spear."

I look up at him, grabbing the spear firmly; I wouldn't put it past him to try and kill me once I remove the spear. If it comes to that, I will have to use the spear.

I give the spear an experimental tug and Skrymsli howls, clutching his tree harder; quiet, this is nothing. I put my weight into the next tug, and it slides out partially. Skrymsli bites his lips, tears welling up at the corners of his eyes; I might die from the impact if one of those hits me. I wiggle it back and forth, then tug backward hard. There's a moment of resistance, the spear sticking in place, my muscles straining and taught, my teeth clenched; I have to get this out! I tug again and the spear slides free easily; I fall backward and so does Skrymsli, dropping his tree. He howls, gripping at his knee, tears splashing onto the ground with such force that I feel the vibrations in my chest. He sniffs then looks down at his knee, rubbing it with wonder.

"It's gone," he says, then looks at me. His eyes spark with something not human, barring his white teeth at me. He grins, looking at his knee, then at me, smacking his lips. "It's been so long since I've had human in my stomach."

I leap back out of his reach, the wind generated by his swipe nearly knocking me back. He looks down at his knee once more, closing his eyes. I take several steps backward, looking from the man-eating giant down at the spear in my hand; it glints evilly in the light, a poisonous green color. It's surface shimmers, and I can't help but follow it, running my hand up the spear until I come to the blade. I pause, my finger stopping at a part in the blade; a piece is missing. I look up and see a small shard of orichalcum glinting in Skrymsli's leg. I turn my back on him, my legs pumping, moving as fast as they can take me. I look over my shoulder, clutching the spear tightly in my hand. His leg appears; and for a moment, nothing happens.

Suddenly, a large explosion sends me flying across the ground and I land heavily, rolling until I hit the golden eggs. My ears ringing, I try to pick myself up but collapse back down, fighting the urge to puke. I try to stand up and am able to this time, shuffling toward him, my feet nearly slipping out underneath me. I'm up to my knees in blood as I wade toward him; he's missing his entire left leg and a part of his left side, blood pouring out of him by the gallon. I wade up to his face, smacking him; he's unconscious. I part his hair and lean directly to his ear, shouting. He doesn't move, and I notice the shards of his floor stuck in his chest and the color leaving his cheeks; he blew himself up—the idiot. Clever giants my foot. I shake my head and begin wading back when my foot bumps something. I grimace, reaching under and pulling out the shard of orichalcum; it gleams wickedly, almost as if it knew the pain it had just caused. *It just saved your life.* How many lives has it ended before this though? *How many have you? You two seem perfectly fitted to each other.*

I cross the drawbridge and make my way back to the beanstalk, looking down.; *Mission accomplished.*

"Well it looks like things got messy," the old man raises an eyebrow. "Let me help you clean up." He snaps his fingers, and the blood disappears from my clothes and skin without a trace.

"Thanks," I say, deciding not to question it. My teacher controls shadows, and I just had a giant explode himself all over me; all I really want to do now is get home.

"You got the spear then?" he says and I raise it, the light of the world glinting off of it, the spear seeming to glow brightly. "I've always wanted an orichalcum weapon," he says wistfully, looking at it with longing eyes.

I look down at the spear, thinking; I don't need to know how he does things—the fact that he can do them is enough.

"You just cleaned my clothes off with a snap of your fingers—what else can you do?"

He grins, holding his hand up. "It depends on what you want me to do," he says.

"First, I want you to teleport me to my teacher's house; his name is Mister E." The man snaps his fingers, and suddenly I'm in front of Mister E's house, the moon high above.

"Is that all?" He sounds disappointed.

"My teacher is currently crippled, and I want his condition cured," I say.

He smiles. "As long as it wasn't caused by a cosmic force."

"He was poisoned."

His smile gets wider as he rubs his hand. "That's good, poison I can do. First though, I want the spear."

I look at the spear, glowing dimly in the darkness; Mister E sent me to retrieve the spear. My mission was to return the spear to him, taken from the giant that sunk his homeland. Supposedly sunk his homeland. This spear could mean so much more to him than I realize, but I realize how much this poison has affected him. It hinders him in everyday life; I see him, a ghost of his former self. He holds his head high still, but the sunken, hollow look in his eyes is enough to convince me of what I need to do. I hand him the spear and he snaps his fingers, the spear disappearing. "I'm also going to want something after I cure him." There's a crash from inside the house and I turn; Mister E?

"You can name your price," I turn my back on him; Mister E isn't in a position to defend himself. If someone else is in there, I have to help him.

CHAPTER NINETEEN

The coppery taste of blood is in my mouth, the scent of it in the air; red stains the walls and the floor. Dead corpses lie all around me and I tug at my bindings, glaring at the figure before me. He squats down and looks at me with hungry orange eyes, reaching out with one gauntleted hand, the metal shimmering a sickening poisonous green color. As soon as the cold metal touches my cheek, I wince, cringing backwards; the touch sends shivers down my spine, leaving an empty feeling in my chest. He grips my hair, pulling me closer and I growl, trying to tug away, but he holds on tighter. It feels like I'm missing a limb when he grips me with those gauntlets.

"Orichalcum is certainly a metal with amazing properties, is it not?" He smirks, revealing the tips of sharp teeth. "Father never thought to use it as more than a rock to chain us to when we were bad; it's a shame really. He could be so creative when he wanted to be. Seems the orichalcum had as much of an effect on his mental faculties as it did our bodies. He was an old fart though; maybe it was just the age."

"Let me go, Verran!" I growl and he smirks again, shoving me backwards. I land with a thud on my back, my head banging against the floor. I tug at my bindings again, but I know it's no use; the chains around my wrist are attached to a large weight with a piece of orichalcum carved in. Mutovinatum won't be able to assist me in any way, though I don't think he would if he could. He always liked Verran; they're more alike than I and Mutovinatum could ever be.

"Now why would I do that? I didn't do it when we were kids, why should I now? I know you're still a kid, but technically I'm a man now," he raises his hands, grinning. "Man of the house now that the old man is gone; patriarch dies and the eldest inherits it all. Pretty convenient, right?" He grips the edge of the kitchen table in his hands, his voice going very soft all of a sudden. "He deserved to die, the worm. May he rot in hell," Verran looks at me, his eyes turning into angry slants beneath his messy mane of dark hair.

"When the island was sunk and all those people were dying, the old man had a choice: grab his youngest son or a hunk of rock that can't be found anywhere else. He chose the rock because it was more valuable to him, but good old mom stepped in and said that he should choose the youngest. The old man said there was no way in hell he was going to leave behind a big chunk of orichalcum when the entire island was sinking. So mom snuck you onto the boat in her place." He tightens his grip on the table, splinters dropping to the floor as it begins to crack. "He blamed you for her death, before he bit the dust himself; we all blame you E. You cost my mom her life, and you're just as responsible for that as the old man. That's why you're going to pay too."

The table cracks into several fragments and he snarls, stalking towards me.

"She was my mom too!" I shout. There's a ringing in my ears as I suddenly find myself looking at the wall to my right; the pain slams into my cheek and I hiss, feeling the heat from Verran's blow. Small rivulets of blood begin to drip down my cheek; he could have broken my jaw if he wanted. He wants to draw it out though; he wants to enjoy himself. Torture was always his specialty, and I his favorite subject.

"You don't have the *right* to call that image of selflessness and perfection the mother of some lowly scum like you," he growls. "But if you're going to call her your mom, then you might as well claim responsibility for her fate. If you don't have the stomach to admit it was your fault, then what makes you think that you can call her your mother? That shouldn't sound right, even to your own delusioned mind."

"Fine! It's my fault mom died! Are you happy?!" I lean forward, the chains scraping against my wrists and threatening to pull my arms out of socket.

"Not as happy as I'm going to be," he grins, whistling. "You were responsible for taking away the most precious woman in my life." Two men kick open the door to the kitchen, swearing as they struggle with something. "I'm just going to return the favor."

They pull in a woman in a thin white dress, a bag over her head. Blood runs down one arm, and the sounds of muffled screaming can be heard under the bag. I roar, tugging at the chains again, trying to get my feet under me and get to her. I'll rip my arms off if I have to!

"No! No! Let her go, you piece of filth! Let her go!" I shout, trying to call upon the shadows. I can feel the orichalcum weighing me down, suppressing my powers and making me weak; I growl, shaking my head. I can't allow this to happen!

"Fair is fair brother," Verran says gleefully, kicking me in the face with a cackle. I reel backward, tripping over the weight and slamming my head against the wall. Verran's mouth is moving as he talks to me, turning to Simiel. He runs a hand over her shoulders, slipping the straps of the dress down slightly, licking a trickle of her blood. I shake my head, blood matting my hair and crusting on my ears. "She tastes yummy; here, have some." He flicks some of her blood at my face and I flinch, then leap to my feet. The chains snap taught, crumpling me to my knees.

"She's your sister too!"

"I know," he says, pulling a dagger out of his belt. It's long and curved, partially serrated; the pommel is a small skull, and red cloth is wrapped around the twisted, knotted handle. Slowly he traces the point against her skin. "If she wasn't, this wouldn't be nearly as much fun."

He slowly twists the point of the dagger into her skin, beads of red welling to the surface. I can hear her muffled whimpers underneath the bag and I slam my palms against the floor.

"Stop it! Stop it! I'll do anything, just stop!" Tears stream down my cheeks and I hang my head, sobs wrenching themselves from my chest. I tremble, shaking my head. "Please just stop; I can't take it if you do it anymore. Please, kill me instead!" I raise my head up, my eyes wide. "Don't hurt her, kill me! Torture me instead!" Verran pauses, pointing the dagger at me.

"I'm not going to kill you, brother dear. Torture you, yes, but I'm not going to kill *my own brother*. What kind of monster would that make me?" He chuckles turning around and slicing one of her straps off, making a thin gash on her skin. He squats next to me, wiping her blood off the dagger onto my face. I lunge forward, snapping my teeth at him, but the chains don't allow me to touch him. He grins, his breath on my face, his face barely an inch away. "No, you see dear brother, I have no intention of killing you, *ever*. Tonight I'm going to do so many things to Simiel, but I won't lay another finger on you. No," he leans in closer, his mouth right next to my ear, whispering slowly, enunciating each word clearly. "I'll make every living moment of hers hell. How does that sound, little brother? Knowing you can't save her must kill you." He pauses, licking his lips. "And I'll make you watch it all E. You'll get to watch every single second and see every single *excruciating* detail. Tonight is about what I want."

I snap at his ear and he leans away, standing up and shaking his head at me. I growl, shaking the chains and heaving my weight against them.

"I could send you to hell, and there they'd play all the horrible details over and over, but you'd get desensitized. Then you'd just wander around, another broken soul. I don't want hell to break you." He turns to Simiel, tracing a pink line across her throat with the tip of the dagger. "*I* want to be the one to break you. No, for you to truly suffer you have to live forever. I'm going to make you immortal, E. I'm going to make you live forever so that when I burn this memory into your mind, you will never forget it. It will haunt you and it will drive you, but it will never consume you, never break you. You won't let it; you'd consider it dishonorable to Simiel's memory. So you'll carry on, but you won't be able to die, outwardly at least. I'm sure you'll die on the inside every day after witnessing what is about to take place." He grins, tracing the tip of the dagger against Simiel's skin, leaving a thin line until he comes to her second strap, cutting it but quickly grabbing the front of the dress, holding it up. He grins and kisses her neck, letting the dress drop to the floor, tracing the knife down.

I roar, slamming backwards against the weight; the bones in my hands and wrist break with several loud cracks. I lunge forward; and after a moment of initial resistance, I slip through the chains, rushing toward Verran. The shadows launch themselves at the other two men, impaling them and slinging them away. A wall of hissing tendrils raises over Verran as I race toward him but he grins, pressing the knife to Simiel's throat. I stop, breathing heavily, the shadows pausing in their assault, hissing and spitting.

"Let her go," I growl, and he shakes his head.

"I don't think so," he says, slowly backing to the door. Shadows wriggle up behind him, hissing and trapping him. "I would prefer to play out my perfect plan; but if you take another step closer, I'll kill her right now; I'm okay with that too."

The shadows move closer, and he presses the dagger harder.

"You or your little shadow pets move, and she's gone," He takes the bag off her head with a flourish, and I almost move forward; she's blindfolded and gagged, tears and snot streaming down her face. Her hair is matted with sweat and she's trembling, a single bruise on her left cheek.

"You hit her," I growl.

"I didn't touch her," he says smiling. "But I will touch her now, and so much more. You won't do a thing about it." His free hand caresses her cheek softly and I growl, all my willpower going into not moving. "You know these gauntlets aren't the only things I got from dad. I got this dagger too," he tilts it up and down, still holding it against Simiel's neck. "I never thought it was very special until I found out what it could do. When this dagger is used to kill someone, it doesn't send them to the Underworld; it kills them, body *and* soul. They're gone, forever, no hope of saving them. Apparently dad got it from some fellow named Beelzebub after he did him a favor; I never saw him use it once. I'm getting much more out of it than he ever did." He kisses Simiel's cheek, keeping eye contact with me the entire time. "I wonder how it feels, to lose your soul as you die. To be erased from existence forever. It must be pretty terrible. Shame we'll never be able to ask anyone."

He removes the gag from Simiel's mouth. She opens her mouth but he speaks first.

"Ah ah, don't go speaking unless I tell you to. You're not the only one I can kill," he gives me a pointed glance, grinning wickedly before returning his attention to Simiel, his meaning clear. "What do you think it would feel like, sister dear?" He moves his hand through her hair, inhaling deeply. "Ah, wildflowers; you always smell like them, even bloody and beaten."

"Run!" She shouts at me, tears streaming down her eyes; she still can't see me. "Just run, please!"

"Answer the question, wench!" Verran roars.

Without a sound, a tendril of shadow wraps around the knife and another wraps around Simiel's waist, yanking her back at the same time that a wall of shadow slams into Verran. He goes flying through the air, and I use the tendril of shadow to wield the dagger, standing over him. My quiet fury emanates in waves, and he grins up at me, slowly scooting backward as I walk toward him.

"You threatened to kill her," I growl.

"Don't do anything you'll regret E. How could you live with yourself if you killed your own brother?" Verran bumps against the wall, looking around quickly, panic setting into his moves. I smile ruefully, licking the sweat off my lips in anticipation; I learned plenty as the subject of his tortures. Perhaps I can try my hand at it as well; it might run in the family.

"Easily," the tendril of shadow holding the dagger rushes forward to impale Verran through the chest. Suddenly, the tendril disappears and the dagger thuds into the wall next to Verran. My legs give out from under me, and my head bangs on the floor. I try to push myself up but wince, my broken wrists and hands unable to support my weight. Verran chuckles, plucking the knife from the wall and looks down at me. How is this happening?! What is this?! Why can't I move my legs?! I snap at his legs, but he just dances back, then steps forward, slamming his boot into my face. It hits with enough force to flip me onto my back, my nose breaking with a sickening crunch, and it feels like shards of bone are being splintered into my skull. I spit out a tooth, glaring at him as blood gushes down my face, my vision hazy from pain and sweat.

"The thing about dreams E," he disappears from my line of sight for a moment. Dreams? What the hell is he talking about? He returns holding Simiel, knife at her throat. "They're part of the mind, and sometimes our minds play tricks on us. It can be a real pain sometimes," he grins, hand tensing. I growl, trying to sit up but I'm unable to; I reach out to the shadows, but they are nowhere to be found. "Let me know how much this hurts you." He draws the dagger against Simiel's throat in a motion so quick it almost looks like it didn't happen. For a moment, I look on in disbelief, the only sign she was injured at all a thin gash in her throat. Blood gurgles out and I roar, trying to lean up.

"No!"

I sit up, eyes snapping open, and I try to stand up, my arms flailing. I fall out of bed, cracking my head on the floor and shaking the shelves in my room. I groan, breathing heavily as the hazy red color clouding my vision slowly clears. I pant, sweat soaking my clothes, pulling myself onto the wheelchair. Another nightmare since the poison began coursing through my veins. I slam my fist onto my thigh, grabbing and twisting the material of my pants as I shake, covering my face. I'm not sure how much longer I can go on like this; useless, unable to move without assistance, the poison turning every sleeping moment into twisted, vivid dreams. I run my sleeve across my face, sucking in a deep breath and unclamping the wheels of the wheelchair, wheeling into the bathroom. I rely on muscle memory to work the pump, staring into nothing; numbly I go over to the sink, washing my face and looking in the mirror.

A tired old man looks back at me, his face gaunt and sunken. Worry lines are beginning to form on his forehead and around his eyes. A once clean-shaven face is covered by a tangle of grey and white beard, and his long, dark locks are in disarray, strands of white now outnumbering their black brethren in his shaggy mane. His eyes are hollow and tired, his mouth turned down into an agitated frown. I reach a hand up and feel the beard on his face. The older man's hand is thin and pale, showing the first signs of emaciation and liver spots. He looks like he is dying; now more than ever, I acutely feel the poison flowing through my veins, sapping my strength, aging me faster than my powers can reverse it. I feel my mortality, for the first time in centuries, like the onset of a disease. The man looks useless and broken, harboring a bitter resentment for the world; I tear my eyes away from my reflection, drying my face off with a towel and wheeling out.

As I make my way to the library, I remember without Scarlett here I can no longer enter; I turn the chair around, heading back to my room when I hear a soft click from what sounds like the front door. I wheel my way into the kitchen which leads into the entrance room where the front door is. The handle slowly begins to turn; is Scarlett worried about waking me? I wonder if she's always this cautious around me, always afraid she'll do something that will set me off; I know she can see my signs of declining health, and we both know the detrimental effects an outburst of rage could have. The door opens and a small gust of wind blows in, whipping the hair of a large man who softly steps into the entrance room. He suddenly goes still, looking at me and I at him; the inaction forces silence until another man steps in.

I quickly wheel to one of the kitchen drawers, taking out several knives. I turn around and throw one at one of the intruders. It thuds into his leg, and he lets out a pained howl. I throw another, the knife bouncing off the closing door, and I hear the lock click. I roll backward toward the hallway, throwing another knife. I miss and jerk to a stop. I turn and slash, but the man that first entered grabs my wrist, twisting it and causing the knife to drop out of my hand as he tips me onto the floor. The knives in my grip scatter on the floor; I reach for one, but my hand is stopped by the hard and sudden pressure of a large boot.

I hiss, grabbing the pant leg of the man and yanking myself forward, sinking my teeth into his calf. He howls, shaking his leg, but I sink my teeth in deeper, the coppery taste of his blood filling my mouth as my hands search around for one of the knives. I feel his boot connect with my head, but I don't have any other choice than to hang on. If I release my grip, I will have given up completely; his boot slams into my head as someone yanks on my legs. I'm wrenched off the man, taking a chunk of his leg with me. I spit it out, reaching for one of the knives, but it's kicked away. The two men who have not been injured bandage their injured comrade's leg and check the pulse of the one I had hit with the knife, confirming his death. The injured man, with the help of the other two, stands up and hobbles over to me; their leader.

My eyes quickly dart around the room; but since the poison entered my veins, my night vision has been in rapid decline along with the rest of my physical functions. The two uninjured men bring the leader a chair who sits down heavily, groaning; my vision is still good enough that I can make out how he winces clearly enough to gain some sort of satisfaction from it. I reach out quickly to grab one leg of the chair, but one of the men stomps on my hand while another kicks me in the side of the head. My vision swims as I reel, my ear ringing.

"He's persistent, ain't he?" one of them mutters, fumbling around the kitchen until he finds a candle, lighting it. The man in the chair is dressed in dirty, ragged clothes; one arm is longer than the other, but his thick, hairy arms both look strong enough to crush a windpipe. His gut sticks out over the waistband of his pants as he wipes sweat from his balding head. A long, scraggly beard gives him a fierce look as he leans forward, wincing as he applies slight pressure to his injured leg.

"My name is Gorival, and the only reason I'm telling you that is because you won't be leaving here alive." He leans back as one of his men search the ice box, bringing him a bottle of ale; I only keep the stuff to entertain guests. He takes a sip and his eyes widen. "That's good; you have good drink, my friend."

"Don't call me your friend," I spit; I am in no mood to negotiate or cater to the desires of these thugs.

"You're not in a position to tell me what to do," he takes another swig, "friend. Now that I've introduced myself and you've kindly given me drink to satisfy my parched throat, let me tell you why I am here."

"You're here to pillage my place of residence," I growl; being beaten by brutish thugs like these is a new low for me. To be reduced to this level, to be reduced to this! It is unacceptable.

"We're not common thugs, friend; actually, we're not criminals at all. My companions here are carpenters and are both happily married with wonderful children. Those kids really do have nice smiles, unlike their fathers," he grins, two silver teeth shining as he drains the bottle and beckons for another from one of his chuckling companions. They seem to be content to let Gorival do all the talking; just backup then. "The man you killed was a locksmith; only one in the neighborhood we live in, so it's a real shame he's dead." He pops the top off of the bottle using the table; I rebuilt that table personally after it was destroyed by my former torturer. I growl and he raises an eyebrow, nodding at one of the men who kicks me hard in the side. I curl up as much as I can without using my legs as Gorival continues.

"As for me, I'm a butcher. I was as happily married just like these two when one day I got terrible news; my wife had been murdered. She was an innocent woman who ran a cart selling jewelry, and the neighborhood was taken aback by how brutal the killing was; she was hollow inside. All this time I've been looking for the one who did it. Now you don't look like a man who could brutally murder and hollow my wife," he leans forward, his eyes bloodshot and puffy; he cried before coming here. "But you have the eyes of a man who enjoys killing. Did you enjoy killing my wife?"

He reaches out, grabbing my face in one of his large hands, squeezing my cheeks so I can't bite. "I know it was you, so I don't care if you deny it or not. You are certainly are a hard man to find, but us Descrans have our ways, and you have more than a few enemies. Tonight I'm going to avenge my lovely Sarbine. I'm going to do the same thing you did to my wife," he lets me go, standing up so tall that he nearly blocks out the candle light, picking the large knives off the floor, holding them in his meaty hands. "I'm a butcher after all, it's in my trade. While I get my tools, I leave you in the very good care of my companions."

He leaves the house, and I turn my attention to his two companions; there's a very real possibility that I could die now.

"I'm a very wealthy man," I say, and one snorts in disgust, kicking me in the side.

"You think you can just buy us off? We have loyalty!" he kicks me again, and the other one lifts me up by the hair, hitting me in the jaw.

"You think it's fun to go and kill innocent women? To cut 'em up and take their insides? You think that's good sport?!"

He hits me again and I absorb the blow, grabbing his arm and pulling him down with me. I dig my thumbs into his eyes as he wriggles beneath me, screaming. I wrap one hand around his squirming tongue as his friend grabs me from behind, yanking me off of him. I take his tongue with me and he screams, blood gurgling out of his mouth. His friend gets down to his knees, panicking, trying to stop the stream of blood coming out of the other man's mouth; I toss his tongue away in disgust, dragging myself along using the counter top. Finally I reach the drawer I'm looking for and open it, pulling out a meat tenderizer. I place it between my teeth and drag myself along the counters until I reach the doorway leading to the entry room where the man is hunkered over his injured friend. I push off the counter, pulling the meat tenderizer from my mouth and smacking the man in the head. He crumples to the ground, and I continue to beat his head in until I have made a sizable enough dent in his skull that I'm sure he's dead. I repeat the process with the man whose tongue I pulled out and lay on the two dead men, covered in their blood and gore. I catch my breath, rolling off the two men as the front door opens.

"What the hell?!" Gorival limps toward me, and I swing the meat tenderizer at him but he steps over the blow, grabbing my arm with one hand and hair with the other. He heaves, swinging me headfirst at the wall. My face crunches against it, my forehead taking most of the impact. He drops me to the ground, wrenching the meat tenderizer from my grasp as warm blood begins to trickle down my forehead. "You killed them! They were good men who didn't deserve to die! You're a sick piece of filth! You can't get enough blood on your hands can you?"

He kicks me in the ribs and I curl up, trying to roll away. He just follows me, kicking at my sides and head; the best I can do is curl up and cover my head and neck with my arms. He continues to kick and occasionally hit me with his fists; I have to take it. I have to take a beating from this scum, this common criminal; no matter what he was before, he's a criminal now. I have to lay here while my body goes numb as he lays bruise after bruise on me, breaking and fracturing my unprotected bones. This lowly, pathetic man is going to kill me. I curl up tighter, trying desperately to move my legs; I am going to die. This man is going to kill me, and I'm going to die in my own home, with no one as witnesses but my murderer and three corpses. I reach out to grab one of his legs, but I realize my arm has been broken from his blows and instead remains covering my head; I'm not sure if I could move at this point if I wanted to.

Slowly, darkness begins to encroach on my vision as the smell of blood wafts strongly in my nostrils; it's my own blood I'm smelling. My eyes, protected by my arms, aren't swollen and flick around the room; I need something, anything. If I had a chance, I'm sure I could move! Without one, though, I can do nothing better than remain like this until I pass out and wake up in another world. My breath, coming in agonizing rattles, hitches as the door opens. Scarlett walks in, lightning flashing that seems to turn her hair into fire.

Her eyes widen in surprise; and before Gorival can react, she's already sent one of her knives spinning through the air. It lands with a thick thud in his chest. I fight off unconsciousness, following Scarlett with my eyes as she strides forward, her anger silent and palpable. Gorival falls backward out of my sight, and all I hear for a moment is the sound of a face being caved in. The low smacks turn into wet crunches, and I can hear the sound of heavy breathing, then the moist rustling as she moves. She kneels down next to me, covered in blood; her long dark hair frames her pale face and orange eyes look at me kindly.

"Simiel," I whisper, the scent of wildflowers the last thing in my mind before darkness envelopes me completely.

I feel the blood pounding in my head, slugging through my veins; my heart beats as loud as thunder, booming and crashing in my chest. My eyelids crack open, and the sound of a tree falling crashes into my ears as my eyelashes bat against each other while I open my eyes.

I'm in my room with two lanterns lit but partially shaded. I turn my head and see Scarlett, asleep in a chair next to my bed. I turn to grab my wheelchair, but it's at the other end of the room instead of where it normally is. I reach out my hand, and a tendril of shadow slithers out, bringing it closer. I blink, looking at my hand, then the wheelchair. I reach out again, and the tendril of shadow pushes the chair away again. It wraps around the chair, and I clench my hand into a fist; the tendril of shadow crushes the wheelchair into a pile of splinters with a loud crack, startling Scarlett awake.

"What?" she looks around and sees me, gazing intently at the tendril of shadow. "You..."

I turn to her and a tendril of shadow wraps around her mouth, silencing her; how long it seems that I've had to wait to do that. A tendril of shadow wraps around my shoulders as I sit up, cooing happily and I pet it slowly; we are both glad for each other's company once more.

"We are not alone," I turn myself and set my feet down, wiggling my toes; the floor feels solid and warm against the soles of my feet. I confidently stand up, and my legs tremble then give out; I haven't walked in some time. I'll have to build my strength up. Scarlett moves to help me, but I hold up a hand, the tendril unwrapping around her mouth and several more moving toward me, wrapping around my waist and lifting up slightly so I don't have to put as much weight on my legs; I can feel their eagerness to be about in the world again, happy to obey me and assist. I walk toward the door when it opens, a small, emaciated man walking in. Tendrils of shadow instantly surround him, hissing and snapping, eager to taste blood after being deprived so long of it. They have worked long and hard to keep me alive, and they justly deserve a reward.

"Mister E, don't!" Scarlett shouts, and I turn to her, the shadows pausing. "He's the one who saved you."

I look at the man, slowly letting the shadows slither off him. He has a beakish nose and a pointed, frail-looking chin; his eyes are beady and sharp, his thin eyebrows lowered in a shrewd glare. He has a few thin wisps of white hair on his wrinkling dome, his mouth turned down in a frown; he's dressed in expensive silk clothes that, while obviously custom fitted to his size, still slightly hang off him.

"My name is Eraxus Prine," he says giving a low, stiff bow.

"That is not your real name," I say coolly, and he grins evilly, pulling a pair of rectangular glasses that look like they would belong on someone much younger.

"I'll give you three chances to guess my real one," he says slyly. "If you can't, I get your youth."

"That hardly seems fair," I say, the shadows circling his ankles slowly.

"That's my price for saving your life and removing the poison from your system," he says shrugging.

"I never agreed to that!" Scarlett shouts, standing up.

"You agreed to whatever price that I named in return for saving your teacher's life," he says, giving me a hard look. "Fulfill your end of the bargain; if you don't, I can easily undo the changes and leave."

Scarlett steps forward, unsheathing her dagger, but I hold my arm out. Up close, I can see the bags under her eyes and the bloodshot veins in her eyes. She made a deal that saved my life, ridding me of the poison; while she may have made it foolishly, I still owe her for it, and she is in no state to negotiate.

"Go get some rest, Scarlett." She looks at me, but in my eyes there is no quarter for questions or argument. "I expect you to actually sleep," I tell her, and she gives one last look at Eraxus and myself before exiting my room. I turn to Eraxus and walk forward, my feet barely touching the ground, supported as I am by the shadows. "I get three chances to guess your name?"

He nods, grinning. "Do your best," he says, confident; he over-estimates himself.

I lean in close and whisper softly in his ear. I lean back to see his mouth agape in shock, his eyes wide. He opens and closes his mouth like a fish, his face turning red and a vein in his forehead beginning to bulge. "How...you..."

"You can still have my youth; I once again have that in an unlimited quantity." He gives me a shrewd glance but puts his hand on my chest. I feel a tug deep in my chest where my soul should be, and I close my eyes, steadying my breathing. When I open them, I see a tall, thin man wearing a dark pinstriped suit, his dark hair slicked back and slanted, dark grey eyes shining behind rectangular glasses. He grins, running a hand to smooth his already smooth hair, leaning against the wall and putting a hand in his pocket.

"You are most generous, Mister E," he says.

"I never told you my name," I say, folding my arms; I'm beginning to tire from having to use the shadows for so long to support me; but after the time I spent in a wheelchair, unable to stand, even exhaustion is refreshing.

"I can see a great many things," he says. "The glasses are just for looks; of course, I chose to call you by the name you call yourself. You didn't reveal my true name; I'll show you the same courtesy. After all, names have power."

I dip my head and my eyes narrow, the shadows covering the door like a black tarp; I won't take any chances with my conversations being listened in on, or any sounds escaping.

"Why are you really here, Eraxus?" I ask and he grins, nodding and pushing off of the wall.

"Ah, yes, *that*. I'm here because you've been a very naughty boy, Mister E," he says grinning and wagging a finger at me.

"I've been in a wheelchair for a long time; I haven't been able to do much of anything," I reply coolly.

"You set that girl up out there; you had her kill Skrymsli instead of you. Very nice." He waves his hand, and a spear materializes out of thin air. It's long, and the spearhead is barbed with serrated edges. It gleams wickedly in the low light, a dark green color shimmering over its dark surface with evil intent. My heart stops, my hands clenching, but otherwise I give no outward sign. He has the spear—my spear. "This is a very nice piece," he says, tossing it into the air, and it disappears again. He looks at the place where the spear was and then at me, nodding. "Oh yes, orichalcum is supposed to have special properties, isn't it? I admit, I like to break the rules a bit; cheating is in my nature, being the embodiment of mischief and all." He chuckles, leaning against the wall again.

"You still haven't answered my original question," I say and he frowns, folding his arms.

"That girl of yours is wanted for killing Skrymsli. The giant was a thug and a bully, not to mention he had terrible breath and manners. But he was a giant, and you know what happens when someone kills a giant. Or a fairy. Or an elf. Or a dwarf. Or any magic folk actually," he strokes his chin. "Stupid minority laws—there are more fairies out there than members of my own race! Would anyone kill my murderer if I died though? *No!* They wouldn't even hold a funeral!" My hands slowly curl into fists and he sighs, holding his hands out. "Fine, fine; I acknowledge your impatience. The girl is expected to appear before the High King above the clouds tomorrow night, in the royal palace."

"She isn't responsible for what happened to Skrymsli," I say in a low tone, and Eraxus nods.

"I know that, and so does the king, but he needs a head to pike. Your best bet is to throw her under the bus; otherwise the High King will be after *your* head as well. Trust me—after his visit with the Red Queen, he is all too happy to use the guillotine."

"I'm not scared of the High King," I retort, and Eraxus shrugs.

"Your funeral; I'm just here to deliver the message." He turns to open the door, but the shadows covering it hiss. He turns to me, and I nod at my legs.

"Do something about these," I say, and he heaves a dramatic sigh, rolling his eyes.

"I suppose you *did* give me your youth." He snaps his fingers, and I stand up, my legs feeling sturdy and strong. I bend one knee then the other and nod. "I'll be going now." He moves his finger in a circle and a bright blue ring appears before him; he jumps into it and it disappears in a flash.

I will pursue the spear later. Now that Eraxus has made himself known, I will surely be able to find him again; for now, Scarlett must be my focus. Hers is the more time-sensitive matter. I sigh, sitting down.

"The High King..." I mutter, running a hand down my face. My fingers come into contact with my beard, and I pluck a strand out angrily; this must go. Upon waking, I have to deal with this new situation with the High King and surely his Council as well. I growl and shake my head, standing up and opening the door; I should consult a few books in the library just in case before we leave.

Opening the library door, Scarlett stands up, pulling a chair back at one of the tables. I close the door and sit down in the offered chair while she sits down in the one across from me. She leans on the back two legs of the chair, putting her feet on the edge of the table, arms folded across her chest.

"I thought I told you to go get some sleep," I say.

"You said you expected me to," she says; I've taught her well enough that I shouldn't be leaving loopholes to be exploited in my orders.

"I'll rephrase that now: go get some sleep." She shakes her head, dropping the chair onto all four of its legs, leaning forward.

"Not until I get answers," she says.

I bite my tongue and consider it; ultimately, I don't have the energy to argue. I'll give her answers, as long as they don't conflict with any goals I've already placed. I barely incline my head, but she knows by now that I have acknowledged her request; she may not see it as a request, but people do not demand things from me.

"For starters, why were those men in the house? Why was that one man attacking you? He said you killed his wife. Is that true?"

I wait half a second before replying; if I wait too long, she'll think I'm lying. And if I respond immediately, it will appear as if I have the answer rehearsed. "I went to the city of Descra some time ago to follow through on a lead pertaining to the whereabouts of Impres. It led me to a merchant woman who sold baubles and trinkets; after questioning her I discovered she knew the Impres's location. She refused my offers to pay her and would not give up her location; I tortured her for the information in an alley, though she still didn't give in. After I was finished, she said she would tell Impres I was looking for her; I couldn't risk the chance she was actually telling the truth. So I killed her." Scarlett tilts her head, looking at me intently; I dip my head down slightly. "I did brutally murder that woman, but I couldn't let her disclose any information to Impres."

"Why did you have to kill her so brutally?"

"I was still obsessed with finding Impres; that singular thought drove me, regardless to any of the consequences. What I did may not have been right, but it was necessary." The shadows needed to be fed; they were getting too rebellious for even me to deal with. She wouldn't understand—she couldn't possibly understand it. Scarlett considers my answer and nods, seeming satisfied.

"Alright, now answer me this: what was the real reason I was sent to kill the giant Skrymsli? It wasn't for the spear, because you let that old man have it," I wait a few seconds before replying this time, letting out a long breath.

"I wanted Skrymsli dead; he represented a failure from my past. He needed to be dealt with, and I didn't let Eraxus have the spear." I look down at the table; with a snap of his fingers, Eraxus has the potential to restore me back to my pitiful condition, and I will not allow that. Regaining the spear will have to wait, but it won't wait long; now that I have it, I can proceed, though with my unlimited youth once more, I can afford to wait a little while.

"Why wait until now though?! Why not kill him once you got stronger?"

I raise my head, looking Scarlett directly in her eyes; she rarely ever looks away from my gaze anymore.

"The orichalcum spear would have negated my powers. While I am fully capable of killing him without my powers, the sudden detachment would have left me off balance and would have been more than enough time for Skrymsli to kill me. Because you don't have any powers, you would not suffer any effects from the orichalcum and would be able to kill him since you are especially deadly in combat." She sighs, shaking her head.

"Alright, whatever. My last question is this: what did that old man really want?" So she could sense it too; there is no escaping this situation; and as it especially pertains to Scarlett, the truth would be the best option here.

"When any magic folk are killed, including giants, it is brought to the attention of the High King. I believed that since Skrymsli was so disliked, by even other giants, that the High King would let it pass, but he did not. He has sent for us to appear before him and his Council tomorrow night."

"Why? Is he going to tell us off?"

"He plans to execute you," I say.

Scarlett blinks then stands up, knocking her chair back. "*What?!* What do you mean he plans to *execute* me? All I did was clean up your mess! It's not my fault!" She slams her hands on the table, her eyes bloodshot and fierce.

"I have no intention of letting him execute you," I say calmly. "You're tired, and nothing can be done right now; the best thing for you at present would be sleep."

"'Nothing can be done right now'? Something needs to be done about this! I will not have myself executed because I simply did what was asked of me! I—"

I stand up, flinging my chair back. I put my hand out, and the shadows grab the table, slinging it against the wall, shattering it. I clench my other hand by my side and the shadows retreat; perhaps I am being a little overzealous with the return of my powers. I grab Scarlett roughly by her shoulders with one hand, and she glares at me, grabbing my wrist.

"Let go of me," she snarls, shoving my hand off and turning her back to me, walking to the library door.

"You're not behaving rationally," I say, grabbing her shoulder again.

"This isn't a rational situation!" she shouts, whirling around. She slaps my hand off again. "I thought I told you to let go," she growls, turning back to the library door. I grab her by the shoulders and spin her around, smacking her hard across the face as she opens her mouth. She looks at me, mouth open as I squeeze her shoulders.

"Acting out against me will not help."

"Get your hands off of me," she snaps, grabbing my wrists, and I growl.

"Stop acting like a child!" I roar, and she breaks away from me, glaring at me.

"*I'm* acting like a child? You are the one who's insisting everything will be fine when I'm facing execution tomorrow!"

"I won't let that happen."

"How?! *How* are you going to stop that from happening, huh? What is your master plan to get *me* out of this?! Why did you send me in the first place?! Why didn't *you* take out Skrymsli when you had the chance?"

"I believed that since you were human, the consequences would be less severe for you. If I had been the one to kill Skrymsli, we would be facing much more dire circumstances."

"*You believed?!* There aren't many more consequences more 'dire' than execution; actually, there aren't *any*! If you were so scared of this High King, how can I expect you to defend me?!"

"Just trust me!" I shout, getting in her face. She glares up at me fiercely, stepping closer. "Just...trust me," I say, softer this time. Her eyes search my face, but I never take my eyes off those orange irises, putting my hand gently on her arm. "I won't lose you again," I say softly.

"Again?" Her green eyes narrow, looking at me intently, and I take my hand off her arm, taking a deep breath. I take a step back, looking at the shelves of books; I need to get a handle on this. With the poison out of my system, my mental faculties should be returning to peak condition as well as my physical; obviously there are some lasting, short-term, effects.

"It's going to be a long day tomorrow. You should get some sleep," I mutter, stroking my new beard. She sighs, running a hand through her tangled, messy red hair.

"You're right; we should both get some sleep, actually." She opens the library door, waiting for me.

"I've been doing nothing but sitting down and sleeping for the past few months; I have no interest in doing either of those right now," I reply, extending a hand; a long tendril of shadow slithers up the bookcase, picking a book from the shelf. I flip through it and growl, shoving it in the direction of the tendril. "That's the wrong one." It hisses, snapping at me; I growl, clenching my fist, and it reluctantly grabs the book, putting it back and getting a different one. I flip through it and nod; it got the right one this time.

"How can I sleep when you're going to be worrying over this? I'll feel your worry." I turn to her; she should have no problem sleeping. I was far more worried when I was in a wheelchair, and she slept fine then.

"You'll be fine," I say and she walks up to me, grabbing the book and setting it on the shelf; that's not the correct spot.

"You've just pointed out the necessity of being well-rested; that applies to you as well. You can't persuade people not to kill me by reading books; you have to do it by talking to people. You'll have a higher chance of success if you get some sleep as well."

The bags under her eyes are dark and heavy, being a very prominent feature on her weary, pinched face; I wonder how long she's gone without a restorative rest if her moods are switching this rapidly. She should know better than to stay up while I'm unconscious, even when I was in my poisoned condition; her worry will not speed up the process.

"Very well," I reluctantly consent, if only to get her to sleep as well, exiting the library and making my way to my room. Scarlett trails behind me and puts a hand on my shoulder as I go to close the door. I turn around, and she looks at my face intently.

"You used to have white hairs," she says frowning. "You should shave that," she says, nodding at my beard and letting me go. I close my door and look at my bed, clenching my fists. I don't know what will visit me in my sleep if I lay down again, but Scarlett's right; I can't afford to be tired tomorrow. With the poison gone, my nightmares should disappear as well, but there is always a chance that there are actual lasting effects. I cautiously make my way over to the bed, stripping down and laying down; I grab the sheets tight, my jaw clenching tight as I force my eyes to slowly close. I have to sleep; I have to sleep. I have to sleep.

CHAPTER TWENTY

I open my eyes and sit up; fortunately, the night passed without incident. It seems that there will be no lasting side effects at least. Opening my closet, I pull out a change of clothes, dressing myself and then putting a spare change in my pack. I walk into the kitchen, and I'm greeted with the scent of grilled mushrooms and onions; I look at the table and see a plate of grilled onions, mushrooms, and green peppers on toasted bread with cooked sausage. Scarlett finishes drying the last pan and sits down opposite me, hungrily digging into her sandwich.

"I wasn't expecting breakfast," I say, cutting the sandwich exactly in half and picking up one of the halves. She shrugs, talking around a mouthful of food.

"I guess I'm used to having breakfast for two," she says, gulping down her food and chasing it with a glass of water.

I pause before I take a bite, looking at her intently; what did she mean by that? Unnoticing, she finishes her sandwich, looking at me expectantly; I take a bite and she nods taking care of her plate. I quickly eat the rest, flicking crumbs off my hands, handing her my plate. I never expected her to develop any home skills, much less in the short time I was poisoned. It appears as if she's been doing it for so much longer... Her voice breaks me out of my thoughts, and I look up.

"Where's this High King live anyway?"

"He has a castle above the clouds," I reply.

"Of course he does," she says. I open the door and walk out into the new spring sun, letting Scarlett follow behind; this is the last time I intend on going above the clouds, at least for the near future.

"Get off my property! You're not welcome here!" Mersa Helvare shouts, brandishing an ax wildly at us.

"Mrs. Helvare—" I start, but she cuts me off.

"I don't want to see either of you ever again!" she shouts, strands of grey hair coming loose from her easy bun, her face red and vehement.

"We don't have time for this," Scarlett mutters, stepping up to Mersa and grabbing the ax handle, twisting it from her grip and hitting Mersa in the nose. Her head rocks back and she stumbles, Scarlett twirling the ax and bringing the handle forward to knock Mersa in the ribs.

I lunge forward and wrench the ax from her grip, tossing it to the ground. Scarlett opens up her mouth, but I hold up a hand and gesture for her to leave; I must deal with this personally. I walk to Mersa, and she holds her hand up, her other hand pinching her nose to stop the blood from flowing.

"You stay away from me," she snaps, turning away. "You're the monster that killed my baby boy," she says, covering her face with her hand. I see her shoulders begin to shake, her entire body trembling; I step forward and wrap my arms around her. I have nothing but respect for this woman, and she doesn't deserve this. She cries out, beating against my chest and I stand there, taking it; she doesn't deserve to suffer like this. A great many people do, but Mersa Helvare never even made it close to being on that list. She weakly hits me again before slumping against me, sobbing into my chest. "My boy! My baby boy! You took him away from me!" she wails, trembling against me; I clutch her tighter, letting loose her hair from her bun. "You took him..." she sobs, crying against me.

She's right; I took her joy from this world, and I can never replace that. I stole her child away from her.

"Mrs. Helvare, I—I am very sorry," I say, pouring as much sincerity and compassion as one can muster without having a heart or soul. "In his last moments, Jack should have been with you; I realize that even though I brought his body down, that in no way makes up for what I did. I know what it is like to suffer through this world without the one you love most. The difference is my suffering will never end; I can end yours."

I take my gloves off and place my hand on her chin, feeling her warm skin and tears; I tilt her head up. I see her slumped shoulders, her red, puffy eyes, and I feel her broken heart, torn and shattered apart, the pieces so far that gods would never find them all. She sniffs, and I softly stroke her chin; her hair greyed before its time, her tears following the few lines on her face. "Please, Mrs. Helvare, I can't do anything about Jack, but I can do this at least. Allow me to end your pain, please." She looks down, trembling.

"I just don't know what to do without him," she mutters, sniffing again. A choked sob escapes her throat, and she grabs me this time, crying into my chest. "I just want it to stop; I can't live like this. Please," she whispers into my chest, hiccuping. I nod, stroking her hair with my hand. I relax my body, holding her closer and tighter than I've held anyone in a long time; I embrace her like a loved one should. No words—no gifts or any other action could possibly ease her pain; I know that, even more than she. A mother should never be without her son; a parent should never outlive their child. I took Jack from her, and now I must reunite them. She buries her head in my shoulder, and the shadows slowly slither up her legs; she starts grabbing at the back of my cloak.

"Shh," I whisper, stroking her hair and holding her close, the shadows hissing eagerly; no, they will show respect. You will show her mercy—you will be kind and gentle, or you will never eat again. Their hissing stops as they snake up her body silently, slowly covering her while I stroke her hair gently. "I'm so sorry I killed Jack, Mrs. Helvare. I am sorrier than you could ever possibly imagine; I can never make up for what I did, and I hate myself for it. Your son was a good man, and I loved him deeply; you don't have to believe me, but letting him die was the hardest thing I've had to do since I came to this forsaken land. I'm sorry," I tremble, lowering my head so my hair can hide my face; I don't want anyone to see. She pats my back as I tremble against her, the shadows climbing higher; a mother until the end. "Please forgive me for what I've done, for the suffering I caused you."

I feel her open her mouth but no sound can be heard; she pats me on the back, kissing my shirt with cold, quivering lips. I gulp, taking a deep breath, trying to still my shaking. "It'll be over soon, Mrs. Helvare; you'll be with your son soon." I hold her against me until the shadows cover her, disappearing into the ground, along with any trace of Mersa Helvare; quickly, without a sound. I run a hand over my face, wiping away any trace and look down at my hands—clean to the rest of the world, but I see the blood on them, the innocent mixed with the guilty. Murder, however merciful it is, is still murder; the cold, hard definition does not discriminate. I walk back over to the beanstalk and look up at Scarlett, who is still climbing. I quickly catch up to her with ease, though it is not as easy as it used to be.

"What was that about?" she asks when she notices me.

"I was doing a favor for a friend," I reply, focusing on my climbing movements.

"I didn't know you had friends," her tone of disbelief is enough to let me know she's being serious, and not simply being rude.

"I don't anymore."

I pull myself onto the clouds and stand up, taking a moment to catch my breath; even though I wasn't completely inactive while I was poisoned, it still wasn't enough to keep me completely in shape. The climb had been easier when I was with Jack. I turn around and wait for Scarlett to make her way up to the top. Once she arrives, she is not smitten with the beauty of the world above the clouds, nor is she attracted to the light of the world like so many are; yes, she must have learned her lesson on her last trip. Experience often can be the best teacher, though I don't want Scarlett seeking so much experience that it becomes her demise.

"Where's this castle of his?" she asks, looking around.

"Observe your surroundings before you ask a question; you'll discover you'll be able to answer it without my help."

She looks around and sees a pair of white marble stairs, then looks up and I can see her eyes widen. A white castle with tall spires and many wide turrets hovers above the clouds, a golden light shining from it that becomes unbearably bright only when you look at it.

"Many people of this world think that the sun is the thing that gives them light and warmth. While that is true on many worlds, that is not the case on this one. The High King's castle provides all the heat and illumination to this world," I say; I became used to this sight long ago, but I allow Scarlett a moment to let it sink in.

"How does it glow so bright?" she asks adjusting her pack, not taking her eyes away.

"There used to be a god that drove a chariot across the sky, which made day and night. The High King grew tired of the god constantly transgressing on his territory and captured the god, locking him away in his castle. Whenever he grows tired of his illumination, the various times of which change with the seasons, he puts a full suit of restraining armor on the god."

"How does he keep a god locked away?" Scarlett asks, and I give her a small nudge to get her moving.

"Orichalcum is the only means by which mortals have any hope of overcoming powers from different entities; but the High King, and people like him, are able to do it with magic. His queen is a very skilled magician and was able to put a spell on the god to keep him from leaving."

"If the inside is just as nice as the outside, I'm not sure I'll mind being executed in there," Scarlett says climbing the steps, trying to make light of the situation.

"The last time I was here, it was very beautiful and ornate inside," I say; I can't go along with her stress-relieving technique, but I don't need to. I won't let her be executed.

Making it to the front door, I look at the large gold double doors, the light gradually growing dimmer as we approach. The High King would not want to blind his guests simply because he liked how his castle lights up. I search for a knocker of some kind but find none; there was one last time. I use the shadows to knock on the door, but they form a wall and slam against the doors, shaking them in their hinges. I hiss, grabbing one tendril and wringing it until it shrieks, letting it slide away; do not act out simply because I did not let you torture her! She did not deserve it; be thankful you got a meal at all.

"Are your powers acting up?" Scarlett asks. She's never inquired about my powers before; her curiousness has never extended as far as me, though I suppose that's because she feels she wouldn't get anything out of me. Her feeling would be correct.

"It's fine," I reply, keeping my voice even; after I deal with this situation, I must deal with yet another one. It's been one crisis after another recently; though after months of inactivity, I won't complain. The doors slowly slide open, and a large figure stands there, arms folded. He has broad shoulders and is taller than myself with arms thicker than my head; all of this is covered by a tuxedo that strains to contain his bulging muscles. He has the head of a bull, with a silver ring through his nose and large tan horns curve out from his head. He snorts, his muscles visibly rippling even underneath his shirt.

"State your business," a high, shrill voice shouts. A small hairy man sits on the beast's head, nearly hidden by the horns. He's slightly larger than my hand and is dressed in a much smaller tuxedo.

"The High King sent for us; we're to appear before him and the Council this evening," I say. The small man's eyebrows, nearly indistinguishable from the large tufts of hair on his head and face, burrow.

"A likely story! If you can't produce a formal invite of sorts, you will have to leave! We will have no gate crashers here!" his shrill voice pipes out.

Scarlett steps up, glaring at the small man. "Shut up!" she shouts.

The small man seems shocked for a moment before he puffs up, his face growing red beneath his hair. "I'll have you know that I am the royal greeter for the High King, and am thus imbued with the powers to—"

"I said shut up!" Scarlett shouts, and I take a half step forward, but she continues. "Has anyone ever told you how annoying your voice is? It feels like a dying cat is burrowing into my ear with a whining drill!"

Loud silence fills the air, and then the large beast chuckles, laughter rumbling from his chest before booming out of his wide mouth. He snorts and steps aside, letting us through.

"What are you doing, you great beast? Don't allow them entry! They haven't got the proper forms!"

The large bull man walks away, his heavy steps echoing throughout. The golden doors automatically close behind us with a loud clang, and that, too, fades into silence.

"Don't say a word from here on in," I keep my voice low, and she turns to me.

"I'm sorry that I'm a little on edge," she hisses back; I'll allow her behavior since she's facing execution. An outburst like that might work on the greeters, but it will only seal her fate in front of the High King.

Suddenly, a large stone man drops from the ceiling; he, too, is dressed in a tuxedo. Large stone wings stretch out from his back, horns spiraling from his head. He bows low, which sounds like rocks grating against each other, talon-like fingers nearly touching the ground. He stands up straight, two dark holes where his eyes should be boring into us.

"If you'll come with me, I'll take you to the Council room," he says, his voice rumbling out like an earthquake. I nod, following him down long corridors with large busts, intricate sculptures, and detailed paintings.

"It's a lot larger on the inside," Scarlett says, her voice nearly drowned out by the clacking of the stone man's talons on the floor. It seems that some sights are enough to take her mind off her imminent trial, but I can allow no sights to distract me. I must put all my effort into keeping Scarlett alive, by whatever means necessary. We come to another pair of large, golden double doors, and the stone man pushes them open, ushering us inside.

"The High King and Council will be with you shortly," he bows low again and exits.

We're in a bright, high room; above us is a silver and gold panel that stretches almost to the door of the circular tower we're in. Behind the panel are several high-backed chairs, with a large, winged silver one in the very center. A large analogue clock adorns the wall behind the center chair, and on the panel in front of the center chair is a large set of silver scales, a wooden gavel resting beside them.

The second hand ticks audibly, the sound of time crawling by echoing slightly throughout the room. Scarlett taps her foot impatiently, biting the inside of her cheek as I close my eyes, taking a deep breath. To call for a hearing and then be late to the same hearing you called is very unprofessional, not to mention rude; I do not care for either, even if it is the High King. I wait patiently, Scarlett's footsteps echoing throughout the room, though not louder than the clock. Her stomach grumbles and she groans; I hear her plop down on the floor, opening her pack. I open my eyes and raise an eyebrow as she pulls out what looks like a toasted fish sandwich with spicy mayonnaise.

"You packed food?" I fold my arms across my chest, looking down at her as she wipes a bit of fish off the corner of her lips, speaking around a mouth full of food.

"Few wan shum?" she asks.

I look at her, then the clock and the doors that have remained closed for twenty minutes now. I can't be seen eating when the High King enters, ready to judge; it wouldn't make a good impression. I also can't allow my mental faculties to be impaired by lack of nourishment. I sigh, holding out a hand.

"I'll take the other one," I say, and she hands me a wrapped sandwich, my stomach grateful she brought two. I sit down next to her and bring out a container of water and two small metal cups from my pack, pouring each of us a drink.

"Did you know I brought food?" she asks after swallowing and chasing it down with a gulp of water, pouring herself some more. I take my gloves off and my cloak, folding them up neatly before I roll up my sleeves in such a manner that they don't get rumpled.

"No, but it's never wise to be gone for more than a day without water." I reply, taking a bite of the sandwich; I keep my face clear of expression, methodically chewing. It's very good, and she certainly has improved; this must be one of the dishes she's mastered. I spot her looking at me between bites of her sandwich. Swallowing, I take a sip of water, wetting my throat. "The High King loves good food; I'd save half a sandwich for him, just in case." She nods, a small smirk on her face; she knows me well enough by now that I don't compliment easily. After we both finish our sandwiches, I lean back on my hands, looking up at the roof of the tower we're in. It's high above, a small gleaming dot of gold and white; the place must be quite the ordeal to clean.

"So..." Scarlett clears her throat, shifting slightly. She takes a drink of water, looking at me over the top of her cup as I raise an eyebrow, looking at her out of the corner of my vision. "At that woman's house..."

"Mersa," I correct, keeping my voice even; I should have known this would come up eventually. I just thought she would prioritize her impending hearing for execution over her curiosity; I should have known better.

"Right, Mersa. At Mersa's house...why did you stop me from attacking her?" She's intently watching my unchanging expression.

"Why did you attack her in the first place?"

"What?" Scarlett asks, surprised.

"You attacked her without any provocation," I say. Scarlett fumbles for an answer, but I continue talking. "It's natural to be nervous when you're facing death." Despite my skills, these could be some of Scarlett's last moments; while I wouldn't particularly care if it was anyone else, Scarlett has been extremely useful to me in her time as my student.

"I've faced death before," she says, finishing the rest of her water, signaling that I successfully changed the subject.

"You're right," I say, finishing my cup and packing them both back into my pack, as well as the container. "And you came back every time alive and relatively well. Why should this time be any different?"

She nods, letting out a long breath. She looks at me, her green eyes sparkling with the reflected light of the room. "It's just—" The double doors behind us fling open, and I slip my cloak and pack on in one motion, on my feet in an instant. I slip my gloves on as Scarlett stands up, looking at the people entering. Twelve hooded figures enter, shrouded in black and white cloaks, climbing up to the panel and sitting in the high-backed chairs.

Last among them is a tall man dressed in long green robes with golden cuffs. Golden thread seems to move around, creating different scenes as he moves; first a fox, then a forest, then a bird flying. The scenes continue to change as he walks up to the last remaining chair in the middle. He wears a golden necklace with a diamond in the middle, golden bracelets on each wrist. A gold circlet with a small emerald in the center rests on his forehead. He has a thin nose and pointed ears, his eyes a bright hazel, yellow color. His skin is pale, though not unhealthily so; long dark hair falls down his back and frames his face as he cups his slight, noble chin with one hand, his thin, long fingers curving up his regal cheeks, settling on his high cheekbones. Several rings clack against each other with the motion and he leans back, his eyes briefly glossing over Scarlett to settle on me; his presence fills the room with authority, but I stand up straight, looking him directly in the eye. My stare tells him that I challenge his authority in his own home, and he knows it; I will not be intimidated into submission. His eyes narrow, his free hand picking up the gavel and twirling it idly.

"I thought that the girl was the only one asked for. Am I correct?" He turns to the other members of the panel and they all nod. Turning back to me, he raises one thin, elegant brow. "Then what are *you* doing here?" He phrases it as more of an accusation than a question, though I answer anyway, keeping my tone courteous.

"I'm here to defend my student, Oberon; I was told I was expected as well."

"You will address me as 'High King' while we are in session. You were not asked for, and now I must ask you to leave." Oberon replies coldly, golden eyes flashing. I dip my head, maintaining eye contact with him.

"Forgive me, *High King*," I reply, doing my best to turn his title into an insult. There's a snicker among the hooded figures, which is quickly disguised with a cough. Oberon's eyes narrow, and he sits up straighter, banging the gavel on the panel. "I simply thought that since she does not know the customs of your people, I should defend her."

"Are you claiming you know the customs of my people?" he leans forward, the cloaked figures murmuring; I do not want them voting against me out of spite. Presuming to know everything about a culture, and simultaneously not being part of it, will always instill hostility; I must have the Council on my side.

"Your wife, the High Queen, and I spent a large amount of time together; and during that time I learned a great many things, among which was the customs of your people. Now," I pause while a few of the cloaked members chuckle, Oberon's face growing lividly pale, "if you are saying that your wife does not know her own customs well enough to teach, then I will happily acquiesce to your better judgment." I need only play Oberon in front of the Council, and our victory in the trial will be all but assured.

"The session will now begin," he says by way of reply, his voice cool, trying to maintain a professional countenance. Still looking at me, he says, "State your name for the record."

"Mister E," I reply, and a small smirk twists the corners of his mouth up.

"Your *real* name," he says, and I stand silent. "If your real name cannot be given for the record, then you will not be allowed to defend the accused," he says, traces of triumphant, smug victory entering his voice.

"I will happily inform the Council and yourself of my true name," I say, looking at each hooded figure for a brief second before returning my gaze to Oberon. I remove a small piece of parchment and charcoal, clearly writing out a single word, then flicking it at one of the members of the Council. After a moment of the paper being passed around with satisfactory nods, it makes its way to Oberon. "I believe that should satisfy you, High King; will that be all?" Oberon's lips twist downwards, the parchment in his hands obliterated suddenly by a burst of flame.

"Your name is noted," he bites out. Turning to Scarlett, he does his best to make himself imposing; I'm sure he thinks that authority will make Scarlett fearful and easy for him to interrogate. He has never met my student. "And your name?"

Scarlett looks at me for a brief moment and I return her look, inclining my head slightly; I will take care of this. All she has to do is remain calm and strong; I'm sure she can do the latter, though I might have to manage her closely to ensure the former; her control will be pushed by the stress of her situation.

"My name is Scarlett," she says, looking Oberon in the eye as well.

"Full name," he says, and Scarlett pauses.

"I don't know," she says.

"You do not know your full name?" he asks incredulously, leaning forward. I take a small step closer to Scarlett, speaking up.

"She has amnesia," I say.

"How convenient," Oberon mutters, turning his now hungry gaze from me to Scarlett and then back.

"I invite any Council member, or even the High King himself, to confirm the truth of her statement with magic." I must maintain control of the situation; that will allow me control the Council, and their deciding vote. The Council turn their heads as one to look at Oberon, who swallows and extends a hand. A small translucent cube appears in front of Scarlett and hovers for a moment, making small whirring noises. Suddenly it turns bright green and beeps; Oberon sighs and leans back.

"It is confirmed: she has had amnesia," he says. His eyes gleam as the cube disappears and he adjusts, straightening his necklace. "As an amnesiac, however, from here on in it is impossible to take anything she says with absolute certainty. As for Mister E, he is obviously emotionally attached to the defendant, and his statements will obviously be biased."

"Actually," I step toward the panel, "I formed a mental connection with Scarlett soon after meeting her, which has allowed her to retain her memories since then."

"This only further proves the point that your statements will be biased, based upon a strong mental connection with the defendant." He continues to try and ensnare me in some clumsy trap; he is not thinking far enough ahead. A trial is not about the truth—it is a game, meant to be played with strategy and personality.

"Then I invite you to question Scarlett directly, since her memories after I met her can be counted upon." I retort. Scarlett looks quickly at me as Oberon smirks, turning his gaze to my student.

"When exactly did you two meet?" Oberon asks, his eyes narrowing with the prospect of capturing his prey.

"Two autumns ago."

His nostrils flair out, and he scratches some notes on a slip of paper.

"Now that the validity of each individual's character has been established," he says, reverting to default protocol, no doubt to allow himself time to think, "we can begin to find out the truth of the matter. Scarlett," she stands up straighter, nodding, "did you kill Skrymsli the giant?"

The High King, Oberon, looks down at me from his chair, high above me, his gaze trying to drill into me. *Think he's overcompensating for something?* Not now, I need to focus. *Quick, snappy comebacks aren't exactly your forte; maybe you shouldn't be the one answering the questions.* Maybe you should just shut up!

"Scarlett, did you kill Skrymsli the giant?"

I look at Mister E out of the corner of my eye; I can do this. I know he said he would take care of everything, but this is *my* trial. I can defend myself; he's done it long enough.

"Yes," I say firmly. Oberon raises an eyebrow, the Council murmuring. *You just confessed, you know that right?* It's all part of the plan, it's under control. *I hope so.*

"Did you do this of your own free will, knowing that it would result in Skrymsli's death?" I pause for a moment; I can't lie, he can confirm anything I say with magic, apparently. *That's cheating.* So is lying. *Only if you get caught.*

"No," I say, purposefully biting my lip.

"No? Are you saying that you didn't kill Skrymsli the giant?" He's positively glowing, and I bite my lip harder, stuttering a little before I find my voice. *What's with the weak act?* Quiet! Acting doesn't come naturally!

"No, I did kill him but...can I please...explain what happened?"

Oberon sits back in his chair, a satisfied smile on his face, the Council leaning in. "Of course, of course," he says smugly.

I look down, hiding my smile; I'm going to wipe that smug look off his face. I raise my face, worry etched all over, wringing my hands.

"Well I went to his castle to retrieve the spear of orichalcum. Skrymsli told me that it could only be removed by a mortal, and it was stopping him from regenerating his leg from the knee down. I pulled it out and...there was still...still..." I suck in a rattling, watery breath, vision blurring with the onset of tears as I subtly pull at my skin each time I wring my hands. "Still a shard in his leg, and when he tried to regenerate his...his leg just...there was so much blood and I...I couldn't stop it! He blew himself apart and I...I couldn't do *anything!*" I let out a choked sob, turning quickly to Mister E, burying my head into his chest. I heave dry sobs, trembling against him and he wraps his arms around me, patting me surprisingly gently on the back. *He caught on, he has to play along to corroborate your story.*

"You were still an accomplice to his death," I turn my head slightly, but my cries only increase in volume.

"This poor girl can't be charged with being an accomplice, much less murder." My cries continue unabated but my ears prick up; I recognize the voice. *It's Eraxus Prine.* Right, Eraxus. *The man who cured Mister E.* Ah yes, alright, I can place him now. "We all know Skrymsli wasn't the most intelligent creature; it isn't this young lady's fault that he blew himself up to kingdom come. I vote we dismiss all charges laid against her. All those who agree raise their hands."

The rustling of robes and cloaks reach my ears. I smile; yes! It worked! "I vote we should also throw little Scarlett here a party, to show our apologies." To show your apologies? A party won't cover up the fact that you tried to have me executed! *They can still change their verdict.* I find myself in the mood to party.

"I—I would like to thank you," I rub my eyes quickly and turn them, red and puffy, to Oberon. "If...if that's okay with your highness, High King Oberon, sir." His mouth opens and closes several times, and I barely manage to suppress a smile; I can't drop the ball now. Just a few more minutes and then I can celebrate.

"I...very well. A party shall be...shall be thrown in honor of Scarlett, to show our most..." he pauses, tugging at his necklace, his eyes fiery golden flames, "sincere apologies." Mister E bows, and I sniff, following suit; suck it Oberon.

Once outside the court room, the gargoyle once again appears, leading Scarlett and myself to what would seem to be our rooms. Opening one door, I silently gesture for Scarlett to follow me in. Closing the door behind her, I point to the bed and she raises an eyebrow but sits, looking at me curiously. I put my hand on the door and shadows slink up the wall, covering the door and pressing against it until it groans with the strain. I grip the shadows hard and they screech under duress, backing off on the door, only covering it now. You got your meal that you so desired, now you are pushing it. After I talk with Scarlett, I will deal with them next.

I sit next to Scarlett, keeping my voice low. "Next time you intend to abandon a plan, I expect to be notified."

"It was *my* neck on the line," she says, turning her head slightly to look at me. "So *I* did something to save it. This was something you couldn't have done, so I did."

"I had it under control," I say.

"What matters is that I'm alive," she says, standing. "Which was your goal, and mine, all along. There's no use in arguing about how it was done; what matters is that it's done now."

I open the door and Scarlett exits quickly; I close the door behind her and grab one of the tendrils of shadow as it tries to slink away.

"Don't think I forgot about you," I growl, squeezing it tighter. It hisses at me, and I throw it to the ground, stomping on it with my heel. "I give you a meal, and you have an attitude because it wasn't done how you want. I will not be tolerating this any longer; be grateful for what you get."

A wall of shadow slams into me from behind and I fly through the air, crashing into the wall. I throw my arms up as the shadows assault me, hissing and spitting, trying to tear at my face; they, too, are frustrated. They wrap around my wrists, slowly pulling my arms apart despite my attempts to keep them closed. I kick one foot up, shoving it through the shadows and they screech, retreating backwards. They begin to disappear into the wall and I lunge forward, grabbing one tendril in both hands and wrestling it to the ground. I pull out my sword, holding it to the tendril. "Mersa didn't deserve a horrible death, you will not ruin her memory with your rebellion." Dark tendrils wrap around my ankles and sling me against the wall. My shoulders take the brunt of the impact, and I quickly pick myself up, rolling away from another attack. I stand, thrusting forward and impaling the shadows, retreating backward. I stumble, feeling blood begin to seep into my shirt. I spin as the shadows plunge toward me, and I slice at the shadows, burying my blade deep. Blood begins to trickle down my arm and I wrench my sword out, glaring at the shadows.

"I am mourning the loss of a friend; I won't indulge you any longer. I won't die simply because you're being stubborn," I sheath my sword and the shadows hiss, trying to egg me on. "No! I will not! You cannot kill me either; we're linked, as much as I sometimes loath it. You will not interrupt my process," I take a step forward and the shadows smack into me, bruising several ribs and sending me crashing against the bed, splintering the expensive wooden frame; Oberon can cover the damages. I stand up, glaring at the shadows as they hiss, swirling angrily, hurt. "That didn't feel good, did it? I try to warn you but you won't listen." I step forward, getting a grip on the swirling shadows and squeezing hard, despite the mounting pressure at the base of my neck. "So listen to me now. You interrupt my process, you rebel at me with petty concerns. I indulge you and satisfy your appetite, despite you making life unnecessarily difficult at times. Remember, I can make your continued existence hell, though that would do neither of us any good. It would be in both of our best interests if we put all of this behind us and began working together again."

The shadows slip through my fingers, hissing their approval in my ear, snaking around me. They coo into my ears, and I pet them slowly; they are not beyond reason. "After we leave this place, I will take you out with me to Descra; we will not be staying here long. I despise the palace as much as you do." The shadows disappear, and I sit down on the damaged bed, pulling bandages out of my pack to dress my wounds, but they've already healed; old habits are hard to forget. I would have liked to crush the shadows underneath my fists until they caved and submitted to my will, but I'm not going to risk bodily harm to ensure I'm obeyed. My will being stronger than theirs, I would be able to take the pain they would inflict, while the shadows would suffer at their own ministrations. It gave me the desired outcome, and that is what's important; the cosmos seems to be trying to drill that into my head recently. The end, while it justifies the means, is not so important that the means must be disregarded. I need the shadows to obey me, and now they do—and the hostility between us has been reduced as well. The means led to the end.

CHAPTER TWENTY-ONE

I turn the knob as a knock sounds from my door; I open it and I remain silent for a moment. The gas lamps in the hallway catch the sequins in Scarlett's long dress, the same color as her hair. A light pink ribbon draws attention to her waist, draping down behind her in a bow, the ends nearly going to her feet.

"It's time for the party," she says, chewing her tongue and purposefully not looking in my direction, her cheeks bright red. "I was sent to fetch you."

"You look..." I search for the proper words, her green eyes peering up at me from dark, thick lashes; is she wearing...makeup? I take a deep breath, allowing a small smile; she needs to enjoy herself here, she deserves it. "Like a fire, all-consuming, devouring the sights of all who dare look at your rapturous inferno." Her eyes widen at such words, then she shakes her head.

"I don't know, I mean it's not exactly designed for combat," she says, holding out the frill of her dress; she can't hide her pleasure from me, no matter how much she tries.

"You are a beautiful woman," I interrupt before she can continue, running a bare hand through her hair. It's soft and smooth, falling down in waves on her left side; just like Simiel's. I quickly remove my hand, putting my fist by my side. "You are dressed much more appropriately than I, it seems." I look down at my cloak and frown, taking it off. Sections of it are burnt almost brown, the edges frayed and tattered, the bottom riddled with holes; this is one of my nicer ones. I toss it aside and search through my pack, but find nothing that would be found at a royal party. I rummage through the closet of my room but find nothing except bright, gaudy royal garb; I decidedly close the closet door, looking once again at my cloak. I don't mind rejecting the standard dress code, but the party will surely be full of powerful members of the magical society. Superficial as they are, I will not be able to gain a word from them with how I am currently dressed; it is their world, unfortunately. I turn around to see Eraxus leaning against the door frame, ignoring Scarlett's bemused expression.

"Somebody's having a wardrobe malfunction," he says in a sing-song voice.

"Why are you here, Eraxus?" His attire has changed very little, the only change being his replacing his neck tie with a bow tie.

"Well I originally came to return this."

He pulls the orichalcum spear from midair, tossing it to me. I catch it and immediately feel a sense of loss from the shadows, and only from force of will do I not crumple to the ground. There's nothing to disguise my trembling as I walk over to the bed and drop the spear onto it. The further away I walk from it, the more warmth that seems to return to my body. Eraxus doesn't say a thing, and I notice his body blocks Scarlett's view of the room.

"My business concerning the spear is finished, and that was going to be that. But after seeing the state you're in...well, now I'm here to fix a disaster."

"I'm fine," I reply, both Eraxus's and my own gaze on my tattered cloak, lying discarded on the floor.

"Trust me, you're not fine. You're the farthest possible thing from fine, and your clothes are a mess as well. Now," he snaps his fingers, and I feel a sudden tightness on my legs and forearms. I turn to the mirror on the wall next to the bed and see myself in a puffy bright blue piece, with tight bright blue sleeves and light tan stockings. I growl at him, the shadows rising up, trembling still from my proximity to the spear, and he shakes his head. "You don't like it? You look darling though." The shadows snap up at him weakly, and he snaps his fingers again. "That should be more your speed," he says, though not sounding too happy about it.

I look in the mirror again; much more acceptable. Black pants and a shirt cling to my skin, large black boots elevating my height; a thin belt holds my sword and sheath, catching the light in an almost menacing fashion. A dark heavy trench coat hangs down, silver borders gleaming brightly, and I flip the collar up, frowning at a thin chain going from the belt to my mid-thigh.

"It's a little tight," I say, trying to pull the shirt away from my skin with little success. I put my fingers on the chain, moving it around slightly. "And what exactly is the purpose of this?"

"They make you look good," Eraxus says, biting his bottom lip. "When you're fixed up a little, you look very nice; perfectly scrumptious, actually," he says, snapping his fingers again. Dark eyeshadow appears around my eyes, and I growl.

"Absolutely not; I am not wearing makeup." I turn to him, and he looks exasperated.

"Is it too much to ask for you to work with me here?! I'm trying to make you look *sexy*," he says. I fold my arms across my chest silently, and he heaves one of his dramatic sighs. "Fine," he grumbles, snapping his fingers, and I feel the makeup disappear. "You suck all the fun out of dress up," he pouts, sulking off to the party. Scarlett looks at me as I reach into one of the pockets of the trench coat, pulling out a pair of new black leather gloves. I roll my shoulders, and I feel the coat shift slightly; it's heavier than I'm used to. I slip on the gloves and flex my fingers, nodding, satisfied. I look at Scarlett and she looks away quickly, folding her arms across her chest.

"What?"

She smiles, tottering a little on heels, closing the door behind me. She faces me, still having to look up to meet my gaze, then she looks back down, grinning.

"Eraxus knows how to clean you up," she says, and I turn her around, pushing her in the back. She stumbles forward, heels clacking against the tile as she struggles to keep her balance. "I'm still getting used to these things!" she says, and I give her another small push;

the entertainment factor of the heels is enough that I may get her a pair. She glares at me, and I snap my fingers, pointing ahead. She grumbles and carefully walks through the halls as I trail behind her until we make it to the main room. The doors are closed, but I can hear the din of conversation and laughter within. I step forward and push the doors open, bright light shining out, and immediately the murmur quiets.

The room is large, with several glass chandeliers bathing the room in a warm, golden glow. Silver platters full of familiar and unfamiliar, more exotic, food gleam from tables on the sides of the wall. On one end of the room, a small symphony abruptly stops playing; someone coughs, and the sound almost reverberates. In the middle of the room are several large, long banquet tables, though no plates adorn them yet.

On the end of the room opposite the small symphony, a smaller, more elegant table sits on a raised platform. Oberon sits there, eyes locked on me, glass paused halfway to his mouth. The silence seems to grow even more pronounced as the woman next to Oberon stands with a glass in hand. She's tall and regal, with high cheekbones and a healthy glow on her skin. Her cheeks are slightly flushed, and her eyes are a warm hazel color, long, straight hair flowing to the middle of her back. She wears a simple silver circlet on her head and a small golden band on her left ring finger. Her robes are long and royal blue, with small threads of gold and silver laced throughout, almost like stars. She extends one thin, dainty hand out and smiles, seeming to light up the room even more.

"Here are the guests of honor!" Her voice is soft and kind, but it carries throughout the room. "Why don't we all show them kindness and courtesy? Most of all though," she raises her slender glass full of thick, sparkling golden liquid, "let's show them how the Royal Family throws a party!" A cheer rises up, and the guests all raise their glasses, drinking from them in one quick gulp. The talking begins again in earnest, guests mingling about while the symphony strikes up a cheerful tune.

I feel a hand on my shoulder and turn quickly. "I hope you enjoy yourself this evening, Mister E," she says, her smile stretching all the way to her hazel eyes even as she rests her hand on my arm.

"I'm sure I will, Tatiana." I reply, subtly moving her hands off my arm, looking from her to Oberon. She's nearly my height, so I don't quite have to look down to look her in the eye. She clears her throat, nodding and blushing.

"Um, yes, well..um…Oh!" she turns and grabs my hand, dragging me through the crowd. I turn quickly and snap my fingers at Scarlett, who waves with a smirk on her face, accepting a glass of the golden liquid; she will be of no help, obviously. I pull my hand from her grasp after we make it to the upper table and she smiles, pulling two women from their chairs and presenting them to me, her hands on each of their shoulders. "These are my daughters. Sindra," she pats the shoulder of one woman; a girl, rather. She doesn't appear to be older than eighteen, with dark, short spiky hair. Her eyes are dark and smoky, her skin pale and slightly freckled. A slip of nice fabric covers only the bare necessities, marred purposefully by several long slits and holes. "And this is Zelraye." Zelraye appears older than Sindra and has light brown hair that falls in curls to her shoulders, with turquoise eyes gleaming behind round glasses. Her golden dress sparkles and shimmers in the light, complimenting her light brown skin. She dips her head courteously, and I turn my attention back to Tatiana.

"They look nothing like you or Oberon," I say and she laughs, a light tinkling sound that brings a smile to Zelraye's lips before quickly disappearing.

"They're both adopted," she says. She pats the shoulders of both her daughters and turns her back with a small flip of her hair. "I leave you in their hands to show you around and introduce you to the different foods. I'm sure between the both of them, they can manage it somehow," she goes and leans over next to her husband, whispering into his ear and smiling. I look at both of them and then back at their mother.

"I don't play well with children," I say, as politely as I can; no use in upsetting the hostess in her own home when her husband is already at the point of wanting to put my head on a pike.

"I am not a child!" Sindra protests angrily, stepping up close to me. "I'm nearly half a millennium!"

"And I'm at least a quarter of a millennium," Zelraye speaks up, standing slightly straighter behind her sister.

"Like I said, children. I think you would have a better time with my student," I turn and point to Scarlett, who is poking at a blue tentacle on her plate. Zelraye immediately looks interested, heading over toward Scarlett, while Sindra stays behind.

"She's mortal," Sindra says, folding her arms.

"So were you at one point," I say and Sindra begins to speak, but I cut her off. "I know all about you and your sister, and how you used to be mortal before Oberon and Tatiana adopted you both. You lived with an abusive stepmother and two half-sisters until you met a man who you thought you would spend the rest of your life with. However, your jealous sisters murdered him and tried to murder you, but you escaped. Tatiana took pity on you and adopted you. As for your sister," I look behind me to see her avidly talking to Scarlett, who is, for a change, remaining quiet. "She was locked in a tower as an infant by a witch and kept there until she was an adolescent. What appeared to be an honest young man used her hair, which had grown quite long, to climb the tower. He was only interested in her for her body, however, and she, too, escaped her confinement. The difference was she had to wander and do whatever it took to survive. It was you who found her though, and convinced Oberon and Tatiana to adopt her." Sindra remains tight-lipped, looking at the ground.

"How did you know?" She looks up at me.

"I make it my business to know, especially when they concern the Royal Family. While you may not rule all of Legend Land, you play a prominent role in its affairs and act as guardians of a sort for Death while he is away. You are also harbingers of peace between the various magic races, also known as the Fae. You keep balance between them all; at least, that's your duty anyway. It doesn't seem like you have any intention of fulfilling that role though," Sindra looks away, her eyebrows furrowing.

"I don't want to be cooped up in this castle all the time," she says, sighing and looking up at one of the small windows high above. "I want to be able to travel, see the cosmos; I know there's more out there than just this world, but my parents want me to stay."

"The cosmos is a dangerous place," I say and she turns to me, eyes flashing.

"I can take care of myself," she snaps, and I clench my fist. I slowly release the tension in my arm and nod understandingly; a rebellious young woman, heir to the throne of the Royal Family. If I could gain a direct link of control to the Royal Family, almost nothing would be out of my grasp.

"I'm sure you can," I say, looking back at Scarlett. "Scarlett has traveled this world with me as my student; you should talk to her about her experiences." Sindra pauses for a moment then brushes past me, walking over to Scarlett and her sister, who were busy with conversation.

"I knew you'd just pass them off to your student," Tatiana says, coming up to stand beside me, handing me a glass of the thick golden liquid; upon close inspection, it resembles honey.

"I don't indulge in ambrosia," I reply and she sighs, tilting her head back and letting the liquid slowly slide down the glass and into her throat. She licks the rim of the glass, lifting it up without wasting a single drop; her tongue darts out to catch a small bit on her cheek and she smiles, swallowing.

"Your loss," she says, turning back; we're both looking out on the party now, which is in full swing. "The last time you visited, we hadn't even adopted Sindra," she says, looking at me out of the corner of her eyes. "It's been too long."

"Oberon would say it hasn't been long enough," I say, and she forces a laugh, shaking her head.

"My husband is just paranoid and prone to jealousy."

"I would say he has a right to be paranoid."

She drains one of the glasses in her hand and holds it out, a servant coming up to snatch it away quickly. She drinks from the other glass and puts her hand on my arm.

"Tatiana," I warn, looking down sharply at her.

"Can you blame me? Oberon's been very busy, and it's been a long time." She leans close to me, her breath on my neck. "I still remember how gentle and tender you can be, and how firm when the urge strikes you," she whispers, squeezing my arm.

"What is it you want?" I ask, and she looks hurt, taking a small step back.

"Just the companionship of a friend," she says, her eyes tracing down my body.

"We're not friends, Tatiana," I say firmly. Indignation flashes in her eyes and I step closer, grabbing the glass and holding it out, letting a servant whisk by and take it. "Don't act so hurt, because that's what it is, an act. I know you well enough, so don't insult my intelligence trying to fool me. You want something, so at least have the gall to ask for it."

"Fine," she says, shaking her head. "Fine. I need your help with a problem," she says, twirling a lock of her hair, leaning back on the table. "Recently I was forced to exile a certain Fae by the name of Nyphra." She stops twirling her hair, pushing herself off the table. "I need her dealt with in a permanent fashion."

"Why should I even consider this?" I fold my arms across my chest, and a sly smirk plays across her face as she slowly walks her fingers up my chest.

"What would you say to a favor from a member of the Royal Family?" she says, picking at the collar of my shirt.

"I don't want any favors from you," I retort, grabbing her wrist.

"Oberon doesn't know your plan; I do. You can be sure that if he were to somehow...discover them," Tatiana removes her hand from my grasp, looking up at me coyly, "he would want to put a stop to them." I lean forward, grabbing both her shoulders, my lips close to her ear.

"I don't take kindly to being threatened," I growl in a low tone and she shudders, stepping closer to me.

"I'd like to know exactly how you deal with it," she says, her voice getting lower, and I separate us, taking a step back.

"You will regret doing this," I say, and she grins.

"Now look at who's making threats," she says, and I grip the table in one hand, squeezing it as the tendrils slither up one of the table legs.

"It's not a threat; it's a promise," I take my hand off the table, the shadows oozing away; if I am to kill Nyphra, I will need to put myself in the proper mindset. That being said, I need to approach this entire situation in a calmer manner. I can't kill Tatiana—one cannot simply kill a member of the Royal Family, and I don't have anything to leverage her with; at least, not anything available to me at the moment. "Nyphra is one of the most powerful Fae in Legend Land; and because of that, I've left her alone, and she has done the same to me. Not to mention she is under direct orders to oversee the Royal Family and report back should anything go awry. Her being exiled will surely incur the wrath of some very powerful individuals."

"Which is why I need you to take care of her before that happens," Tatiana says.

So I'm the cleanup crew then. Should anyone be sent because of the breach of balance, I will direct them to Tatiana, and she will be dealt with in what will surely be a severe manner. If no investigation is launched, I can always draw their attention.

"I'll leave first thing tomorrow and take care of it," I say. I grab one of the silver knives and stab it deep into the wood near one of Tatiana's hands. "But if I, or any ally of mine, is ever threatened by you or any member of the Royal Family, I will slaughter every last one of you." I let go of the knife, leaving it quivering in the table. I cannot simply kill a member of the Royal Family, but I'll be damned if I let them harm Scarlett or myself. I turn my back on the party and quickly make my way out of the room, closing the door quietly behind me with tense muscles.

Making my way back to my room, I slam the door closed behind me and rip off the closet door, swinging it at the wardrobe; I am not just some attack dog! The wardrobe cracks, collapsing in on itself while the closet door splinters apart. The shadows shoot out, wrapping around everything in sight, and I growl. They tighten and yank, wood and glass flying everywhere. I glare around at the room and kick at the remains of the bed angrily; the shadows know how I feel in this situation, very accutely. I pick up a small wooden chair that had only been knocked over and I prop up a table now missing one leg; it's better to release my anger now, so I can enter a calmer mindset. I will need to confront Nyphra as soon as possible; and afterward, now that I have the spear, I can finally begin the final stage of the mission.

CHAPTER TWENTY-TWO

"It'd be nice if we could stay a little longer—take a break," Scarlett says, waving goodbye to Sindra and Zelraye from the top of the beanstalk.

"We have a job to do," I reply shortly, beginning my descent down the beanstalk. I had woken Scarlett up early and rushed her out of the castle; I hadn't given any thanks nor any goodbyes, and I received the same treatment. I had made sure to let Scarlett know that I approve of her friendship and communication with Oberon's children; the parents were of little use to me, but the children more so. Afterward, however, I asked for silence; I do not like this situation Tatiana has placed me in.

"We were only there for one day! What kind of job would require us to leave so quickly?"

"The important kind," I retort and she huffs, going silent and climbing down after me. After we make it down several yards, I speak up again; I'm not angry at Scarlett—I shouldn't focus my anger on her just because it's convenient. "A Fae, Nyphra, has been exiled and now needs to be dealt with. Since you've never fought anyone this powerful who uses magic before, I've decided to take you along; it will be a good learning experience. You'll be able to see what someone powerful in the arcane arts can accomplish."

"This should be easy using the orichalcum spear though," she says, nodding at the very same spear now strapped to my back alongside my pack.

"You'll have to get close enough to use it," I say. Scarlett remains silent for the rest of the climb down, and we make it back to the ground around late morning; we made good time, even with my powers hindered by the spear. Scarlett bends over, catching her breath.

"Climbing is a much different exercise than what I normally do," she says, straightening up and pulling a container of water from her pack, taking a long draught before putting it back. "Where are we going to find this Nyphra?" she asks. I hand her the spear and take several spaces away, my connection growing stronger with each step. I close my eyes, putting my hands on two nearby trees. Shadows embed themselves in the ground, squirming down until they're anchored deeply, like roots. I extend my senses out, traveling through the trees and through the ground; it's only possible to find extremely powerful individuals in this manner. Impres is not nearly as powerful as Nyphra, or else I would have used it to find her when I was pursuing her. I feel two echoes back and I open my eyes, the shadows rising from the ground and retreating quietly.

"There are two possible locations." I tell her one of them. "You'll be going to that one." I nod to the orichalcum spear, and she holds it out to examine it in the sunlight. "You'll need that."

"What if she's at the location you'll be at? With as big of a deal as you're making out of this, I would think that you could benefit from some orichalcum as well." I nod and think it over; orichalcum can rarely be broken unless it's by another piece of orichalcum.

"You're right," I look at the slightly broken point of the spear and hold out my hand. "When you killed Skrymsli, there was a piece that was broken off; giants' bones tend to do that to things, even to orichalcum. Do you still have it?" Scarlett thinks for a moment then rummages through her pack, pulling out a small jagged piece of orichalcum, less than half the length of her own dagger.

"I kept it in case it could be put back on the spear," she says, and I take it.

"This is all I'll need," I look at Scarlett; I could say something to her, to give her confidence. She's faced things with me before, but she could possibly end up facing one of the more powerful entities in Legend Land, on her own. I put my hand on her shoulder and look her in the eyes. She nods and dips her head for a moment, putting her hand on my arm; all is said. I take my hand away and turn my back on her. "When she's dead, we meet back at the house." I sense Scarlett nod behind me, and I begin to walk away. The moment I detect that Nyphra is not actually at the location I'm going to, I will make my way to Scarlett as quick as I possibly can. Knowing that, I hope my location is where Nyphra is residing. I slip the orichalcum sliver into my pocket; a small piece like this still allows me to feel the shadows, though they are out of my control. All I need is to be able to detect them; I can feel their restlessness, their hunger. They were not satisfied with their last meal. I will allow them their satisfaction with Nyphra; I truly hope she is where I am heading.

I set my hand on a tree to steady myself, sucking in a quick breath; even though I am only carrying a small amount of orichalcum, it is still enough to reduce my stamina. The only thought that comforts me is that the orichalcum will effect Nyphra as well, though I'll have to get close to kill her. I plan on killing her with the orichalcum piece; I simply can't take any chances by using any other method. I must keep it close; if I lose it...Nyphra will be able to overpower me quickly.

The wind whistles above, rustling the leaves of the trees, shaking the branches. I look up and see a green leaf slowly floating down; I hold a hand out and the leaf lands on my hand. I stare at it for a moment, looking at its shiny surface and the thin, light green veins underneath its surface before the wind picks up again and blows it away. I continue walking through the forest; even with all of the time I've spent in the Kingdom specifically, walking its roads and forests, I have yet to explore all of the woods in the Kingdom. I come to the edge of the tree line and look out; thin, green blades of grass sway in the breeze and not too far off the beginning of the mountain ridges that shelter the northern borders of the Kingdom.

I make my way quickly across the grassy areas toward the mountains, not letting the orichalcum's effect on my stamina stop me. The sun beats down on my head and begins to warm up my body underneath my dark clothing. Even though the weather is on the colder side for the Kingdom, no matter what the season, with the sun out and multiple layers on, it's very easy to heat up quickly and possibly catch heat stroke. I stop for a moment and take the small sliver of orichalcum out of my pack, setting it down on the ground and walking several paces away until I can no longer feel the effect it has on me.

I feel the shadows slither up and over me, blocking me from the sun and allowing me to cool off. I take water out of my pack and drink heavily from it. My tongue feels dry and limp, almost like a shriveled pepper; I shake my head in disgust, putting the water back in my pack. Because Scarlett is mortal, she does not suffer from the effects of the orichalcum; her only limitations are her mortality, and that is not of her own choosing. In my case, though I will not age, it is still possible to kill me by even the most simplest of mortal means; that includes heat stroke. This is compounded by the fact that orichalcum, while extremely rare, can allow anyone to have the upper edge against me; even a sliver is enough to reduce me to mortal standards. The shadows hiss at me and I reach out, grabbing them, but this time to assure them rather than to harm them.

"You don't need to worry about me; I am still a very dangerous man. You will get a meal soon as well, I promise you that. Check your impatience for just a while longer, and you will get the meal you so desperately crave." The shadows hiss, content for now, and sink back into the ground, exposing me once again to the elements. I pluck the orichalcum from the ground, and the now-familiar feeling of detachment and weariness settles over me as I settle into the mindless repetition of moving one leg after the other. I keep the orichalcum clutched in my hand; I may have to use it at a moment's notice. The sun has passed its highest point by the time I see the cottage at the base of the mountains. As I get closer, I'm able to make out more details.

Several trees are bent over, forming the cottage; a door has been made out of several branches, and the same for the windows. The trees appear to be dead, and the tips of the branches are in a state of decay. They are still rooted, however, like a giant hand bent them over and keeps them there under pressure. Once I can see the glass of the windows clearly, I stop, setting the orichalcum down and once again walking away from it. I drink more water and notice with a start how hungry I have become; I glare at the sliver of orichalcum, barely distinguishable between the blades of grass. I reach into my pack and find only a small ration bar; it will do. I cannot afford to turn my nose up at any source of nourishment when nourishment is required; I quickly eat the ration bar and pick up the piece of orichalcum, making my way to the cottage.

"Not one step closer, thank you!" a woman's voice shouts. A small, thin person walks out of the house, covered in a heavy dark robe. There's no hair on the person's head, or anywhere on their body that is visible; angry red scars crisscross their head and extend down their throat. Filmy white irises gaze off blankly into space; blindness has struck. "I know who you are, and I have no business with you." The voice is a woman's, though I wouldn't have known it by her appearance; she looks completely genderless, almost like a separate species altogether.

"I want to talk," I say and she smirks, several of the scars wrinkling up on her long, pale face.

"I know you're lying," she says, revealing several chipped and pointed teeth. "I know what you're thinking at this very moment, Godkiller. You were just wondering how I could see you; and since you traveled all this way, I'll tell you. The answer is simple, young man: magic. Magic can do everything for me, serving in place of all of my dead senses. Well, almost everything," she says bitterly, feeling her face. "I found a way to achieve everlasting life, so long as I am not killed, though by that time the disease had taken a firm hold on my body. Thanks to my magic, I was eternally trapped in that one moment, with all of the disfigurements and pain that came with it. I know you share my curse—everlasting life. What is the price for yours?"

"You already know," I reply and she grins, letting out a sound halfway between retching and chuckling.

"I want to hear you say it though, young man,"

"I'm not here to discuss my past with you," I reply, setting my pack on the ground. "The High Queen has sent me to make sure that you don't do anything that might alert higher powers to what has happened recently."

"You mean you're here on that sadistic wench's orders to kill me so that nobody learns that wise, kind Tatiana banished me?" she says, more of a statement than a question.

"I'd prefer not to kill you," I say, taking a step forward. "I know how powerful you are, and I have no love for Tatiana. If you give me your word that you will not do anything that will threaten the High Queen's position, I will leave you be." I know she will not accept my offer; but on the slight chance that she does, it would be worth it to see Tatiana's face when she learns that her problem was solved in a way that did not end in Nyphra's death.

"No deal, young man," she says, shaking her head slightly. "I'm afraid I've already sent for an Enforcer to resolve the problem; he should be here shortly. I applaud your desire for a peaceful solution, though I share no such desire. Tatiana breached the balance; and anyone who has any association with her must be dealt with."

What a hopelessly extremist point of view, though I notice some of my own thinking within; I have changed, though. Not enough to prevent me from killing her, however.

"Then I'll have to make this quick," I reply, dashing forward. It's not fast enough, hindered as I am by the orichalcum, and roots snap up from the ground, wrapping around my feet. I'm able to keep my balance, and I unsheathe my sword, hacking at the roots. Nyphra yawns, waving her hand dismissively. A gust of wind slams into me, raising me up, and the roots extend, pulling me back to the ground. I slam into what feels like concrete and then begin to sink slowly into the ground.

"Fortunately for you, my curse leaves me weak in other arcane arts besides nature ones, the one thing that will weaken me also weakens you. How ironic."

The ground has nearly risen above my shoulders and I squirm, trying to get out. I strain and wrench my arm free from the ground, throwing the orichalcum shard at Nyphra. She dodges it easily and it thuds into one of the trees that make up her cottage. "You missed, you know."

"I'm well aware," I growl, and the shadows shoot up from the ground, yanking me along with them. I flip in the air over a root, and several tendrils of shadow shoot towards Nyphra. A wall of flame rises up, and the tendrils screech, slithering away, singed and smoking. I land on the ground and extend my hand; if the shadows desire a meal, they will assist me. The tendrils reappear indignantly and shoot through the wall of flames, which quickly disappears. Roots have wrapped around the shadows, holding them off; Nyphra hasn't moved once the entire time.

"I could have defeated you easily by now if I wasn't required to use such earthly magic. If I had dabbled and mastered the more abstract arts before my experiment 'succeeded', I could have easily killed you by now." Wind buffets me, nearly knocking me off my feet; I grit my teeth and dig my heels in, more tendrils of shadow appearing and wrapping around my arms, shooting themselves into the ground. The ground around them turns to liquid and the wind increases in force, flinging me into the air. I shoot my hand out, but the tendrils are buffeted back, wriggling useless in the air. I look up as the sky rumbles. Dark clouds swirl above, blocking out the sun, the wind tearing at my hair.

A flash of lighting streaks across the sky, and I pull out my sword, a tendril wrapping around it and connecting itself to the ones near Nyphra. Far below, I can still see her eyes widen, and too late she realizes what is about to happen; it's already out of her control. Even as she throws herself out of the way, lightning strikes the sword with a thunderous roar, like a blow from the gods themselves, and travels through the tendrils of shadow in a rippling current, exiting near Nyphra. It doesn't hit her directly, but strikes the ground near her, sending her flailing through the air. I suddenly find myself falling through the air and smoking tendrils wrap around my ankles, slowing my descent marginally and slinging me at Nyphra. I tackle her as she begins to stand, rolling across the ground until we slam into her cottage. I pull her up and slam her against the wall, her eyes fluttering.

"Why am I...so...weak?" she sputters, coughing up blood. The green shard of orichalcum shimmers, embedded in the wood, and her neck.

"You grew complacent in your position of power," I growl, my eyes searching her face. "I thought you were powerful; I was genuinely *worried* that you would pose a serious threat. In the end, you're no different than the others I've faced; you're a disappointment and an embarrassment to all practitioners of the arcane arts. I did not defeat you because I was more powerful, or because you were weak; I was more intelligent than you. You spend your eternity developing your magic, and your strategic mind has suffered." I hold her there, my arms trembling from the combination of not only my close proximity to orichalcum, but also through the effort of holding up Nyphra in my weakened state. As I wait for the life to drain out of her, I glare at her scarred, disfigured face; she was a disappointment. Scarlett could have easily killed her, and I was worried she would pose a serious threat; rarely do I overestimate someone, but it seems that was the case.

I squeeze her shoulders hard, the orichalcum digging into her neck deeper. I drop her to the ground, her eyes flicking underneath her eyelids. I kick her away from the orichalcum until I can no longer feel its effect. The shadows slowly rise up from the ground, hissing and snapping at her, but doing nothing. They turn to me, making an inquisitive hiss.

"Have at her," I say, and they turn to her, snapping. They begin by nipping at her exposing ankles and wrists gently, taking small bites of skin. Nyphra's eyes flutter open, and a gasp escapes her thin, pale lips; she already looks like a corpse. The shadows hiss gleefully and dive onto her in earnest, tendrils of shadow burrowing into her, biting and snapping. She screams, unable to do anything as she is devoured by the shadows. The scream finally stops, echoing throughout the empty plains and mountains like a pitiful wail. The shadows swirl around Nyphra and then sink back into the ground, leaving nothing behind; there was no sign she was ever there.

I wipe blood off my forehead with a finger, and a single tendril of shadow appears again, slowly wrapping around my finger, cooing. I remain absolutely motionless until it unwraps from my finger, the blood having disappeared as it lethargically slips away; they were useful in defeating her after all.

I feel a shudder of the earth underneath my feet, traveling up my entire body in one single shiver. The trees shake in the distance, the grass flattening as a gust of wind slams into me, and I'm barely able to keep my feet on the ground. The echo of a roar hits my ears, and my breath catches; Scarlett. Nyphra had sent for an Enforcer already; it must be locked onto her energy. With Nyphra dead, that only leaves the other energy source that reeked of her; Scarlett will be dealing with the Enforcer now. I screw my eyes shut and clench my fists, letting my shoulders lower; one thing after another stacks itself against me. I can't let Scarlett die, but the repercussions of killing an Enforcer...to say they would be great and painful would be an understatement. My eyes open, my breath coming out slow and loud to my ears; I can't let her die though, no matter what. One foot steps forward, almost without conscious thought; I will have to kill the Enforcer. My other foot moves forward, and then again, and again; I have to get there in time. I pick up speed, blurring across the plains; I will not let her die again!

I look into the clearing carefully, surveying it, holding the orichal-cum spear tightly; there's nothing there. Mister E sent me this way, there being a chance Nyphra was actually here, but she seems to be a no-show. I hear a rustle in the trees behind me and I turn quickly, thrusting the spear forward. There's a loud yelp and I stop quickly, my heart hammering; oh god.

"Gods!" Wilhelm shouts, holding a hand to his chest. "You almost impaled me!" *How often does he say that to you?* Just stop already. He bends down, collecting his basket of different herbs and fruits; he's out gathering?

"Don't sneak up on me like that!" I hiss. "What are you doing here anyway?"

"I always come in this area to gather my herbs; recently I've had to go in further to find the good stuff. There's some in the clearing, which is where I was heading. What are *you* doing here?" I lower the spear; he has to leave quickly.

"I'm here on a mission," I look around, leaning in close. "You have to go, *now.*"

He smiles, walking past me. "I will, as soon as I get some more herbs." He walks into the clearing and I spin, following him.

"Wilhelm you have to—" The ground rumbles and I turn, swearing. The earth shifts and churns in the middle of the clearing. Slowly, a large, earthen humanoid rises out of the ground, growling and rumbling. "Run," I whisper to Wilhelm who's frozen in place. "Run!" He turns but gets smacked back by another one of the things. It roars, and I roll out of the way, stopping near Wilhelm. I check his pulse and breathe a sigh of relief; he's alive, just unconscious. I turn to the two things who are making their way closer, rumbling and shifting. They appear to be earth golems, creatures created by magic to protect a space sacred to a magician. *Mister E's library?* Mister E's library.

"This is not going to be fun," I sigh as one charges at me. I rush in quickly and thrust my spear at the earth golem. The force of the impact on the spear knocks me to the ground, but the golem disappears in a cloud of ash. The other one charges at me, and I sweep the spear at its legs; it topples forward, and I spear it through the head. It too disappears in a cloud of ash. I stand up, wiping my hands off on my pants; that wasn't so hard. The ground rumbles again and several earth golems appear, roaring; oh gods, at least it couldn't get any worse. Above me there's a low rumbling and I hear the trees shaking and writhing, the air crackling with energy. *You spoke to soon.* I didn't notice! I level my spear as the golems charge me, a loud thunderous boom shattering the sky above me; I won't die here today!

CHAPTER
TWENTY-THREE

I race through the forest, hand clenched around my sword as the trees blur past; she is in danger. I gnash my teeth; how could I have been so stupid?! I will not let something like this happen again, not ever again. I speed into a clearing, my form a mere blur, slicing my sword at the large mass in front of me and I dig my heels in, coming to a halt. I quickly clench my fist and bring it up; tendrils wrap around the feet of the creature and sling it into the air; I spin and splay my hand, and the tendrils shoot from the ground, piercing the creature and holding it still. I slowly lower my hand, and the pierced creature lowers closer to the ground until it comes to the height where I can look into its icy blue eyes.

Thick, dark green scales cover its large reptilian form, the segmented plates covering the creature to the tip of its long, python-like tail; large metal gauntlets with needlepoint claws adorn its large hands. Several teeth jut out from its jaws, which widen into a grin when it looks at me, a long slimy pink tongue slithering out of its gaping maw that smells of putrid things and rotting flesh; some of the spit drips onto the ground and the grass sizzles, an acrid smell rising up. The tendrils move the alligator further away from me, keeping it eye level; this creature threatened Scarlett—nearly succeeded in killing her. I will extract the information I desire, then I will end this creature; it will not live beyond this day.

"Why hello there," it rumbles with a deep, smooth voice; obviously male. "I believe introductions are in order. I am the Investigator," I remain silent and he coughs. "And you are?" A dagger spins through the air from behind me, and I catch it before it can embed itself into one of the Investigator's eyes. I turn around, the tendrils of shadow moving the Investigator so that I can keep him in my sight; I walk closer to Scarlett and flip the dagger around, holding the blade and handing it to her. She takes it slowly, looking at the Investigator cautiously. She stands protectively over the form of a huddled young man, and I grit my teeth; him again.

"You cannot kill him yet; he still has information. He is an Enforcer, sent by gods to correct breaches in the balance; we have made an enemy of one and must be prepared for what will happen next. Stay out of this."

"He tried to kill me; I was holding him off until you showed up. I think now I'd like to finish him," Her glare is murderous, completely fixed on the Enforcer; perhaps I'll unleash her after I get the information I desire.

"Stay out of it," I repeat. She's never dealt with an Enforcer before; I want to handle this initially. She crosses her arms, but stands back, glaring at the Investigator, who clears his throat. "Yes?"

"I'd like to explain why I'm here now; there's been a breach in the balance, and I must correct it; that means that young man and woman have got to go, not you. I originally just had to kill the girl, but he sided with her, so he has to die as well. I'm just doing my job, you see—nothing personal. I'm sure you understand." He smiles, and I nod.

"I understand," I say, and Scarlett draws her dagger.

"You can't let him kill Wilhelm," she whispers, knuckles tightening on her dagger.

"I understand," I say again. "However, I cannot allow you to kill her." The Investigator's eyes narrow. "I would be fine with you taking him; he is of no use to me, but I cannot allow you to kill the girl. She is with me." If he insists upon taking that man, Wilhelm, I would not deny him, no matter the emotional angst to Scarlett, but he has threatened my student; such an action must not go unpunished.

"Perhaps some sort of deal could be made," the Investigator suggests, and I straighten up, looking him directly in the eye.

"You can have the man, but I will not budge on the girl. That is the only deal I will make; and if you refuse, you will receive neither kindness nor quarter from me."

"Is there nothing that you wish? I can give you nearly anything, simply name it." he says, and I smile ruefully, giving a soft, bitter laugh.

"So sure of yourself," I say, shaking my head. "You cannot give me what I desire; if you do not accept my offer, I will kill you for threatening the safety of my student." The Investigator sighs and shakes his large head.

"Diplomacy never works," he says sadly. "You must understand that you are siding with the girl and boy now, and thus I must kill you as well."

"I understand your sadness over the failure of diplomacy; believe me, I have no desire to make an enemy of your masters. Many beings more powerful than you have threatened to kill me, yet here I stand." I reply, drawing my sword. "I invite you to try though."

"Don't take this personally; I'm just doing my job," the Investigator says, and I thrust my sword at one of his icy blue eyes; his long pink tongue lashes out and I dodge quickly, my sword still on course. The Investigator twists his head quickly and my sword hits hard scales, bouncing off; he thrashes his head and catches me in the side, sending me tumbling backward. The Investigator thrashes his entire body, muscles rippling, and the tendrils strain, then shortly afterward, break. He rushes at me, wicked steel claws whistling through the air; I parry the blows and tendrils of shadow come from behind him, wrapping around his hands as I thrust my sword up toward the unprotected underside of his jaw. His snake-like tail wraps around one of my feet and hoists me into the air, and the tendrils disappear; a dagger spins through the air and imbeds itself in the tail, causing its grip to loosen and drop me.

I roll away as Scarlett dashes past me, plucking her dagger from the thrashing tail of the Investigator and running behind him; a tendril of shadow wraps around one of the Investigator's legs as he tries to turn. Scarlett leaps up and over his head, grabbing his jaw and swinging herself around, her dagger aimed at his eye. The Investigator's tongue lashes out and Scarlett drops down, rolling away as I block a blow from one of the Investigator's claws. I disengage, dodging as the Investigator slices at me, retreating next to Scarlett.

"Next time, cut the tail off," I tell her.

"A thank you would be nice," she retorts, and I clench my sword tighter.

"Thank you, next time cut the tail off." She flashes me a ferocious smile, then executes a roll in the opposite direction of mine as the Investigator lunges at us. We stand at the same time, though I notice before her the glance that the Investigator throws to Wilhelm, still unconscious.

"No!" Scarlett shouts, the Investigator's claws swiping down; I take a deep breath and time stands still for a moment. If I let the young man die, Scarlett will trust me less, and that carries its own risk. However, if I save the young man, then it just prolongs the battle and puts myself in danger. I let out my breath and reach out; a tendril wraps around the young man and yanks him back, slinging him behind me. The Investigator slices through empty air and then rushes at me; I parry several swipes of his claws, but he continues to drive me back. A tendril of shadow wraps itself around the young man and then slings him over the Investigator. The Investigator turns as Scarlett rushes forward to catch the young man; I lunge forward, imbedding my sword between two large scales in the Investigator's side.

The Investigator roars and turns quickly, wrenching the sword from my grip and sending me flying through the air; I slam into a tree and try to stand up as the large reptile turns toward me. My head throbs, and I barely register that blood is trickling down my face; my legs wobble as I try to stand and then collapse out from under me. The Investigator stalks toward me, and I reach out with one hand, gritting my teeth; the shadows don't move. I shake my head, and my eyes burn as I try once again; the shadows retreat away from me with a low hiss and I growl, shaking my head weakly, the shadows moving further away as the Investigator stalks closer.

"Not like this," I growl, gripping the grass with my hands tightly. Once again I try to stand; I make it to my feet and my vision swims, and I sway as the Investigator comes to a halt. I blink, my vision clearing; I take a step forward, but my legs give out and I drop to one knee. "No," I mutter shaking my head. "No! No! No! Not after everything, to end like this!" I pound the ground with my fist, and the Investigator chuckles.

"You threatened to kill me," he rumbles, the acrid smell of his saliva reaching my nostrils. "Many beings more powerful than you have threatened to kill me, yet here I stand." I look up at him and his mouth is split in a large smile. He raises his claws and I roar, leaping forward; his tail whips around and catches me in the side. I go flying through the air but manage to wrench my sword from his side as I go; I land on the ground and roll backward before slamming into another tree. My head slumps to the side, and I faintly register that footsteps are approaching; so this is how it ends. Despite my best attempts, darkness has finally won out and is coming to engulf me; seconds are all I have left.

"You said you were here because the balance had been breached," I say, and it's only now I realize I cannot move my limbs; from the neck down is numb and cold; I no longer care. Numbness, no feeling, is not a new sensation. Just as well that I cannot feel anything; I do not relish the prospect of suffering before the end. The Investigator stops and nods slowly, steel claws clinking against each other as he wiggles his fingers. "What was the breach? Was it Nyphra?"

"You mean you don't know?" The Investigator chuckles, and then laughs, his laughter booming out and echoing around the forest, sending birds flying from the trees. A single black crow circles overhead, cawing out; it can sense it will soon have a meal. "The famous, all-knowing Mister E doesn't know why I'm here?" I open my mouth and he cuts me off; the shadows beside me wriggle slightly as my anger mounts; if there was any possibility of me making it out alive,

I would take it and kill this rude beast right now. He is nothing but a thug, and I have been in a similar situation with thugs; it did not end well for them. "Oh yes, I know of you; Benson speaks often of you." My jaw clenches and the Investigator chuckles, arching where his eyebrow would be. "I know all about you Mister E, and I must say, I don't like you. Not one bit. That's why I'm going to kill you, and you're going to die without knowing; let that follow you into hell," he growls.

His steel claws slice through the air with a hum toward my neck, and the crow caws; I stare into his icy blue eyes calmly and the shadows hiss, but do nothing more. I have been abandoned in my time of greatest need; I will die alone; and after years of fighting it, the darkness will engulf me. I have been abandoned before; why should death be different?

The claws never reach my neck; something is stopping them. I blink and notice Scarlett, standing over me, blocking the attack with her dagger. Her heels dig into the dirt and sweat pours off her skin with the strain.

"Move," she growls, her arms beginning to tremble as the Investigator's claws slide slightly along her dagger, metal screeching against metal.

"I can't," I reply, and she turns to look at me, her green eyes filled with determination and resolve. I look deep into them, and they go soft as Scarlett realizes she will die here as well, that she will die trying to protect me; and in her eyes, she forgives me. She understands, and she forgives me for that; the Investigator's other hand comes down and his claws pierce Scarlett through her chest. He lifts her up and flings her away; her mangled body flies through the air, red hair streaming around her, blood spraying through the air and coating the trees.

My head snaps up to the Investigator, and there's a flash of white; heat flushes into my body, into my bones, and with it pain. Immeasurable, immense pain, but I move; I stand up quickly, and the shadows shoot from behind me, emboldened by my rage, impaling the Investigator and sending him up toward the sky. He is slammed back into the ground, and I'm standing above him; his tongue flicks out as his mouth opens to cry out in pain and I grab it, his acidic saliva burning into my skin. The smell of burning flesh fills the air, and I rip out his tongue; he screeches and I growl, stomping my foot. Shadows impale him again and again, and his screams fill the air; I grind my heel into the ground, and the shadows burrow and twist into him.

My sword is in my hand, and I stab into the Investigator and his screams stop; I stay there, my sword embedded in his thick hide. The image of Scarlett being whipped through the air flashes before me and I scream; I do not roar, I scream, wrenching my sword out and bringing it down. I bring it down again and again. The sky darkens as I wreak havoc on the Investigator's corpse; a high-pitching screaming reaches my ears, and I realize it's me. I'm still screaming, and my hoarse cries are joined by the hissing of the shadows as they rip and tear at the remains of the beast; we have both suffered an immeasurable loss. I drop to the ground and tear at it with my own hands, tossing them behind me as I rip away chunks of flesh and scales. Only when my hands hit the ground underneath do I stop; there is nothing left of the Investigator's corpse. My hands are covered in guts and gore; I am stained in it. I look down at my hands and laugh; it's here! It's all here! I laugh and screech, rolling around in the blood-soaked grass; death! Death is here! Death is all around me! Why fight it any longer?! Everything is gone!

I laugh maniacally and lick my palms, as if trying to quench an insatiable thirst; I see the pale skin underneath the red and stop; red on pale. Scarlett. I feel a strange tightening in my chest and slowly turn my head to look at the mangled corpse of Scarlett, resting on the ground in a pool of blood; I crawl slowly over to her and cradle her head in my hands. Her eyes are dull now and stare vacantly into space; her blood soaks my hands, turning them red once again. That is how they should stay, red, with blood; blood that is never mine. I clutch her to my chest; it is never my blood.

"Simiel," I groan, closing my eyes and clutching the still-warm body to me. I feel a hand on my shoulder and whip around, ready to tear apart whoever it is that dares to disturb me. A woman looks at me and smiles, her auburn hair flowing in loose curls around her angelic face, her bright eyes looking into mine.

"It will be okay," she says softly, kneeling down in the grass, ruining her white dress with blood. "You will move on, you always do. You will adapt and survive; that is in your nature." I have no urge to hurt this woman, and she pulls me close, putting my head to her chest and I close my eyes, listening to her heart. "I am here to make that transition easier for you; I am here to help you forget so you can move on quicker, so you can continue with your plan unhindered."

I push away from her and she falls onto her back, blood splashing up from the grass and soil; how does she know of my plan?

"Who are you?" I demand, scooting back and staying next to Scarlett's body.

"I'm here to—"

"*Who are you?!*" I roar, and she closes her mouth, responding slowly and carefully.

"My name is Evermore," she says with a smile, and I slowly lower my sword, which I hadn't realized I had raised. I sheath my sword; I don't sense that she's going to be a threat, and I pick Scarlett up, cradling her in my arms. "What are you doing?"

There is no reason to relinquish that information; I take a step toward the dark forest, and she calls out. "Wait!"

I stop, one hand tangled in Scarlett's red hair, and I keep it loose.

"You can't save her; she's already dead. All you can do now is forget about her."

"I cannot forget about her," I growl and I turn around, glaring at her. "I don't need your help!" She opens her mouth and I roar, "*Go away!*" The shadows rise above me, illuminated by the bright moon, tendrils writhing, but Evermore stands her ground, looking at me calmly.

"You're in denial," she says and I growl, the shadows swarming around her. "You need to—"

"Don't tell me what I need to do!" I shout, and several tendrils of shadow shoot toward her; I grit my teeth, and my legs wobble as the tendrils are vaporized by a wall of bright white light that appears in front of her. The shadows inch backward slowly, and I step forward; their retreat halts, and the shadows begin to creep warily toward her, with the same hesitation they had showed the Investigator.

Evermore looks at me thoughtfully, then continues speaking, slowly, as if she's puzzling over something. "Maybe you don't need to forget her," she says, and the shadows continue to creep toward her. "Maybe I can help you move on and continue with your plan; you can honor her memory and remember her, give her a proper send off."

The shadows pause in their advance, hissing quietly, like thousands of murmuring voices.

"I don't need your help to do that," I retort, gritting my teeth, the shadows hissing louder in agreement.

"No you don't," she says, taking a step forward, and the shadows retreat as she walks toward me. "But I can make it easier for you; doing this alone will be difficult." She's standing in front of me now and puts her warm hand on my cheek. "You went through this alone once, but you don't have to do it again."

Simiel.

The thought flashes through my mind without provocation, and I close my eyes; her beautiful dark hair, her orange eyes flashing green when irritated, a playful smile on her lips. Her beautiful white dress, fluttering in the breeze; I take a deep breath and can nearly smell the fragrant scent of wildflowers. Her toes curl in the bright flowers, white dress flowing. White dress being ripped apart, her pale skin marred by ugly dark bruises and long red cuts. Blood seeping through the thin cloth of her dress; red, warm blood all over her pale skin, glistening in the moonlight. Red on pale; Scarlett; my eyes open, and I can see my reflection in Evermore's eyes, my black eyes flashing a bright orange with shoots of green. I failed once, I shall not do it again; there is still time.

"I lost someone once," I whisper, stepping backward away from the comforting warmth of Evermore's hand as Scarlett's cold, pale one brushes my arm, falling and remaining limp by her side. "I will not let that happen again; I can still save her."

"Why do you even care?" Evermore asks, stepping forward, a hint of anger in her voice. "Your sister is dead; trying to save this... this girl won't bring her back."

I look at Evermore coldly, and the shadows move closer to her, hissing and clawing at the ground; we care in our own ways, each of us. These shadows...they loved her, as I still love her; I can still save her, I know I can.

"This *woman* is my student," I retort fiercely, taking a step forward. "I have invested more patience and more energy in her than nearly anything else in my otherwise-useless life. This *woman*," I gently set Scarlett down in her own pool of blood, slowly rising, my eyes on Evermore's, "gave my life meaning; my mission was just that—a mission. With Scarlett by my side, it became something more; it had more...purpose, more life in it. This *woman* has earned a privilege many are unaware even exist; my love."

I close the distance between myself and Evermore, a hand wrapping around her throat. The pain is instant and blinding, white hot light coursing through me; the sensation is familiar, almost rejuvenating in my otherwise-numb body. I grit my teeth and lift her off the ground, her toes barely scraping the grass, slamming her against the tree; she looks at me calmly and the shadows hiss, crawling up my arm toward her face. The shadows hold her eyes and mouth open, crawling into her throat and nose, wriggling around to slither inside her ears. She starts screaming, fear lighting up her eyes. She begins to glow brightly, her eyes rolling back into her head.

"Do not *dare* bring up my sister again!" I roar, slamming her against the tree again, and her head shakes around limply. "Do not ever talk about my student! Do not let the name of any of those I love cross your lips." I put my lips right next to her ear, my voice a low growl, reverberating through the shadows. My mind is in another place, the shadows crawling in my skull as much as hers, and I welcome them. "You think simply because you have this...light, that you are safe? Is that it?" I chuckle, and several tendrils of shadow claw at her exposed skin, creating small gashes in her tan skin, drops of blood running down her arms. "You are vulnerable, weak, exposed; you have power, but you do not use it. You let it control you; this…light, has mastered you. This harsh, painful light has blinded you and turned you into a mere slave. It has coddled you so you remain blind, so you notice nothing; the darkness does no such thing. It does not coddle; it forces you to keep your eyes open to everything, even the pain. You have the potential to be strong though—let us see if that can happen, shall we?"

The shadows retreat from her quickly, and I drop her to the ground; she lays still for a moment before stirring, looking up at me wearily, her eyes not quite so bright any longer; I will remove the light from you. I will obliterate any illumination from your soul until it is as nonexistent as mine; I will ensnare you, and you will be as soulless as me. I will paint you black.

"Why are you doing this to me?" Evermore asks in a hoarse whisper; I raise my hand and she flinches, but I just put it on her head, tangling it in her hair.

"Someone once told me that through the fires of hell are wills of iron born," I say, and I grip her hair harder and she winces, tilting her head back in an attempt to ease the pain. "I live by that philosophy."

I let go of her and walk over, picking Scarlett up gingerly. "You now understand that you have much more power at your fingertips than you thought, correct?" I turn and she nods slowly, the white light around her fluxing in different levels of brightness. "You will take me to this location, and then I will reveal to you the full extent of your power."

She pauses for a moment, then slowly stands up, her entire body shaking, and the light around her slowly retreats within her body.

"How do I know you won't kill me?" she asks, doing her best to smooth out her dress, red with blood and torn by the shadows.

"Even if I said I would, would that really matter to you?"

Each obstacle requires a different path to be taken; violence cannot always be used—it has its place, but Scarlett made me realize that other ways are needed. Sometimes more subtle methods are required; for each new enemy, there is a new weakness. It's important to find the weakness within someone, or else risk them gaining leverage; sometimes the weakness is violence. Other times, it is the lure of power.

She walks toward me and puts her hand on my shoulder, warmth seeping into me; for everyone there is a weakness, even for someone who flaunts their power.

"No, it wouldn't," she says softly, looking at me with her bright eyes. I need her to save Scarlett while she can still be saved—Scarlett is my mission now. Outside her field of vision, my hand clenches itself into a fist in Scarlett's hair as I smile; I will do whatever it takes to complete this mission. White light engulfs my vision, and then darkness ensues.

CHAPTER TWENTY-FOUR

I stand in a dark, dimly lit corridor; I am perfectly clean, and I stand up straighter before noticing Scarlett is no longer in my arms.

"I trust you have not been here before," I say; I would prefer to be here alone, but this place is outside of my normal reach. Death is no stranger to me, though certain parts of the Underworld are out of reach for many, even a Godkiller.

"No," Evermore says, perfectly clean and healthy, not a scratch on her; I long to change that. She intruded upon me, but her intrusion was a gift—one that I intend to use. "What exactly is this place?"

For someone of such power, her ignorance of the cosmos—of its places, hidden and in plain sight, of its workings—it truly astounds me.

"The passageway to the Underworld," I retort, walking down the corridor; voices hiss from the shadows, and Evermore opens her palm, a small ball of white shining light illuminating our surroundings. A gruesome, grey figure leaps forward, shrieking and howling; Evermore jumps back, but I remain unmoved. The thing thrashes at its bindings, however it is securely shackled to the wall and no threat to me. In this forsaken place, in this darkness stained with grey things and nightmares, the shadows are at home, and I feel their contentment as my own.

Evermore steps closer, peering at it curiously; it screams, lunging forward at her, and I pull her back. She tumbles back into me, breathing heavily. I let go of her and move on, trusting she will catch up; something that is of no threat to me obviously is much more of a threat to someone of lesser intelligence; Scarlett never would have made the same mistake. I begin to bring my feet down with a little more force than necessary with each step; I have been so careless—so careless, with everyone around me! Another shriek comes from my side and Evermore turns, shining her light upon it; a small, thin, pale child with long dark hair wearing grey rags is shackled to the wall.

"Help…me…" it whispers in a hoarse voice, looking at me; its dark eyes flash, and I clench my jaw. Shadows wriggle toward the child and shield it from Evermore's light; screaming can be heard and blood begins to seep down the wall, but I turn sharply on my heel and start walking again. This nightmare sphere will play tricks on the mind. It will try to confuse me; but with my resolve, the conjured fears cannot sway me.

"Why didn't you help that child?" Evermore asks, staying a pace behind me.

"Some things are worth saving," I reply, stopping and turning to her, the screams still echoing down the hall. "Some things need to die," I say, grabbing the ball of light in her hand and crushing it, the bright white light disappearing. "The corridor is lit enough to be able to see; no need to investigate anything that should stay hidden—it will only slow us down."

"You said the darkness forces you to keep your eyes open, but maybe you just don't want to see clearly."

I ignore her and just keep moving. She will be silent soon enough; but for now, she must be tolerated. Some part of me tells me she is right; but with the assistance of the shadows inside, I crush it; I will blind myself if necessary so that others cannot use my eyes against me. As we continue to walk, the hallway begins to fill with a dark, tar-like substance. I continue walking through it easily, keeping my gaze set straight ahead; it takes a moment for me to realize I am the only one making any progress. I turn around to see Evermore trying to walk, tugging her legs in vain at the black ooze that engulfs her body up to her waist.

"How am I supposed to walk through this?" she asks, white light glowing around her but doing nothing to the ooze.

"Focus on one thing; this thing must drive you, fill your being. It must be the reason you move—the reason you continue on at all. If your mind is not consumed with thoughts of this thing, you will not make any progress." I turn and set my gaze straight ahead; Simiel.

I hold her close, breathing in her scent—lavender and wildflowers. It fills my nostrils and makes my head cloudy, filled with visions that make me sway. I caress her soft, pale face, and our eyes flash at the same time. I put a finger to her small lips and hide her away; I know they are coming, and I am not strong enough to protect her. I must keep her hidden or else she will die, and I will not continue living. Her breathing is slow and steady; she knows better than to be loud. I close the door and creep throughout the house; their footsteps are loud enough to wake the dead, and I track them easily. I remove the small knife I hid in my boot, my hands slick; I lick the salty sweat off my lips nervously and crouch down, creeping into the same room.

"They're not here," a gruff voice growls, and there's a loud noise as one of the intruders stumbles into a wooden chair hidden in the darkness. A loud swear pierces the brief silence, and I skirt the man's stumbling form, my eyes already adjusted to the dark. He is joined by two more, all large and bulky, all stumbling about through the house like elephants. I see the sharp outline of an ax and follow the man quietly, not even daring to breathe. He sticks his head into one of the rooms, and I creep silently behind him. The stink of him mixed with the scent of rain hits me, and I lift the grey rag of a shirt over my nose. I grip the small knife tighter in my thin hand, my heart hammering so loud I'm afraid he might hear; I have to do this. I am a hunter, from a family of hunters; we are the last of our kind. I must do this for Simiel—anything I do must be to protect Simiel, no matter the cost.

I dash forward, slicing at his calves; he howls, turning around, grabbing me by my thick mane of dark, knotted hair.

"Why, you little—"

I bite deep into his hand and he swears, jerking it back. I stab my knife into his other hand and grab the ax when it clangs loudly onto the floor. The steel of the blade embeds itself deep into his leg and he cries out, dropping down. I yank the knife out of his hand, jamming it into his eye. I keep my mouth clamped shut, sheathing and unsheathing the knife in him until he stops jerking and twitching. I gasp out, my stomach heaving, but it has nothing to spit up. I wipe my mouth and grimace, the coppery taste of blood wetting my lips.

I shakily get to my feet then collapse onto the corpse, my thin shoulders trembling; I…killed a man. I *had* to do it—to protect Simiel, I had to! I did it…I did it for her. I did it for her, Simiel…

A blade screams toward me through the air, and I wrench my feet from their stationary position in the ooze, drawing my sword and parrying the blow, sliding my sword along the blade and sending my elbow into the throat of my attacker. I run my sword through the chest of my attacker, and it drops down, dead. I turn to see Evermore battling a large creature with wings, hissing and spitting at her as she throws bolts of white light at it. I reach out my hand and the shadows respond, rising up and capturing the creature, pulling it down into the muck and its cold, murky embrace. It shrieks and screams out before being pulled under; the ooze bubbles for a few moments, then grows still once more. Evermore turns to me, and her light glows brighter for a moment before the scene suddenly shifts.I turn around quickly, pointing my sword at the open door before me.

"Why is all of this happening?" Evermore asks me, and I slowly take a step toward the open door.

"Retrieving a soul from the Underworld is not as easy as Orpheus made it out to be," I say, stepping through the door. Evermore walks in past me and the door slams shut behind her, disappearing; I pull her back before she can take another step, and she looks down. A dark, yawning chasm lays open before her, screams of agony and pain echoing off the hot stone walls, bursts of fire shooting up occasionally. Evermore begins to walk toward the small, narrow wooden bridge that spans the chasm to the other side, and I kneel down on the edge of the chasm. I put my hand on the rock, but the shadows remain silent and unmoving; some things cannot be done the easy way.

"Come on!" Evermore calls, and I put my hand on the edge of the rock, squeezing it until it cracks.

"That is not the way you go to retrieve a soul," I warn and begin to climb down the chasm; Evermore looks down at me and I up at her. After a moment, she follows my lead and begins to climb down with surprising ease; we make the descent at roughly the same speed. The rock grows hotter beneath my hands and feet as we near the bottom. I finally make it to the bottom and it's sweltering hot, sweat dripping off my skin, slicking the inside of my gloves; Evermore looks down at her feet, and I follow suit.

We stand on a writhing sea of bodies, screaming out and crying, reaching out for us with desperate hands. I begin walking toward the river of magma beyond this sea of the damned, stomping hard on anything that reaches out for me. I feel a thin hand on my shoulder and I turn, growling as one of the bodies grasps at me. I tear at the hand, but it's joined by another and another, the sea of bodies surging toward me, trying to engulf me. Hands grab at my clothes, my limbs weakened from the climb and the heat, my throat parched. It feels like a thousand hands are grabbing my throat and more hands grab my ankles, pulling me into the mass; I reach out, clawing at the ground, desperately trying to fight my way above as I'm quickly devoured by the horde of screaming, writhing bodies.

I feel myself falling, surrounded by darkness, then I feel sensation slip away from me all at once. I feel nothing around me, or underneath me; I can feel nothing; I cannot see if there are any clothes left on me, nor can I feel them. There are no sights or smells; I reach out with my senses, trying to detect something, but there is only nothing. Suddenly I feel something solid collide with my feet and I crumple, sprawling out on the solid thing beneath me. I shake my head; I heard nothing when I landed. I feel distinctly the vibrations of the screams within me now, the echoes from the writhing of the bodies in my very bones, shaking me to my very core, yet I hear nothing. The screams are there—I can feel them now—but I hear nothing;

I do my best to stand and suddenly tilt to the left before collapsing once again on the ground. I try to reach out, but it feels like my hand is disjointed from my body; I grasp at the ground and feel something smooth and cold beneath my fingers. Not quite metallic, more slippery like plastic, and I latch onto the cooling sensation that erupts when my fingers come into contact with the surface. I latch onto this sensation as my stomach battles with itself to keep me from retching all over the floor.

My mind battles with the incomprehensible fact that there are no sounds and that my body will not obey my commands; I do my best to curl my left hand that is in contact with the floor, and my right arm merely twitches in response. I growl and feel the vibrations within my chest, tremulations within my very bones, yet my ears detect nothing and my world seems to spin. I can no longer tell if I am lying face down or face up, or whether I am lying down at all; my breath comes in quick gasps that I cannot detect, and I suddenly wonder if I am even breathing at all. I open my mouth and a scream issues forth, my vocal cords going raw from the effort, but my ears detect nothing.

I stop and suddenly retch over the smooth surface of the floor, and the smell hits my nose. The smell makes my stomach turn again and makes my eyelids flutter, invoking a subconscious response from my gag reflex, yet nothing comes out. I can taste the bitter flavor in my mouth and I spit, wrinkling my nose and twisting my mouth into a grimace from the multiple unpleasant sensations. I try to scoot away from the vomit and end up partially rolling and flopping instead, though fortunately away from the puddle of puke. My eyelids flutter again, and I realize they are closed; with a great effort akin to that of wrenching open the earth and forming a canyon, my eyelids slowly pry themselves apart.

Bright white light hits my retinas, my pupils contracting. The sensation is almost surreal as I struggle to sit up and finally manage to do so, slowly surveying my surroundings. As my vision adjusts, I find myself in a long, white hallway with no visible lighting fixtures or an end to the hallway in sight. I notice that the smell of vomit is gone, but the bitter taste in my mouth remains and my stomach feels no less empty. I turn around slowly, my vision swimming, but I cannot find the vomit anywhere. I slowly run my hands over the cool, slick floor, and a chill comes over me. Clenching my fist, I feel my nails hit skin. Where are my gloves? I squeeze tighter, feeling the pulsing of blood in my veins beneath my fingers, my nails making deep indentions in my warm, scarred palms.

I continue turning around, trying to get my bearings when I see Evermore. She lies face down, sprawled out, her short, thin white dress immaculately clean once more; not even the lace on the bottom edge is torn. Her short sleeves do not cover much of her thin, tan arms, and her back seems to stretch against the thin fabric with every intake of breath. Her long, tan legs spill out from the dress, and my eyes trace the curves down to her white sandals; my vision travels back up her body to rest on her auburn hair, spilled out over her back and covering her face. I take a deep breath and the faint, but unmistakable, scent of wildflowers trickles into my nose and down my throat like a soothing balm.

"I never thought you were one to ogle, especially a lady. Seems we learn new things all the time," a scratchy, hoarse voice says from behind me. I stand up shakily and slowly, my vision swimming, and I feel my body sway from side to side as I turn around to the direction of the voice. A tall, black figure stands before me; it stands on two legs and is the same shape as a human, though instead of skin or any discernible features, there is just a long stretch of darkness covering its body, like a dark canvas. On the face there are no other features other than a large red smile, red paint splashed onto the canvas.

I take a step forward, my leg buckling as soon as it comes back into contact with the floor, and I nearly fall. The figure chuckles and I grit my teeth, standing tall and clamping down on the unpleasant flipping sensations within my stomach.

"Then again, she is very attractive, though not as attractive as this young beauty I just caught."

A single dark tendril comes out of the figure's back, slipping into the white floor like it was water. The tendril removes itself slowly from the floor, and a bright red lock of hair can be seen. More slowly reveals itself; a head appears from the floor, and then the rest of the body is suddenly yanked out by the tendril. I make no move towards Scarlett—instead, I stay perfectly still, my eyes intently looking at her deathly pale face and closed eyelids before my ears detect a soft, slow intake of breath from her direction. Her chest moves only a mere fraction, but enough to let me know she is alive.

Without warning, relief crashes through my body, but I quickly clamp down on the sensation and keep my eyes fixed on Scarlett, even as the figure begins to talk. I must stay focused here.

"This young redhead here is attractive but quite the screamer. A remarkably high pain tolerance though; it took every ounce of skill I had to illicit any sort of vocal reaction from her; but once I did, it didn't stop—thrashing her head around, that hair flying, as she screamed her soul out, her entire body tense. But that wasn't anything compared to what happened next. She started crying and begged; she begged like a blubbering child—she begged for you to come and help her. 'Oh Mister E, please help me! *Please!*' It was pathetic, though, really," the figure said, chuckling.

I clench my jaw briefly before relaxing it and my entire body; I have come all this way to get Scarlett, and I will not have her life extinguished because I cannot control my temper and lash out.

"What, no reaction; nothing? I knew you were cold, but this is really a new low for you."

"What do you want, Mutovinatum?" I ask, turning my attention from Scarlett to Mutovinatum.

His smile grows wider; I keep my voice even, my body loose and relaxed, despite my mounting fury. "It's been so long since you said my name," Mutovinatum coos, a tendril of darkness reaching out and caressing my face slowly.

"How are you here? You are supposed to be powerless," I say, and the tendril wraps itself around my neck, applying a bit of pressure but I remain still, staring at Mutovinatum.

"Yes, that's what you would like, isn't it? For me to be powerless, weak and destitute; is this not enough for you? I'm still trapped inside that prison you made for me!" Mutovinatum's voice has dropped in pitch to a low growl, and I can feel the vibrations through the tendril.

"Then how are you here?" my gaze flicks briefly back over to Evermore; I can stall until I feel capable of moving, at least.

"I may be trapped, but I have ways of getting things done; as much as you may believe this is the case, you are not all-knowing. Even your designs have loopholes, and I am more than willing to exploit them; do not forget you learned your cunning ways and trickery from me. Also—" the tendril squeezes my neck tightly for a brief moment before beginning to pull away; it halts for a moment and Mutovinatum frowns, before the tendril slithers away with a parting caress on my chin. "You stole your power from me, though I will always have a small hold on that."

"You make me repeat myself," I say, shaking my head slightly. "What do you want?"

Several tendrils wrap themselves around Scarlett, and Mutovinatum makes a disapproving noise.

"I think we've had enough questions out of you for now." The tendrils move, and I can hear the sound of them slithering along Scarlett's clothes, tightening their grip; I nod, and the squeezing continues for a moment before they stop. "I'll be asking the questions, and you will answer them," Mutovinatum states. "First: why did you journey all the way to the Underworld to save this girl?"

I grit my teeth, glaring at Mutovinatum when I hear the sound of the tendrils tightening, and I relent, speaking. "She's my student," I growl; there is no need to give away any information that is not explicitly asked for. I even out my voice so I don't give Mutovinatum any reason to do anything rash. "She's a major investment."

"Still so technical I see," Mutovinatum says chuckling, nodding. "I assume you got here through her?"

A tendril slithers over to Evermore, moving a piece of hair from her face; Mutovinatum hisses and the tendril recoils immediately, smoking. I feel a small amount of satisfaction but quickly banish that so it doesn't show on my face. "What is she?" Mutovinatum hisses, red mouth twisted into an angry snarl.

"I have no idea," I respond calmly, and Mutovinatum growls, tendrils circling around Evermore like sharks having caught the scent of blood.

"You didn't answer the question!"

"Perhaps you should ask better questions then," I retort, and the tendrils tighten around Scarlett. A sharp snap echoes through the air; her eyes flutter open, and she gasps before the pain hits her. She groans and tries to move, but the tendrils squeeze tighter. There's no hesitation as I rush forward, hand extended, and the tendrils halt their progress. Mutovinatum now stands a mere foot away, and the red mouth is once again smiling.

"You have a weakness now I see," Mutovinatum laughs, a sharp, grating sound that sets my teeth on edge. "You used to be invincible; with me, there was nothing you couldn't accomplish."

"There was one thing you could never get me," I growl, and Mutovinatum sighs, nodding slowly.

"Yes, I'll admit that I could never give you that. But really—are you closer now than you were before you sealed me away? I feel like you've taken a step backward…or maybe you ran in the opposite direction, rather. Now you allow yourself to get emotionally attached to this…*girl?*" Mutovinatum spits, growling. "I can manipulate you so easily now; you have a weakness that is beyond your control. Her life could be threatened, and you would risk yours to try and save it. You journey into the Underworld simply to retrieve this lost soul! She is lost, you know. More lost than you even know—she is a burden to you! Such weakness."

Weakness? I am being accused of having a *weakness?* I look at that red smile, and a high pitched whining fills my ears—that red smile. It fills my vision, and my sight begins to go red; I feel a growl deep within my bones and then I am moving, rushing at Mutovinatum. My hands pass through Mutovinatum like smoke, and I feel a tendril smack into my side, sending me flying. I land and skid along the cool floor; when I look up, Mutovinatum is standing before me. He brings a hand down to backhand me, and I raise an arm to block it, but the hand goes through my arm before it connects with my face, sending me careening onto my back.

"Oh how the mighty have fallen," Mutovinatum growls, stepping to the side so I can see the tendrils squeezing Scarlett tighter, and she drifts into unconsciousness once more, the pain obviously too much to bear in her current state.

I will not let him harm her anymore! I swing my legs at Mutovinatum's legs, but they simply pass through and several tendrils wrap themselves around me, keeping me down.

"Such pathetic display of human emotion and weakness," Mutovinatum says distastefully, red mouth pulled down into a grimace.

"This is not weakness," I hiss, and Mutovinatum chuckles, kneeling beside me.

"You are trapped, your student is dying, and the vessel that brought you here is in no condition to save you. And you still say this is not weakness?" Mutovinatum strokes my cheek with a sharp talon gently, barely cutting the skin. "I fail to see your logic."

"She saved me," I say, looking at Scarlett. "If it were not for her, I would be dead. She gave me purpose."

"Purpose?" Mutovinatum spits disdainfully, waving his hand dismissively.

"I may not understand humans," I say, struggling under my oppressive bonds as they begin to constrict around me, "but I understand human emotion and the power behind it. You do not let these emotions control you, but rather you control them. If you are able to manage this, you can have the drive to accomplish anything."

"Is that what has driven you all along? Human emotion? No wonder you are failing so miserably," Mutovinatum chuckles, slapping my cheek lightly. "Though pray tell, what human emotion drives you? Is it hate or envy? Possibly jealousy or greed?"

I look into Mutovinatum's blank face, save for the ghastly red mouth, and I square my shoulders, my bonds loosening slightly; I hear another crack and know both of Scarlett's legs are broken, but that changes nothing for me at this point. I can save her, but not if I let Mutovinatum know what he is doing to me; I must keep myself centered.

"The human emotion that drives me," I growl, digging my fingers into my palms, squirming as the bonds begin to loosen slightly once more, "is love."

Mutovinatum chuckles, standing up. "Love? Oh that *is* rich! Love!" His splattered mouth grows into a wider grin. "And what do you, broken, soulless little man, know of love?"

"I know love as a driving force—how it can urge one to do amazing, impossible things. I know love," I squirm subtly against the tendrils, my fingers slowly stroking them underneath me, "as a means to an end, as a lie that is told; I know love as something true. I know human love as something that is forced between two creatures that should not be able to feel it."

The shadows slowly begin to uncoil under my ministrations, cooing so softly that I can barely hear it. "I know the feeling of love, ripped away, torn unwillingly from my heart; I know how it feels to spend millenia unloving, uncaring. Love is not something that you choose, and it is not something you can fight; you cannot control love." The tendrils slip away, stroking me as they disappear.

"Your love is false. I know you, and you do not feel love." Mutovinatum growls; I roll as a tendril of shadow appears, spearing itself into the floor where I had laid just a moment before.

"Perhaps I do not feel love, but I know its power. The love of a mother for her son," I leap forward to dodge more tendrils, Mutovinatum's mouth twisted into a snarl. "The love of those too young to fully understand it," I say, grabbing the tendrils as they lash out at me. My grip is firm but not crushing, the shadows wriggling at me. "The love of a brother for his sister." The tendrils slip down from my hands, despite Mutovinatum's frustrated growls. "Love is as useful as any emotion—fear, greed, jealousy. But humans motivated by love will go to any length; love does not have the same limitations as fear. Perhaps I do not feel love or understand it, but I recognize its power, and power is something I am quite familiar with."

I reach out with one hand, and the tendrils around Scarlett disappear, slinking into the floor. Mutovinatum growls, mouth open, revealing a gaping dark maw full of teeth built to rend flesh from bone like razors. Mutovinatum rushes at me, arms now long, thin, inky black blades that are being swung at my neck and chest. I step back, dodging, sending several tendrils shooting at Mutovinatum's chest, but they slip right in and I gasp, feeling like part of me was just ripped away. I stumble back as Mutovinatum slices at me once again, several tendrils appearing from the ground to wrap around Mutovinatum, but they are just absorbed into the dark canvas that makes up Mutovinatum's body, save the awful red mouth plastered onto the face. I throw my arm up as one of the blade arms comes down at me, but no tendril responds to my call. The blade sinks into my arm, biting bone before I fall back, blood seeping down my forearm.

"You preach about love," Mutovinatum growls, swinging the blades at me, and I roll out of the way, pushing myself up and retreating back. "Yet when the die are cast, those whom you love desert you."

Several tendrils appear from behind me, but I turn and grab them all with one hand; they hiss and writhe but soon slither into my arm with a contented purring sound, easing the pain of my injury. Mutovinatum snaps angrily, lunging at me. I step backward quickly, ducking to his side, aiming a kick at his ankle. My foot fades right through and I continue the motion into a roll in order to avoid decapitation.

"You stole your power from me! It is *mine!*"

"You say I stole this power, but it never belonged to you." I hold out my hand, a wall of shadow appearing as several more tendrils shoot out, but the wall absorbs them. "You stole from the Queen of Darkness that which was never yours."

Mutovinatum roars, slashing at me with the blades, but again I bring up a wall of shadow; Mutovinatum slips right through it, but I am already several feet away. "It was always mine!"

He spins around quickly, slashing at me, but I duck and then drop to the ground in one smooth motion, rolling away and coming up near Scarlett. I wrap several tendrils around her and sling her across the floor, her body sliding across the slick, cool surface, bumping into Evermore; I leap at Mutovinatum to stop him from pursuing her. The thought of Mutovinatum capturing Scarlett once more—of torturing her, of her begging for it to stop—the thought of Mutovinatum's dark, cold hands touching her face…the thought burns through my mind, and I collide with Mutovinatum. He turns around, mouth agape with shock, and I grab his head, slamming it against the floor before sinking my hands into the inky dark canvas of Mutovinatum's chest, my hands sinking in to my elbows. I grab and twist inside as the demon screams.

"I will not let you take her from me," I gasp out through heavy breaths, twisting my hands inside him deeper. "You took her once," my grip tightens inside of him, eliciting another screech. "You are responsible for what happened to Simiel," I punctuate her name while tugging my hands, the black ooze of Mutovinatum's body slipping from my elbows. "I will not allow you to do the same to my student!"

I jerk my hands up and out higher, the pain mounting inside with the pitch of Mutovinatum's screeches and screams; I must do this. I must ensure the safety of Scarlett. "I understand the power of love, but fear and pain have their uses too. I know them intimately." My hands rise out of Mutovinatum to the wrist; hands turn inside him, my fingers gripping even harder, arms shaking with the effort of pulling. I lean my trembling form down, my lips close enough to Mutovinatum's ghastly maw that I can smell his rancid breath. "This power is not yours. This power—" I jerk my hands out of him savagely with a resounding snap, the tendrils screeching and slithering into me, his cries threatening to split my skull. "—is my inheritance!"

I stand up shakily, panting, taking a trembling step away. My legs give out and I threaten to drop, but the shadows reappear, pushing me back up. I pet them and nod, my feet sliding against the floor, the shadows supporting me around the shoulders. They deposit me next to Scarlett, my hand instantly going to her throat; I let out a long breath, her pulse beating faintly but steadily against my fingertips. I slump over her, softly moving a hand through her hair; it's going to be alright now. Everything is going to be fine, I promise.

"I will not be trapped again!" I turn quickly, tendrils shooting out of my arms, embedding themselves into Mutovinatum's charging form. He doesn't stop, and the tendrils remain held in place, rooting me to the floor; no, no! "I was hoping to not have to kill you, but that is no longer an option."

Several more tendrils shoot out but they, too, simply absorb into Mutovinatum, whose blade arms are raised above me. I tug again as I hear the blades come down toward me; I am so close! I growl and tug, but to no avail; I cannot fail! I made a promise! Suddenly Mutovinatum flies backward, my arms free once again, the shadows retreating back into me. Mutovinatum is pinned to the ground by a shaft of crackling white energy. I turn and see Evermore slowly stand up, her auburn hair swaying slightly, her eyes glowing brightly, the white aura around her shining. I extend my hand, and several tendrils of shadow slither quickly across the floor before stopping near Mutovinatum, refusing to go any further. They circle, hissing as Evermore throws another bolt of energy into Mutovinatum, who screams, writhing on the spear of energy. "I'll kill you!"

"May I do the honors?" Evermore asks, and I nod. I have fought Mutovinatum too many times now to care. I have retrieved Scarlett, and that is what matters. She walks up to Mutovinatum, the shadows on the floor parting before her, and she leans close to Mutovinatum's red mouth; her lips move but I can't detect what she's saying. A bolt of white energy appears in her hand, and she shoves it through Mutovinatum's chest. He wriggles and writhes, squirming as the bolt burrows itself into his chest. I let out a deep breath and several tendrils appear, shooting in every direction, burrowing into the white corridor from all sides. It is over, now we must leave.

After a moment, a click echoes through the newfound silence in the corridor, and a portion of the corridor wall slides back, revealing a dark opening. The tendrils retreat back within me, and I look down again at Scarlett, putting my hand on her head.

"Is she injured?" Evermore asks and I nod, pausing to think for a moment as I put my hand on one of Scarlett's legs and she groans.

"Thank you," I say slowly, the words moving uneasily through my throat. For a moment, there is only the sound of Evermore's heavy breathing, having brought my own under control several moments before.

"You are welcome," she says, putting a hand on my shoulders; pleasant warmth spreads throughout my body, but my head begins to throb. I scoop Scarlett up in my arms and stand up, pulling away from Evermore's hand.

"This is the exit," I say, walking over to the dark opening in the corridor.

"I got us in here; I can get us out." Evermore says, and I raise an eyebrow at her.

"You are welcome to try, but getting into the Underworld is far easier than getting out. There is only one exit, and it is this way." Evermore looks at me for a moment, debating, before she follows me into the dark opening.

CHAPTER TWENTY-FIVE

I stand with Evermore in a stone room, lit dimly by sputtering torches that could go out easily at any moment. Chains adorn the walls, holding up bodies in various stages of decomposition; one opens its mouth with a dry creaking sound, but only a hoarse rasp comes out.

"Oh shut up," an old woman hobbles into view from the shadows, pointing a wrinkly, gnarled finger at the corpse and several stitches appear, sewing its mouth shut. She keeps a liver-spotted, grisly hand on a twisted, gnarled walking stick, her shabby black cloak hiding everything else from sight. She taps the stick on the ground several times and the stones move slowly, sliding and grating against each other to make way for a large opening in the floor. Slowly, rising up, a large throne comes into view, made up of old bones and sinew. She slowly makes her way over to the throne and gets onto the throne with what appears to be a large amount of effort. She nestles into the throne with a sigh, and a bone hand dislodges itself from the chair, scurrying into the darkness and coming back with an old, rusty goblet. It scampers up the throne, spilling half the contents onto the old crone's cloak. "Idiot!" she hisses, snatching the goblet, and the hand sinks back into the throne. She moves the hood of her cloak back and takes a sip from the goblet, smacking her thin, pale lips with satisfaction.

Out of the corner of my eye, I see Evermore looking at her with disgust, but I keep my expression impassive, looking the old woman's face over. Her skin is thin and hangs off her face in bags; her veins are prominent, and portions of her skull peek through the translucent skin. One bright blue eye rests lower than the other, which is simply an empty eye socket. Liver spots and warts are numerous in number on her face, and long, greasy, stringy locks of white hair droop down, barely hiding her scalp. She opens her mouth and only has four brown, misshapen lumps which were probably teeth at one time or another.

"Who the hell're you, and what're ya starin' at, boy?" Her voice is coarse, like sandpaper, and Evermore shivers visibly beside me.

"I am someone who seeks a way out of the Underworld," I say, adjusting my grip on Scarlett; this old crone is the way out of the Underworld, and I refuse to be stuck here because I cannot show some manners. If Evermore cannot control herself, however, I will have to deal with her; she averts her eyes from the old woman's hideous visage, and I squeeze my hand in Scarlett's hair tighter; now is not the time to be superficial. I have done what is necessary to secure Scarlett, and I will not let Evermore sabotage this now.

"Doesn't everyone?" she grumbles, taking another swig from the goblet. "That's all they want is to get out; the dead can't get outta the Underworld, so stop tryin'!" she shouts, and several of the corpses groan pitifully.

"I'm not dead," I say, and she looks at me shrewdly with her one remaining eye, leaning closer.

"Yer not dead, eh?" she says, looking me up and down before turning her attention to Evermore, who shifts uncomfortably, her white aura all but gone. "Well you gotta be dead, or else you wouldn't be here pining for a way to get out!"

"She is dead," I say, raising Scarlett up a bit. "I came here to retrieve her and bring her back with me."

The old woman sits up a little higher, seeming to be interested. "And what made yeh come all the way down here for that young thang?" she asks, pointing at Scarlett with her walking stick.

I pause for a moment, carefully thinking over my answer. "She… is a valuable resource," I say, and the woman stares at me hard for a moment before leaning back and cackling, her shrill laughter echoing around the room before she begins to hack and cough; the horrible, phlegmy sound reverberates just as well throughout the room.

"Oh boy, that's a good one," she says, beating her chest so hard I wonder if it will cave in as her coughing fit passes. "The ones that come down here usually do it for things like *love* or for a *quest*," she says distastefully, spitting on the floor, and Evermore takes a small step back. "Like that Orpheus fella—he was a looker but not many worms in the apple, if yeh get my drift," she said, smiling ruefully. "Seein' as how yeh introduced yourself, we'll continue with the introductions. Who's the thing yeh got in yer arms?"

"My student," I reply, and she snorts through her large, beak-like nose.

"More clever answers, eh? I'll respect that," she turns her gaze to Evermore. "And who're you?" she barks.

"Evermore," she responds through clenched teeth, keeping her eyes averted.

"You gotta problem, Evermooooore?" the woman growls, sounding like she's chewing her way around her name.

I look at Evermore, and she glances my way, seeing the look in my eyes.

"No," she says, relaxing slightly, looking the woman in her eye for a moment. The crone waits a moment, then sits back in her throne.

"Good," she says, taking a swig from her goblet then taps her stick against the throne; a long bone arm reaches out into the shadows behind the throne, pulls out a pitcher, and refills the goblet, putting the pitcher back in the darkness and sinking back into the throne. "I am Valkyrie; and in case ya haven't gussed it by now, I decide who getsta leave the Underworld. Normally, I would have ya 'mpress me in some way or another, but I was woken up from my nap, so I'll let yeh get out the easy way. Sacrifice," she says, and her blue eye sparkles as she slurps at the goblet greedily.

"A sacrifice has already been paid," I say, to which she just chuckles.

"I don't think so," she says when her eye glazes over with a white film, before returning to its normal color. "So it has," she says, sounding amused. "One of ya getsta leave now I 'spose," she grumbles.

"One?" I question and she sighs.

"You seemed like an intelligent fella 'til just now. Let me explain, and ya better pay 'tention," Valkyrie wets her lips again with the goblet before continuing. "One sacrifice means one of ya getsta leave. More than one of ya wantsta leave, gotta sacrifice 'nother being," Two bone hands come out of the throne, taking her walking stick and goblet so she can spread her hands and shrug. "That's the way it is."

"I see," I say; and without hesitation, several tendrils appear, slamming into Evermore and wrapping around her. They sling her into a wall and wrap around her, slamming her into the floor, and the torches shake in their brackets. She glows bright white and the tendrils hiss, snapping off of her, leaving black marks on her tan skin.

"What are you doing?!" Evermore shouts at me, and I look her in the eyes coldly.

Evermore saved my life, and she got me this far, and for that I will not kill her. However, she interrupted my period of grief and tried to convince me to forget about Scarlett; I do not want her as an ally. "I came here to retrieve Scarlett and bring her back with me; you are no longer necessary."

I duck as a bolt of white energy flies toward me, and a small wave of shadows appears beneath Evermore, flipping her up into the air. Several tendrils shoot out and wrap themselves around her, slamming her into the wall. The tendrils slam her against the wall again, her head banging against the stone. A white wall of light appears, cutting the tendrils apart, and I grit my teeth as Evermore drops to the ground. She glares at me, several bolts of white energy flying at me; I dodge them and several tendrils wrap around some of the chains on the walls. They fly at Evermore, tangling her in them and stringing her up against the wall. Her white aura immediately disappears and she shakes, trying to get loose.

"I brought you here!" she shouts, and I turn my back on her, looking intently at Valkyrie.

"I'm sure this will suffice as a sacrifice," I say, and Valkyrie stares hard at me for a moment before waving a hand, and a door appears. I kick it open, revealing a bright white opening.

"I saved your life!" she shouts, the chains rattling as she struggles.

"And that is why I do not kill you. You tried to convince me to leave my student—to forget about her. I will do a great many things to ensure her survival and the success of my mission, but the former is far more important than the latter. She has taught me that," I say, falling backward into the light with Scarlett in my arms, the door slamming shut in front of me.

CHAPTER TWENTY-SIX

I stare emptily at the space where a door had been previously. I helped him here…and he left me; my body hangs limply from the chains, and I let my head droop. I was a fool, and I failed. I thought I could play him, but I was tricked and left here to rot. He left me here to die—chained and shackled away from the world. I screw my eyes shut as angry tears run down my face, leaving salty strands on my cheeks. Why did he do this? When did I give myself away? My body trembles in its chains, the cold metal biting into my skin; how could this have happened?!

"He…he left me," I gasp as my throat constricts, trying to cut off my air; a tear drops down onto my bottom lip and I bite it, digging my teeth in.

"Oh shut up," the old woman growls, hobbling over to me; I avert my gaze. "Yer actin' like this is the first time you've been left by a man," she says, poking me with her walking stick. I try and shy away, but these chains hold me too well. They hold me; I shake in the cold shackles, yanking at them desperately, digging my fingernails into my palms, rubbing my wrists raw on the unrelenting metal as I tug and pull.

"Let me go!" I scream, shaking and trembling, tears flying out into the room like tiny little crystal droplets. "Let me out!"

"Calm yerself, deary."

"*Let me out!*" I glare vehemently at the woman, leaning forward as far as these shackles will let me. "Unchain me now, you ugly, horrendous bag of—"

The slap hits me square in the cheek and snaps my head to the side; I gasp and stay still out of sheer shock. Anger mounts in me, and I glare at the old witch. "You—"

My body trembles with the aftershock behind the next slap, my cheek burning.

"Gawd yer such a little pest," she spits on my face, and I recoil and bite the inside of my cheek hard, the coppery taste of blood hitting my tongue. "I dunno why that woman even trusts you to get the job done; you got yerself trapped here. Ye failed horribly, dear," she says, then chuckles a little. "Quite funny, if I think about it."

I tug at my chains, trying to pull out or kick or…or something!

"Yer not goin' anywhere unless I want you to," she cackles.

I snarl and tug harder, my hair matted with sweat from the effort.

"Ooh, that's not a pretty face now, is it?" She snarles, leaning close to me so I can smell her putrid breath.

I lunge forward, snapping my teeth at her nose, but she pulls back.

"Feisty are ya? I thought *her* assassin would be better than this. But, I have to say, I'm a bit disappointed."

I stop, glaring at her. "What are you talking about?" I whisper, and she comes closer again, grinning, showing the old, crooked remains of her teeth. "How do you know her?"

"Would you like to see a pretty face dear?" she asks.

"Just answer the question, hag!" I spit and her one eye flashes, but she does nothing.

"You first," she says and I sigh, hanging my head.

"I don't care," I say, annoyed; I just want to get out. I need to get out.

"I'll take that as a yes then," she says and hobbles out of view.

How long am I going to remain here? Will my body rot away? Or will I remain here, trapped, shackled away, forever listening to the ramblings of an insane old hag? How could he leave me here to this?! When did I get sloppy and give him any reason to doubt?

"Why don't you take a look at that pretty face you wanted to see, dear?"

The voice is cool and soothing, washing away my agitation like a cool stream. I look up and widen my eyes in astonishment.

"Surprised I see," the woman before me gives an amused chuckle that sends a small spark through my nerves. "Who knew behind that old bag of wrinkles and that wretched accent lay this vision of cosmic beauty, correct? I admit," she walks toward me slowly, her feet bare on the cold stone floor, and I take a deep, shuddering breath. "The need for a disguise I sometimes find…superfluous—but at other times it's quite necessary. And amusing," she adds with a smirk.

The edge of her dark blue robe skims the floor, light blue designs of vines and flowers adorning the shimmering piece of clothing. My eyes follow the flowers, taking in her pale legs and traveling up; her robe is fastened with a single, gold tie around the center. Her choppy black hair falls in jagged layers to her chin; her bright purple eyes are thin, sharp, and mesmerizing, in sharp contrast compared to her delicate cheekbones and light blue lips.

"Come now—you can't be struck *that* speechless," she raises a thin, dainty hand and traces a long, opal white nail down the curve of my cheek. I let out air I hadn't know I'd been holding, and I can see my breath in the air as a shiver races through my body, a spark crackling up my spine. "Pity, I expected more from someone *she* said to watch for personally." She shrugs and turns, her slight shoulders barely holding up the robe. "What a shame."

"Wait!" I call out, leaning forward, and she turns around with a playful smirk, tapping her lips with her finger. "I—I'm sorry for how I acted earlier. Please, forgive me." I lower my head and stare at the floor, the streaks left by my tears freezing on my face in the cold air. My breath frosts in the air, and I suck in deep breath after deep breath; I can't seem to get enough air. I feel a cool, smooth hand on my chin and it lifts my head up; I look into her bright, violet eyes and she smirks, tilting her head slightly as spots dance in my eyes. My eyelids began to droop, darkness creeping at the edge of my vision as I try to keep eye contact. My chest continues to tighten, and I can't even breathe anymore; I try to gasp and pull away. Her hand tightens on my chin and holds my head in place; the chains coil tighter, spreading my arms farther apart, constricting my breathing even further. A plea for air wells within my soul, but the pain within my lungs drowns it out; my head aches, and my eyes feel like they're going to pop out of my skull.

"I do not care *who* you serve," she says, her voice sharp and biting now, cutting into me like daggers, and I begin to shiver uncontrollably. My teeth chatter and my fingers begin to turn blue. "You will not disrespect me in that manner ever again. Do you understand?"

I try to speak, but I don't have enough air to do much of anything right now; it's all I can do to keep my eyes open, and even then I can only see those violet irises boring deep into me. I can hide nothing; I am laid bare, trapped; trapped once by him, now I am pinned under the gaze of this woman.

"I know you do, which is why I'm going to let you go." She releases her grip on my chin and steps back. My head droops, and I take a large gulp of air; my vision returns, and my teeth stop chattering. My lungs cry out in relief and my body stops trembling, color returning to my fingers as I greedily gulp in another breath. The chains suddenly uncoil, and I drop to the cold stone floor; pain shoots up my body from my knees and I crumple, sprawled out on the floor. I shakily put my palms down and raise myself up, running a trembling hand through my auburn hair.

"You have strength dear, I'll give you that."

I take a deep breath and smooth the edge of my dress nervously before tilting my chin up slightly and looking her square in the eye.

"Do you work for *her?*" I clasp my hands together in front of me, trying to keep a certain amount of poise in my posture.

"I do not work *for* her," she replies, settling into her throne of bones, accepting a small crystal chalice and taking a sip of the dark red liquid inside. "We are…familiar, with each other; I am doing her a favor. However, I have had to do quite a bit more work than was agreed, so I am considering our contract…null." A piece of old, yellow paper appears before her, then goes up in flames, the ashes swirling towards me. I scrunch my eyes closed, waving them away.

"Then why did you help me?" I ask, flicking a piece of ash off of my dress.

"You're really going to question why I saved you?" She raises a thin eyebrow and smirks around the chalice as she takes another sip. "She certainly didn't choose you for your intelligence—I can tell that much."

I blink, my white aura beginning to glow around me once more; my soul lets out a shudder of relief, and my aura glows brighter. The feeling of power rushes back into my system, white hot relief coursing through my muscles, penetrating, burrowing into my bones. It is soon replaced by a chilling feeling of contentment, and I tilt my chin up, eyes glowing brightly as my soul coos, readily accepting the familiar, unique flavor of my power.

"It didn't take long for your abilities to return."

"I'm talented," I say moving toward her, my aura glowing brighter with each step. "If you're not working for her, then you didn't have any motivation to help me—unless you want me to work for you." My aura dims considerably as I reach a hand out and place it on one smooth, pale knee, and two thin eyebrows raise up, violet eyes widening, blue lips opening as a small gasp escapes from within. For a moment, those violet eyes glow white before I take my hand away, and my aura glows bright once more. "She may not have chosen me for my intelligence, but I can tell that's definitely going to be a factor in what you decide to do with me, Valkyrie." I lift her chalice from her dainty hand and gulp its contents down in one swallow; the coppery taste of blood fills my mouth and slimes its way down my throat. I smile, setting it down lightly on one armrest. "You should think carefully before you make any hasty decisions."

Valkyrie peers at me with a neutral expression from behind her bangs, tapping one long, opal fingernail on her chin. "Do you wish to work for me?" she asks and I smile, taking a step back, licking some of the red stain off of my teeth slowly.

"Not *for* you," I reply and she smirks, waving a hand; a small, white door appears beside me. I look from the door to Valkyrie and remain where I stand; I have a rule not to trust anyone I can't kill, and I'm weak enough in here that Valkyrie falls in that category.

"If you're going to work with me, you'll have to lose the dress," she says, standing up and waving a hand. A long rack of clothes appears, and she moves her hands over the clothes. What's wrong with my dress? "Here we go," she waves her hand and the rack disappears, an outfit suspended in air before me. It consists of heavy looking black boots, segmented black metal plate leggings, and a light black metal breastplate with a single pauldron and gauntlet.

"I won't be able to move in that," I say, frowning.

"You'll die in anything else," she says. "You're going to start this relationship out by questioning me? An interesting concept on how to improve your standing in my eyes, but not very effective I'm afraid."

I take a step forward and put my hand on the black metal breastplate; it shimmers for a moment before turning into a white sleeveless shirt with small metal scales adorning the front and back. The plate leggings change into simple, loose white pants, the boots into small, slip-on shoes, and the gauntlet transforms itself into two fingerless white gloves. I begin undressing and putting the new clothes on; Valkyrie looks at me with interest for a moment before turning around and settling back into her throne.

"I see you like that color," she remarks; I have an affinity for certain things and colors. "Do you know what you'll be doing for me?"

"Something similar to what I was doing before," I say, slipping on the armored shirt and then the gloves. I run my hands through my hair and shake my head, whipping my hair about and running my hands through it again.

"Not quite," she says smirking; I can do whatever it is she tells me to do. "You'll be overthrowing a government and raising an army, for starters."

"Is that all?" It's outside of my area of expertise, but I'm a fast learner; I'm sure if other people with no abilities can accomplish such a feat then so can I, but better.

"No, but I'll let you know what else when the time comes," she says.

"I prefer to know what I'm getting into," I take a step forward, white aura fluxing slightly. "All of it."

"Noted," Valkyrie says, then sighs. "I'll tell you when you need to know; and if you can accomplish what I told you before, I'll let you pursue some of your other interests."

My aura flashes brightly, filling the room for a brief second with blinding white light before it returns to its normal brightness. One thought flashes across my mind; revenge. Revenge against him for leaving me here; revenge for shackling me—for trapping me. Revenge for choosing that *girl* instead of me; revenge for lying to me—revenge for betraying me.

"Fine," I say; overthrow a government and raise an army; how long will that take really?

"Do you know the situation?"

"What situation? I know my way around the land well enough, and there's always some war or another being fought; what else do I need to know?" I say folding my arms; every second that ticks by now is another moment that is being wasted.

"I hope you learn to bite that tongue of yours," Valkyrie mutters before standing up, walking toward one of the bodies hanging on the wall and stroking its cheek slowly. "I'll explain, and I expect you to listen, or you can forget about your...extracurricular activities. Legend Land is a dimension ruled by Death; it is separated into two landmasses, the Kingdom and Vis Land. You were in the Kingdom. However, Death has strangely been gone recently, and four entities are making a grab for Legend Land: Fate, Luck, Artemis, and Malus, some of which are Death's own siblings."

"What role are my actions playing in all of this?"

"You'll be making sure that Legend Land stays in the control of Death during his...absence."

"Why do you want Death to remain in control of Legend Land? This would be a perfect time to take control; it would even be easy."

"Because whoever takes control of Legend Land has to deal with Death in the case of his return," she turns to look at me, slashing the body with one of her long fingernails, and it disappears in a burst of flame without the chance to scream. "When Death gets angry, there is always a…reckoning; and when the time comes, it is best to be on the right side."

She's kissing up, but that's fine; less work means I have more time to pursue him. "Then I have no time to lose; lower the barrier around this place."

Her eyes twinkle, glowing brightly for a moment and then she nods. I take a deep breath, putting my hands together, my aura glowing brighter. I will overthrow this government and raise Valkyrie an army—a simple task. Then, I will get my revenge. My aura flashes brightly, hot, white light coursing through me, burning into the room and searing my retinas, but then I'm gone.

I arrive in a clearing within a forest; the ground has been gouged out in some places, and dark craters mar the setting. Trees have been toppled, and the remnants of what looks like a house are strewn throughout; the smell of charred flesh reaches me, and I wrinkle my nose in disgust. There are several rotting corpses laying about; some have been ripped apart, others look like they were killed more cleanly. I take a knee, putting my hand on the ground; a white shimmer glimmers over the bloody, trampled grass, and festering bodies. Several small dark wisps of shadow appear from around the bodies, retreating with a hiss. A solid cube of light appears around the wisps, and they begin to hiss louder; I stand up and put my hand on the cube. It glows brighter, and the wisps began to shriek and scream before disappearing along with the cube.

He was careless enough to leave a trail behind, which means I have something to follow. I feel something clutch at my ankle, and I spin around. One of the bodies, severed in half along the waist, is grabbing at me, snapping at me with its partially decayed mouth, tongue lolling out, eyes rolling. I wave my hand dismissively; several spears of light pierce it, and it stops moving. I don't have time for these things. I go to the spot with the most wreckage and put my hand on a charred board; white light shimmers around it, but nothing happens. There's a faint rustle, and several small boards move; is someone here? I squat next to the small boards and put my hand on them; several spears of light appear over them. Whoever, or whatever this is, it survived a fight with him and several other forces that look just as powerful, meaning it will be nearly as powerful as me; caution is the best principle to follow after what just happened. The boards tremble again, and a groan comes from beneath them; I hesitate for a second before shifting some of the boards away. My eyes widen in shock; this… this can't be…this can't be what stood up to him. I don't believe it!

A small dog with black, curly fur lies in the rubble; it has several cuts and scrapes on it, and parts of its fur are matted in blood. A small brown belt is buckled around the dog's thin waist, and attached to the belt is a shiny metal rapier, small enough to be a toy for children. I frown and put my hand on the dog who whimpers; *this* is the thing that stood up to him? This is the thing that has powers that nearly rival mine? A white light shimmers over the dog briefly, and several green sparks snap up from its body; I jump back, a wall of white light appearing between me and the dog. That wasn't his doing; someone else was with this dog. That must be the power I'm sensing.

A shiver makes its way up my spine and I shudder, the wall of light disappearing; the power is cold and seems to contain an enormous amount of unbridled fury. I put my hand on the ground, white light shimmering over it and the rubble; green smoke rises up from the ground, and the temperature slowly drops as the smoke rises. My breath crystallizes in the air, and the green smoke begins to swirl around, hissing and snapping like a dying fire. I hold out a trembling hand, and a cube of white light appears around the smoke. As soon as it begins to form, the smoke hisses louder and passes through the cube like it wasn't even there. It slowly drifts over to me, until its right in front of me, hissing and spitting like a monstrous snake. There is a sense of old, ancient power within this mist, though the mist itself is a mere fraction of the power that must lie at the source.

I reach my hand out and touch the mist with just my fingertips.

As soon as I do, my arm snaps rigid, and my body freezes in place, my mouth open, eyes wide; I'm unable to move. The mist trails up my arm and my shoulder, leaving small electric snaps in its wake as it travels up my body. Finally it comes to my mouth, and I fight my invisible bonds; I can't be chained again! I won't be chained again! I desperately try to wrench myself free, or snap my mouth closed, or *something* to get away from this intangible invader. It slowly inches its way into my mouth, and I can do nothing to stop it; it slides in my mouth and down my throat, leaving a taste like old, musty carpet and rotting flesh in its wake. I try to gag but can't, and it trickles down my throat until it nestles in my belly, curling around my stomach.

Icy pains shoot up through my body, shocking my system like ice water. I fall onto my hands and knees with a gasp, sucking in air and glowing brightly; white hot light glows on my skin and penetrates deeper, soaking into my bones and down into my stomach. I feel the mist squeeze tighter and I clutch my stomach, groaning as flashes of hot and cold shoot through my body. Cold sweat appears on my burning skin, and I curl up tighter, gagging and feeling like I could retch. Icy spikes of pain drill themselves into my bones as hot light courses through my veins; I'm searing and freezing inside. I clutch at the grass, scrunching my eyes closed and curling my knees up closer, trying to will it away.

Well this is certainly an interesting predicament you find yourself in. That raspy voice…I know it; for a moment my mind focuses on that voice, desperately trying to reach back, but then a new wave of pain hits, banishing all attempts at recollection from my brain. *You don't remember me? I'm a little offended, I must admit, but we didn't know each other for very long. I am Mutovinatum; you need not introduce yourself, I've been rooting around in your mind for hours now. I know who you are, Evermore.* I bite my tongue so hard I feel like I'm going to bite it off as the mist spreads itself throughout my body, pressing at my organs and bones, straining against my skin. *Looks like you could use some help here.*

"Are…you…offering?" I spit out between clenched teeth, writhing and groaning as several flashes of heat burst through me like my blood is boiling; I clamp on my bottom lip to keep from screaming and alerting whatever is in the forest to my presence.

I am offering, but I'm equally content to just wait this out; very powerful forces are battling for control of your body right now, but I always found power struggles to be a…spectator sport—at least until both sides are tired and weak; then I play a very active role.

"So are you…just…going to wait…this out?" I gasp, heat flushing up my neck as my fingers begin to turn blue, numb from the cold in my hands. *That depends on how I feel; right now I'm feeling a bit tired. I think I'll just wait until one or the other wins, then I'll take the prize.* I groan as a new wave of pain hits; but instead of shying away, this time I lean into the pain. I dive into it and search inside. My body is behind me, in some other place where there is grass and clothes and pain; in here, there is nothing like that. I sift through the green mist, the bright white light and I delve deeper. I find a black figure, the size of a small child, curled away, hiding in a dark corner. When the figure senses me, its bright red grin drops into a frown. I wrap both hands around its neck; its small black fingers clutch at mine, but it can do nothing, though it continues to try and pry my hands off.

I return to my body with a gasp, my fingers curled in the grass, trying to rip up chunks of earth. Waves of pain wash over me faster than before, tremors wracking my body, but I don't fight it; don't fight it or it hurts worse. Instead, I keep a tight grip on that dark figure inside me, fingers digging in; my fingers dig into the dirt, and my arms unwittingly clench, pulling me across the ground, closer to the rubble. *What…what do you think…you're doing?*

"If I go…you go with me," I hiss, before a cold wave crashes into my throat, constricting my airway; I try to suck in a breath but end up choking on my own built-up saliva, coughing out precious air.

You're…you're going to disappear…before I do.

A low, rumbling sound echoes around in my head that I realize is laughter, and I scrunch my eyes tight, digging my fingers into the ground, legs twitching and kicking, sending dirt and grass and earth flying everywhere. "Get…out of my head!" The laughter grows louder, replacing my thoughts; there is only laughter in my head. A new wave of pain hits, but this time I don't just let it hit me, but I don't resist; I grab it. I grab that pain, and I let go of the figure, but I grab that pain and I twist it. I twist it until it screams in my bones, my body shaking, tears streaming down my face. I stand up, trembling as a shiver starts at my shoulders, making its way down my body. I let go of the pain and it is replaced by cool comfort, trickling down my body; I wipe spit and bile from my mouth. I slowly flick sweat off my face, working my jaw loose of the death grip it had on my tongue.

"Where is your laughter now?" There is only silence in my head, and my aura glows brighter. "Answer me!"

What would you have me say? Your question is rhetorical; and if I give a wrong answer, then you will just make me disappear.

"I'm going to do that anyway," I spit blood out of my mouth and the ground shimmers with white light; nothing appears, and I nod. "You said you were going to take your 'prize' after someone won? Well, what are you waiting for?"

I don't feel like it.

"Oh, poor baby doesn't feel like it? Are you not feeling well?" My aura glows brighter, and I hear a shriek in my head.

Don't…do that.

"Why not?" My aura glows brighter, lighting up this devastated clearing, and the shriek gets louder, threatening to split my skull, but I just laugh a harsh bark that hurts my vocal cords but I don't care. "What are you going to do? I can get rid of you whenever I like."

Then you won't have any answers.

"I don't have anything I want an answer to that I don't already know."

That's a lie, and you know it! You have dozens of questions swirling around in that pretty little head of yours, and I can give you the answers.

"The only thing in my head right now is you, and I want you out!" I spit out, my aura glowing brighter, skin heating up; power courses through my veins, white hot power, and I laugh louder. It feels good—great even—and I burn brighter, white light shining through the clearing.

Don't you want to know how to beat him?! There's a note of desperation to Mutovinatum's voice, but I stop, my aura fluxing slightly before slowly fading to a soft, white glow.

"What do you know about him?"

More than you could ever imagine. I gave him his power, and then he stole it from me; I was with him for so many years. I shared every experience with him; his every thought was privy to me. I knew his every desire, just like I now know yours; I know you want answers, and I can give them to you. You don't have to like me; because if we're being honest, I don't like you—but we can coexist. To do that, though, you have to not erase me.

I remain silent for a moment, thinking it over; if I let this… creature, Mutovinatum, remain inside me, then I must always be on guard on the inside. I must always remain aware of everything inside; and if I slip, then I'm doomed. I can surely get my revenge without Mutovinatum; is the advantage really worth it?

I know what you're thinking; and yes, it is worth it. How can you defeat an enemy if you know nothing about him?

"I don't want to defeat him," I reply, folding my arms. "I want revenge."

There's no difference.

"If you can't tell the difference, then how can I expect you to be able to help me get my revenge? Knowledge is one thing, but useful knowledge is another."

Wait!

My aura glows brighter, and I smirk smugly. "You have nothing to offer me; goodbye."

I can tell you his real name!

I pause, aura dimming once again, and I sit down cross-legged in the rubble. "Tell me."

His name…is Eurael.

CHAPTER TWENTY-SEVEN

Sensation crashes into me in one single blow. Sound penetrates my ears, burrowing into my skull as blades pierce my skin, gusts of wind tearing me apart. A myriad of tastes and smells assault me, trying to deny me any sense at all. My eyes flick open, and I see the small blades of grass pressing gently against my skin, a single bird chirping occasionally, a soft breeze cooling the sweat on my face. I pick myself up off the ground, stifling a groan. I sit up and let out a long breath, running a hand through my hair. I look at Scarlett and reach out, feeling the warmth of her skin; I feel the steady beat of her pulse, and I retract my hand. It worked. I sigh and keep my eyes on her, interlocking my fingers and resting my chin on them; it worked. I was able to prevent demise from permanently visiting her; it worked.

I close my eyes and allow myself a small smile; I did not fail this time—I was successful. I open my eyes and look up at the clear blue sky, the white clouds like cotton, lazily drifting across the sky. The sun does not beat down harshly on my back now, but warms me pleasantly. I lay back, spreading my arms and legs out, soaking up the sun; rarely do I ever just take a moment to experience. Experience itself is not inherently good or evil, positive or negative; it just is. I reach a hand up to the sky, the scent of wildflowers tickling my brain.

"You did it," I turn and see her dark hair laid out on the grass, just barely touching my cheek. She has a small smile on her face and I nod, bringing my hand down from the air to cup her face.

"I did it," I affirm, stroking her cheek with the pad of my thumb. "I finally saved you."

"Thank you," she says with a smile, and I take a shuddering breath, closing my eyes.

"I know it wouldn't have been required if in the first place—"

"You succeeded," she says, cutting me off, and I open my eyes. "I am safe; you no longer need to worry about that. You saved me."

A gust of wind blows through, and I see Scarlett's eyelids begin to flutter, her red hair barely touching my cheek; I quickly pull away, sitting up several feet from her. I look at my hand and close my eyes; I succeeded in saving Scarlett. I saved Scarlett, my student.

Slowly her eyelids flutter open, her green eyes shining brightly. Her lips part barely, and a soul-searing scream looses from her mouth. She turns onto her back, gripping the grass hard, screaming at the sky. She shudders and shakes, choked sobs intertwined in a long, painful note. I put a hand on her shoulder, looking down at her as she shakes her head, tears streaming down her face. I can see the strain in her neck, her face red, her eyes glazed over; she must be experiencing her own death.

I move my hand to her hair and touch my forehead to hers, letting out a long breath. Slowly her screaming ceases and she merely sobs, shaking; I bring her into my arms, holding her to me and shielding her from the world as she cries into my chest.

"I died," she sobs, curling my shirt in her hand. "I died!"

I stroke her hair, keeping a firm grip on her as she trembles in my arms; I allowed her to die. I sent her into a situation where she could have ended up facing an enemy far out of her league, and she fell right into a trap. I allowed this to happen; I am responsible for her pain. A teacher should only inflict pain on a student if it will benefit them in some way; I look down at Scarlett, snot and tears streaming down her face, soaking into my shirt as she hiccups and cries. There is no benefit to this, no lesson to be learned here; the pain is pointless. I can say nothing, and I do not try; I communicate through my arms, holding her close. My hands gently stroke her head as she lets out her sorrows and fears in the most primal, human way possible. I dip my head and I hold her closer; she is my responsibility, and I will never let something like this happen again. Never.

"Eurael," I work the word over in my mouth slowly, and I feel a small amount of bile creep into my throat; the name makes me sick, much like the person it is attached to. "Tell me more about him."

Does this mean we have a deal?

"Tell me more about him, and then we'll talk about a deal."

There is a contact, Benson, who can tell you all you need to know.

I nod, my aura glowing brighter. My limbs tremble as heat flashes through me, my blood searing through my veins.

What are you doing?!

"What use are you, when this 'Benson' can tell me all I need to know?"

Wait!

"I'm done waiting."

White hot light tears through me, burning deep inside. I grit my teeth, my eyes burning, Mutovinatum's screams splitting up into my skull. With a bright flash, my aura dims down to a normal level, a cool sensation washing over me, muscles untensing. I check inside and sigh; he's gone. I don't like voices in my head, dirty little thoughts rooting around my mind; it's just unpleasant.

A rustling in the rubble draws my attention—another corpse? A low groan rises up, a small furry paw appearing through the splintered remains of the cabin. I cautiously inch forward, a spear of light appearing in my hand; I'm not taking any more chances. A furry head pops up, swiveling around until it sights me, the rest of it clambering out of the rubble; the dog?

"You got anything for these wounds?" His voice is deep, a thick Scottish accent rumbling through his words. A talking dog. I slowly lower my spear but keep it handy; I'm not going to underestimate him. He clears his throat and winces. "Perhaps introductions are in order," he bows and howls, quickly straightening up. "I am Totomir, of Kansas." He extends his paw up to me, trying to turn his snout into a smile. His curly dark hair is covered in blood, several scratches and burns dotting his small body; this dog went through hell, gods. I reach down, shaking his paw; I can't underestimate anyone, but I also shouldn't overestimate them. An injured dog that barely comes up to my knees, even if he is standing on two legs, can hardly be considered a threat.

"Evermore," I reply, wiping my hand on my pants after we shake.

"So, Lady Evermore, do you have anything for these wounds?"

I eye him up and down; I shouldn't let anyone know the full extent of my powers, at least not yet. Not until I get stronger.

"I'm heading to find someone by the name of 'Benson'—I'm sure he will have medical supplies." The dog's ears perk up, an actual smile growing on his muzzle.

"I know Benson," he says with a mischievous twinkle in his eyes. "But I'm not sure if I'll be able to make it all the way there in my current condition." He holds his arms up to me, and I look down at him dubiously.

I shake my head; I am not carrying you, dog. You shed fur—I do not like fur.

"I thought not," he says with a sigh.

I nod ahead of me, gesturing with my spear, "Lead on."

He hangs his head, trudging ahead of me while I follow. Above his pointed ears, several spears of light follow him, heads pointed directly at him. Overestimation is not the same as overkill, and there is no such thing as the latter.

CHAPTER TWENTY-EIGHT

Scarlett stares blankly down at the book laid open before her. I look back down at several sheets of paper on my desk, then back up; she hasn't stirred. It's been like this for weeks; I didn't expect her to recover immediately, but I had expected her to make *some* progress. A small amount of drool forms at one corner of her mouth; death has changed her. I stand up and walk over to Scarlett, putting a hand on her shoulder. The small amount of contact is enough to shake her out of her numb reverie, and she looks up at me, slightly confused.

"Did I...fall asleep?" she asks, wiping her mouth.

"Yes," I say; I have no intention of letting her know how damaged she truly is. As far as she knows, she is doing remarkably well. She nods, looking back down at the book, frowning slightly and then taking notes on a piece of paper beside her. I look at the paper and see several rough, jagged lines, but no coherent symbols or words. A small crack resounds throughout the room, but Scarlett doesn't seem to notice, her normally bright eyes glazed over. I turn and see Eraxus standing there, shoots of grey in his dark hair now.

"She looks terrible," he says, his glasses shining in the bright light of the room.

I begin walking to the library doors and open one silently; he makes a motion for me to exit first and I do, closing the door silently behind him as he exits after.

"What do you want?"

He takes his glasses off, rubbing them clean with a bit of cloth produced from his suit pocket. Finished, he settles his glasses back on his nose, holding out a hand. "First, I would like to offer my sincere condolences for your loss and congratulations on recouping said loss."

I fold my arms across my chest; I am in no mood for his games.

He waits for a moment longer then lowers his hand. "I'm here on a matter of business though; I have a task for you. In the mountains of north there is—"

"No," I say, cutting him off. "No tasks, missions, or jobs. I will not be doing anything for anyone until Scarlett has recovered."

"Mister E, I really think you should—"

"*No!*" I bark, taking a step toward him. "I did a job for Tatiana, and that ended up being the death of my student; now that I have recovered her, I discover she is damaged—broken. I will not be devoting time to anything else except to Scarlett for the foreseeable future. I appreciate your visit, but I will not be doing any more jobs until she has made a full and complete recovery."

Anger enters Eraxus's eyes, but I'm beyond caring; I am responsible for her state; and until that is resolved, I will not be focusing on anything else. Scarlett is my responsibility, and she did not leave my side while I was poisoned. She did not abandon me because I was frail and broken; I will not betray her.

"I cured you of your ailment; I removed the poison from your body. I made what could have been a much longer and more painful process short and easy for you. Now when I come to you for aid, you scorn me? I thought you were a fair man, Mister E," he says, his thin eyebrows frowning, his lips curling into a snarl.

"Can do the same for my student?" He removes his glasses, looking hard at them.

"We both know the effects of the Underworld are not so easy to undo,"

"When I was suffering, Scarlett stayed by my side and cared for me, and would have done so if my ailment had continued. I will show her the same courtesy until she has made a full recovery. Now," I say by way of a reply, moving to the side, and pointing in the direction of the front door, "unless you plan on somehow doing the same for Scarlett as you did for me, I suggest you leave peaceably before I am forced to physically remove you."

He brushes past me with several long strides, then turns around, the small gleam of his glasses hiding his eyes. "Your student will be the death of you, Mister E," he says coolly, disappearing with a small snap.

I look at the empty space where he was, resting my head back against the wall. I'm not sure I would have let Eraxus cure her anyway; she is my student. I am responsible for her current state—I must be the one to fix it. I was the death of her; it would only be fair.

Scarlett's breathing remains normal as I put my fingers on her throat, checking her pulse. She's been asleep for several hours now, but since Eraxus's visit a few days ago has made no more progress. I sit up quickly, alert; a knock resounds from the door, and I quietly close the door to Scarlett's room, quickly making my way to the front door. I open it quickly, the shadows curling and hissing behind me out of sight. A young man stands before me, shaggy brown hair getting in the way of wide, innocent brown eyes. He's dressed in plain pants and a plain, loose shirt; the rain patters quietly on the roof, his hair wet and his shirt hanging off of his body, weighted down with water. Bright flowers, protected by clear wrapping, are clutched in a trembling left hand, his other one clenching and unclenching nervously at his side.

"What do you want?"

He clears his throat, looking up at me and swallowing hard. "I'm here to see Scarlett; I heard she had an...accident, and I wanted to wish her a speedy recovery."

"I'll tell her you came by," I reply and quickly move to close the door, but his foot stops it from closing completely. I open the door and he moves his foot back, wincing; it must have hurt. Perhaps that will deter him from visiting again; Scarlett can afford no distractions.

"I was actually hoping to see her now," he says, craning his neck trying to look past me.

My grip on the handle of the door tightens, the shadows almost hissing loud enough to be heard over the rain as I speak through gritted teeth. "I do not know you, and Scarlett is not in any condition to see you besides," I reply, trying to close the door, but he sticks his foot in again. I resist the urge to slam the door on his foot repeatedly; the door is sturdy, his foot would break first.

"We've met more than once actually," he says, shivering now from the cold rain. "I was unconscious at the time, but Scarlett saved my life. We get together often enough; I know who you are, as she never stops talking about you. You're her teacher, and I know you have her best interests at heart." He takes a small step forward, his entire countenance pleading. "Please, let me see her." A captured heart will do many things to grant it relief; I look coldly down at him, and he trembles harder now.

"No," I say, my voice deadly soft. "You will not be seeing Scarlett; and if you do not remove yourself from my property immediately, you will never see her again."

He takes a step back, looking hurt. "But—"

"Now!" I roar, and he stands there a moment, shivering and shaking in the rain.

His wide eyes begin to moisten, and he hangs his head, his hair hiding his eyes from view as he awkwardly thrusts his arm out, flowers quivering in his shaking grip. "Please make sure Scarlett gets these," he mutters.

I look at him for a moment, then knock the flowers from his hand. He slowly bends down and picks them up, dripping in mud and hanging down pathetically, sodden. He turns and stiffly makes his way toward the road, not once looking back. I slam the door closed, and I feel the entire room shake. I sit down at the table, a tendril of shadow rising up next to me. I turn to it and shake in my chair, almost as if I had been the one out in the rain.

The man didn't seem to be lying; why would she keep her relationship a secret? I believed that we trusted each other; did her training suffer because of her relationship? I look down at the table and the shadow moves to me, but I grab it and toss it away. It snaps at me, then slinks away, the shadows retreating, leaving me alone. Why wouldn't she have told me?

CHAPTER TWENTY-NINE

I crouch low atop a hill overlooking a small village; the wind rustles the leaves on the bushes in front of me, shaking a few of the smaller branches of the tree behind me. The village looks sleepy and peaceful this early in the morning; no lights can be seen, the only sound being the occasional whining of an early risen dog. The village itself consists of a tightly clustered group of brown buildings made of clay bricks with wood and straw roofs; a small dirt road makes its way through the center of town.

"You're sure this is where Benson is?" I whisper, and Totomir nods, his furry arms crossed over his chest, his muzzle barely coming level with the top of the brush.

"That's the place," Totomir affirms, his large brown eyes glinting as the tip of the sun just begins to peak out over the horizon—the grey morning light gaining a subtle hint of gold, the brown ground turning a slightly more orange shade—and I stand up cautiously, wetting my lips. "We can just walk in you know; Benson and I are friends."

"We're going to do things my way," I retort, taking one last look at the village before coming out from behind the brush.

"I'm in no condition to be sneaking around," Totomir says. He brushes past me, barely coming up to my knee. "I came here to get bandaged up, and that's what I'm going to do." I raise my glowing palm as Totomir walks down the hill, head held high, paws barely making a sound on the sparse grass. It would be so easy. And, after all, I can't let him expose me—not when I don't know whether this Benson person is a friend or foe; I'm not just going to kill an innocent bystander though. I lower my palm and take a few short, quick breaths before letting out a long stream of air slowly, my aura fading to a dull shimmer that is barely separated from my skin. I creep after Totomir as the ground turns brighter, the whining keel of that single village dog growing louder in pitch.

As I crest a small hill in the road, a building, larger than the others, dominates the view. It's built with old, faded bricks and stained wood with a rusty metal roof, but it's larger than any other building around. There looks to be a single entrance, and Totomir is already halfway there. I quickly catch up to him, grabbing him by the shoulder and looking around, keeping my voice at a low whisper, my lips right next to his ear.

"We can't go in through the front door," I whisper, and he rounds on me, eyes flashing.

"I'm in a lot of pain here!" he hisses, tugging away.

"If Benson is your friend, why are you whispering?"

He pauses, looking down. "I, uh...don't want to wake him," he says, more of a question than a statement. I raise an eyebrow; I knew this dog had some things he wasn't telling me.

"What happened last time you two were together?"

He drags his foot through the dirt lightly, avoiding eye contact. "We played dice," he mumbles. He meets my eyes and sighs, shaking his head. "Okay, fine. He's angry because I cheated. I'd be too if I lost as much as he did," he adds with a small snicker.

Maybe this dog will be of use after all; if he has wealth, and knows Benson, perhaps I can use him to my own advantage.

"I need information from Benson, but I can get you medical supplies and protect you."

He looks at me cautiously, taking a small step back, frowning. "And what do you want from me?"

Clever doggie.

"To start, what do you know about the place?"

He thinks for a moment, scratching his chin. "Well, it's commonly deserted at this hour, but it doubles as a meeting spot and a bar. The only entrance is the one at the front. Benson practically lives here though; he's commonly in his office. He has an alarm system set up on all the walls."

I walk around the building but find no other entrance than the single door in front, just as he said.

"If you're going to try to get in, maybe sometime before sunrise would be good," Totomir says.

I frown, looking the building over again; an alarm on all the walls, huh? Well the roof is too high to climb onto without a boost up, and that isn't an option with the little dog. I look around and smirk as I look at the other small buildings common around this little village.

I rub my hands off on my pants and run at one of the buildings, jumping up and scrambling onto the top, taking a moment to judge the distance between this building and Benson's—a manageable jump. I lean over the edge and hold my hand down; Totomir looks at me dubiously then sighs and runs and leaps, grabbing my hand, and I hoist him up easily. Even if he isn't strong enough to boost me, he is fortunately light enough for me to lift him.

"Now what?"

I grin, looking at the distance, my aura glowing slightly brighter.

"I make an entrance." I run across the roof and leap, extending my arms out. I hoist myself up quickly onto Benson's roof before I can smack into the side, breathing easy; this is nothing. I take a deep, cooling breath, putting my hand on the roof. A flash of heat surges through me and into my palm, a thin ring of white light expanding outward from my palm. I feel my skin flush, the ring spinning rapidly with a soft whirring sound. I catch the sheet of metal roof before it falls, raising it out of the roughly shoulder-width hole, setting it beside me. I turn to Totomir and beckon for him to follow. Even on a separate rooftop, I can hear him heave a sigh, wincing with each step he takes. He leaps across the small distance, falling faster than he moves forward. I quickly reach a hand down, snatching him up and placing him next to the segment of roofing I removed. He gasps, looking at me with wide eyes, his breathing heavy.

"You...have...powers?" He manages to get out through his labored breathing, looking at the circle of cleanly removed metal from the roof. I nod and he lets out low chuckle. "Why didn't you just use your powers to get us up here?"

"I need to stay in practice; I can't rely too much on my powers or else when I find myself unable to use them, I could end up dead. Or I could end up like you," As I look over his injured form, I can't decide which would be worse. He nods, managing to push himself to his feet.

"I don't think I've ever met someone as determined as you," he says, and I flick a strand of hair out of my face, crouching low.

"Well I'm not like most people," I mutter, slowly lowering myself into the hole and holding onto the edge with my hands. I deftly swing myself through the air and let go, hitting the ground with a soft thud and rolling, coming up behind the bar counter, right where Totomir said it would be. I close my eyes, catching my breath behind the counter, recalling from my memory the view I got of the room. As the dog said, it appears to be a bar, the room I'm in now being the main room. It's filled with small round tables and wooden chairs, the bar counter being made of thick, solid wood, and behind the counter are several shelves of liquor. Close to the front door stands another door, probably a small closet, and off to the side, there are two more doors.

I peek over the edge the counter cautiously and stand up, going over to the entrance I made in the roof and helping Totomir down into the building alongside me. He looks around and walks over to one of the doors, sniffing and pressing his ear to the door.

"We go through the other door," he says quietly, and I walk over to him, frowning.

"How can you be so sure?" Just because I've taken him with me this far doesn't mean I'm going to start blindly trusting him.

"I have a superior sense of smell to humans, as well as hearing. I also happen to know from personal experience that employees and customers alike who end up completely drunk are thrown in here to spend the night." I put my hand on the floor, and I can almost taste the salty tang of sweat as a shimmer passes over the floor into the room filled with employees and patrons alike; he was right after all.

"Very well, you're right. Just to be safe," I stand up, putting my hand on the door, and it shimmers white for a moment before resuming its natural color. I walk over to the other door and pause, looking down at the dog. "You said this was Benson's office?"

"Unless he's moved, yeah," he replies.

"You're going in first," I say, willing my aura to a shade of dimness where it was almost invisible and pressing myself into the shadows beside the door.

"What?! Why me?" he exclaims as I open the door, pushing him in.

"Don't worry, I'm right behind you," I assure him with a gleam in my eyes, warm, yellow light spilling out over his form.

"Why Totomir, this is a surprise! I wasn't expecting you back so soon; are you in need of more laborers?" The voice that rolls out is deep and silky smooth, issuing out an air of sophistication and command that is not altogether unpleasant.

"Um...hey Benson."

I cringe inwardly at Totomir's attempts at conversation; I should have handled it.

"Or perhaps you came to swindle me for more money?" the voice drops to a low growl.

I quickly spin around into the room, my aura flashing brightly, filling the room with white light. The light disappears, and I take in my surroundings in a blink in case I have to blind everyone else once again. Several spears hover near the beast directly behind a desk. The room is small and neat with rich, dark wood walls. Several shelves of the same wood house various books of different shapes and sizes bound in leathers, also containing framed papers and small knick-knacks. Dominating the room, against the back wall, is a large ebony desk, in front of which are two dark leather chairs. Behind the desk is a tall, wing-backed chair, and an open lantern sits atop the desk along with papers and pens. I slowly move to stand behind Totomir, looking the beast over.

Standing behind the desk is a large wolf with black fur, his ears brushing the ceiling; he has calculating yellow eyes and wears an expensive-looking grey suit that strains to contain his large frame; his hands are the size of my head, and his fingers are tipped with long, sharp claws. One eyebrow arches itself in amusement as he looks from Totomir to me before he seats himself once more, gesturing to the chairs in front of his desk.

"Please sit," he says, his voice like the slow, soothing tide of the ocean.

I remain standing and so does the dog, but Benson simply shrugs, placing his papers in neat stacks and setting his pen in its stand, interlacing his fingers and peering over them at me.

"My name is Benson Barry Wolf," he moves the shutters of the lantern slightly closed. "I would shake your hand, but I fear you might try to kill me," his eyes shift from mine down to the dog's. "I see you've attained what appears to be a new...partner." He says the last word carefully, turning his gaze back to me, his brown eyes flicking from me to the spears of light still hovering around him. "Now, why don't you tell me why you are here, young lady?"

"For the record, I'm not here to kill you," I reply, my palms still glowing, spears spinning slowly around the wolf. "I can recognize an Immortal when I see one, and your kind is just so difficult to kill."

"I assume you've come here because you want something," Benson says sighing, leaning back in his chair.

"That's the only reason I ever seem to be visited these days."

"I'm here to contract your services," I say. Benson clicks his claws against his desk slowly.

"What do you expect to pay me with?" I pause for a moment; payment. I have no money, though that will change soon enough, but Benson won't follow me on promises. If he is one of Eurael's contacts, I have to be careful; I can't have him telling Eurael of my return.

"I brought you the dog; I know you have a quarrel with him." Totomir looks up at me quickly, paw going to his rapier.

"You backstabbing—"

I snap my attention to him, eyes flashing angrily; don't push your luck, dog. He gulps, nodding quickly, holding his hands up.

"I do not want the dog," Benson says.

"I'm *right here*," Totomir mumbles under his breath, but neither Benson nor I pay any attention.

"Then what do you want?" The spears of light glow brighter, my skin heating up as my aura starts to fluctuate out. I take several deep breaths, focusing on the spars again, my aura dimming down to its normal level.

"The first rule of negotiations is to never let the other side know you are willing to comply to any demand," he stands from his leather chair, the spears following him, but he pays no mind. "You Godkillers are all the same; arrogant and brash, especially the new ones. A rare breed though you are," he turns to me, tapping his chin with a claw. "You still have yet to get a handle on your powers, though you have so much untapped potential. No wonder Eurael used you." I open my mouth, but he continues, nodding. "Ah yes, I know all about your quarrel with Eurael; information is my specialty, after all."

"What are you two talking about?" I turn one of the spears to Totomir, and he mutters an apology.

"Then you should know that I am here to enlist your help in fighting him," I say.

Benson smirks, transforming his snout into a wolfish grin. "I owe Eurael a favor or two, not to mention we have known each other for far longer than you have even been alive. That incentivizes me to remain with him," he snarls quietly, sitting back in his chair, taking one of his papers and reading it over. "What do you have as an incentive for me to join you?"

"I incentivize you with my skills," I reply. For now, they are all I have, but that doesn't make it any less of a good deal; I am a very skilled individual.

For a moment, Benson says nothing, then leans back, chuckling, his muzzle turning into an amused grin.

"What makes you think that I'm interested in your skills? Eurael is already quite the skilled individual; why would I choose you over him?"

I lean across the desk, and I can smell him now, like pine needles and subtle cologne. The spears of light disappear from around him, a soothing cool flushing through my veins, my aura fluctuating slightly.

"If I'm going after Eurael, it is because I am confident I can defeat him."

"Or you are very foolish."

I stand up straight, taking a step back. "Either way, you are at an advantage. On one hand, you will have a new ally even stronger than Eurael, who is willing to do anything to get revenge. On the other, you will have a foolish tool that you can use; you benefit both ways." If he can gather such information at as quick a pace as he just demonstrated, I will need him. And if he's known Eurael for a long time, then his information could be invaluable to my revenge.

Benson smirks, standing up and extending a paw. "I will consider your offer; for now, let us do a trial run. Do something for me, and I will consider the deal done and valid."

I take his hand firmly, my palms heating up, but his expression remains the same and he doesn't move his hand, even when the tips of his fur begin to singe.

"Tell me what it is, and you can consider it done," I reply, shaking his hand firmly.

Totomir looks between us and pulls himself up onto the desk; Benson looks at his dirty, blood-matted paws on his desk, the light shining off the rich surface, but says nothing.

"I propose we screw that option," he says.

Benson remains quiet while I glare at Totomir, taking a step toward him as he continues talking.

"This woman obviously has balls coming to you, and she says she has skills; so give her the chance to prove it."

I yank Totomir off the desk sharply; he's lucky I don't kill him here and now.

"The original deal is just fine," I say, forcing a smile; I sure as hell can't take down Eurael without any allies, which means I can't anger any potential ones.

"No," Benson says, his eyes twinkling. "I like this idea."

My eyes flick to Totomir, and he gives me a thumbs up. I grip Benson's desk, my aura glowing slightly brighter.

"We have a deal in place already," I remind him, maintaining my smile.

"I don't remember signing anything," Benson says, his expression neutral. The smile drops from my face and I lean back, folding my arms; he wants to do it like this, fine. I'll play his game, but I will not put myself in a position of weakness; all that being said, I'd still prefer not to have to kill Benson.

"What exactly do you have in mind to test my skills?"

I shake my head, standing in a large, open area outside of Benson's place; I can't believe this. The giant wolf stands before me in loose black pants and nothing else, his fur barely covering his large, rippling muscles; he's obviously physically stronger than me—that much he has made clear. The sun has risen completely, and the entire town has come to watch the mysterious stranger take on Benson.

"You'll do fine. With your powers, this should be a snap. This way, you don't have to do Benson any favors to get his help. Sweet, right?"

I flex my fingers, aura fluctuating with my breathing, keeping my eyes closed; I don't want to kill Benson. I'll have to make this quick and incapacitate him before he can become a real threat to me.

"If I die, Benson will definitely kill you." I open my eyes, letting out a long, cool breath.

"And if you live?" he looks up at me hopefully, bandages wrapped around all his wounds; he wouldn't stop nagging about them.

I stand from the bench, turning my gaze to Totomir, who shrinks under my hard glare. "You better hope he kills me," I retort coldly, brushing past Totomir and into the circle.

"If your opponent yields, then the fighting stops; otherwise, there are no rules," Benson says, and an assenting cheer rises up from the town.

"Let's just get this over with," I reply and he chuckles, beginning to circle me. I spot Totomir going through the benches, taking slips of paper, writing figures down; he's taking bets? That dog better hope I don't make it through this. I turn my sole focus back to the impending fight; Benson circles further to my left so that I can no longer clearly see him, but I flick one finger, and a wall of light raises up, stopping him. The wall of light extends in a circle around Benson; I hear him growl, slamming against the wall of light. Mere physical strength is not always the deciding factor in a battle; I raise my hand and enough spears of light appear to hit every spot inside the light wall, my hair practically smoking with the heat pouring off of me. The crowd gasps, then cringes as they all thud down into the circle of light.

Silence stretches out for several seconds, not even the wind daring to stir; maybe next time he'll think twice about going back on a deal. As an Immortal, he won't die that easily; Godkillers still cannot kill gods like any other being—they are too stubborn to just die quietly and quickly. I wave my hand and the wall of light disappears; I blink, my eyes widening. No...this, this can't be.

The spears of light have only pierced the ground, and there's no sign of Benson. I look at the crowd, their eyes glued to something over my shoulder. I turn and see Benson grinning down at me, completely unharmed; he should still have been damaged by my attack! I barely have time to raise a small shield of light before his paw slams into it, breaking through it easily and colliding with me. I fly through the air when something grabs my waist, wrapping around it easily and slamming me onto the ground. My face smacks against the earth, and I spit out dirt, smacking my hand on the ground. Two walls of light rush at Benson who is still holding me down, the grass beneath my hand blackening under my glowing palm.

He disappears again, this time reappearing in front of me. His foot comes down to stomp on my head, but it never reaches. He stumbles back howling; I stand up and grin, looking at the spear of light embedded in his foot with appreciation. One must have quick thinking to deal with an Immortal, but the same can be said when dealing with Godkillers; he underestimates me. Good, it will wound his pride all the more when I crush him.

He rips out the spear and throws it at me, but it just disappears, a small cooling sensation trickling down my spine. He sets his foot down and winces; I take the opportunity to raise a block of light from the ground, lifting up suddenly. He tilts backward and lands heavily on his back. I rush toward him, slamming him down with another large block as he tries to get up. I sling a spear of light at him, and he disappears. I feel a whistle of wind and duck underneath his swipe, turning around and smacking my hot palm on his injured foot. He howls and I stand up quickly, a block of light smacking him in the chin, knocking him onto his back once more; not fast enough, Benson.

I stand over him, hand raised. Spears of light dot the sky, like stars in the day, covering the entire area, including the crowd. Everyone wanted to see what I can do—I'll show them.

"Yield," I say coolly; I'll only make the offer once. Benson looks up at me seeming impressed; he should've taken my deal beforehand. Allies are important but not necessary; I am not like Eurael. I don't need a network of informants and allies or leverage on individuals to have them do my bidding; I rely completely on myself and my own skills. Now he should see that my skills are a sufficient enough incentive for him to join me, or they may be the end of him.

"I yield," Benson says, holding up his hand. I wave my hand, and the spears of light disappear. I walk over to one of the benches, letting Benson pick himself up off the ground; he was rude to me by reneging on the deal, I'll show him the same courtesy.

Benson walks over to the bench, sitting down heavily, making the bench creak and groan. A smaller wolf comes over, handing him a large bucket of water. He holds it up and his tongue lolls out, lapping at the water. Totomir walks over, pulling himself up onto the bench as well. I glare at him; it was because of him that I had to go through this in the first place. He was right though; I didn't have to do Benson any favors to gain him as an ally. Not that I'll admit that to the dog.

"Looks like you won," he says, holding up a bag of coins with a grin. "And we got a pretty decent haul from it too."

"I could have died," I growl. He waves his paw at me dismissively, peeking into the bag.

"I had every confidence in you," he says, closing the bag tight and clutching it close. "I always hedge my bets, after all." I bend down, putting my face directly in front of his, livid and cold; this dog assumes too much.

"This is my money," I snarl, snatching the bag from him and hooking it onto my belt. "You're lucky I'm even going to let you live. From now on, you will do what I say; and when I am negotiating, you will *not*, under *any* circumstances, speak."

"You mean I'm going to stay with you?" the disappointment in his voice is obvious.

My aura glows brighter, my voice a poisonous hiss. "You think after that stunt you pulled I'm just going to let you get away? No," I put one palm on him and he yelps, leaping backward, smoke curling off his singed fur. "You're not going *anywhere*."

"It seems your skills are quite extraordinary," Benson says from behind mes. I turn to him as a wolf brings him a loose shirt, and he slips it on—even the loose shirt strains to contain him. "I believe you now, and I believe I can use your skills."

"No," I say, and Benson raises an eyebrow.

"We had an agreement," he says, frowning as his glasses are brought to him. He puts them on the end of his nose, looking down at me.

"I don't remember signing anything," I retort.

Totomir snorts beside me, then quickly covers it up with a cough. Benson leans back, his eyes growing cold while I maintain my resolute stare. I wouldn't unnecessarily anger him if he hadn't done the same to me; fair is fair Benson.

"Very well. What is your new deal?" he asks, his voice dropping in temperature.

"You will provide me with the information I seek first," I say. If I don't offer to help him and be of use to him, there's no way he'll accept any deal from me, and he may choose to rat me out to Eurael later. My biggest advantage right now is that Eurael doesn't know I'm in Legend Land; I will not lose the element of surprise. "Then I will complete a task you assign me." Benson's expression returns to a more neutral one; he knows the deal is fair, considering the circumstances.

"Alright," he says, lapping at the bucket again. "What do you want to know?"

"It's not so much of what I want to know, as much as what I want you to do," I reply.

"I'm an information broker, young lady; I detest field work," he says, pausing on his way down to begin lapping at the bucket again.

"No field work," I assure him, and he resumes lapping at the bucket. "If Eurael comes to you for information, I want you to turn him away. You will not aid him in any way."

He sets the empty bucket down, water droplets dripping off parts of his fur. "I don't think that will be a problem, considering he currently doesn't even know I'm in Legend Land."

That's a pleasant surprise; I should have asked if Eurael knew he was in Legend Land or not to begin with. That's an advantage of total surprise then—even better.

"Now if that's all—"

"Not quite," I interrupt, stopping him as he begins to stand, and he slowly sits back down. "I do want information," I look firmly at Benson, keeping eye contact. I was sent here with a mission to accomplish: conquer a kingdom and raise an army. It burns me to think of Eurael unhindered, living contentedly; but if I don't do this, I could make at least one very powerful enemy, and enemies are not something I can afford to have in abundance right now. "I want information on the current ruler of the Kingdom and on its capital building. I need the current ruler's history, allergies, and known enemies; I want the building's history, layout, and blueprints if there are any. I want everything on them."

"Consider it done," Benson says without hesitation, turning to one of the wolves and whispering in his ear. The wolf nods then scurries inside. "It will be ready shortly, though I must ask what you're planning on doing with this information." If I tell him the truth, he could easily go to the ruler of the Kingdom and tell them my intentions, and they could prepare for my arrival. If I don't tell him, he may go to the ruler anyway, and I don't want to start a partnership by lying. I need a stable foundation, and right now that's Benson.

"I plan on usurping the throne," I say calmly. Benson's expression doesn't change; he simply nods.

"You plan on doing *what?!*" I ignore Totomir's outburst and Benson does the same; overall, it really is better to just ignore the dog.

"In that case, I have in mind the task I want you to do for me," he says, his eyes gleaming brightly; he's an intellectual, this one. He has enormous physical strength, yes, and many might underestimate him for that, but he excels in intelligence and cunningness. He is, true to his nature, a big, bad wolf.

"Name it," I say, preparing myself; I might have to undertake something very large and time-consuming to pay for the amount of information I just requested. Of course, I will have to do it quickly; I have a schedule to keep.

"Once you're on the throne, I want you to publicly sponsor and endorse me," he says leaning forward. "I strive to run a generally honorable business."

I keep my face calm; I wouldn't call what he runs an honorable business, but I'll just keep that to myself.

"But some still see me as disreputable," he continues.

I look behind him at the wolves who keep their mean eyes flicking between the gathered town and me; I wonder how anyone would get that impression.

"I'd like to change that. If the new ruler of the Kingdom were to endorse me as a reputable broker of information, among other things, then a great amount of new clients would flock to me; I despise being seen as a wolf in sheep's clothing. This would benefit you as well," he says, and I raise an eyebrow; he certainly does know how to sell a point, I'll give him that. "As my client base grows, so will the amount of information that is constantly available to you."

"Do you plan on making this information available to me for free?" I ask.

He lets out a loud bark of laughter, and it turns into a rumbling chuckle; he wipes a small tear from his eye, sighing. "That's a good one," he says, chuckling again. "Free information! Oh you're a funny one. You would have all of the resources of the Kingdom at your disposal; you could afford it."

"Fine," I say, shaking his hand once again; hopefully this deal will be more final, though I plan on negotiating on the amount that I have to pay for information in the future.

I make my way to the front, the dog following behind. A young wolf runs out, a large briefcase in hand. He hands it to me, panting for breath and I take it from him, smiling gratefully. He holds himself up a little higher, his chest swelling out a little and he nods, walking away. I shake my head and smile to myself; men. I open the briefcase, sorting through the papers; it all seems to be there. I close the briefcase and begin walking, Totomir struggling to keep up, panting slightly.

"I thought that went well," he says, his small legs moving quickly to keep pace.

"It could have gone better," I say, glancing down at him, then back in front of me; he should learn the very valuable skill of knowing when to shut up.

"You got what you wanted, right?" He asks.

"This is merely the beginning."

Totomir speeds up, standing in front of me; I stop, looking down at him. It is a little amusing to have such a stubborn, hopelessly stupid mind trapped in a small, cute body as that. Honestly, I'd like him better as a regular, non-talking dog. Oh gods the silence would be heavenly.

"What's your beef with this Eurael person?" his eyes flick over me, searching; you will find nothing to use against me, mutt. "If I'm going to stick with you, I should know what I'm getting into."

"It's not important," I reply coolly; just because I use him does not mean he gets to be privy to my machinations. "You should focus less on asking questions and more on what will happen to you should you continue your pestering."

"I'm not moving until I get an answer," he says firmly.

I get down on one knee, dropping to his level. "I will not argue with a dog," I state simply, my aura shimmering, fluxing out brightly.

"You owe me for back there," he says, keeping his feet firmly planted, a paw on his rapier.

"I don't owe you anything," I snap, standing up and stalking off. He thinks because he was right about a few things that I suddenly owe him? Because of him I could have died fighting Benson; I didn't, but I *could* have. Even if he has wealth or possible connections, it doesn't matter enough to me to deal with his infuriating mannerisms.

"Where do you think you're going to stay?" he shouts out from behind me.

I stop, swearing softly under my breath; I don't have much money either. I close my eyes, forcing my aura to stay dim, a pleasant cooling sensation rewarding my efforts. I turn, opening my eyes, forcing a small smile on my face. "I hadn't figured that out yet," I say, walking toward him; one of his infuriating mannerisms is that he constantly seems to find ways to be useful.

"I happen to have a place you could stay," he says grinning.

I could just take it. He would tell me, I could kill him and take it; it would just be that easy. This could all be so easy. As infuriating as he is, though, he still continues to be useful at every single turn, surprisingly so. I will put up with him—for now.

"Are you offering for me to stay with you?"

His grin grows even wider, becoming an almost wolfish smile. "Of course," he says, and I nod. "As soon as you answer my question."

I inwardly sigh, my aura fluxing out; I can tell him, without telling him. I just have to choose my words carefully. "This man, Eurael, betrayed me," I say; just a little more and that should be enough for him. "He left me alone, to die. I survived, and now I'm exacting my revenge." No need to get into the specifics really; there are some things that are just personal.

"Men," he says disdainfully. I raise an eyebrow, and he shrugs his shoulders. "I'm a dog, it doesn't really apply to me. People automatically love me."

I'm not sure "love" is the right word there. I gesture in front of me, coin purse swaying slightly; ah yes, I do actually have money.

Some things are just easy to forget; but if there's an option where I don't have to pay for residence, why waste money on one where I do?

"A deal is a deal," I say, forcing a small smile; hopefully smiling will just start coming naturally. What's the expression, kill them with kindness? I suppose I can try anything once.

"I don't remember signing anything," he says with a smirk.

I glare at him, light burning through my system as my aura glows brighter, my tongue feeling like a fork of fire in my mouth.

"It's a joke. Gods woman, don't get your knickers in a twist," he grumbles, stepping in front of me, walking as quickly as his legs can carry him. As long as he continues to be useful, he's safe; but if he cracks one more joke, even that may not be enough to save him.

CHAPTER THRITY

I sit by Scarlett's bedside. The summer is now in full swing, and her condition has yet to improve. Her breathing is deep and steady, her face clear, like the calm before a storm. I have spent the last few weeks discovering everything I can about the man that came to visit Scarlett, and in that time I have learned much.

His name is Wilhelm Ludwig, approximately twenty-five years of age; he lives alone in a cottage off the side of the road outside of the capital of the Kingdom. He has no friends, but no enemies either; he does odd jobs and whatever else he can to earn money. Recently he tried mercenary work; he failed miserably at his first job. He has not realized he isn't cut out for mercenary work and has actually been trying harder to improve his combat skills of late, most likely due to the fact that he does not want to appear weak to Scarlett. In relation to Scarlett, they are together often, even during times when I had sent her out to train. I look at Scarlett's hair and gently take a strand of it between my fingers. I am not against Scarlett having personal relations with someone, save for the fact that she did not tell me. Her mouth opens partially, but her eyes remain closed.

"Wilhelm," she mutters, turning over in her sleep, her hair slipping from between my fingers. I stand up, turning on my heel and walking to the door; I should have kept a closer eye on her. While this man, Wilhelm, does not appear to be dangerous, he could have been. Scarlett needlessly risked her life, all because I was careless.

And she didn't tell me, even after all we had been through together. I close the door behind me and lean against it, letting out a long sigh.

A scream wrenches me from my bed. I fling my door open, flying down the hallway to Scarlett's room. I twist the knob and find it locked, growling. The shadows slam themselves against the door frantically, and it finally bursts open, allowing me to rush in. Scarlett lies on her bed, convulsing and twisting about, her mouth open, jaw locked. Her throat strains from the effort of maintaining the scream, and I leap onto the bed, holding down her body. Her mouth snaps shut, her body arching up, the tendrils wrapping around her wrists and ankles; they care about her safety nearly as much as I.

"Help me, please! Help me! Mister E!" I gesture for the shadows to release her, and I hold her body to me, trembling and shaking. "Oh gods make it stop! Please! Mister E, help me!"

My hands curl in the material of her shirt, burying her sobbing head into my chest; I can do nothing to help her. She relives her torments in the Underworld, and I can...I can do *nothing* to stop it. I bite my tongue, trembling against her; *useless*. She sobs into me profusely, trying to move her arms, but she won't let herself.

"Please..." she chokes out, her body tense and rigid against me. "Please kill me. Mister E, please." Her shoulders slump, her body going limp against me. I stroke her hair gently, drops dripping from my chin, wetting her hair; I can't do it. I know it isn't her, but I can't...I wasn't there for her. I know she won't remember any of this, as she never does, but I still let her go, and she suffered for it. But I can't...I can't kill her. I can't end her pain.

"I'm sorry," I whisper, kissing her forehead, the salt of her sweat on my lips. "I failed you again. Simiel," I press my lips to her forehead again, a new kind of salt joining the taste. "I'm sorry."

"You look stressed about something," Scarlett leans in the doorway to the library. I look up to see a playful smile on her face, barely crooking up one side of her mouth; I have been lax lately in her studies and training. I fear that by pushing her too far her condition will only worsen. I look back down at the papers, keeping my hand steady as I write, my expression carefully neutral; it is nearing autumn now. Spring faded and summer burnt itself out, but there is still no change. Outwardly she is herself, but she continues to suffer breaks and episodes. I keep myself there for her during them, but she doesn't know I'm there. She can't know what's happening to her; I can't give anything away. To know of her inner torture would be...it would be hell; I can't let her know. It's best she doesn't remember her episodes or her time in the Underworld; it's better for everyone.

I glance up from my work; returning from the dead isn't easy on everyone. To wrench the soul from death and bring it back to the land of the living...it is not the easiest thing for the mind to cope with. While I thought I had stopped Scarlett's amnesia, her recent episodes might be a sign that it could be returning. I know the mental block I have put in place is now under more pressure, its hold fragile at best. Returning from the Underworld would have placed an immense amount of stress on her mind; it managed to keep the mental block there, but barely. She's lucky her mind didn't simply snap; I could have done nothing for her then. My hands clench around my pen, my fingertips shaking; I have not delved into Scarlett's mind to fix its workings yet because I fear that her mental state could be irreparably damaged in her current condition, or that the mental block I had instilled upon first meeting her would crumble.

"You are stressed about something, or at least thinking about something." she walks over, leaning over the desk to look at my papers; but before she can do so, I give her a firm look and she stops.

"I'm fine," I reply, looking back down. In addition, since Wilhelm's first visit, he has visited twelve more times; each time I have turned him away. I don't believe he would attack me even if he had the skill to hold his own against me, but I cannot allow him to introduce more chaos into the situation. In Scarlett's current state, any turbulent or more potent and powerful emotions could throw her over the edge; after all the work I have done to prevent that, I will not have it undone by a fool. Especially one she did not feel was important enough to mention to me.

"I don't believe you," she says, folding her arms across her chest; without any tampering of her mind, she might resort back to childish ways and mannerisms in order to cope with her most recent ordeal. This could be the onset of something much worse; I might have no choice. She could be reverting back to her old self—the one that existed before I met her. That would be disastrous. I stand up and walk close to Scarlett, keeping my expression neutral even as my hands quiver; she is broken, not stupid.

"It doesn't matter what you believe. All you must believe is that, right now, you are asleep." I put my hand on her head, holding her in place as she tries to jerk back.

"What?"

I focus intently on her, and her eyes roll back in her head, her knees buckling as she slumps to the ground. Gently I lay her downand kneel over her, my hand first checking her pulse then resting on her forehead; she is steady and well at least. I look down at her sleeping form, calm and peaceful; I cannot allow this to continue anymore. The body will eventually fix itself if given the proper tools; but the mind, while resilient, can and will eventually break. To the untrained eye, it would even appear that nothing is wrong with Scarlett until she suffers an episode. But I can tell. Every day I notice the difference. She is not herself; and if I don't stop it, she may never be again. The constant drifting to an unconscious state, lack of motor skills, and resorting to a more childish behavior in order to protect herself is all done subconsciously. I have to take control of this and restore order; I will not lose my student, not even to herself.

I close my eyes and take a deep breath; I will have to alter her mind without breaking it, without her detecting me, and without removing the mental block. It must be done carefully and cleanly; this cannot be rushed or forced. I take my glove off, putting my skin against hers, feeling the warmth travel all the way up my arm in a single, small wave; I have no choice.

CHAPTER THIRTY-ONE

A great emptiness swamps me, threatening to pull me under; not emptiness, but an absence of anything—light, memory, sound—a great, vast nothingness. I tremble and trudge forward blindly, unable to see even with my enhanced vision; this is what plagues Scarlett now. It is a vast wasteland of emptiness, space that has yet to be filled—a blank slate on the edge of consciousness, always waiting to take over. A scream echoes, and I whirl around, but I can see no one. I feel wind rustle my hair, a playful laugh rebounding around endlessly before abruptly ceasing.

The temperature has gotten low enough for me to feel it despite my clothes and natural resistance, my breath becoming visible puffs in the air. Slowly the darkness around me begins to fade, as if a picture is finally becoming clear. Dead grass crunches under my feet, barely held by the brittle, dry soil. A harsh wind tugs at my clothes and at my exposed skin, like it would want nothing more than to tear me away forever. The sun shines bleakly overhead, barely giving enough light to discern color, everything appearing in grey-scale. In the distance, a large grey wall looms, though even from this distance I can tell it is crumbling—a weak, dilapidated barrier that is barely keeping this dead wasteland from overcoming everything.

A stronger gust of wind tugs at my hair and whispers in my ear, but I keep my eyes firmly set on the wall. The sound of crunching grass gets louder and I stop, the sound stopping as well. I take a step forward, the crunch of the grass louder than it should be. I take a few steps forward then whirl around, swinging my sword through empty air. A small peal of laughter wavers in the air, and I hear the sound of something hitting the grass repeatedly.

A small red ball bounces of its own accord before me. Its maximum height doesn't reach my stomach, but it continues to bounce. The grass underneath remains untouched, and the wind does not move it. The red paint on the ball is chipped and faded, several holes poked clean through, though it still retains its round shape. Grass crunches behind me, and I extend a hand quickly, willing the shadows to find the disturbance. Instead, they simply rise up and circle around the ball as it bounces, hissing and spitting at it. I slowly reach a hand out and the wind picks up, howling in my ear, angrily tugging at me. The ball begins to bounce faster, becoming a blur now as it slams itself down against the ground, as if trying to break free. A low buzzing fills my ears, crackling in the air like broken sound; white noise. My hand closes around the ball and the wind suddenly stops, allowing me to perfectly hear the scream from behind me.

"Don't touch my ball!"

I turn around, ball in hand, and see a small child glaring at me. Her skin and clothes remain in the grey-scale of the rest of the world; she's wearing no shoes, her feet bare against the grass. She's wearing a small pair of overalls, one strap nearly sliding off her shoulder, a small shirt underneath. Her small hands are planted firmly on her hips, her lips turned down into a scowl, her nose slightly scrunched, eyebrows furrowed. Her green eyes shine brightly, glaring at me and her red hair falls down in gentle waves to her waist, those two features breaking the grey-scale rule that seems to apply to everything else; they rebel. She stomps up to me, barely coming up to my waist; she glares up at me fiercely, seeming ready to attack me if necessary.

"That is my ball, and I want it back! You shouldn't be touching it! Give it back!" She's missing two of her top teeth and one of her bottom ones, the air whistling through them as she speaks.

"Did you lose some teeth recently?" I ask, keeping my voice calm; I have much less power here than this girl, and I am not sure if

I would win if it actually came to it. I am an intruder here, and she the warden; with a single swipe of her hand, she could erase me if she wanted, though she may not even know it.

"Yeah," she says smiling and pointing to her teeth. Her eyes narrow and she points up at me, glaring once again. "Don't try to distract me! I want my ball!"

"Well so do I," I reply, holding the ball high over her head; experimentation must be done, even if it seems foolish at the time. I risk losing myself in this action, but I must know. The wind picks up again and she clenches her fists, her eyes shining brightly.

"I WANT MY BALL!" she shouts, a gust of wind slamming into me, nearly knocking me off my feet.

I hold out the ball and it stops abruptly, her small hands reaching out to grab it. Just as she's about to grab it, I pull it out of her reach. She glares at me, a high pitched whining sound filling my ears, drilling into my brain; just as I thought. "Let's make a deal."

The whining stops, and a bit of the anger leaves her eyes as they start to become curious.

"What kinda deal?" she asks, suspiciously.

"You can have the ball if you walk with me to that wall over there," I say, pointing to the barrier in the distance.

"That's a long way," she says, folding her arms across her chest.

"I'll carry you if you get tired," I say, and she unfolds her arms, all anger gone from her eyes now.

"What if you try and hurt me? I know some men like to hurt little girls," she says, her bright eyes watching me warily for any sign of violence.

"I won't hurt you," I say, and she frowns.

"Promise?"

"I promise," I reply, and she holds out her hand, her smallest finger extended.

"I want you to swear on your life you won't hurt me," she says seriously. I hook my finger around hers, and her finger curls around mine, not letting go immediately. "The pinky promise is the most binding contract in the universe; you can't break it," she says and I nod, my finger slipping loose.

"Don't worry, I won't; since I swore on my life, I'd die." I hand her the ball and her eyes light up as she holds it to her chest, walking quickly to keep up with my long strides as I began walking to the barrier, a warm breeze trickling over me as she whistles happily.

"Have you ever died before?" she asks inquisitively.

"Yes."

"What was it like?" her eyes are wide and curious; I look away from her, keeping my eyes on the barrier. The innocence—the mind of a child—I won't spoil it.

"It's not fun."

"Huh," she says, looking back down at her ball. "My name's Scarlett, by the way." She remains looking down at her ball, holding one hand out and up to me.

I shake it, my gloved hand engulfing hers like a dark maw.

"My name is Mister E."

"That's an interesting name," she says. She frowns, looking up at me in an accusing fashion. "Is that your real name?"

"No," I say and she glares at me, then she smiles, the outside of her mouth barely crooking up.

"Well Scarlett isn't *my* real name either," she says, holding the ball close to her chest.

"Then what is it?" I look down at her; she's begun walking by doing a sort of march, keeping her legs stiff and swinging them out in front, then planting her foot, sending up a small puff of dirt, then swinging her other foot forward. Children get so bored with the mundane quickly; in their defense, the mundane is often boring. Despite the seriousness of my mission, I pay special attention to the girl; she is important to understanding Scarlett's mind and her past.

"It's...Queen Countess Hismalin of Ballinra," she says, looking up at me, her eyes twinkling.

"Well Countess," I say and she giggles, hiding her face behind her ball, "I have a question for you."

"What is it, Mister Fakename?" The same spark has apparently existed her entire life; clever, rebellious, stubborn. No matter who she is, or what she forgets, perhaps she will always be herself. My eyes flick down to the little girl, then back ahead; perhaps she will always be like this. Maturity growing and receding with age, but her personality staying the same; perhaps the Scarlett I know is the same Scarlett who has always been, and all I have done is give her the tools to discover it for herself.

"What would you have done if I hadn't given you the ball?" These echoes of herself, of her memory; they are an insight to who she is—insights she herself is not even capable of making.

"I would have bit you," she says without hesitation. I raise an eyebrow, and she bounces the ball hard on the ground, catching it as it comes back down. "It would have hurt a lot," she assures me confidently.

"But you're missing teeth," I point out. "That would reduce the amount of pain you can inflict with a bite."

"Oh," she looks down, reforming her perfect plan mentally. "I would've asked the snakes to bite you then," she says.

"Snakes?"

She points to the tendrils of shadow slithering along the ground behind us. I wave my hand subtly, but they simply slither over to Scarlett, swirling up her legs. She giggles as the tendrils hiss and coo at her, several rising up behind her silently. I clench my fist and make my next step much more forceful, causing the shadows to shake and slither away regretfully, disappearing; they cannot interfere with this, with her. "I'm not sure they would have bit me."

"You're making it difficult on purpose," she complains, bouncing the ball again. I sigh, speeding up, and she has to run to keep up now. "You're going too fast!" I stop suddenly and she digs her heels in, sliding to a stop. "You said you would carry me," she says, lifting her arms over her head and I pick her up, setting her on my shoulders—children. They are the most unique creatures, and yet the most baffling. She keeps both hands on the ball, resting it on my head, her legs kicking gently against me.

"There," I speed up again, and her heels dig in slightly to keep her balance.

"This is weird," she says after a moment, turning on my shoulders to look around.

"What is?"

"Being this tall," she says. "No wonder adults aren't any fun; you're always looking down on everyone. You can't help it though, because you're all so tall, and it just becomes a contest to see who can look down on more people. That's why people grow," she finishes her sentence with a firm nod of her head.

"That's a very interesting theory," I say; it's no worse an idea than what's been put forth in the Kingdom. The Kingdom is not exactly the most...scientifically advanced realm I have traveled to, and its medical knowledge has suffered because of it; she might be hailed as a genius back in the Kingdom. "But adults are no fun," I continue, "because they have lots of things to do, and they don't use their brains to be as much fun because they have other things that they need to think about."

"I have lots of things to do too," she says, holding the ball with one hand and holding up fingers as she names each thing. "I have to breathe, my heart has to beat, my blood has to move, my bones and muscles have to work together. I have to use the bathroom, sleep, eat, remember dates and faces, remember to blink, and learn. I still have fun though, even though I have a lot of things to do all the time; I don't see why adults can't do it."

I nod, thinking it over; the argument does actually carry some weight. Obviously not all of her traits were developed because of my training, least of all her argumentative intellect.

"You're right," I say, tilting my head back slightly and moving my eyes up as far as I can to look her in the eyes. "Adults really have no excuse to not have fun. What about me? Am I fun?"

She pauses for a moment, holding her ball with one arm and using her free hand to tap my nose as she thinks.

"You're...interesting," she says as I lean my head forward again.

"Which isn't the same thing as fun. I only met you two seconds ago though."

"It's been far longer than two seconds."

"I'm not allowed to have a concept of time until I'm at least ten," she says.

"I still don't have a concept of time," I reply, and she looks down at me, leaning over my head to look me in the eyes.

"Are you a really big ten-year-old?" she asks seriously, her hair hanging down to my stomach.

"I'm much older than that," I assure her, and she leans back, resuming her former position.

"That's just weird then," she says factually.

"Why is it weird?"

"Because you're an adult, and I'm a kid; some things that kids do are weird when adults do them."

"Like have fun despite being very busy?" I can feel her scowl, heat radiating from her small body in a larger amount.

"That's not fair; you tricked me!" she says, bouncing the ball on my head.

"You tricked me though," I say.

"How?"

"You made me think that you were just a very small ten-year old with a concept of time for the first two seconds I knew you," I reply, and the heat from her body gets greater, then dissipates as she laughs, grabbing a strand of my hair and letting it run through her fingers.

"You are fun, Mister E," she decides, patting me on the head.

We travel in silence for some time as the barrier grows closer. Scarlett tugs my hair gently, and I turn my head slightly to show I'm listening; she's quieter as a child actually.

"I know why you're here Mister E," she says, much more serious than before. I continue walking, inclining my head a little, showing her that I want her to continue. "I know something is wrong behind that wall; I can feel it. Adults don't feel things as much as try to explain them; I can feel that something is wrong here. This is a dead place outside of the wall, I know it; I am trapped here, on the outside, unable to join with the rest." She kicks her legs and I kneel down, letting her slide off my shoulders. She looks up at me, clutching her ball, her eyes serious and determined. They hold an amount of focus that is uncanny in anyone, much less a small child, or at least an echo of a memory of a child. "But I am here with others like me," she gestures around, to the faint whispers and soft voices that make up the wind. The blades of grass whistle slightly in the wind of voices, and faint specters have begun appearing the closer we got to the wall. "We are all trapped, unable to be remembered; we live a miserable life here. Please," she grabs the leg of my pants, looking up at me, pleading now. "Fix it so we may join the others. Please. We are echoes and shadows of memories, unable to be recalled; that barrier keeps us out. Please fix it, help us."

I look down at her and place my hand on her head, letting her hair slide and slip through my fingers. "I put that barrier there," I say, and she looks up at me, pulling away.

"What?!"

"When I first met you, you continued to forget everything that happened at random moments; you were stuck in this wasteland. I created a safe place for you to reside, but I could not make it very large. That barrier remains in place to keep you safe; if it were to fall, everything would be engulfed by this wasteland. It's for the good of everyone."

Hurt flashes across her face, and she backpedals away from me, clutching the ball to her chest.

"You keep us here! You keep us trapped!"

I remain silent, standing still as tears well up at the corner of her eyes. "You keep us imprisoned!" The wind begins to howl stronger, whipping at me as tears leak down from her eyes.

"You'll always be trapped here! Nothing can be done! I can't do anything to change that!" I shout over the roar of the wind. The wind stops suddenly and Scarlett turns away, her small shoulders shaking.

"Go away," she mutters, dropping to the ground. She clutches the ball, shaking and trembling, her hair spread out over her shoulders, covering her face. I walk past her toward the barrier without a second glance; I cannot afford to look back. She is just an echo.

I'm close to the barrier now, and I can see up close how weak it has become. Supports are barely keeping it up, holes appearing, big enough for the wind to whistle through. Grass has begun to grow through the cracks, and small portions seem to crumble and drop off every minute. I walk closer to the barrier and it sparks, gleaming brightly for a moment. A man stands before me, dressed in shabby black clothes resembling my own. He's slightly stooped, his face pale and lined. Hard, black eyes gaze out from their deep sockets, his grey, matted hair falling to his shoulders in a mane.

"Who are you?" his voice is low and gruff, telling the experience his lines show.

"I am you," I say, looking him over slowly. "Or, rather, you are me."

"I highly doubt that," he says, straightening up slightly.

"Gods you are stubborn," I say shaking my head. Was this what I was like before I met Scarlett? Next time I shall not place myself as a guardian; I'm far too difficult for even me to deal with. "I don't have time for this." I take a step forward and he thrusts his hands out, tendrils of shadow shooting out toward me. I hold my palm out and they slow, curling up my arm, cooing as I stroke the tendril with the pad of my thumb. It disappears into my skin, and I unsheathe my sword, stepping forward again. He thrusts his hand out, but nothing happens this time; I grab him by his shoulders and pull him toward me, thrusting my sword into his stomach and up into his heart. "You are an old fool," I growl, thrusting it in deeper. He is my mistakes, my failures; he is my past, and the past is exactly what I am here to fix. "And you are no longer needed." I yank the sword out and he drops to the ground, slowly sinking down until he disappears. I sheathe my sword and shake my head; I simply can't stand myself. Placing my hand on the wall it shimmers, becoming translucent for a moment, and I step through, the wall becoming solid once more behind me.

Dirty streets with dilapidated houses twist and turn around me, deserted except for garbage and loose pieces of paper. Ahead at the far end of the road lies a glimmering golden palace, shining brightly; the memory palace. I quickly stride down the roads, noticing spots of dead grass crawling up through the cracks in the road. Voices whisper softly, and I hear a steady thud on the street; I speed up, blurring through the streets. The wasteland is quickly making its way beyond the barrier, and I must find the solution to this problem before it absorbs Scarlett's mind completely. I will have to start over from the beginning then, or Scarlett will be broken beyond repair; neither of those options is a viable one. Nothing else matters now; I cannot lose Scarlett.

I stride up the steps to the palace, the shadows twisting out and pushing the doors open, then slamming them shut behind me. They hold themselves against the door, hissing as I stride through the palace; I am looking for a specific memory. The shadows will hold, at least for a moment; they can sense the danger Scarlett is in, as much as I feel it where my soul used to be. I stop, looking around; all around me are doors. Hundreds of doors everywhere: on the floor, on the ceiling, and on the walls. It will take too long to search all of these rooms! The chandelier overhead swings, its crystal pieces gently hitting each other. The shadows hiss louder from the front as a voice shouts out, the wind beginning to audibly howl through the walls.

"Let go of my ball, snakes!"

I close my eyes, placing my hand on the ground; I have to find it quickly now. I extend my senses out, taking a deep breath as I push them out throughout the palace. The howling of the wind grows louder, and I feel the shadows slither back into me, retreating from the door. I feel grass tickle my wrists and I open my eyes; upstairs. I race up the stairs, chased by the voices.

"Don't run from me! That's no fun!"

A loud cackle of laughter peals out from behind and I turn, tendrils of shadow wrapping around the single staircase. With a loud crack it crumbles and I turn, racing through the halls. Grass clutches at my feet now, and I have to yank my feet up with each step to continue moving, the wasteland spreading like a virus. A single door gleams on the left, and I unsheathe my sword, slicing at the grass and the air around me. The wind blows out the window at the end of the hall, pushing against me; I grit my teeth and the shadows dig into the floor, pulling me toward the door. My trembling hand reaches out for the doorknob and I wrench it open, throwing myself inside.

The door slams shut behind me, and the shadows cover it, the wind straining against it. Before me is a small picture frame, with one memory in it; a single memory on loop, playing over and over. The Investigator impales Scarlett again and again, the same few seconds on repeat. I can clearly see where his claws push through her, gripping, preparing to toss her; this memory leads to all the other ones she has of the Underworld. If I destroy this memory, then the rest will follow—a domino effect. I pick it up, turning it over in my hand; the other memories should remain untouched and undamaged, but it is possible that this could be the catalyst; it could break Scarlett. I grip the frame harder, squeezing my eyes shut; I don't have a choice though. If I let things go on how they are, all my work will be destroyed anyway. This is the most logical solution, the one that gives me what I want; I squeeze the frame tighter, the glass beginning to crack underneath my gloves.

I stop, shaking my head; it could hurt Scarlett. I could damage her by doing this; I could destroy her. I could lose my student, and I would only have myself to blame. The logical solution...I shake my head. Behind me, the door slings open, the shadows flying against the walls and then disappearing. Scarlett's echo stands in the doorway, holding her ball, glaring at me.

"Stop!" she shouts vehemently; I turn and she screams, lunging at me.

The ball bounces once on the floor before I catch her, throwing her against the wall. I hear footsteps above, and I grip the frame tighter in both hands; Scarlett's consciousness is aware now. In a few short moments, she will be in this room, looking at an echo of a memory and me; I have to destroy this, logic be damned. Somewhere where my soul used to be, where Scarlett has touched, tells me to destroy it; she is strong enough, she will survive it.

"Don't destroy it," The echo says, standing up as the glass frame cracks and falls out, the wood beginning to splinter. "If you do, you'll seal the rest of her memories away, stuck in that wasteland. You'll seal me away!"

"You are an echo," I say softly, unsure if she even hears me. "I have to save the you that exists, now; I'm sorry." The frame breaks with a loud snap, the picture tearing in two. There's a loud scream and she fades away, the grass receding. I find myself flying backward, retracing my steps through the memory palace. I exit and the doors slam closed behind me. I pass through the wall without incident, flying across the wasteland, an explosion of light chasing after me.

CHAPTER THRITY-TWO

I look at the sheets of paper spread out over the table before me, gripping my head in my hands. I dislike the idea of attacking head-on with an army, but a small force wouldn't be able to get very far in a castle like this. A small creature runs up to me, giving me a cup of water. I look at the creature, taking the cup; it is small, barely coming up to my waist. Its skin is a dark green color, and it has large floppy ears, a pointy nose, and round, pure black eyes. It has long, thin arms and short legs, with two tusks curving out of each side of its mouth. I pat its head, and it snorts its appreciation, waddling away. These creatures make up the underground "army." Totomir has an extensive array of mining tunnels—and enough of these creatures to fill a city. He said he acquired them all through a game of dice; maybe this was what he stole from Benson.

I sip from the cup, looking back over the blueprints and layout of the castle; I am very apprehensive of the skill of this army. Totomir seems keen on a frontal assault, taking the enemy head-on. It's only natural that he wants to do that, with his untrained mind, but it's not the best option. Ever since I revealed my plan to attack the capital of the Kingdom, Totomir has been surprisingly on board. The dog is a true glutton—money, power, glory—he can't stop himself. He wants it all, and he sees me as a way to get it; his ambition will get him killed, and his stupidity might have me share his fate.

I stack the papers up neatly, moving them aside, getting the other stack and looking through them. The current ruler of the Kingdom is Artemis, a woman who is said to be a legendary combatant. It is rumored she fought her way up from the gladiator pits and took on the capital single-handed, just as I am about to do. Her skill with the bow is said to be unrivaled, and she's a fierce close-hand combatant, rumored to be blessed by the Goddess of the Hunt in all her endeavors. As an opponent worthy of my time, consideration, and respect, it wouldn't be wise to underestimate her. She's managed to keep her throne for several years, despite multiple challengers and various nobility trying to usurp her throne.

I set the papers down; I have to think this through, though it has to be done quickly so that I can begin pursuing Eurael. I stand up and walk out of my room; so far I have managed to keep the dog from digging too much into my mission, doing my best to distract him with the most trivial matters. I walk through the tunnels that the creatures are digging; they are almost constantly digging and mining, slaving away for that pretentious canine. Precious stones and gold abound in these tunnels, a very fortunate fact; if only these creatures could comprise a formidable army. I walk to the end of one of the tunnels, my aura shining brighter to provide the proper illumination; these little goblins can see very well in the dark, but my eyes aren't so keen. I come to a set of large stone doors and push them open easily, closing them behind me.

"I've come to the conclusion that this is where I belong," Totomir says gleefully, looking down at me.

The throne room is large and long, barely lit by gas lamps, which only lengthen the shadows cast by them. Large stone steps lead up to the throne itself, which is high enough that the person seated can look down on the entire room. Totomir is seated atop the throne, which gleams even in the sparse light; it's made entirely out of shining, bright gold with a small cushion on the seat. A small golden crown with several precious stones sits loosely on his head as he grins. With my tales of conquest to drive him, he has come to fancy himself the king of these creatures and his underground "empire." I see the way he looks hungrily at the plans for the capital, the way he salivates looking at the building in the distance; I will have to rid myself of him. The creatures are bound to him in a way that I don't quite understand, and his desire for power will make him a dangerous ally to have. I can't have dangerous allies when I have dangerous enough enemies as is.

"Oh is it now?" It can get difficult at times to keep my eye on Totomir; he has the habit of slipping away without me noticing and returning with a sly look scrawled over his mangy face. "Have you come to any other conclusions? Such as how we might get into the castle to overtake it?" I climb up the steps; he may play the part of a king, but that does not make him one.

"We attack head-on and crush them," he says.

A head-on assault will never work. Rarely is a head-on attack the best option, no matter what the situation. "That won't work with this army," I say. "And I use the term 'army' very loosely."

"There's a lot of them!" he says, gesturing around. "These tunnels are filled with the things! We can win through sheer numbers. These creatures are as valuable a resource as the precious stones and metals they mine; no human would subject themselves to mining all day and night for no pay."

"I have to deal with the people afterward," I snap, my aura fluxing out, causing Totomir to shy away slightly. "I can't slaughter thousands of soldiers who are simply defending their queen and expect the people to follow me."

"They are subjects who must obey their king," he says dismissively. He looks up at me and gulps, quickly doing his best to cover up his verbal slip. "Who must obey their queen, of course." He confirms my suspicions; he wants the throne for himself.

"I want my subjects to respect me," I say; I don't know why I bother to tell him anything at this point. All he wants is war, so he can gain power. My aura flashes as I straighten up, eyes shining brightly as I look down at him. "What do you intend to do after we take the capital?"

He looks up from inspecting a ruby the size of my fist, tossing it back into the bucket of a passing goblin.

"Same 'ol, same 'ol I suppose."

"You mean you don't plan on trying to take the throne for yourself?"

He splutters, seemingly offended, which I don't buy for a second. "*Me?!* Usurp *you?!* I may like money, but I'm not completely *daft,*" he says, taking his crown off of his head, turning it in the dim light. "I'm happy with my little underground empire, with all the servants and gold I could ever want."

Even if what he says is true, how long before he starts desiring more? The dog is a glutton by nature; he will covet, and his desire will only get stronger with time. After I conquer the Kingdom, I will crush any underground rebellions, suspected or otherwise.

"Why the frontal assault though? Why end thousands of lives unnecessarily?" I've killed a great many people—some I regret, some I don't—but it has to serve a purpose. To just needlessly charge, thousands dying on both sides, it...it would just be a complete and total waste.

"Look," he says, glancing up at me, his eyes appearing as dark as the goblins' in the low light. "Evermore, I've been stuck in this world for a long time. I mean, this isn't even my homeland." He flips the crown slowly over, watching the jewels catch the light. "Here, I have power. Before, I couldn't speak, much less rule an empire," he looks down at the crown, spinning it around one wrist. "If there's one thing I've learned by being here, though, it's that only the strong survive, and they take from the weak. I'm tired of being weak; a frontal assault will show everyone that we are, above all else, *strong.*"

I shake my head; I can't believe this. Gripping one arm of the throne, I lean in close, my voice as hot as the blood boiling in my veins.

"Listen here you arrogant, selfish, pompous little bag of fur," I growl, my aura shining brighter, heat racing through my body, concentrating in my hands. "I don't care about you wanting to be strong; I don't care about appearances. The only thing that matters is the result; the end justifies the means, but there is always another option. A frontal assault will do nothing but waste otherwise useful lives," I stand up, straightening my shirt, breathing deeply, leaving two red hot hand prints in the golden throne. "I'm going to run a clean, covert operation to secure the throne of the Kingdom, with minimal loss of life." He nods slowly, and I turn on my heel.

"I'll come with you then," he says, hopping down from the throne.

"Why?" I snap back. Whether he gives me a satisfactory answer or not, I'm going to let him come with me; he will be away from his workers, vulnerable. Now that he's all but made his intentions clear, I can't let him live; the risk he presents is no longer outweighed by his use. In the heat of battle, accidents are bound to happen after all.

"I want to see how your definition of strength matches up to mine," he says, eyes flicking knowingly between the hand prints left in the throne and me.

CHAPTER THIRTY-THREE

I look at the castle, holding my breath as a guard walks by. The castle is lit by lanterns and other powerful lights, so it's easily visible in the night; a symbol. It towers tall and strong, its dark grey stones standing the test of time and armies that have laid siege to it in the past. Tall turrets allow sentries to keep watch during the day and provide a perfect place for archers to fire invisible arrows on enemies under the cover of darkness.

"You should have dressed in black," Totomir says, his dark fur making him nearly invisible in the night. "I mean, you're practically glowing."

I look down at my own white clothing which, while not very easily visible, still allows me to be spotted easier. I shake my head, dimming my aura as much as possible with a few deep breaths; just focus. You've completed far worse tasks in the past; after this, you can finally begin hunting down Eurael. You can do this.

"There are times when you have to adapt to the situation, and other times when the situation will adapt to you." I watch the guards patrol, keeping on schedule to the letter. I close my eyes, slowing my breath, preparing myself further; I've got this. I feel cool sensations travel pleasantly up my spine, and I have to resist the urge to shudder. The sensation almost grows to be unpleasant, but I simply control my breathing, making sure my aura remains dim almost to the point of invisibility. I begin counting in my head; three. The wind blows quietly, just barely teasing my hair, causing the leaves to rustle over-head. Two. I can hardly hear my breathing. One. I flex my hands once, sweat forming on my skin as my aura gives a small burst of light before becoming nearly invisible once more. Zero. I open my eyes, seeing the guards patrol regularly. I look around cautiously; it's time. Seconds tick by slowly, the patrol uninterrupted, the night still as can be. Something should have—

A loud explosion booms from the west, plumes of fire emerging at the same time; a nearby village, already evacuated, has just played its part in the diversion. The guards take off running toward it; common sense will kick in, and they will return to the castle in a moment to alert Artemis and the soldiers. But for now, a window has been opened. I dash forward across the open field that lies around the castle, keeping low to the ground. The only way I am able to tell that the dog is following is by the soft sound of his footsteps racing on the ground slightly behind me. I come to the castle wall and pause, catching my breath as he races up beside me. His breathing is steady and calm, only panting slightly, his tongue barely lolling out.

I shake my head and gasp out, my skin feeling flushed. My aura begins to glow brighter, fluxing out almost to a dangerous level given the circumstances, and I put my hands on my knees, taking a deep breath in through my nose. I force my aura to dim, heat flashing up and down my skin as I take deeper breaths until it returns to its former brightness. I look up and Totomir takes a step closer, almost touching me. A block of light erupts from the ground, shooting us upward. I pull myself over the side of one of the turrets, landing in a crouch. The guard atop turns at the small noise and I rush forward, hooking one of my legs under his and grabbing his throat. I sweep, throwing him off balance, plucking his helmet from his head so it cracks against the stone. I set the helmet on his chest and it moves in time with his breathing; I want a fighting army, capable of standing a chance against an opposing force if need be. It would be best, and easiest, if I convinced these men to join me; I can't do that if they're all dead. Totomir drops next to me, having struggled to make it over the side.

"A little help would have been nice," he gasps.

"Perhaps our definitions of strong are more radically different than you thought," I respond, and he says nothing. I smirk, quietly heading down the stairs of the turret. I come out at a walkway which leads to the ramparts; two guards stand at attention on the portion of the rampart I can see. I slowly make my way to the walkway and look down; below is the courtyard, where several guards are stationed. Totomir starts to move, but I stop him. He shrugs me off, starting to run at the two guards. I swear and bite my lip, thinking quickly; he will undoubtedly cause a commotion and draw unwanted attention from the guards below if he is allowed to engage them. He's trying to prove a point to me, but it's going to blow our cover and get us killed! I shake my head; there's no avoiding killing these two, unfortunately. I would prefer to keep as many as possible alive, but there are casualties in every battle—you just have to make sure they're not your own in the end.

A thin bolt of white light crackles in my hand and I send it forth, speeding through the air for only a moment as a quick white blur. It passes easily through the heads of the two guards, disappearing as soon as it does so, leaving small holes in their helmets and heads as the only sign it was there at all. A small white box appears below them, gradually shrinking, lowering them both to the floor soundlessly. I look at the guards below; one scratches his ear and another coughs, but neither seemed to notice anything. I let out a sigh of relief, quickly making my way to the two fallen guards.

"I could have taken them!" Totomir growls, his sword drawn, glaring at me.

"You could've exposed both of us!" I hiss. His jaw locks, but he remains silent; if he's going to be this quiet, I should've been taking him on missions since the beginning.

I turn to the guards down below and raise both hands. A large wall of light appears, turned flat so it resembles a flat piece of paper. I bring it down, and there's only a startled yelp as it crushes the guards in the courtyard. I hold it there, stepping off the ramparts; a block appears and lowers me to the ground. I spread my hands and both constructs disappear; neither of the guards remains conscious. I hear a low growl and look up, waving my hand dismissively; a block appears to lower the dog to the ground. He hops down and walks over to one of the unconscious soldiers, placing the point of his rapier against the soldier's neck. He brings it up, then back down but I wave my hand, a small white wall appearing over the guards' neck; the rapier glances off and Totomir turns to me.

"We can't leave them all alive!" he hisses; bloodshed is pointless when it serves no purpose besides satisfying some macho pride.

"These soldiers make a formidable enough army—more formidable than the one currently at our disposal. I can't use them if they're all dead," I hiss back.

"Leaving them alive is weakness," he says, stepping up to me.

"Killing them won't make us stronger," I snap, my aura glowing brighter. "You want strength? Watch, and don't interfere." I take a slow breath, my aura slowly dimming back down; I can't let the dog get under my skin. He'll be dealt with soon enough anyway. I turn to the doors leading into the castle, opening them silently; the corridors are brightly lit, decorated with banners and polished suits of armor. I slip inside and the doors close behind Totomir louder than I would have liked; a large, portly guard spins, noticing us.

"Hey!" He shouts, but the dog is already moving. He runs close to the wall then leaps onto a suit of armor, leaping onto the wall and bouncing off it onto the guard's face before he has a chance to react. I blink, my hand glowing, but he has already stabbed the man's eyes out and slit his throat. I run quietly over to the man, bleeding out on the floor; he stabs him several times in the throat for good measure, licking blood off the blade.

"That is how you show strength," he says.

I glare at him and look at the man, smiling as an idea flicks through my head. I quickly remove the guard's uniform and slip the uniform and helmet on. Looking down the hall, I notice that a closet lies not too far down on the right.

I use a block of light to slide the guard down the hallway to the closet door. I open the door, and the block of light pushes him in as I quickly close the door, taking a deep breath to cool off. My aura dims back down, the sweat cooling on my palms while I look down the hallway, taking in the trail of blood and the puddle of it where he had first collapsed; I set my hand on it, the trail and puddle shimmering with white light for a brief instant. A bright flash fills the space; but afterward, there's no trace of anything that happened, save the faint smell of burnt liquid. I grab Totomir who begins to wriggle as I move him toward me.

"Stop squirming! You need to get in the uniform to help fill it out, and hide."

"I won't get in that!" he protests.

"You have no choice," I hiss, shoving him inside the uniform. He claws at me, and I glow dangerously bright; he yelps as it gets uncomfortably hot and stops, settling around my stomach. I close my eyes, concentrating; when I open them and look down, the uniform looks filled out nicely. I feel the heat of the various objects of light I had to create to fill it out; hopefully Artemis is close. I pick up the man's helmet and tuck my hair underneath it. Blood sticks to the front of his uniform from where it had spilled and I dab my hand in it, smearing it across my face and hands. Lastly I pick up his pike and grit my teeth at the awkward weight of it; this is why I don't use actual weapons.

I rush down the hallways, recalling the layout from memory; left, then right, right again, then left. I stop and turn; was it two rights? I turn around and see a guard turn the corner; he spots me, and I immediately tense out of habit, then relax. I jog up to him, gasping for breath; luckily the helmet hides my face, but that won't do anything about my voice.

"Good gods, what happened to you?" the guard demands, sounding worried as he reaches out to touch me.

"It's not...my...blood," I gasp out, taking a subtle step back, wincing at how false my voice sounds, but the guard doesn't pay any attention.

"You should still see someone about this," the guard says, moving to grab my shoulder.

"I'm fine," I say, regaining my breath and brushing past him.

"I just returned from the village that exploded and have something the queen should hear."

"I'll escort you there," the guard says, shutting down my protests. He remains silent as he walks beside me, expertly navigating the halls, the heat growing within the uniform. He stops in a large space filled with guards; beyond all of them are two large doors leading to the throne room. The guard with me pushes through the guards, helping me to the door; I'll try my best to make sure he remains alive. He pushes open the door, ushering me inside.

"What's the reason for the sudden intrusion?!" a woman at the end of the room barks from a small, modest throne. Her skin is tan, her grey eyes slanted slightly upward; she has pure white hair, despite the fact that she has very few lines on her face. She wears thin, segmented silver armor everywhere save her head, where a silver circlet rests above her thin brow. A metal bow rests in a quiver on her back, and each finger of her gauntlets ends in a sharp point. On her each of her forearms is what appears to be a razor-sharp armblade, gleaming in the light.

"This man has news regarding the explosion to the west, ma'am!" the guard says, saluting.

I push my hand out, and a wall of light catches him in the back, slamming down on top of him, crushing him against the floor. It disappears, along with the objects of light in the uniform, and the doors behind me shimmer brightly for a moment, then return to normal. The woman doesn't waste any time with speech, pulling out her metal bow; it bends easily to her pull as she knocks an arrow, firing it. I throw up a wall of light; commonly, projectiles are much easier to block than blades. My eyes widen as the arrow passes through my wall of light without disrupting it, and I barely have enough time to dodge it. Several more arrows whistle my way, and I roll behind one of the columns that lines the throne room. I remove Totomir and shed the uniform, tossing it aside. An arrow whizzes past, spearing the uniform; I take the opportunity to duck out, shooting a bolt of light at the woman. She dives behind her throne; we duck out at the same time, just as she lets loose an arrow, and I a bolt of energy.

"Artemis, I presume?" I call out. I receive an arrow in response and nod; seems about right.

"Just who the hell are you?" she calls back.

"My name is Evermore," I shout out, raising my hand up. A block of light appears and slams down toward her. I hear her roll out of the way and turn, several spears of light forming and shooting at her. She leaps over them, her gauntleted fingers digging into one of the columns. I throw a bolt of light at her and she leaps off, firing several arrows at me. I roll out of the way, a wall of light slamming into her before she can land. She rolls backward and then out of the way to avoid another wall of light pushing against her. I duck behind one of the columns, breathing heavy, my clothes smoking slightly. I gulp in a few deep breaths, allowing the cool sensations to wash back over me, my mind focusing on the task at hand.

"What do you want, Evermore?"

"Your throne!" I call out, hurling a bolt of light at the column, but it just smacks into it without doing any damage; I have no interest in having this castle crumble down around me. After I defeat Artemis, it will be my place of residence, and I dislike the idea of living in ruins, or of expensive renovations for that matter.

"Over my dead body!" Artemis calls back out and I laugh; I like her. If I didn't have to usurp her, I'd probably want her as an ally.

"If you insist!"

She rolls out from behind the column, firing several arrows at me. I dodge them, a block of light raising her high off the ground as she rolls. This doesn't faze her, and she simply leaps off the block, landing behind her throne with cat-like reflexes. Out of the corner of my eye, I spot Totomir behind one of the columns; go ahead, do it. He rushes toward the throne and I do the same, hurling bolts of light at it; I take opportunities when they present themselves. The dog doesn't have the power to stab me in the back during the middle of combat, and the queen can't as easily fight the both of us off. Artemis stands up between bolts and shoots an arrow at me. I dodge to avoid it, and she turns her bow to the dog, knocking an arrow. I wave my hand, and a wall of light smacks into her as Totomir leaps toward her.

A small thud fills the silence as I sling a bolt of light at Artemis who rolls out of the way, then stumbles and stops. She groans, dropping her bow, slamming her palm on the floor.

"No!" she growls and I stop, hand poised; what exactly happened? "No!" she screams, launching herself at me. I sidestep, her arm blades whirring by, slicing off pieces of my hair. I catch her ankle with my foot, a blast of energy erupting from my palm as I slap it on her back. She goes flying across the room, smacking into the wall with enough force to crack it. She stands on shaky feet, blood seeping through the segments of her armor; Totomir must have wounded her. My eyes follow her as she stumbles to one column, leaning onto it for support; an injured animal is the most dangerous kind. She blurs toward me, and I fire blasts of white hot energy at her. She leaps over me and I barely have time to throw up a wall before her claws hit it; the wall shatters, sending me flying forward. I roll into it, spinning and hurling a blast of energy in her direction. She bends backward underneath it, scampering out of the hole in the wall out into the night. I rush to the hole, hurling several spears of light out into the darkness, but none hit their mark. I put a quivering hand on the stone, closing my eyes; just one more thing. I feel a flash of heat suffuse the room briefly; Totomir isn't here. That damn dog...he's slipped away. I open my eyes, letting the cool night wind wash over my hot skin, my clothes feeling like they are sticking to me from the sheer amount of sweat. I may have gained the throne tonight, but I made two enemies in the process.

I stand on the balcony that extends out from the royal bedroom, looking down. I immediately gathered all of the soldiers down below in the field at the very first hint of morning; all had obeyed my summons, fearful of my power. The soldiers shift below, uneasy and nervous, murmuring amongst themselves. I clear my throat then speak, my voice carrying out across the field in a powerful wave.

"Soldiers of the Kingdom!" I shout, and they all stop murmuring at once, looking up at me. Some are fearful, some hopeful, and some hateful; they are open with their emotions, easy to read. "Your queen has fled! After battling me, it was made apparent she would not be able to defeat me, and she fled. Your queen has deserted you!" The soldiers begin to murmur again, some shouting out. I speak up again, and they quiet once more. I don't need to intimidate them. I don't need a gruesome display to instill fear; the fact that I stand here, unchallenged on the balcony, says enough. "I plan on taking the throne and offer all of you a choice. If you do not wish to be part of my army, you may leave; set your weapons down and leave. Follow a career of your choice or leave the Kingdom altogether; it's your choice. I warn you, though, that those who seek to rebel or fight back will be dealt with swiftly."

My gaze sweeps through the crowd, and at once a shiver passes through them.

"For those who remain, you will join my army; you will be treated with the utmost respect and decency; and if you are crippled in battle, you will be taken care of. If you die in battle, your families will be taken care of; I don't wish to have to take either of those steps though. I have no intention of beginning a war on any nation. I am not a warmonger; I only want what is best for my people, if you will have me." The crowd remains silent before one man steps forward, shouting so his voice can carry up to me.

"Why should we believe you?" he shouts, and a chorus of assent erupts from the crowd. "Why should we follow you?!" A cheer erupts from the crowd; but as I open my mouth, they all quiet at once. They are not truly rebellious—they are simply afraid. We are all afraid of the unknown; they are like children, they just need to be comforted.

"I have not killed you all," I say; there is dead, absolute silence. I lean forward, turning my voice to an imploring tone. "Please, believe me when I say I value life; I have no intention of going to war or putting your lives on the line unnecessarily. I will invoke radical change throughout the Kingdom, but I will endeavor to improve conditions for you as much as I am able!" I take time to look several soldiers in the eye, slowly scanning the crowd. "I would prefer not to even require a standing army, but not everyone feels that way, and I would rather be prepared than caught off guard by a surprise attack. I only do this to protect the Kingdom—to protect your families, your spouses, and your children. If there were no threat of war, I would ask you all to please leave. As it is, war is not a phantom or an idea, but a very real thing that could break out anywhere, at any moment, and so I must ask you to stay. Please," I let my aura shine a little brighter as the sun's first light begins to turn the horizon a light grey color. "I ask you to help protect what you hold closest and dearest to your hearts."

Silence rings out through the field, and then one soldier sets his weapons down. Then another, and another. Soon soldiers are dropping their weapons and turning their backs in the hundreds. I wait with baited breath as the ones who do not wish to stay clear out; will there be enough for an army? Valkyrie told me to raise her an army; while I have no intention of mistreating these people, I *must* have an army. They finish leaving, and I let out a sigh of relief; it appears that over half remain. I smile and stand up straighter, my aura shining brighter.

"Thank you for remaining! You brave souls who remain, from the bottom of my heart, thank you." A single person cheers, then another, and then it begins in earnest, the soldiers cheering up to me as I smile.

CHAPTER THIRTY-FOUR

I look at the basin of water in what is now considered to be my room. A four-poster bed with rich, red silk sheets is partially obscured by thin white curtains around it. My own, private bathroom lies just on the other side, a large closet adjacent. I had room made for a desk and several chairs, a full-length mirror hanging on the wall, runes and carvings etched into the rich golden frame. My face looks back at me in the clear basin, tired but content. Now I can begin to track down Eurael; I look away, shaking my head slightly. I will have to do it with the help of Benson, or locating Eurael may be next to impossible. I splash water on my face and turn to the mirror, the surface rippling. After the mirror clears, a face is visible: Valkyrie. Her blue lips curl into a smile. I can hear the sound of clapping, but I'm unable to see her hands.

"Well done," she says, the clapping coming to a stop. "You did that swiftly; I'm impressed."

"I figured you would be," I say with a grin, and her smile grows wider.

"I see I made the right choice in deciding to release you; she must not have realized how good of a find you are. Her loss," her violet eyes sparkle, and my heart beats quicker in my chest, heat flushing to my cheeks, but I keep my composure.

"I've done as you asked, and now I'm free to do pursue my... extracurricular activities." I state, and she nods.

"Though I do have another task for you," she says.

"If it's as easy as the last one, I'll gladly take it on," I say, and she leans her head back, a breathy laugh escaping her lips.

"Someone's quite confident," she says with a smirk. "I have a feeling you'll like this next one," she leans back; now I can see her slender neck as well as her face. "Eurael is planning on constructing an item known as 'Ragnarok'; I want you to put a stop to that."

My hands grip the basin tighter, my aura spiking out quickly; finally, I can begin my revenge.

"What's a Ragnarok?" I ask and she grins, shaking her head, her choppy black hair swaying slightly.

"I can't give everything away; you'll have to find out what it is, and how to stop it, yourself. I'll know when you've finished."

The mirror ripples again; and when it clears, my face looks back up at me, eager. I turn and call out; a perk of being the queen is that I now have messengers to send. It's very helpful; I don't have to go everywhere myself anymore.

"Hekras!" I shout. A young lanky man quickly appears in my room; I've learned he's very quick, and the best messenger available in the castle. "I want you to send a summons for Benson Barry Wolf." I say. True to our deal, after taking the throne, I soon after publicly stated that I endorsed and supported his perfectly legitimate and honorable business; I was not allowed to choose my own words.

I sit up a little in my throne as Benson walks into the room, thanking the guards. I nod and everyone exits, leaving me and Benson alone; another one of the perks of being queen. He grabs a chair from one of the tables by the wall, bringing it up to the dais with him, setting it down and sitting.

"I really must congratulate you on how quickly you took the castle, with barely any bloodshed. It's quite admirable." Benson has been reliable in the information he has provided so far, though I have not been extensive in my asking for information on Eurael; I want to do this right. I can be patient; I will have my revenge, but it can't be rushed. "Now, I was told there was an urgent matter which you wished to discuss with me."

"What significance does the word 'ragnarok' have to you?" I watch his expression carefully, but it doesn't change.

"In some languages, it signifies the end of the world; but other than that, nothing," he says. I reach beside me and grab a small bag weighted with coins. I sit it at his feet; he looks down from the bag to me and grins.

"What about now?"

He picks up the bag of gold and weighs it in one large paw, then nods, tucking it into his suit.

"Ragnarok is a fabled spear that holds tremendous power. It was rumored to have been used by Father Time to first bring souls into the cosmos; it is said to have the power to be able to not only manifest any soul in a physical form, but also to steal souls as well. However, it is a myth; many have tried to find the fabled spear and none have succeeded. There are rumors that you can turn a spear into Ragnarok, but it would be impossible to do."

The spear sounds powerful, but what would Eurael want with it? He is powerful enough already; what use is such a spear to a man like him? I open my mouth, voicing my question.

"What would Eurael want with Ragnarok?"

Benson's face goes blank once more, his voice sounding slightly amused but nothing more. "I haven't the faintest idea."

I sigh, reaching over to my side and dropping another small bag of gold in his hand. He frowns, and I toss him another two bags. He catches them all in one paw and tucks them into his suit as well.

"Eurael, for as long as I've known him, has had a fascination with the fabled spear Ragnarok. I don't know what he might do with it; it would be difficult to tell. If it can steal souls, then not even Immortals would be safe; being able to create Ragnarok would allow whoever wielded the spear to become a Godkiller."

I sit up straighter, clenching my jaw but keeping my expression neutral; that would be disastrous. Godkillers are only created in an instance where an Immortal has stepped out of line; to have that power able to be moved from person to person would be very dangerous.

"Eurael, however," Benson continues, "knows how dangerous this would be; he's not stupid enough to try and create the spear."

"How easy would it be for him?"

"He's collected artifacts over the years, but he would need—" Benson stops then swears, standing up quickly, a low growl rising up from his chest.

"What?" I stand up as well, my aura glowing brighter with my mounting curiosity. "Benson, tell me."

"He would need an orichalcum spear. Orichalcum is a nearly indestructible metal that is incredibly rare; orichalcum naturally negates the powers of anyone near and is rumored to be able to kill spirits. I got word that he was recently called to court due to an incident involving the giant Skrymsli." I raise an eyebrow, and Benson explains. "Up until this point, Skrymsli has had the only large piece of orichalcum, in the form of a spear stuck in his leg, unable to remove it. If Skrymsli is dead and Eurael was called to court about it, then that would mean he has the spear." He begins to pace, shaking his head. "How could you be so stupid, Eurael? I warned you..." he mutters.

He begins to walk to the door, but I call out. "How will I know when he tries to create it?"

He turns, looking at me gravely, his voice low, tinged with worry, "You'll know."

This isn't right. There's a sense of unease in the air, like the calm before a storm. I pace in my room, my hair hanging down, whipping about as I turn sharply when I get to one end of the room. The ability for anyone to become a Godkiller? That shouldn't be possible—it's abhorrent. Abominable. Something that defies and defiles the very laws of nature. But Eurael already seems to possess the powers of a Godkiller—why would he want Ragnarok? There has to be another reason! My aura fluctuates out and I sigh, sitting and resting my head in my hands; there has to be another reason, *think*.

Benson said I would know—he said I would know when Ragnarok was created; how will I know? What if I can't stop it? What will happen?

CHAPTER THIRTY-FIVE

I gasp, reeling backwards, landing against my desk as I'm forced out of Scarlett's mind. She lies on the floor of the library, her eyes closed, taking slow breaths. I lean forward and her eyes fly open as she gasps, sucking in air. She sits up quickly, then groans, putting a hand to her head. She looks around blearily and her eyes settle on me, then she clamps them shut, groaning again.

"Ugh, what happened?"

Confusion would be normal, normal is good.

"You passed out," I respond, and she shoots me an annoyed glance; annoyance is also normal, normal is still good.

"I gathered that. Thanks. But why?" She tries to stand up, and I quickly make my way over to her as she collapses, setting her back down.

"Why don't you tell me the last thing you remember?" I say, my eyes scanning her face; she should be disoriented enough to be unable to coherently lie about this. "That would help pinpoint the cause of this."

"The last few months are fuzzy; only bits and pieces come through. The last clear thing I remember," she pauses, looking at me, "is fighting that alligator."

"You must have had a lasting concussion as I thought," I say and she frowns, looking down. "That would explain why you suddenly passed out; your mind was trying to reorient itself. I noticed strange

367

behavior in you, but I didn't know the cause; when you passed out, I did research and made a solution for you that would hopefully negate the effects. It seems to have worked."

She nods, shakily standing up on her own, running a hand through her hair. "I guess so," she says, shaking her head. "Thank you." She looks at me, then away toward the door. "What was the solution you used?"

"Admer's Revival," I respond, and she frowns.

"I didn't know that was used for concussions," she says, and my expression hardens slightly, but I quickly return it to something more neutral.

"It's actually used more for fainting spells, which is originally what I thought this might have been the beginning of. However, I did some examination and research; and upon altering it slightly, I was able to devise an apparently successful revision of Admer's Revival."

Scarlett looks at me for a moment then nods. "You should take notes on what you did, in case this happens again. I feel like I need to lie down now though." She walks to the door and looks back at me again, frowning, then closes the door.

I walk over to my desk and put my hands on it, leaning against it. It's very possible that she might remember parts of what transpired in her mind. Given her behavior, I wouldn't doubt that she has her suspicions; but as long as I continue to do things accordingly, they will remain simple suspicions. Then they will fade, and things will return to a more normal state, and normal is good. I will have to observe her for some time though to be sure that she has recovered and, more importantly, remains unaware of what truly transpired. I want what is best for her, and it would be best if she remembered nothing of what happened; death is not for everyone. I will deal with that, if it proves to be true. For now, I can begin the last phase of my mission. I back off my desk, blowing out the lights in the library and closing the door behind me; there is work to be done.

The grass sways gently, far below the balcony. I grip the rails, my aura dimmer than it has been for a while; I have to save my strength. If it comes to it, I will have to pit myself directly against Eurael; I have to destroy that spear. I can't allow Eurael to create Ragnarok, as that would make him unstoppable. Benson said I'll know, and he hasn't been wrong before. I haven't been able to find him, as no one has heard from Eurael for weeks. Has he been preparing himself? Or has he been too preoccupied to do anything? I have to know when this is happening; I have to be able to stop him.

CHAPTER THIRTY-SIX

I make my way through the twisting halls of my house until I come to a small door tucked nearly out of sight in a corner; I pull a key from my pocket and unlock it quietly. Scarlett should be getting some rest, but it's best to be cautious. Inside, the room is dark and musty, many boxes littering the dusty floor. I go over to the right wall and count three boxes, picking up the third and setting it atop another box. I search my fingers along the seam between two beams of wood and find a small crack, which I press against. A small panel slides open, revealing a lock; I maneuver my hand so I can actually insert the key, twisting it. For a moment nothing happens, then the lock clicks and I slide back two boards. Stairs lead down into darkness and I descend, sliding the boards closed behind me. I slide one hand along the left wall for sixteen steps until it comes across a lamp. My left hand continues sliding along until I find a small rock, which I strike against the stone walls. There's a shower of sparks, then a small light shines forth, barely illuminating the darkness.

I walk through the dark stone corridor until I come to a large room, nearly empty. It has the appearance of a small maze, and I step into it, navigating by memory, avoiding any hazardous offshoots of the maze. I pause and hear a low growl coming from my right, turning left; I always need a reminder at that section. I come to the center, which is a small circular area with a stone wall blocking the only other exit. A padded stool and a viola sit in the center of the area. I sit down on the velvety red cushion and pick up the viola. The instrument is a rich, dark brown, untouched by dust. I pick up the bow next to it and slowly draw it across the strings, producing a long, low note.

Removing my gloves, I place my hands once more on the warm wood, closing my eyes, letting my breathing become deep and steady. I draw the bow across the instrument again, feeling the vibrations through the viola into my arm and throughout my body. The single note echoes throughout the maze in such a way that it sounds like an entire symphony is playing, in different pitches and volumes, complimenting the one note; it is not merely a maze, but an amphitheater of sorts. Setting the bow on the instrument again, I begin to play it slowly and methodically, producing a slow string of low notes which reverberate around the maze.

I draw the bow sharply across the viola, interrupting the steady rhythm I had built up until that point, cutting across it sharply. The sharp squeal echoes back as almost a scream in some places, almost a roar in others. I begin to mount an aggressive attack on the viola, furrowing my brow; it is push and pull, give and take, rise and fall. I draw the bow harshly against the strings then smooth the sound over as I push it back, now barely touching the bow to the strings. The viola gives off a keening whine, almost as if begging to be played more. I press the bow down slightly harder, producing short, deep notes that resonate deep in my chest, humming at the base of my skull. Music is supposed to be an expression of human emotion. I push the bow slowly across, letting the sound taper off like the final word rolling off a dying man's lips; my music is an expression of the absence of human emotion. It is pure, unfiltered, unhindered, unemotional, and therein, the greatest emotion awakens.

As the note finally fades, I stand, putting my gloves on once more, setting the viola and bow down on the stool, looking at the stone door. It slides open with a grating sound, which echoes around the maze until it finally opens with a loud thud and I step through, carrying the lamp with me. It slams shut behind me, the sudden gust of air nearly blowing out the flame of the lamp. I wait for a moment until it begins burning brightly once more, then continue down the dark passageway; as accustomed as I am to the darkness, in here light is necessary for even my survival. I come to a wall made up of several identical doors. I choose the third from the right and step through into a small room. Illuminated by the small flame of the lamp is a tall wall with a small opening at the top, a crawlspace a few feet above my head.

I hoist myself into the cramped dark tunnel, crawling on my hands and knees, holding the lamp by its metal handle between my teeth. The tunnel continues to grow more narrow, pressing tightly against my shoulders and bearing down on my back. I'm barely able to move through the tunnel, and I have to do more of a writhing, squirming motion to make it through at all. Suddenly my hand meets empty air and I stop, looking down. I know the hole below me is several dozen feet deep; one could, at minimum, easily break their leg or ankle from the drop, and then be unable to continue. Or at the very least, it would be quite difficult. I shimmy my way out of the tunnel, only falling for a brief moment before the shadows catch me, slowly lowering me toward the ground.

I transfer the lamp to one of my hands and as soon as I do, the shadows deposit me neatly on the ground. My knees pop as I stand, straightening up and walking into the darkness until I come to a door with no knob, though it swings open as soon as I approach. The door swings silently shut behind me, the only clue I have to its closing being the soft gust of air brushing against the back of my neck, followed by the clicking and turning of an innumerable number of locks settling back into place. The room is dark, but I walk around easily, keeping my hands on the walls, lighting each lamp I come to on the wall until light fills the room. The room is large and circular with various glass cases placed neatly and carefully around the room on pedestals. There's barely enough space for me to walk through due to the amount of cases; and in some places, I have to turn sideways to slide through.

I stop at one and look in, seeing an old shriveled up hand, smaller and darker than a human's. It's wrapped in linen that is falling away and is suspended in midair inside the case; its pinky is broken at an awkward angle. I had only tried to use it once before deciding it would be better suited to remain below in this room with the other items too dangerous to let remain in the world; the results from the object had been...unfavorable.

I pass the paw and stop again at a small pale white doll with long black hair. Dark buttons are sewn on for eyes, and it wears a small surgical mask over its mouth.

"Am I beautiful?" a faint voice whispers from the glass, and I quickly move on; summoning spirits normally ends in an untimely end for the summoner, especially vengeful ones. I make my way to the end of the room and walk up a small pair of stone steps to a stone altar. I grab one hand to stop it from shaking, locking my knees to keep myself standing up straight. Behind a tall glass case is the orichalcum spear, glimmering a poisonous green color in the light. I jerk my leg forward and press my hand to the glass; after all this time, I have the spear. Having been occupied with Scarlett, I have had little time to follow through with my plans; no more am I occupied with the problems of others.

I move my hand over the glass slowly; now I am free to continue. I was never able to collect the ingredient needed from Impres, but now I have the spear. With that, I can continue no matter what might stand in my way.

I lift the glass case off of the spear, my arms trembling under the weight and awkwardness of it; I grit my teeth, and they stop as I set the glass case down gently. Removing the spear from its brackets, I clear the altar and place it next to it. From beside the altar, I remove the full-length mirror, placing it on the altar, the runes and inscriptions in the ornate golden frame glowing in the sickly green light of the spear. I turn to the room and walk to one of the glass cases, carefully removing the case and retrieving the object within. Returning to the altar, I place a large black book on the altar, its binding thin and loose pages threatening to fall from it. Spidery cracks of age line the color, deforming the golden cross on the front, courtesy of Solomon.

I once again go back into the maze of glass cases, returning with several items. I place a small golden crown on the book and pour a small vial of ambrosia onto the book. The golden liquid runs off the book, filling the small grooves in the altar. I place a heart, smaller than a human's, on the book, and it beats once; Fae hearts are much more difficult to obtain than human ones, but they are much more powerful in their magical properties.

I look down at the last item I grip in my lands. It's a long curved dagger, partially serrated with a small skull for the pommel. Faded red linen is wrapped around the handle, but it's beginning to unwind from it; I turn the dagger over in my hands, controlling my breathing. I cannot stop my own heart from beating faster; the body's responses to memories are not always logical and not always in my control. With a shaking hand, I place the spear next to all of these items on the mirror. I turn the blade downward, gripping the handle tightly in my hand; I glare at the heart and grit my teeth, jabbing the blade into it. A loud scream echoes throughout the room as blood spurts out, trickling over the book, joining the ambrosia in the grooves of the altar. I let go of the dagger as the blood and ambrosia mix slowly and make their way to the spear. The spear begins to gleam brighter, soaking up the mixture.

By its very nature, the orichalcum should not be able to be enchanted, enhanced, or changed in any way through magical or alchemical means; there are ways of circumventing that, if one has the right tools. I smear the mixture across the mirror, murmuring softly.

"Mirror," the spear glows brighter, its light leaving dancing spots across the walls and cases. "Mirror." A low hiss snakes out from the mirror, a green fog settling over the altar.

"What is it you seek?" the hiss forms words, slithering into my ear.

"Ragnarok," I whisper breathlessly, the green vapor growing thicker.

"Ragnarok!" the mirror chants back, a low rumbling echoing throughout the room, shaking me to where my soul used to be; another price for what must be done—what I must do—I must have Ragnarok.

The spear glows brightly, light fluctuating in waves from it, the green metal shimmering and changing like thousands of snakes crawling across the surface. I take a step back, feeling immense heat from the spear, and the ambrosia mixture begins to boil, steam rising. Suddenly the book catches fire, instantly turning to ash, steam coming from the mixture. Next the crown and heart disintegrate in a burst of flames, the mirror cracking underneath the spear.

"No!" I shout, slamming my palms down on the altar. I yank my hands away immediately, hissing as my gloves melt off my hands, the poisonous vapor spilling over the sides of the altar. "No! This has to work!" Could the final ingredient have prevented this? No, this is something else! I reach for the spear, and a blinding white light shoots forth, blinding me. I close my eyes, squeezing them shut, backpedaling away from the altar. How can this be happening? What power is interfering with this? I can't let myself be thwarted when I'm closer than ever! *I must have Ragnarok!*

I rush toward the spear, gripping it in both hands despite the searing heat. I only feel the blazing heat intensify, scarring my hands, but I grit my teeth; I can't afford to lose this, not now! A high pitched whine fills my ears, and I grit my teeth, dropping to one knee.

"I've come too far!" I scream, gripping the spear harder. The spear glows brighter as I force tendrils of shadows down my arm. They protest, screaming and screeching, but I pay them no mind; this is the culmination, I cannot be thwarted here! Suddenly the light stops, and I look up at the orichalcum spear. It crackles with energy and then it explodes, destroying the altar in a blast of hot energy and sending shards of orichalcum and stone out into the room. I'm thrown backward by the blast, crashing into several glass cases. The cases shatter, sending glass shards flying outward, cutting me. The walls shake, dust dropping down from the ceiling. I cough and pick myself up, my arms trembling. Orichalcum shards lie across the room, bits of stone and glass littering the floor.

"Am I beautiful? Am I beautiful? Am I beautiful?" The phrase repeats itself over and over, growing louder each time. I grab a piece of orichalcum off the floor, looking around. I spot the white doll and step toward it on trembling legs; when the orichalcum was concentrated in the spear, it was easier to handle. Spread out all over the room, the effect is much more potent. I take another trembling step forward as the doll shifts. It begins to morph and grow, bones snapping into place and skin crawling over the newly formed muscles. Her head hangs back, then snaps up, turning slowly to look at me. "Am I beautiful?"

I hear a rustle to my left and my eyes dart over, seeing a woman crawling to me. Her body is cut in half along the waist, her bones and entrails hanging out. No blood smears the floor as she rasps, dragging herself along the floor. A skull begins to shake on the ground, lifting into the air. Slowly a large man materializes, dressed completely in black. He wears large boots and gloves, a long coat, splatters of blood covering his pants and shirt. His collar is turned up, but that cannot hide the fact that he is missing a head. He grabs the skull and places it where his head should be. It floats in place, turning to me, settling its hollow eye sockets on me, its jaw clacking.

"No," I growl, the shard of orichalcum cutting into my skin. "No, this couldn't have happened!"

"Am I beautiful?" the severed woman leaps at me, screaming. I turn and can do nothing more than raise my arm as she slams into me, clawing at my face. I stab her with the orichalcum, and she disappears, turning to ash. I try to stand but feel a large boot slam into my side; I slide across the floor and settle against the wall. I blink, my vision swimming as the orichalcum drops from my hand. I reach out toward it, but that same boot kicks it away. The woman with the surgical mask crouches next to me, the skull dagger in her hand. "Am I beautiful?" she whispers, tracing the point of the blade against my skin. I manage to pull my arm away and she giggles, taking a step closer.

"Leave him," a deep voice rumbles. She hisses then stands, leaving my side to walk over to the headless man. "Nightmare!" He holds out his hand, and a large smokey black horse materializes, its eyes bright red, shining like blood as it snorts a small flame from its nostrils. The headless man makes a circular motion with his finger, and my ears detect rustling, the shifting of glass and stone. I manage to sit up, watching as dark shapes and figures collect the artifacts that haven't been destroyed. I try to stand, but my legs give out and I collapse, my head banging against the wall. My vision swims again and I reach out, trying to pull myself forward, but I can't get a firm hold on any of the stones. No, it wasn't supposed to happen like this! It wasn't supposed to fail! I cannot allow this to happen!

"Stop!" I croak, gritting my teeth at my own weakness. The rustling pauses, then begins again in earnest, picking up pace. The figures begin to disappear, taking with them the artifacts. No! I can't allow them to do this! I growl and push myself up, leaning against the wall, shaking; these items are too dangerous to be out in the world. I feel something grab my hair and spin me around, smacking my face. I land heavily on my back, and I find my arms and legs pinned down, points of orichalcum poking against my skin through my clothes. I struggle to move but am unable. No! I can't be paralyzed again; I cannot be rendered immobile again. Not again! I shake and tremble, trying to throw my assailant off, but all I do is rock him a little. His breathing is heavy and ragged, almost sounding strained. I can only make out a vague outline of him, but I can clearly see his mouth open wider, his tongue lolling out. His head lowers close to mine and I try to raise my head up, but my neck refuses to cooperate; move! I have to move! My chest rises and falls faster as his warm breath hits my neck, his tongue slowly dragging over my skin. He moans, the vibrations reverberating through his body into mine.

"Humans can lick too," he whispers in a choked, breathy voice. He scrambles off me and disappears, along with the rest of the spirits and phantoms.

I screw my eyes shut, my jaw clenched, my chest rising and falling rapidly as I struggle to bring my breath under control. I gasp out, my fingers slowly curling into a fist, my eyes opening wide. I sit up all at once and scream out; a loud, throaty scream rises up from my core, carrying with it the weight, anger, and fury all built within. I curl my hands around shards of orichalcum, letting them cut into my skin, blood dripping down my arms as I scream, the cords of my neck straining against my skin. It wasn't supposed to happen like this! I slump forward, screaming into the floor, pouring every ounce of anger and rage I have into that scream; it should have worked!

My breathing is erratic, hitching and stopping as my heart pounds, beating the blood out of my wounds faster. Anger shoots through me like poison and lifts my arms up, and I slam my palms down on the floor. They are stains, and I will wipe them away; I will burn them, tear them, rip them! I curl up into a ball, then turn onto my back, roaring my rage at the heavens.

"I will kill every last one of you!" I roar, slamming my fists against the stone once more. "This will be the last mistake you ever make!" Something flicks in the corner of my vision, and I struggle to turn, but nothing is there. I turn over and large yellow eyes look at me, then blink. I reach out toward it and it hisses, jumping onto my chest. The thing looks down at my chest then raises its claws, slicing through the fabric of my shirt and leaving long, shallow scratches in my chest. I sit up, making a grab for the creature, but it disappears in a puff of smoke. I look down at the wounds and I slump backward, my head banging against the stone. I blink furiously, my vision swimming. Complete darkness encroaches on my vision; I growl, trying to shake my head, but I cannot move. Not again, not again...

When I awake, darkness surrounds me. I reach out a hand, but nothing happens—the orichalcum. I turn to the wall and pull myself up, struggling and trembling as I reach for the cracks between the stones. A small shard of orichalcum cuts into my hand, and I look at its shimmering green surface. A small flash of white streaks across it for a brief instant, and my eyes narrow. I growl, tossing it away; it should have gone right. It would have gone right, I'm sure, if someone hadn't interfered. Final ingredient or no, I enacted the ritual flawlessly; it should have worked! So much...so much time went into one ritual, one reverent experiment, and for one very brief, fleeting moment, I felt that I had succeeded. Ragnarok was in my grasp, and with it, I could change the past; I could make everything right. Then it was all ruined!

I drag myself along the wall until I come to what had once been the altar. I bend over, but collapse once I take my full weight off the wall, though I have collapsed close enough to where the altar had been that it doesn't matter. I run my hands over what remains of the stone base of the altar and a shock of white flashes out, searing my hands. I growl, gripping the stone base harder; someone is responsible for this. I hold a piece of the broken mirror, my dark eye glaring back at me.

I look down, shaking my head. "I do not know who you are, but I will find you; and when I do, you will know what it is like to have lost. To have suffered. To feel the immeasurable depth of your complete and total despair, and the inescapable fate which you are now doomed to. You stole my last chance—and for that," I look forward, my jaw setting as I slowly push myself up, "I will kill you."

A searing pain in my chest jerks me awake from my sleep. I sit up, my aura fluctuating rapidly, my chest tightening. I gasp, feeling as if my breath is being stolen from my lungs. Rivulets of sweat run down my arms and face, my clothes sticking to me. Flashes of heat arc up and down my body; I double up and groan as the pain spreads to my stomach. I stumble out of bed and shuffle to the basin, my face contorted in pain; where is this coming from? Is this it? Is this the moment Benson was speaking about? I try to cool myself off with the water, but it turns to steam as it hits my skin. If this is the moment…I turn quickly to the mirror, the surface shimmering. A room appears in the basin, filled with glass cages. Suddenly the image is dashed by shadows, and I place my hands on the the frame of the mirror, my nails digging into the runes and inscriptions; I'm sure this is the moment Benson was talking about. Taking a deep breath, I put my hands on the cool surface of the mirror.

Gasping, my aura fluctuates brightly and I whirl around, the shadows clearing. I'm in the room, and at the end of the room a man stands over an altar, a gleaming green spear in the center. I suck in a quick breath, squeezing the mirror frame that I can no longer see, barely even feel; Eurael. Time seems to have no limits here; this ritual could be taking mere seconds, or days; it's impossible to tell. My aura shines brighter as I walk closer to him; he must be doing it now. The ritual begins and I groan, doubling over, feeling pains shoot up through my stomach; I know this cannot be right. This unnatural ability for anyone to be a Godkiller upsets everything that the cosmos is built upon! I blindly lash out toward the altar, and the pain eases. The book has turned to ash, and Eurael is frantic. He lunges for the spear, grabbing hold of it and I grab it as well.

"You will not destroy us all!" I growl, holding onto the spear as he tries to yank it away. I feel my power mounting, my skin heating up, my aura fluctuating rapidly, shining brighter and brighter still. His face is contorted in rage, a mirror of my own. His perverted mission cannot succeed!

"I have come too far!" he screams, tugging at the spear.

I dig in, heat flashing up my arms, the spear beginning to glow. I cannot let him win! Shadows begin to envelop the spear, in small tendrils; I grit my teeth, pushing my aura out farther. This has to be destroyed! I refocus myself, plunging my power into the spear; don't fight Eurael, you just have to destroy the spear. I feel my body overheat, my arms trembling. I have to hold on—I can't let him accomplish this twisted ritual! Ragnarok must be destroyed! My aura blasts outward with blinding white light, throwing me backward.

I land on my bed, my muscles seizing, my aura fluctuating rapidly. I cry out, curling in a ball as icy spikes of pain pierce every inch of my body, my skin heating up. This is the price I pay for destroying such an object? I cry out again, gripping the sheets, nearly biting my tongue off. No, please; I was helping. I was helping! The pain slowly recedes but does not vanish completely as I let out a choked sob; I was trying to help.

"Hekras!"

After a moment, Hekras appears, running toward me in a nightgown.

"Yes ma'am!" he says, saluting. My eyelids droop, but I take a deep breath, standing up straighter despite the cold spikes of pain icing through my stomach.

"Send for Petravin; tell him I need him immediately." He nods and then he's gone, racing away, almost at the end of the hallway already. I close the door and go to my closet, sliding it open; I guess I'm about to have company. I double over with a hot flash sending me to my knees, nearly pulling the handle off the door; I have to get ready for Petravin.

I sit on my throne once more, fighting sleep, exhaustion, and the constant echo of pain still making itself known, unable to leave me in peace. I hold a sheet of papers, selected from the list of Eurael's known contacts Benson had given me. It had cost a much larger sum than anything I had paid him since, but it was well worth it. The doors burst open, and a young man strides up to me. He's dressed in dark green and brown clothes with his hood pulled down; he has short, messy brown hair sticking out everywhere, a pointed noise and ears and a mischievous grin constantly playing at the corners of his lips on his impish face.

"I hope you have a good reason for waking me this late," he says, his eyes bloodshot and angry; he must have been roused from his sleep. Welcome to the club. Petravin and his mercenary group, the Lost Boys, had been referred to me by Benson almost immediately after I took the throne; he said they would one day come in handy. Now is the time to test it.

"I want you to find these twelve people and kill them," I say yawning, too tired to phrase it eloquently, holding out the sheet of paper. I fight down a searing pain racing through my arms, doing my best to keep them from snapping back to my body. Petravin stalks up and snatches the papers from my hand, looking over each one. "I want them all killed within the hour—immediately."

He looks up his eyes wide; the shock has woken him up. "Twelve kills in an hour will be..."

"Difficult?" I offer, and he shakes his head, grinning.

"Expensive," I heave out a bag of gold and sling it at him, the icy pick of echoing pain digging into my head with each physical movement I make. It catches him in the chest nearly causing him to tumble backward. He steadies himself and nods, awkwardly shuffling out. I stand up and make my way back to my room, collapsing on my bed still dressed in my day clothes, bursts of pain causing me to curl in a ball; blessed sleep, please come to me.

CHAPTER THIRTY-SEVEN

I lean heavily against the door, locking it behind me, looking down the hallway that is brightly lit in comparison to the tunnels below. It was not impossible for me to make my way back through the different challenges set in place in the tunnels down below, but it was far more difficult than it had been the first time. I take a step forward and stumble, falling onto the ground; I hold out my hand, but the shadows do not come. I push myself up, my arms shaking with the effort, blood seeping down onto the floor; I'm as disgusted with my weakness as they are. I hear footsteps running, and then Scarlett turns the corner, spotting me.

"I've been looking for you for hours!" she says, running up to me. She stops, looking me over. "You look terrible!"

"Something happened," I reply, my voice hoarse and rough.

"Obviously," she says, wrapping one of my arms around her shoulders, supporting me. I try to remove my arm, but she holds it firmly, helping me whether I want it or not. "But I have news." She says, making way to my bedroom.

"It can wait," I say, but she stops, looking at me.

"No, it can't," she says as she opens the door, setting me against the bed. I work my arms, turning them, and feel several pangs in my chest and back; my injuries could be worse. "Twelve known members of your network have all died within the last three hours."

I try to stand but collapse on the bed, the shadows remaining hiding; they will not come to my aid. The orichalcum seems to have had a lasting effect this time; it must have been the metal coming into contact with my blood; something must have been carried into my bloodstream. I growl, slamming my palm on the bed.

"How did this happen?!" I roar, and she shakes her head.

"I don't know, but I'm going to leave right now and find out," she says, checking to make sure she has all of her daggers. I clench the sheets, turning them red; I don't care about my network. I failed; how could this have happened?

"No," I move to stand up and do so successfully this time, putting a hand on my bedside table. "I will deal with this myself." Whoever is taking out my network so soon after my failure, they are most likely the same person who destroyed my chances at Ragnarok; they will not get away with this.

"You are in no condition to deal with anything," she replies, and I glare at her.

"Neither are you."

Her eyes narrow, and she shoves her dagger into its sheath. "I know my skills have deteriorated slightly over the past few months; you've expressed that much. But I'm not the one who can barely stand."

I stand up straighter, glaring at her, my arms trembling, and her eyes focus on them.

"I'll take care of this; it shouldn't take more than a night for you to recover. I'll have something by then." She closes the door behind her as she exits, and I slump onto my bed. I growl, throwing my hand out, but the shadows remain still. I thrust my palm out, but they do not move.

"Obey me, you useless pieces of—"

They shoot out, wrapping around me, forcing me to lie on my back in bed. I struggle, but they curl tighter, refusing to obey. They stop when they are tight enough, not going to the point of being uncomfortable. They remain silent, simply holding me against the bed; the message is clear. I sigh, glaring at the ceiling; I have no choice but to remain here while my network is under siege, trusting it in the hands of my student who has been in a dream state for months! I slam my head back against the pillow underneath my head, growling. I cannot just lie here and do nothing! I squirm, trying to squeeze my hands and draw blood, but they are held firmly open and down against the bed; there is no escape. I struggle, but the shadows hold me securely, not allowing me to move.

"Let me go! I have to solve this! This is my problem, I have to fix it! I cannot remain idle while everything is destroyed before my eyes! I will not watch this kingdom I have built burn!"

They tighten their hold on me slightly; I have already failed, and they will not let me solve it—they do not trust me. I roar at the ceiling, but the shadows remain deaf to my cries.

CHAPTER THIRTY-EIGHT

I open my eyes suddenly, looking around me. I'm on the floor of a dark room, mist swirling around my knees. On a long dark couch made of bones is a woman. Her legs stretch out from the darkness, but her top half is covered by shadow. I gulp, moving to stand up, but suddenly an immense pressure presses down on my shoulders, keeping me from moving.

"You were to report back after your task was completed," her voice slithers out from the darkness, powerful and penetrating. The power behind it reverberates in my bones, and I try to stand again, but the pressure increases, forcing my head and shoulders lower.

"I—"

"After the task you were assigned, which you *failed* to complete," her accusation is like a knife, cutting into my soul. It tears into me, twisting, trying to drain as much blood from me as possible.

"I can explain—"

"Explain how you failed at your mission? Explain how you failed to report back nonetheless? Explain how you *abandoned* your duties to join that lowly Underworld watcher Valkyrie?"

I remain silent, not offering a response this time, and the pressure slams down on my back, forcing my nose to the floor. The mist swirls up, filling my nostrils and slipping into my mouth. It clogs my airways and I gag, trying to move, but the pressure keeps me still. The mist chokes me further, and my aura begins to glow, but the pressure exerts itself on that too, forcing it to remain dim.

"I am very disappointed in you, Evermore," she says. After a moment, the pressure eases, the mist curling out of my mouth, swirling around me again. I gasp, sucking in gulps of air, tears at the corners of my eyes. I sit up, my back protesting at the sudden movement.

"I am deeply sorry, my queen," I reply, bowing my head; I hold no power here. She is the most powerful person I am aware of, and I have disappointed her. I have abandoned her and disobeyed her; I did not make wise decisions in my pursuit of revenge. The thought of revenge reenters my mind suddenly, my aura glowing brighter slightly; my power is not all gone—not even here.

"At least you have kept yourself busy," she says, her voice almost sounding amused. Her statement doesn't require a response so I stay quiet; there are strict rules one most follow when communicating with her. "Do not disobey or abandon me again, Evermore; complete your task and then return to me. Your next reminder will not nearly be as pleasant," she says coolly. I nod, looking up, but she's already disappeared. The mist swirls around me, rising up, filling me once again. I choke, fighting back as darkness encroaches on my vision, the mist filling me. My aura fluxes feebly, cold chills trickling over my skin, my body slowly going numb. Darkness fills my vision and I fall backward into nothing.

I gasp, sitting up in my bed, gulping in breath after breath of fresh air, taking advantage of the ability to be able to breathe again. My aura is so dim that I can't see it if I hold my hand an inch from my face; I rub my arms and feel goosebumps on my skin. My tongue feels swollen, my body sluggish, little pricks of cold torture needling up my legs. I take a deep breath in my nose, breathing out my mouth; I repeat this several times until my heart stops hammering, my aura shining slightly brighter, some warmth returning to my body.

"Ma'am!" Hekras bursts into the room and I turn to him; he looks at me in my day clothes, panting, and blushes, dipping his head. "Ma'am, Petravin is here for you. He says it's urgent."

I go to the door that leads to the balcony, peering through one of the glass windows in the door; it's still dark outside. I rub my eyes and stifle a yawn, making my way down to the throne room. I lean on the doorway to the entrance of the throne room, putting a hand to my stomach, a small amount of warmth seeping in to try and ease the tundra-esque pains. Petravin waits impatiently, his eyes lighting up when he sees me. He runs to me then stops, remembering my position; he takes a few hasty steps back, allowing me to sag into my throne, unable to suppress the yawn that is building within. My mouth stretches wide and my jaw pops, the yawn keeping my mouth open for a full ten seconds. I snap my mouth shut, trying to keep my gaze pleasant enough; even if my sleep had been unpleasant, sleep is sleep, and it is still something I long for, if nothing more than to forget about this accursed pain.

"We've completed the task," he says, almost bouncing from one foot to the other.

"Is that why you're so excited? Did you—" I yawn, then shake my head, aura fluxing; I have to show a little control. "Is that why you're so excited?" I ask again. He shakes his head quickly, shaking his hands a little.

"No; I'm still just working off the adrenaline and energy I got from it. Combat gives me a rush," he says with a wild grin; forest boy.

"Why are you here then? Not to be rude, but it's very early in the morning, or very late at night. Either way," I make a gesture behind me to outside, "it's still dark out there. The sun has yet to rise; roosters have not crowed. Sleeping should be the action I am doing right now, so I would appreciate it if you got to your point." The last part comes out almost as a snap. I try to smooth it over with a tired smile, rubbing one of my temples with one hand, trying to ease the hot headache that continues to build, like steam gathering pressure.

"After we had finished off the last person on your list, someone came to stop us. She was good, *really* good;. She looked spectacular in combat." A large smile begins to spread on his face; I blink rapidly, waking myself up, my aura glowing slightly brighter as I sit up.

"Who was she? What did she look like?"

"I don't know who she was, but I'll never forget what she looked like. She was graceful, with pale skin and bright red hair and the most stunning green eyes you will ever see. She..."

He continues talking, but his words fall on deaf ears. The world seems to be spinning very quickly, and I lean back in my throne, eyes wide, aura fluxing rapidly. It's her, that girl that I helped Eurael save—the one he left me in the Underworld for. She was the reason he betrayed me and left me to rot in hell for eternity; my fingers grip the arms of my throne tightly, my aura beginning to glow brightly, heat radiating from me in such a degree that it begins to turn the throne red. It's because of her that he saw through my ruse; she was the catalyst for my failure.

"Find her," I say softly, snapping Petravin out of his reverie. "Find her and kill her."

"Kill her?" he seems confused, tilting his head at me. "Someone as graceful, as splendid as her should not—"

"I said find her and kill her!" I shriek, my aura flashing, and I stand up, molten metal dripping from my hands, my aura fluctuating rapidly. "I want you to kill her, no matter what it takes; and once you do, I want you to bring her body to me."

He backs away, his eyes wide. "I—I d-don't think—"

"Before you deny me, *think* of your group," my voice drops low, white light crackling around me. He gulps, getting the message and quickly leaves the room. I sag down into my throne, my aura dimming back down, the metal having cooled quickly after I removed myself from the throne. I rest my head in my hands for a moment; I must kill her before I kill Eurael. She was the reason I journeyed to the Underworld with Eurael in the first place, and she is the reason I was discovered, betrayed, and left to die. I stand up, shaking as I make my way back to my bed; I need to rest.

I drop onto my bed, looking up, the echo of pain reverberating through me, but I do my best not to pay attention; that's not my concern right now. I can't believe she's interfering with my plans. Of all the people, it would just have to be her. I turn over onto my side, smacking my pillows; maybe it's a good thing it's her. This way I don't have to track her down; it's easier this way. She came to me, and then I will bring her body to Eurael. I will lay it at his feet and tell him that it is his fault—that he is responsible for her death; he drove me to this point. I will lay her battered, broken body at his feet, and I will tell him it didn't have to be like this, that he is to blame for her death. I nod to myself; that's good, I should write that down.

I turn over onto my other side, smacking my pillow again. After a few minutes I squirm, adjusting myself. I give up and smack the mattress, laying on my back breathing heavy; doesn't this bed have one comfortable spot?! My back is riddled with hot and cold spots of pain, and this blasted mattress only seems to make things worse. I look up, trying to see the ceiling in the darkness, but I'm unable to. Visions play in front of my eyes, phantasms sliding in and out of my vision. Mocking laughter fills my ears and I turn, covering my eyes with the pillow.

"She was chosen over you," a voice whispers, the pillow doing nothing to block it out. "She's better than you," it hisses. I curl up tighter, pressing the pillow harder against my ears. "He will protect her; he will ensure her safety," the voice whispers.

"Quiet," I murmur, waving my hand at the air. "What do you know? You're just a voice."

"Or maybe I am the one hallucinating, and you are just a voice," I sit up, looking around, but see nothing.

"You're not real," I say, a little louder than necessary.

"Look again," I turn and start back, my heart leaping into my throat. She stands there before me, that girl. Her green eyes shine brightly, her red hair falling in a wave to her shoulders. Her mouth is twisted into a cruel grin and she looks down at me, contempt etched into every curve of her face.

"You're not real," I repeat in a choked whisper.

"There's no use in saying that if you're the one that's not real," she says, taking a step forward. "You don't even exist. Why should you anyway, when someone like me was chosen over you? I'm obviously stronger, more powerful, or why would he have chosen me at all? And he *did* choose me." Her grin gets larger as she steps closer. I scoot backward, heart hammering, my aura fluctuating; she's not real, she is *not* real. "He saw through your disguise, and he chose *me*."

"Just get...get out," I breathe and she cackles, jumping onto the bed, crawling toward me on all fours.

"But why? We were just about to have some fun," she stalks closer. "Or I was, anyway. How can you have fun when you don't exist? You are nothing."

"Be quiet," I murmur, looking away.

"You are pathetic," she says, her eyes shining brighter.

"Be quiet," I say a little louder, glancing up.

She's stopped, her mouth carving itself into a snarl. "You are weak."

"Quiet!" I shout, my aura fluxing brighter.

"You are useless, pathetic, weak; you are nothing. You are garbage, you are filth, you—"

"Shut up!" I scream, leaping at her. I collide with nothing, a bolt of energy hitting the balcony doors, sending them flying over the balcony ledge. I crash against the wall and remain motionless for a moment. I slowly pull myself up, looking at my room, but it remains empty. The wind whips my hair, tugging at it, howling in the darkness. I pull my knees up, holding them; she'll be dead before sunrise. She'll be dead. I begin to murmur to myself, rocking back and forth slightly.

"It'll all be over soon, it'll all be over soon, it'll all be over soon..."

CHAPTER THIRTY-NINE

I dodge past a tree, a branch smacking me in the face, leaving small cuts. *Hurry! They're coming!* I know! I leap at a branch, swinging myself up as an arrow thuds into the thick trunk, whoops and hollers echoing through the dark forest. I don't stop moving, climbing higher and leaping to the next tree, scampering lower and then dropping, rolling into brush. I clamp down on my breathing, my nostrils flaring out, the scent of dirt and forest thick in the air. Who are these people? *Does it matter? They're trying to kill you.* It matters; if I know who they are, I can track them down later, and make sure that they don't ever come after me again. *It seems that, for once, you are making rational decisions.* The leaves rustle above me, and I roll out of the way as a small figure leaps out of the trees above me. I slice at the dark creature, gasping for breath. I flip up a hood and stand up quickly; it's a girl, even younger than me. *She tried to kill you.* They're just children! A ghostly blur flies past me, and I take off running; they're kids. I can't...I can't kill kids. The whoosh of something swinging through the air reaches my ears right as someone collides into me. We go rolling and I find myself on top, dagger poised to kill.

"Who are you?" The only response is a low growl as the hooded person rolls me off, small daggers swinging at my exposed face. My arm locks out of its own accord, and my attacker drops off of me, my dagger sliding out. I throw back the hood and stifle a cry, the frozen face of a boy no more than twelve looking back. *You must do what you must do in order to survive.* I trip over the boy's body, an arrow thudding from one of my pursuers into their own comrade, my legs pumping, urging me to leave these child murderers behind.

One of the children rolls out of the brush as I race by. I plant on foot on a tree, making it a few quick steps up before I push myself off, grabbing the head of my would-be assailant, my knee cracking into their head. They slump down and I roll underneath an arrow, flinging one of my small knives at the silent archer as I'm coming out of my roll, planting my palm on their soft face and slamming their head onto the ground. My legs snap out behind me, rolling like a log away from the unconscious form of the archer, leaping at the child who had just had a sword at my neck. My elbow crushes his temple, breathing heavily. I take off before any more have the chance to join the fray. An arrow whistles by, leaving a thin cut on my leg. I weave between the trees but still receive several more cuts on my arms and legs.

I skid to a halt as I come to a clearing, a small cabin standing in the center, light flickering out its windows. My eyes flick to the trees and I take a running leap, smacking into the child on the rope, dragging them down. Before they can try to attack me, I slam them into the wall of the cabin, dagger at their throat.

"Why are you trying to kill me?" The door to the cabin opens, the kid taking the chance to drive their foot into my leg. The steel of their dagger catches the flickering lights of the cabin, glinting off the blade even in the darkness. Before I can blink, my hand grabs the child's wrist, my forearm snapping their elbow then sliding up their arm, driving my dagger deep into their neck. I blink, the child falling off my dagger, bleeding out on the ground; I didn't want to kill him! *Get it through that thick skull of yours. They are trying to kill you; you can't let that happen. Think of your teacher, think of Wilhelm; you have reasons to live, and you have to do whatever it takes to survive, no matter what the cost.*

"Miss?" I turn and see an old man carrying a lantern, peering at me through the night. A whoop of laughter rings throughout the clearing, a rustle of leaves my only warning to duck as one of the group swings over my head. I grab their legs and wrench them down, but they quickly kick me off, scampering backward. Unlike the others, this one doesn't retreat, unsheathing a thin sword and a dagger, the light from the man's lantern revealing his unhooded features. Short, messy brown hair nearly looks black in the low light, his pointed ears and nose turning his mischievous, impish features almost sinister.

"Get inside!" I urge the old man, but he remains frozen in the doorway. My opponent dances forward, sword streaking through the air. I unsheathe a second dagger and his sword glances off, my own blade unable to touch him as he blocks with his small dagger. "Who are you?" I growl as he dances backward, laughing.

"The name is Petravin," he says with a grin. He takes a running leap at me but disappears over my head. I barely have time to turn, blocking his sword as it races at my head. I catch his blade between both of mine, dragging him with me as I roll onto my back, planting my feet on his stomach and pushing off. He flies behind me, but remains suspended in the air; he can fly. He flies toward me, my daggers blocking his thrust at my heart. He flips over me, leaving a deep gash in my arm, pushing off of me with his boots. I stumble forward, blood seeping through my shirt and down my arm as he lands lightly on the ground.

"Why are you trying to kill me, Petravin?" He raises a thin eyebrow, twirling both blades in his deft hands.

"I was hired of course."

"By who?"

He lunges at me, soaring through the air by way of response. I lean backward, our blades sparking as they slide against each other. He passes me, his blade sinking into the old man. "No!" He was innocent. Petravin pulls out quickly, his front covered in blood, flicking his sword in my direction. I bat it aside, rushing at him. He ducks underneath my blade quicker than anyone but Mister E, his dagger slipping into my stomach as he pulls us both to the ground. I push him off, his dagger sliding out of me with a wet, sucking sound. My breath rattles in my throat as I force myself to stand, one hand sheathing my dagger, holding my hand over the wound. *You have to get out of here.* I can't...I can't let Petravin get away! *You can't do that if you're dead!* I roll sloppily under his next flying attack, pausing at the old man, his fingers trembling, his hand reaching out to me. *You have to leave him.* He's an innocent man, he had nothing to do with this fight; I can't just let him die! *You can't save him!* "I'm sorry," I whisper, pushing myself up, taking off into the forest.

I blearily lift my head up as someone knocks on my door; it still isn't light out yet. I crawl over to the door and pull myself up using the knob, making an effort to straighten out my clothes. I pull the door open, blinking at Hekras.

"It's Petravin again ma'am," he says, sounding understandably annoyed; I nod weakly, brushing past him. My foot slips on the stair and Hekras rushes toward me, but I hold up a hand, moving down the steps slower, each step another needle jabbing into my feet. I don't even move to sit in my throne, instead leaning on the back of it, openly glaring at Petravin.

"Well?" I snap. Petravin is covered in blood, yet has no visible wounds on him; that better be the redhead's blood on him.

"We found her but," he licks his lips, swallowing hard. "But we weren't able to kill her." I remain silent, my aura glowing steadily brighter. Seeming to sense my anger he speaks quickly, trying to smooth the situation over. "We wounded her badly in the fight! There were a great many of us and we tried our best but—"

"But you failed," I whisper, my voice dead. "I gave you a task, and you failed."

"My people were tired, and she is incredibly skilled," he protests.

My light flashes out brightly. "You didn't kill her! She's still alive out there, right now! I told you to kill her, but you couldn't!" I give him *one* job, one *simple* job and he can't accomplish it?! Why do I even hire pathetic forest rats like him if they can't get the job done?! Anger wells within my chest, my hands glowing brighter, clamping down on the throne.

"I—"

"Get out!" I scream, my hair flying around me, my face turned red with rage.

"We—"

"Get out!" I scream again, hurling a bolt of light at him. He scampers back. "Get out! Getoutgetoutgetout!" I shriek, hurling another bolt of light at him. He quickly scurries out of the room, the door slamming shut behind him. I bite my tongue, blood filling my mouth as the throne melts. He failed and now that girl is still alive! I scream, my aura filling the room with blinding white light; she's still alive!

CHAPTER FORTY

My head snaps toward the door as a step creaks outside. My eyes focus on the doorknob as it slowly twists, and the door opens slowly on silent hinges. Scarlett stands there for a moment, then takes a step forward and collapses. I move, and the shadows uncurl from around me instantly; my foot hits the floor, and I drop to my hands and knees as my leg gives. I crawl over to Scarlett, turning her over onto her back. Her face is smeared with blood, her hair matted with it. Long gashes wound her arms, several smaller cuts having broken through her pants. I set my hands on her stomach where a large stain has appeared, continuing to blossom outward. I raise my hand up, but the shadows don't move.

"She's dying!" I hiss, but they remain still, unfeeling; do not punish her for my mistakes. They disappear completely; no! You cared for her! I growl, pulling myself up and out of my room. My legs burn as I walk through the halls to the medicine closet. I remove a bowl, a small wooden knob, several plants, and a large amount of gauze. I return as quickly as I am able, dropping to my knees next to her. I mash up the plants in the bowl until it turns into a sort of goo, spreading it quickly on the gauze. I remove her dagger and cut away the fabric, revealing her wound. I swear and stand up again, getting a small bucket of water and a cup. I clear away the blood from the wound, grabbing one of the lamps in my room. I hold the open flame to her wound and she tries to move, but I hold her still, cauterizing the wound. Her eyelids flicker, and I apply the gauze with the mixture on it. Instantly her face relaxes, and I bind the wound tightly, though lax enough that it can still breathe slightly. I bandage the rest of her wounds after cleaning them, standing up and leaning against the wall for support.

Someone not only interfered with my plan and caused the escape of several phantoms, but they also killed several members of my information network. Now they have attacked and wounded my student; I stand up straighter, clenching my fists. With the destruction of Ragnarok, I would have hunted them to the ends of the earth; now, hell itself will not stop me. No one shall harm my student without being punished.

I bend down and pick Scarlett up, quickly setting her on my bed before my arms give. I pull out my sword, and it is relatively undamaged from the explosion; I sheathe it again. I step toward the door and falter, but I take a deep breath; this person must be stopped at all costs. I take another step forward and falter again, but am able to step quicker. I make my way to the door and throw it open, stepping into the hall. With each successful step, my footing grows surer, and soon I am striding through the halls. I sling the front door open and it slams shut behind me; I will find the person responsible for this. My anger drives my footsteps forward, my eyes glaring into the night; I will make them pay.

CHAPTER FORTY-ONE

I slam the portly man against the alley wall, lifting him up by his neck.

"If I find out you are lying, I will come back and rip your tongue from your mouth," I growl and he shakes his head quickly, face turning red.

"I...I'm—I'm not lying, I—I swear," he gasps out, and I drop him unceremoniously to the ground as he sucks in a rattling breath. I plant my boot on his head, pushing down slowly until his forehead is touching the concrete beneath, his sweating, putrid mortal body shaking and trembling; I will not be denied my revenge. I want to make sure that this man knows that I am serious about my threats, or else he might very well still lie to me. "Please..." he groans, and I move my boot from his head and he sighs in relief. I stomp on his hand, and several bones break with small snaps. He whimpers, trying not to scream; good man. I grind my heel and he howls softly, biting on his knuckles of his unbroken hand. I lift my foot off and he quickly snatches his hand back, cradling it to his chest. Scarlett taught me that there are other ways than violence to get what I desire; she is lying on my bed, grievously wounded. I am no longer in a diplomatic mood.

"I do not make empty threats," I assure him, and he nods quickly, sniffing and wiping tears from his eyes. I turn on my heel, quickly exiting the alley. I stride down the street and exit the city in a matter of minutes, walking toward the forest. The people responsible for

Scarlett's condition are said to inhabit this portion of the forest, high in the trees. I enter the forest and look up at the top branches high above; I hold my hand up and the shadows slither up but do not aid me. I growl, grabbing one tendril, squeezing it hard, but it merely spits and hisses at me. I throw it to the ground and unsheathe my sword, impaling the shadow. I feel a sharp pain in my stomach; but instead of stopping, I twist the sword around, digging the point into the tendril as it screeches and squirms.

"I will not be denied now; I am not in the mood for games. I tried to love, and you simply continue to spurn me; Scarlett nearly died. Do not punish her for my failure. There is no other option except for you to help me," I shove the sword deeper into the ground, further impaling the tendril and it shrieks louder, a small dab of blood leaking from a new wound. "Do I make myself clear?!" I roar. The shadows coo their assent, and I remove the sword, sheathing it once again, my eyes flashing; I am done playing games. They lift me into the tops of the trees, and I look through the thick branches, then lower myself back down. I place my palm on the ground, extending my senses out, taking a deep breath; I must find these people.

I open my eyes and stride forward through the forest, picking up speed. The trees blur by, and I only stop when an arrow whizzes past me. I dig my heels in and turn, slicing another arrow in half. I extend a hand and a tendril of shadow shoots out, wrapping around my attacker, dragging them down. The young man who would appear to be my attacker rolls on the ground as the tendril releases him. I walk over and kick his bow away, yanking him up and holding my sword to his throat.

"Tell me where the rest are," I growl, pressing the blade harder against his throat. He glares at me but says nothing, tilting his chin up in scorn at me. My hand tenses, and a small bead of red trickles down his throat when a voice calls out.

"Wait!" I turn, holding the boy in front of me as a shield. A boy of about eighteen stands in front of me, holding a small sword. He's dressed in dark green and brown clothing to blend into the trees, a hood resting unused on his back. Short coppery hair sticks out in a wild mess, not fully covering his pointy ears. Bright blue eyes gleam with cunning, a mischievous smile played out on his impish face. "You wanted me, and now you found me," he says, holding up one of his hands. "There's no reason for you to hurt the boy—just let him go." There's a barely audible creak and I turn quickly, holding the boy out. His eyes go wide, and he gasps as I drop him to the ground, an arrow shaft sticking out of his back.

"No!" A young girl runs out of the brush, dropping her bow, kneeling next to the fallen boy, shaking him. I grip her hair and tilt her head back; she squirms, but I smack her in the temple with the pommel of my sword and she slumps. I drop her to the ground, turning back to the leader; I will enact my vengeance in full on those responsible. His eyes remain on me, his stance wary and ready to flee at a moment's notice.

"Will I have to worry about any more surprises?" I point my sword at him, and he shakes his head, looking past me to his two comrades, then back to me.

"No; they were the only two."

"Do not lie to me," I growl, taking a step forward.

"I'm not lying! I brought my two lieutenants with me to check the disturbance; the rest are back at our headquarters, under the assumption everything is taken care of. It's just the two of us now," he says and I nod, keeping my sword pointed at him.

"I'm here to kill the people responsible for attacking and injuring my student," I growl.

"I wouldn't know anything about that," he says, and I swipe my sword at him; he dodges, dancing out of the way.

"I told you not to lie to me!" I roar, and he holds up his hand, nodding.

"Alright, alright; I'm sorry. I know who you're talking about," he confesses. I growl and take a step toward him, but he backs up, dropping his sword and holding up both of his hands. "Just listen to me for a moment!" I stop, the tip of my sword quivering; I will kill him regardless. He is undoubtedly the one who attacked Scarlett; I can smell her blood on him. Taking this as a sign of my cooperation, he begins speaking again. "My name is Petravin, and I run a group called the Lost Boys. Recently we were hired to kill a young woman, with bright red hair and green eyes. The job paid good, so we took it; she fought us off and managed to escape though. It wasn't personal, it was just business; I will gladly give you money that we received. It's yours—you can take it; we haven't spent a coin yet."

"Who hired you?" I growl, tightening my grip on the sword.

"A woman; she was taller than me, dressed all in white. Fair skin with auburn hair and bright eyes," he says.

I suck in a quick breath—Evermore. I left her in the Underworld, chained and sure to rot for eternity. How could she have escaped?

"Listen, you know what you want to know now; there's no reason to shed any more blood over it," he says, looking at me cautiously. These people still tried to kill Scarlett; they attacked her and injured her. By accepting the job, they accepted all the responsibilities attached to it; I will make sure they realize how grave their mistake was. I lunge forward, and Petravin flicks his sword up using his foot, parrying my blow. He twirls away, but I grab one of this thin wrists, pulling him forward, bringing my forearm down at his elbow. He brings his sword in, and I have to make an adjustment to my grip so that I can block his blade with my own. Using that moment, he slips free from my grasp, flying up into the air to avoid my next swipe.

"You can't touch me up here," he says laughing. He swoops down, taking a swipe at me with his blade, which I block, reaching out to grab him, but he flies out of reach. "Too slow!" he says grinning.

Anger boils up, and I feel the shadows swirling inside me; we are in agreement then. They will not rebel when a clear path of revenge, for the both of us, is so close. A tendril of shadow shoots from the ground, and he narrowly avoids it, his eyes going wide. Several more shoot from the ground and he has to fly quicker, twisting and turning in the air to avoid the tendrils. One finally catches him, smacking him in the stomach, sending him crashing to the ground. He picks himself up, quickly dodging another tendril.

"Let's be honorable about this," he says with a grin, wiping blood from his bottom lip. He knows he can't win against me with the shadows; he's trying to appeal to any sense of honor I have. "Give yourself a chance to avenge your student, with dignity and honor."

It won't work. I glare at him, leveling my sword at him; he grins, twirling his blade. The end will justify the means, and the means are unimportant. Honor, morality—they are outdated concepts—they are useless. Victory, by any means, revenge by any means—he appeals to the wrong individual.

He rushes at me, light on his feet; my other hand twitches, and a tendril of shadow wraps around his foot, slamming him against a tree. The tendril slams him against the tree again, and his blade drops from his grasp as I sheathe my own. The tendril slings him to me, and I throw my fist out, catching him in the jaw, sending him to the ground. I kick him in the side and he groans, rolling several feet. Tendrils of shadow wrap around him and sling him into the air, a wall of shadow slamming him against a tree, then, holding his face against it, drags him down, sliding him across the ground. I pick him up and blacken his eye with another blow, kicking him in the chest, sending him flying. A tendril of shadow smacks him back toward me, and I grab his face, slamming him onto the ground, feeling his pointed nose crush against my palm. He tries to gasp for breath, but is unable, merely coughing and gurgling as blood trickles underneath my palm down his face. You tried to kill my student, whelp.

"Tell me where the woman is," I growl next to his ear. "And I won't make you watch while I slaughter your 'Lost Boys'."

Finally regaining his breath, he takes a rattling gulp of air, breathing heavily against my hand. "I…don't know…where she is," he wheezes out. I pick him up by his hair and look him in his one eye that hasn't swollen shut; it's wide with fear; but with his people at risk, he would not dare lie.

Tendrils of shadow wrap around him, trapping his arms to his sides and his legs together, wrapping around his mouth to keep him quiet. I place my palm on the ground, extending my senses; I will find the others as well. Nodding, I stand up and the shadows hoist me in the trees. I make my way from tree to tree; and as I draw closer, I can hear alarm bells and voices. My ears detect the sound of bows being drawn when the tendrils of shadow move Petravin in front of me. No shots are fired, and I land on a wooden deck with a large wooden platform before me.

Dozens of young men and women stand before me with bows, swords, axes and knives drawn, looking from me to their leader. They're covered in dirt and dressed in the same attire as Petravin. The shadows, keeping Petravin bound, lower him to the ground, and I grip his head firmly in my hand, keeping it still as I place my blade against his throat. They look at me warily, some angry, some fearful; if they attack me, they will all die.

"I came here to get revenge on someone who you were hired to kill; you didn't succeed, but, nonetheless, you tried to kill her. I came here to kill each and every one of you." The creak of bows about to be let loose fills the air, but I continue. "However, I ran into Petravin, and he convinced me that no more blood should be shed; I am here now to return your leader and collect the money you were paid to assassinate my companion." There's a soft murmur as they converse among themselves, not taking their eyes off me. Their distraction is all I need; tendrils of shadow rise up, hissing and snapping. In a moment, if they deny me, the will all die.

"Stop!" I search the crowd and look beyond them as someone pulls themselves onto the platform. The person pushes through the crowd, coming to the front, and I tighten my grip on my sword, pressing the blade harder into Petravin's neck; not this. "Don't kill them," Wilhelm says, looking up at me, pleading.

I growl, letting go of Petravin, though the shadows remain wrapped around him. I reach down and yank Wilhelm up onto the raised ledge with one hand, dropping him next to me. I point my sword at him as he tries to rise and he gulps, remaining on his knees. This man was responsible for Scarlett not focusing entirely on her training; perhaps if she had focused less on him, she wouldn't have nearly died. I should kill him now.

"Why?" I growl through gritted teeth, and he wets his lips.

"Because..." he says and I bring the point of my blade closer. "Because if you do, then you'll have to kill me as well!" he says hurriedly.

"I don't see a downside to this," I press the point against his throat, and he swallows hard.

"If you kill me, Scarlett will know; we're connected in a way. She'll investigate," he says. I growl, my hand tensing and he looks away, clamping his eyes shut, wincing; coward.

I release the tension in my hand, the shadows slithering against him, then hissing confirmation of what he had said. I should just kill them all now, consequences or no; I slowly move the sword away, sheathing it with a jerk of my arm. No, my revenge is against Evermore; I cannot let myself be distracted by these... children.

"Very well," I growl, and Wilhelm visibly slumps with relief, letting out a heavy breath. "If I do this, you will remain with the Lost Boys. You will not visit Scarlett, and you will stay away from her at all times, until the end of your days." I see Wilhelm look behind him at the Lost Boys, taking in their faces; he's conflicted. He is a man of conscience; that conscience makes him weak. He sighs, looking pained, nodding. He will no longer be a distraction to Scarlett; this situation will never happen again.

"Alright," he says. The shadows toss Petravin into the crowd and I jump down, the shadows lowering me to the ground; now I must find Evermore.

CHAPTER FORTY-TWO

I stand on a wooden ledge looking at large platform, high above the trees. The sun is high overhead, and I'm dressed in finer clothes, my hair styled back elegantly; I hold a large bag of coins in my hands, waiting patiently. I acted out last night; I made a mistake. I let my anger get the best of me, and I might have scared away one of my allies who has only failed me once, on his record. The girl will die anyway with time; I will simply hire someone else to kill her, or do the deed myself. Finally someone walks out of one of the wooden huts, dressed in dark green and brown. He has shaggy brown hair and wide brown eyes, which look me over searchingly; the eyes speak of a certain innocence not found in many in this land, especially in adults.

"Hi, yes, I'd like to speak to Petravin please," I say with a smile, holding up the bag of coin slightly. He waits a moment to speak ,and I notice he has no weapons on him. Smiling comes more naturally now, even with the constant echoes of pain in my body.

"Petravin is seriously injured right now," he says. I widen my eyes for the man's benefit; who would have attacked him? Was it Eurael?

"How? Where is he?" I step forward, but he steps in front of me; he does it in such a way that it doesn't come across as hostile, but almost apologetic.

"He's not accepting visitors," he says, his eyes sympathetic.

"I can heal him; I assure you, I'm a friend." I say, trying to step forward but he doesn't move.

"The Lost Boys is under new leadership, and we're instructed not to let anyone visit Petravin," he says, taking a step back to seem less confrontational; I do the same, speaking as politely as I can.

"Then I would please like to speak to this new leader," I say with a small smile; I need answers.

"Currently speaking," the man says with a nervous grin.

"I've never seen you before," I say, my aura shining slightly brighter. "When did you join?"

"Yesterday,.

"Oh," I look him over slowly; he seems harmless enough, not the type to lie intentionally or do any real harm at all really. He looks almost like a lost puppy, and I feel a twinge of sympathy.

"They thrust the position on me after I saved their lives from...a man," he says, looking uncomfortable. "You seem like a regular, so you should know that we won't be taking jobs for a while; and when we do accept jobs again, we won't be doing assassinations any longer."

I nod; I will have to find someone else to continue destroying Eurael's network then. I have a kingdom to run now that I am queen; I cannot exactly be seen killing people left and right that happen to have a connection to one man. I smile, holding the bag of gold out to him.

"If you're not going to be taking jobs for a while, you might need this." I say. He takes it with trembling hands, looking up at me with wider eyes, if that's possible.

"Thank you," he says, sounding stunned. I nod and smile, turning to leave. I wave goodbye behind me and he returns the favor, nearly dropping the bag of gold; he's cute, I like him. "You should know, Petravin remained loyal to you. He lied to the man that came here, and said he didn't know where you were. I just thought you should know."

"And do you know where that man is now?"

He pauses a moment before answering, grip tightening on the bad of gold. "It was dark—I didn't get a good look at him."

My eyes narrow slightly, but I manage to keep my aura from brightening; he's lying. That's fine; I don't need to get to Eurael right now anyway. The moment isn't right.

CHAPTER FORTY-THREE

Scarlett parries my blow, ducking underneath the next one and flipping back, rolling backward to avoid a thrust. Her arms shudder as I bring my practice blade heavily down onto hers, but she slides mine off and rolls away, coming to a stand.

"We lost another three today," she says and I swing at her, but she blocks it easily. I step in, closing the distance and forcing a bladelock; I jam my knee into her thigh and she crumples slightly, for a brief moment. I twist the blade, smacking her in the face with the flat of her own, catching her in the chin as I bring my elbow up. Her head snaps back, and I slice across her exposed neck quickly. She rubs her chin as I throw my practice blade at the ground, the point embedding into the dirt.

"I cannot stand my network being attacked like this," I growl, pacing. "Something has to be done about it, but no one seems to know where Evermore is."

"Why are people protecting her? Why is she even doing this? I know you have plenty of enemies, but I've never even heard of this woman before she started targeting you." Scarlett gets a drink of water, sipping at her cup.

"She appeared from the blue; I have no idea why she'd be doing this." I shake my head in anger, gritting my teeth. "I've never met her before; I can barely find anything on her, and her whereabouts are all but impossible to track." I wrench the practice blade from the ground and bring my arm back, throwing it as hard as I can. It disappears into the distance and I clench my fists, shaking my head. I have to deal with the situation without letting Scarlett know about what truly happened, managing two fronts at once. Her memories of the Underworld are supposed to have been erased, but there's no telling if a trigger will bring them back; she can't know what truly transpired. She can't know the truth about Evermore.

"At least we know what she looks like," she says.

I slam my fist on the wall of the house, glaring at the ground. I was careless; I left her in the Underworld without any consideration of the consequences. There could have been another way to handle it, but I spurned a potential ally and turned her into an enemy. I let my emotions get the best of me; I let my emotions about Scarlett cloud my judgment. I wouldn't care so much if I regretted it, but I don't; I don't regret one thing I did to ensure Scarlett's safety. Now it has come back to me, and she is doing more damage than I thought possible. She knows where to hit and when, how to get around my defenses, almost seeming to know what I'll do ahead of time.

There is no doubt in my mind that Evermore is the one who sabotaged Ragnarok; my emotions for Scarlett cost me my mission. They cost me a chance to right things, to bring back something from complete erasure. Simiel, I'm sorry; my emotions cost me your only chance.

" A physical description is very helpful," I spit sarcastically, slamming my other fist against the wall.

"We'll beat her," Scarlett says, putting a hand on my shoulder. "We haven't been beaten before, nothing will change."

"She *is* beating us!" I roar, turning around. "Don't you see that?! She's not about to start beating us, she *is* beating us! We don't know where she is or what her next move will be; we're completely blind! She's been targeting me for months now, and I haven't made one successful counterattack! My network is in shambles, and there's absolutely nothing that can be done about it." She takes a step back, her eyes narrowing as she glares at me, her voice loud and vehement.

"I was just trying to help. She's winning because *you* are giving up; you're losing it because for the first time you're facing someone who has actual skill. You need to snap out of it or you really *will* lose!"

I roar, taking a step toward her, but she unsheathes her dagger, dropping into a fighting crouch. "You need to go, now. Don't come back until you've cooled off," she says.

I clench my fists; she's right. I clench my fists and spin; I have to find Evermore and put a stop to this.

The doors to Oberon's castle slam open, and I race inside as they swing, partially knocked off their hinges.

"What are you doing?! This is trespassing! You can't be here!" The small man shouts from the bull man's head. I lash out with the shadows, but they only go halfway before stopping, hissing at me. The bull man rushes at me, and I throw myself to the side, swinging my arm. He trips over my arm and I quickly move on; I'm not here for him. I have to go to Tatiana; she can help. I have to! I race frantically through the halls, taking turn after turn. I skid to a halt at a dead end, swearing; no, not here! I race back, turning nearly at random now; I will search this entire palace if I must! Finally I see a set of double doors with two guards dressed in steel armor standing outside.

"Stop!" they shout in unison. I continue running; they will not stop me here! I shoot out one palm and the tendrils wrap around one of the guards. The other thrusts his spear at me, and I spin out of the way, feeling a slight cut in my side. No mind, no mind; this is not my concern. I grab the man's spear, yanking it from his grasp, smacking him in the skull until he crumples. The other man slams his spear into me, the shadows having let him go, and I fall toward the wall. I spin, unsheathing my sword, hacking at him without elegance or pattern. Finally, he drops to the ground and I stop, pushing the doors open. Tatiana jumps, turning from her mirror to look at me.

"What are you doing here?" she says, standing up, but I'm at her in an instant, forcing her back down.

"Where's Evermore?!" I shout, the doors swinging back shut behind me.

"Alright, just calm down. It's alright—no need to get angry over anything," she says, holding up her hands. "Just ask your questions, and I'll answer them as best I can."

"Where is she?!" I take several steps toward her, breathing heavily; I am on the edge, and I will go over if it means finding her.

"Who?"

"Evermore! I know someone with that much power wouldn't escape your attention! You know where she is, and I expect you to tell me, *now*." I tighten my hold on her shoulders, itching to reach for my sword; she has to know where Evermore is.

Her eyes grow cold, narrowing as she reaches up, flipping a strand of hair over her shoulder. "I have no idea who you're talking about," she says coldly.

I roar, grabbing a chair and shattering it against the wall before I realize what I'm doing. I cringe inwardly at the sound, struggling to keep my breathing under control; Oberon will already know I'm here—I don't want him to come looking for me just yet. Not until Tatiana tells me what I need to know.

"Do not lie to me, Tatiana!" I hiss, stepping close to her. "Do not play games with me! Now tell me where she is." She looks up at me coolly; I unsheathe my sword with one jerk of my arm, holding it to her throat. "Do not test me—just tell me where she is."

"You're in dangerous waters," she says softly, leaning forward, pressing her throat against my sword. "I don't know who you're talking about; but if I did, I wouldn't tell you." She glares up at me and I shake my head, my grip tightening on my sword; I just need to know this one piece of information! I don't require anything else; all I need is for her to tell me where! I turn back to Tatiana, desperation fueling every word and action.

"Tatiana, tell me where she is; someone as powerful as her wouldn't have escaped your attention. Just tell me where she is, that's all! I took care of Nyphra, you owe me!"

Her cool, angry eyes shoot daggers into me; I won't get anything from her. This entire trip was useless! Now I might have to send a message; even in this time of desperation, I can't afford to be seen as weak. The muscles in my arm tighten in preparation, almost eager to draw the blade across her neck, when the doors fly inward off their hinges, bright light shining forth. I turn my head quickly, squinting until the light dims, revealing Oberon glowing with power, accompanied by several guards. His eyes narrow once they take in the sight before him, his voice bursting forth like a dam that had been in place for far too long.

"Step away from my wife!" he shouts, a bolt of energy flying out toward me. The shadows shy away from the energy, and it smacks me in the chest, sending me across the room. I crash against the wall, smoking, struggling to my feet, the shadows disappearing from the room.

"Oberon, it's not what it looks like!" I hold out a hand in an effort to placate him; I will not fight him in his own castle. A ripple of energy erupts near my feet, and I throw myself out of the way, barely able to keep from being vaporized. I clench my teeth, sharp pangs shooting up through my chest, my hand trembling.

"Tell me what it looks like then, Eurael; to me it looks like you were threatening my wife at swordpoint."

I stand up straighter, sheathing my sword, taking a deep breath; just explain the situation.

"I came here seeking information—that's all. Tatiana was unwilling to give, so I—" Another bolt of energy blasts me off my feet.

"Information! You threaten my wife over information?" Oberon is looming over me before I have a chance to stand, his eyes mere slits of vehement rage. "I will not have you lay another hand on my wife, not ever again!" I sense his power building and I roll, knowing it will do little when he decides to unleash it; I can't die now! No, not when Evermore is still out there; I cannot let her win!

"Wait!" I stand up quickly when Oberon doesn't obliterate me, putting my hand on my sword; I won't go down without a fight, despite Oberon's power. Tatiana hangs onto Oberon's arm, looking up at him with big, round eyes. She leans up to him, whispering in his ear, and his eyes grow hazy and unfocused, his power beginning to fade. I step around him, slipping between the guards; I have to find where Evermore is, but I won't do it here. An entire waste of time! I rush through the palace again, finally making it back to the front door. I stop when I see a tall man in a dark suit leaning against one of the columns, watching me from behind his glasses. I walk up to him; his expression is neutral and his hair is fully dark once again.

"Eraxus," I say, barely containing my desperation; this is my last chance to make sure this trip wasn't an utter failure. "I know that you know where Evermore is," I say. He looks down at me, standing up straight.

"I do," he says—finally! This is all I need; now I can track down Evermore and end her, end it all. I will be able to avenge Simiel and the destruction of Ragnarok.

"I need to know where she is!" I exclaim, taking a few eager steps closer.

"That's nice," he says, turning and beginning to walk away. I reach out and grab his shoulder, spinning him around.

"Tell me where she is," I nearly beg. He brushes my hand off his shoulder, his eyes narrowing.

"I needed your help not so long ago, and you turned me away. No, you didn't just turn me away; you spurned and insulted me," he says coolly. "I will not help you."

"Just tell me where she is!" I shout, hand clenching on my sword; he cannot deny me here! My last chance to make something of this trip, to make sure I find Evermore and put a stop to her, to get revenge.

"Good day, Eurael." he says, turning away from me. I roar, unsheathing my sword, swinging at him; he will not stand in my way! I have to know! He turns, glasses shining briefly as he snaps. My swing meets empty air and I turn around, but only see the storage shed. I turn and look at my house, then shove my sword into its sheath. I storm into the house, slamming the door behind me so hard it cracks. I stride through the house, knocking things aside, tipping chairs and tables over; Scarlett went out, I can feel it. I come to my room and wrench the door out of its frame, slinging it down the hall; violence, rage, desperation. My thoughts swarm in a discordant cacophony, threatening to overwhelm me.

I growl and run my hands through my hair, pacing in my room. I sling my coat off, slumping on my bed; I require assistance in this matter. I have to find Evermore before she destroys any more of my network—before she causes any more damage. I lean back on the bed, closing my eyes, forcing myself to take a deep breath. The scent of wildflowers slams into me, overpowering all my other senses.

"You idiot!" I turn to see Simiel glaring at me, her face livid with rage. "You dolt! You stupid, idiotic—"

"Just tell me what can be done!" I shout. She glares at me, stepping up close to me, poking me in the chest.

"You screwed yourself this time, big bro," she bites off that last word with disdain. "You could have found another way out of the Underworld, but *noooo*, you just *had* to leave Evermore there as a sacrifice. What were you thinking?"

"It was the quickest and most effective option," I defend and she snorts, shaking her head.

"Obviously it was not the most effective option, or else you wouldn't be in this mess. Your actions have consequences, Eurael," she turns away from me, covering her face with one of her hands. "You shouldn't have left her."

"I did," I reply, stepping up to her. "I can't change that, but I don't know what to do." I look down, looking at my hands. "I don't know what to do. She outsmarts me at every turn; she knows what I'm going to do before I do it. If I try to be unpredictable, she just resorts back to taking apart my network piece by piece. I don't know how to stop her," I say, my voice low and quiet.

"You're screwed," Simiel says. I look up and she looks at me with disgust. "I can't believe you allowed yourself to get put in this situation."

"You're supposed to help me!" I shout, my eyes wide. "How is any of this helping me?"

"You're supposed to feel guilty!" she shouts, her face turning red with anger. "You left her there to rot, and you don't feel any remorse over it; you don't feel anything. She's acting out against you because she does—she feels hurt and betrayed. She was an ally and you betrayed her, but you don't care. You don't care that you hurt her. Maybe if you felt guilty, you would understand her, and you could beat her."

"I don't know *how* to feel guilty," I protest.

"That's right, because all you know how to feel is rage. You just feel anger, because you can't handle anything else. You don't know how to deal with those other emotions; you just get angry. But I'll teach you how to feel guilt," she steps up to me, placing her palm on her chest. "When you couldn't stop me from dying. When you couldn't do anything, you were helpless; when you were paralyzed, unable to move. When I was beaten, bloodied and bruised; when I was cut and torn apart. When I was bled dry, and you did nothing. That feeling that you get, when you remember that, when you remember vividly the look of pain and anguish on my face as I died and you did nothing, that feeling is guilt." She presses her palm into my chest harder and I feel a pang in my chest. I groan, dropping to my knees and she follows me, keeping her palm on my chest. "You never even once told me you were sorry for not acting; you just vowed you would avenge me. But you never told me how sorry you were for doing *nothing*. Then, when you had a chance to redeem yourself by creating Ragnarok and bringing me back, you *failed*."

I look at her face, twisted in rage, and something inside me breaks. I sputter, leaning forward, shaking. "I'm sorry," I whisper, watching as drops drip from my eyes, landing on my hands. "I'm sorry."

"I hate you," she spits vehemently, her fingers digging into my chest, as if trying to rip out my heart. "You let me die, Eurael! You watched me die, and you did *nothing!* You never apologized, never tried to comfort me; instead, you made this illusion of me in your mind to help you, to *use*. You have the audacity to use me, but barely even apologize?" She stands up, shaking her head. "I'm done with you Eurael; I'm done." I look up quickly, reaching my hand out.

"Simiel, wait!" She disappears before my hand can close around her dress. I remain there, my hand outstretched, trying to grasp something that is already gone. I slowly retract my hand, shaking. I grip the grass in my hands, touching my head to the grass as my tears trail down my nose, dripping onto the ground; I never once said I was sorry. I throw my head back, the sun seeming blurry from the tears in my eyes which stream down my cheeks.

"I'm sorry!" I cry out. I rip at my shirt, exposing my chest to the sky. "I'm sorry! I never said it, but I am more sorry than you could ever possibly know! I hate myself! I hate myself for not doing anything, for never feeling sorry or guilty; I hate myself for not allowing myself to feel anything! Please," I choke, a lump welling in my throat, the salt of the tears stinging my eyes. "Please forgive me." The wind whistles quietly, messing with my hair slightly; the grass remains still. I look around, waiting, hoping. "Please forgive me," I say, but receive no response, no sign that I was forgiven. I slump forward, choked sobs wrenched out from where my soul should be, spilling out of me; I couldn't even forgive myself. How could Simiel ever forgive me? Forgive me for my rage, for my anger, for my failure. How could she ever forgive such a failure? I look up, my eyes red and swollen. "Please...I'm sorry."

CHAPTER FORTY-FOUR

I grin as I dole out a small bag of coins to the rugged man in front of me, and he takes it, counting the coins then turning around. I have the guards escort him out of my room and then the castle; I've been conducting business and other affairs in my room since I damaged my throne room. I look at the sheets of paper before me and put my hand on one; my hand warms up, a flash of heat racing through my arm and the paper disintegrates. One more down. I look at the few sheets of paper left, smiling; thanks to Benson I've been able to keep ahead of Eurael every step of the way.

I can imagine how stressed Eurael must be, unable to do anything as I destroy his network piece by piece, tearing his work apart. Sometimes he tries to be unpredictable, but he doesn't succeed; he's soundly losing, and I'm confident he knows it. When he tries to retaliate, I tear apart his network. When he tries to defend, I make it personal and send him a message. His allies want nothing more to do with him; after all my work, the pieces have all *finally* come together. I lean back in my chair; now I think it's time I drove the point home. There's a knock on the door and I turn to face it, putting on a pleasant smile.

"Enter," I say, and Benson walks in, stooping underneath the door frame.

"What is it you want today, Evermore?" He asks, sitting down in a chair opposite me.

"First, I wanted to tell you how much I appreciate how much you've done for me," I say; I must do this properly. Nothing else will do for that final blow; when I confront him, I want him to know that all the shock, all the pain, was from me. Benson is the perfect messenger for the job.

"I've enjoyed it," he says, his eyes twinkling; I've probably paid out half the treasury to Benson, but I regret no part of it.

"This should be the last thing I require of you related to Eurael," I say, and Benson leans forward, curiosity dancing across his features.

"I'm interested," he says, his glasses gleaming slightly in the light.

"Eurael must be sweating by now, considering the state his network is in," I say, and Benson nods. "I believe he knows how hopeless it is to continue to try and outwit me."

"You want to break him," Benson summarizes, and I nod the affirmative. He leans back, folding his arms across his chest, the chair groaning under his weight. "What did you have in mind?"

"I want you to summon him," I say. His eyebrows raise in surprise, his fur swaying slightly as the surprise moves through the rest of his body. "I want you to do it under the guise of offering help, and then I want you to betray him; show him that he is utterly and completely alone, without allies or connections. Then I want you to bring him to me."

"This puts me in considerable danger," Benson says leaning forward, and the chair protests again. "If Eurael loses it and his anger overcomes him, I will be forced to fight back; you are well aware of how I detest field work."

"I will make sure that you are compensated well," I say; poor baby doesn't want to get his hands dirty. Well you're about to rub them in the mud, Benson, get used to it. He nods, standing up.

"This will be the last time I help you then," he says, straightening his suit. "You are asking me to betray a friend for monetary gain; I won't do anything for you again Evermore."

"You've been betraying him all along," I say, and he shakes his head.

"No, I have been helping *you*, there's a difference. It was due to his own lack of skill that he has been bested until now; this is direct betrayal."

I nod understandingly, handing him a large bag of gold as I do; whatever you need to do so you can sleep at night, Benson. He looks at it for a moment then takes it, sadly slipping it into his suit, ducking under the door frame on his way out. I sit back down grinning; while losing Benson will be unfortunate, the gain is much larger. I must now make preparations for the aftermath of this; I stand up, grinning happily. Finally, I will have my revenge.

CHAPTER FORTY-FIVE

I sit up in bed, swinging my legs over the side and setting them on the floor. I lean forward, putting my elbows on my knees, looking down at my hands. She didn't forgive me. I'm content to remain in this position until the house around me crumbles, and I with it, as my body expires from lack of care; I don't care anymore. The rapid sound of footsteps racing through the halls reaches my ears, but I do my best to ignore it; I have no interest in any affairs that are not related to Simiel. Scarlett bursts into my room, not seeming to notice that I'm missing a door; I suppose it could be considered a trivial detail. She doesn't seem to notice or care about my condition, jumping straight into her point as usual.

"One of your contacts said that he knows where Evermore is," I remain silent, calmly observing my hands. "Didn't you hear me? He knows here Evermore is!" She puts her hands on my shoulders, pushing me back so she can look in my eyes. "You have to get up and go check it out!"

"I have no interest," I reply numbly, and she steps back, shocked.

"You lost your mind earlier about finding Evermore, and now you don't care?" I say nothing and she shakes her head incredulously. "No, I don't believe it; you need to get up and go find out where Evermore is."

"No," I say quietly. She glares at me, placing her hands on her hips. "I no longer care about finding Evermore."

"You don't *get* to not care!" she shouts, sticking her face in front of mine. "You have put me through hell trying to find that woman, and now that she's within reach, you say you don't care. No, you *have* to care!"

"I'm sorry that I caused you pain in my pursuits," I reply softly. Her eyes widen and she opens her mouth, then closes it again. She kneels in front of me, looking in my eyes, taking a deep breath.

"Okay, if you're really sorry, then you'll have to make it up to me," she says, calming her voice.

"Very well," I say, looking down again; if it's necessary to apologize to Scarlett, then I believe I should do it. After all, she might forgive me if I can do this; then I will have at least made up for one mistake.

"To make it up to me, you need to go to this contact and find out where Evermore is," she says. I look up and sigh, standing up and slipping my coat on.

"Very well," I repeat; I will do this, but not one step further. I will give the information to Scarlett, and she may do with it as she pleases. "Who is the contact?"

"He said his name was Benson Barry Wolf," she says. I feel a small spark in my chest but quickly crush it, clamping down on the feeling until it goes away. I nod, walking through the empty doorway and out of the house.

"Please, have a seat." A large black wolf stands before me, towering over me by several feet. His ears brush the ceiling, and he has small wire-frame glasses perched on the end of his long snout. His face looks like it is constantly smiling, and his grey suit struggles to contain his rippling muscles and black fur. He extends one paw the size of a large dinner plate with long, sharp claws at the end; I shake his hand, his fur as soft as I remember. I sit down on the offered chair, my shoulders slumping forward, and I remain looking at the floor. "I'm surprised you didn't contact me when you first had this problem. Did you even know I was in Legend Land?"

"No," I answer truthfully, and he lets out a loud, barking laugh.

"It sounds like you need a drink, my friend," He takes a bottle filled with dark amber liquid and two small glasses, pouring each one nearly full to the top. He hands me one and I take it, downing its contents in one gulp. A faint searing sensation bubbles up in my throat, but I don't pay it much attention. Benson raises an eyebrow, looking surprised. "Well that certainly is a first; for the centuries I've known you, Eurael, I've rarely seen you drink. I didn't think your powers let you get drunk, but perhaps I was wrong. Nonetheless, it must be pretty rough for you."

I wordlessly place the glass back on his desk. He sits in a large leather chair behind his expensive wooden desk. There are several small shelves in the room, containing bottles, pictures, and awards.

"Well let me solve that for you. I'll tell you where Evermore is."

"Alright," I say, paying as much attention as I can to his words; I have to remember this to tell Scarlett.

"That's it? 'Alright'? I thought this was going to be more difficult, to get you here, alone, but it wasn't hard at all. You're not even suspicious of my intentions," he stands up, his glass untouched. I feel my muscles begin to seize up and lock; I try to move a finger but cannot. The sensation is familiar, and I simply let it overtake me; I can do nothing to stop it. Ever since I talked to Simiel, not even the shadows have approached me. He notices my lack of resistance or emotion and frowns, leaning in. "What is wrong with you?"

"She didn't forgive me," I whisper, the poison affecting me from the waist down.

"When has being forgiven, or lack thereof, mattered to you? The Eurael I knew wouldn't have given a damn."

I bring my eyes up to meet his, my reflection staring back at me from his glasses, my haunted, orange eyes looking right through me. "That Simiel is dead," I reply. "Along with any chance of forgiveness."

"Obviously," Benson says distastefully. "This is pathetic, Eurael; Simiel would be disappointed." The poison stops me from slumping at the mention of her name, but a lump still forms in my throat, blinking away tears.

"She already hates me," I croak, looking back up at Benson. "Just kill me, please." He steps back in surprise, eyes widening behind his glasses.

"What are you saying Eurael? I didn't send for you to kill you."

I blink, salty trails of wet dripping down my face. "Please Benson, I can't take it anymore. This...*this* guilt is eating me alive! I don't want to deal with this, I can't."

He steps closer again, his voice soft and low, "Eurael I—"

"Please Benson," I do my best to lean forward, my breathing choked and shallow. "Kill me."

His claws suddenly sink into my chest until I can feel his soft fur. He keeps his eyes on me, his expression unreadable as blood seeps from the wound. My head lolls to the side; with the spreading of the blood, my numbness is replaced with a warm, fuzzy feeling that suffuses my body. "Thank you, Benson." I whisper, the coppery taste of blood in my mouth mixing with the tingling scent of wildflowers, my eyes flickering closed.

I scream angrily, my aura fluctuating out brightly, white light crackling at my fingertips. My blood boils, my face flushed as anger rises up in me, burning through. My hands feel like they will light afire, my skin hot and feeling like it will melt in a moment. My vision is red, my mind filled with white noise as I scream louder, my vocal cords at the verge of snapping from the strain. I stop, my throat feeling raw, my vision clear; I breathe heavily, angry tears at the corners of my eyes.

"What do you mean...he's dead?" I hiss, not able to get enough air.

"The man Benson summoned is dead, ma'am." Hekras says, looking at me nervously. "I went to check like you asked and—" My face contorts into a snarl, and I hurl a bolt of white light; it pierces Hekras through the chest. His eyes widen in shock, his mouth gaping open before he crumples as I pace.

"That *idiot*," I hiss, my aura glowing brighter. "Benson wasn't supposed to kill him—that wasn't part of the arrangement, and he knew it. Why would he do that? Why?!" I turn, hurling a bolt of light at one of the columns, chipping stone off. The air shimmers from the heat radiating off my body, my hair sizzling. I was betrayed once and now it has happened again; I asked for aid, and this is what I receive. I didn't want Benson to kill Eurael! He hadn't been broken to the extent that I desired! I twist my hands, clawing at the air by my sides. "I was going to break him," I snarl, eyes shining so brightly that it hurts to see. "I was going to make him suffer like he planned on making me suffer; I was going to make him watch as I killed his darling student right in front of his eyes. He was going to pay for what he did to me, but now he's dead!" My aura flashes, filling the room and someone screams. I take a deep, angry breath, hurling a bolt at the wall next to the doors leading out of my room.

"Guard!" I shout. The door opens and a guard hesitantly steps in, sweaty; he better not screw this up. "Take as many soldiers as you can round up in ten minutes and march for Benson. I want that backstabbing wolf found!" The guard throws up a hurried salute, mumbling before he races out. I stomp up to my room, hurling a bolt of white light at my door, blasting it off its hinges. I wrench the doors open to my closet, yanking my battle clothes out.

I grit my teeth, forcing down the pain that threatens to rise, aura flashing. I slip on light metal guards on my shins and boots, wrapping around my calves. I strap similar guards on my thighs and arms. I keep my hands free and slip on a light breastplate and two pauldrons on my shoulders; the armor was designed to be able to be put on by a single person. I snap on a white robe around the armor, flicking my hair out so it falls down to my shoulders in an auburn tangle, my eyes flashing as I look at myself in the mirror. I toss a bolt and the mirror shatters, its metal flying out around the room. A piece of it pings off of my breastplate and I nod; good enough.

I join my soldiers marching to Benson's establishment; he should still be there. The soldiers march in silence, casting nervous glances at me occasionally. I keep my gaze set on the horizon as Benson's town begins to come into view, the heat of my aura keeps me from focusing on any echoes of pain; I will slaughter Benson. I will make him pay for what he did; betrayal will not be tolerated! As I promised these citizens when I first took the throne, rebellions *will* be crushed. Striding into town, I turn sharply to my soldiers, my voice cold and quick, leaving no room for argument.

"Search the entire town; if anyone resists, I expect them to suddenly become a corpse. If someone finds Benson, call out; we will not let him escape. Clear?" A soldier shifts uncomfortably and another one shuffles in place slightly. "Clear?!" I shout, my aura flashing dangerously.

"Clear!" they all shout, quickly moving past me to fulfill their orders. I make my way to Benson's building as screams begin to rise up from the buildings around; they must be resisting then. A wolf turns, his eyes widening when he sees me; he brought me a briefcase once. I strike him down with a bolt through his chest, and he flies backward, slamming into the wall. I blast the door open, stepping through the charred remains. The bar stops as its patrons all hush, looking at me.

"You're not welc—" I turn to the wolf who spoke up, and two walls of light appear, slamming into him from opposite sides. His nearly two-dimensional corpse drops to the ground, no one else speaking up as I scan the bar.

"Benson!" I call out, taking deliberate steps through the bar. Someone nervously sips at their drink and another one coughs. "Benson, come out! Come out, come out wherever you are!" I shout, cackling. I stop in front of his door, waiting for only half a second before I blow it open. I step into his empty office and quickly scan it; no sign of him. I blast apart his desk and howl, tossing bolts of light at the shelves on his walls. I scream, destroying any trace of anything Benson left behind; he isn't here! He betrayed me then left, deserting! I exit his room, fuming; the audacity of that flea-ridden canine fur ball!

"Listen, none of—" I blast the wolf, and he drops down, dead. Another one stands up, and I kill him with a bolt of white light. They begin to rise up quicker now; one runs at me, and I flick my hand. Three spears of light shoot up, impaling his leg; he cries out, falling down. Another bolt of light takes off his head; I turn and raise my hand, three spears of light impaling another to the wall then disappear. A wall of light appears behind me, and a would-be attacker smacks into it; I'll kill everyone who ever worked with Benson!

I smack several to the ground with a block of light and crush their backs with it. I turn and grab a patron's head as he tries to sneak up on me, slamming my metal-covered knee into his stomach. A spear of light materializes in my free hand, and I stab him through the back. I turn and slice a charging bull across the throat with the spear, stepping back a little and smacking a large man in the stomach with the other end of the spear. I turn and impale him through the skull, turning as several of Benson's employees howl. I run toward a charging wolf and leap at him, stabbing him through the chest. He drops backward, and I fling myself through the air with the momentum, bringing the spear with me. I land on another and stab him through the skull, wrenching the spear out in time to impale another one through the chest. I turn and hurl the spear, catching a charging wolf in the chest; he stumbles and then drops to the ground, sliding to a stop at my feet.

The rest of the patrons have congregated on the opposite side of the bar, glowering at me but staying put. I hold up my hand, my aura glowing brighter; I will not leave one alive. They all worked with Benson; if they were stupid enough to stay behind, they deserve death. They begin to retreat nervously as my hand glows brighter; they will all die, every single one. My aura flashes out, light erupting from my hand; their screams reach my ears, and my mouth twists itself into a smile. I lower my hand, breathing heavily, beads of sweat dripping down my forehead, my aura dimming down again; half the bar is turned to ash.

I double over, dropping to my knees as a wave of pain slams into me; I smack my palm on the floor, trembling. I don't have time for this! My aura flashes out, my shaking legs barely supporting me as

I swallow bile; I will not let anything stop me! I kick through the ash but find nothing; I walk into the street and see the townspeople gathered on their knees, a circle of soldiers standing around them, pikes and swords at the ready. I step up to the people, dimming my aura slightly, smiling at them.

"I will ask all of you this once," I say, my voice cheery. "Where is Benson Barry Wolf?" Several of them sniffle and a child cries out, sobbing. My aura glows brighter, my hands clenching at my sides. "Where is Benson Barry Wolf?!" I snap, and several recoil.

"Please!" a man shouts out. "Don't hurt us! We don't know!" A spear of white light silences the rebellious vermin, and I turn my back on them in disgust, turning my glare to one of the soldiers. He immediately snaps to attention, looking at me nervously, sweat dripping down his neck.

"Captain," I whisper, coming closer to him. He begins to sweat profusely, the heat from my aura cooking him in his armor. "Kill these people and burn this village to the ground." I hiss.

"Ma'am?" he says, looking down at me, confused.

"Did I stutter?" I hiss, and he shakes his head.

"No ma'am, but..." he says, eyes flicking between the villagers and me.

"Do you have a family, captain?" My aura glows brighter as I put a palm on his metal armor.

"Y-yes ma'am," he stutters, the metal glowing red beneath my hand.

"Do you want them to end up in a similar situation as these people?"

He twitches in place, itching to move away. "No ma'am," he says firmly, despite the heat.

"Then I suggest you follow my orders," I growl.

"But ma'am—"

"Now, captain!"

He meets my eyes for a moment before lowering his defeated gaze. I take my hand away as he looks past me to the other soldiers.

"You heard the queen, men," he says in a broken tone, moving past me.

"Oh and captain, hang their bodies up on some of these buildings, and don't burn those. I want to make an example of them."

There's only silence behind me; does he really think he's going to disobey me now? I turn, my aura glowing brighter. "Captain?" The captain drops down at my feet, a hole in his neck.

"Run!" I look at the woman; her green eyes focused on me, her bright red hair swaying softly. "Run!" she shouts to the villagers again.

"You," I say, shocked. She runs to me swiping at me with her dagger. I numbly raise a wall of light; here is this woman, the one he chose over me. She's here, in front of me, but Eurael is dead. Killing her is pointless when I can't drop her corpse at his feet. I lower the wall, and she swipes at me again; I turn, dodging the attack, and she follows the movement, sweeping her leg behind me. I simply kick her leg away, throwing her off balance, pushing her away with a block of light, sprawling her out on the ground.

The reason he abandoned me in the Underworld; she's just... here. My aura glows brightly as my jaw clenches, my eyes shining; he may be dead, but she is alive. I cannot kill Eurael, but I can send him the soul of his precious student. If he is dead, he cannot return them both to the land of the living; her death will not be pointless after all. In death, he will know he failed; I grin as she picks herself up off the ground, the villagers scattering.

"You're the one who's been targeting our network," she accuses.

"I am Evermore," I smile eagerly; I can still have revenge! "And you are?"

"Scarlett," she bites out, glaring at me.

"Scarlett," I say, trying the word out; it leaves a bad taste in my mouth. I grimace, walking to her with deliberate steps; she will not escape. There is no one here to rescue her this time. She throws several small knives at me, but I stop them with a wall of light. She rushes at me, then feints left; I raise several spears of light at her, but she leaps up, grabbing one of the spears and swinging herself at me. Her boot collides with my breastplate, sending me tumbling back. I send a bolt of light at her, but she dodges it easily, streaking toward me. She slices low, but I step back, though slower than I would be without armor; she comes up, slicing the dagger at my face. I duck back, but still receive a small cut on my cheek. I raise a block of light but she just uses it to leap off of, flipping toward me. A block of light comes out, slamming into her, sending her flying through the air. Another block slams down on her, and her dagger skitters across the ground.

I remove my armor, leaving myself in my normal attire; I can be quicker now. I don't want to kill her with my powers, protected by armor; I want to feel her life fade underneath my own hands. I want her to know how hopelessly outmatched she is as death comes for her.

I raise my hand up and the block disappears. Scarlett picks herself up, glaring at me, then looking at her dagger. I swipe it far away with a block, and her eyes rest back on me.

"No powers," I promise, and she cracks her knuckles, running at me. I dodge her jab and duck under her hook. She brings up her knee, and I'm forced to use my hands to stop it; she slams her elbow onto my back. I grit my teeth, taking the blow, throwing my shoulder into her stomach and standing up quickly. With the proper leverage, I toss her over; I turn and aim a kick at her face but she rolls out of the way. I leap on top of her, scrambling to pin her. She twists and writhes underneath me, not allowing me to get a firm grip.

Suddenly her knee slams into my ribs, loosening my hold. She twists her hips and jerks her body, throwing me off. We both roll back, coming up at the same time. This time I race forward, throwing several quick jabs out. She blocks them easily then comes in with an elbow, which I swoop under, jamming my elbow into her side and then sweeping her legs out from under her. She lands hard on her back, and I'm on top of her, my hands around her throat, my aura glowing brightly; finally, I have her. I grin wildly as I squeeze the life out of her, her face turning red. She grabs at my wrists, trying to pull me off; she scrambles at my wrist and twists, trying to get out from under me, but I have her pinned. She reaches down further, straining, and something flashes in the corner of my eye.

I feel something dig into my side and I gasp, my hands slipping off of her neck. She twists out from under me and I roll off of her, clutching my side as blood quickly begins to soak through my shirt. I glare at Scarlett and the small knife she holds in her hand. I wave my hand and a bolt of light hurls at her, but misses widely. She begins walking toward me slowly as I throw another bolt, missing again. She dashes in quickly, and I throw up a wall of light, but she skirts around it, slicing at me. I stumble back but still receive several cuts on my arms and a small one on my neck. She advances on me, and my aura grows dimmer, fluxing out weakly. Suddenly she stops, looking behind me; I turn my head as I drop to my knees, my legs no longer willing to support me. The group of soldiers looks at her for a moment. Her words are lost to my ears, but she leaves with the group of civilians, the soldiers watching her leave, silently.

"No, after...her," I order weakly, collapsing onto my stomach, darkness closing in.

CHAPTER FORTY-SIX

I stand in my armor as my soldiers battle for their lives. I hear the sound of a horse galloping and duck underneath a scythe. I turn quickly and toss a bolt at its dark rider, who keels over the side. I look down at the man, or rather, thing. He's dressed in old black clothes that are falling apart. In one hand lies a battered, serrated scythe. He has several bloody wounds on him, but no blood pours out of him; he has no blood to give. A yellow head is tucked under his arm—his head. His collar is turned up, but you can clearly see there is no head there. It has lanky strings of hair, most of it gone. Its eyes are wide and white, its lips gone, its teeth rotting and fallen out. Its skin is a sickly yellow color, rotting and puffed up with puss in some places, resembling rotted cheese—a dullahan. It disintegrates before my eyes, and I turn quickly.

A woman missing the bottom half of her body runs at me on her elbows, her clawed hands holding a scythe which scrapes against the ground producing a *teketeke* sound. She screeches, leaping at me, her face disfigured and bloody, entrails trailing out of her. Several spears of light shoot out from above, stabbing through her into the ground. She disintegrates after a moment as well—the teketeke.

I throw up a wall of light, shielding me from a blast that kills several of my soldiers. An old hag hurls a bolt of energy at me, and I twist out of the way, returning the favor. She suddenly disappears, and a dark black cat with a single white patch on its chest scurries away. I throw a bolt at it, and it dodges deftly, turning to me. It begins running at me; and as it does, it transforms. Its legs elongate, and its torso grows larger, its skull snapping and breaking then reforming as it grows. It leaps at me with a deep roar, and I duck underneath it, several spears of light shooting up from the ground. The creature lands on the spears, impaling itself. It lets out a howl, wriggling on the spears; its fur is dark and missing in patches, revealing pieces of bone. Its spine strains against its skin, almost to the point of ripping it. It has large wicked paws and a large patch of white fur on its chest. It has two large, pointed ears which normally hang down, a twisted, snarling snout and two ferocious, golden eyes—a catsith. It too fades and I turn, surveying the battlefield.

My soldiers fight against these beats valiantly; but every time they bring one down, it seems to get back up a few moments later. The only exception is my powers. I've been searching for a weapon that can kill these demonic creatures, but so far I've found nothing. A dullahan gallops toward me; a spear of light materializes in my hand, and I leap up, impaling the dullahan then throwing her off. I ride the horse, slicing apart dullahans, teketekes and catsiths left and right. The horse disintegrates; it too is part of the dullahan's manifestation. I land heavily and roll, impaling a catsith through the skull.

I stand and see a teketeke slice one of my soldiers in half with her scythe. The soldier falls to the ground, bleeding out. He twitches and writhes for a moment before going still; then his chest rises up, his face contorting into a pained snarl. He reaches for his sword, his hands turning into long claws. He begins pulling himself along the ground, but I throw a bolt of light at him and he disintegrates. The roar of the battle drowns out any one plight; and amidst the carnage and confusion, my soldiers must fight for themselves, as I am forced to do. Several teketeke converge on me, hissing and shrieking as they launch themselves at me. I impale them all with spears of light, but a catsith lands heavily on my back. A wall of light slams into the catsith, knocking it off, and I angrily pierce it with a bolt of light. I look to see my soldiers dying left and right; I have to end this.

"Retreat!" I call out. My soldiers immediately disengage, running as quickly as they can away from battle; none of them want to be here. The creatures are in hot pursuit, but I raise my hand and they slam into a large wall of light. I concentrate, and the wall of light encloses around the creatures, trapping them. My aura glows brighter as I raise my other hand, enough spears of light forming that they momentarily block out the sky and give a harsh, stark look to everything. I lower my hand and they scream to the ground, leaving no piece of ground untouched.

I keep the spears coming and falling, sweat dripping down my neck, my armor heating up until the screaming and rustling finally stops. I let the walls fall and the spears disappear with a gasp, sinking to my knees. I draw in a raspy breath, shaking as my aura fluxes brightly, then goes dim. Icy spikes of pain dig into my spine, my lips turning blue, my aura dimming to the point of invisibility, leaving me shaking and cold.

The soldiers watch me, their gaze nearly as cold as my trembling body. I hold out a hand; and after a long moment, one of the soldiers tosses a canteen out, letting it roll in the dust. I crawl over to it, draining the entire container to quench my parched throat. I stand up, shaking, and look at my soldiers. I have done what must be done to destroy this plague, and the plague of rebels led by Scarlett; my army barely obeys me. They know if they desert me, they will fall to the ghouls; they have no choice but to follow. Shortly after Eurael died, these creatures began showing up, attacking everything and everyone.

As our numbers fell, theirs grew, and we lost entire cities to the plagues, especially the teketeke. The catsith are the most rare, but are some of the most deadly; if they come in contact with a corpse, it will become a dullahan; no one quite knows how, including me. The dullahan are especially dangerous; dark, undead knights that no door or gate remains shut for. I personally have to secure each and every door and gate to make sure it will not suddenly spring open for the dullahan. The only comfort I have is that the ghouls attack the rebels as much as they do my own forces.

All-out war has been declared on the Kingdom by the insurrectionists, or, specifically, me. None of my soldiers openly support them, but every day my numbers shrink and theirs grow.

My soldiers are afraid and tired. I make the motion and they turn, beginning the march back to the capital. They are bruised and bloody, dirt and grime staining their uniforms and armor. It's only a matter of time before they lose all hope and desert me completely. The massacres will begin soon after if they do; their families will pay if they become insubordinate. Nothing will stand in my way—not these ghouls, not my own soldiers—I *will* find Scarlett.

When we near the capital, I hold up my hand, and the soldiers all but drop to the ground, taking out canteens and distributing rations; with the creatures and mass death came the rats and famine. Crops die earlier and earlier; two weak harvests later, and the Kingdom's population has all but been decimated. I hear a rustle and turn, my aura flickering; I'm still weak after clearing the battlefield. A soldier cries out and we turn, seeing an arrow protruding from his chest. The rest scramble to their feet, reaching for weapons, but a voice calls out.

"I wouldn't do that if I were you!" Petravin steps out of the forest, along with a great many number of Lost Boys. On their shoulders, they each have the symbol of the insurrectionists, the letter "E" with a sword through it; the message is clear.

With the recent battle, our current party is outnumbered and in no position to fight, but I can't afford to show weakness. The group with me now is all but ready to desert me. I don't need their loyalty, I need their lives; I can't waste them in a petty skirmish, at least—not until my power returns.

He smiles at me, whistling. "We were just out here to scout around, but imagine our surprise when we spot the queen with her merry band of men." A chorus of laughter rises up, and I glare at them; just keep talking, forest rat.

"What do you want, Petravin?" I stand up straight, forcing my aura to glow brightly, the icy cold in my body replaced with torturous flames licking at my insides; I can't show weakness to these insurrectionist scum.

"I just wanted to scout around up here, but now I'm not so sure what I want," he says with a crooked grin.

"Why were you scouting up here?" I ask; he likes to talk, I'll let him talk, and he'll play right into my hands.

"Ah, now that's a surprise," he says winking, his eyes glimmering. "I can't spoil it; but trust me, it's good. I'll let you live to see it, but your soldiers aren't as necessary." He raises a hand, and several bows are drawn back.

"Wait!" I say, stepping forward. They halt, and he raises an eyebrow. "Petravin, you used to work for me; you said you wouldn't be doing any more assassination jobs. This is worse; you're killing men who are loyal to a cause, just like you." His grin fades and he snarls, glaring at me. If he's willing to kill my soldiers, no matter what he says, I won't trust his word to spare me.

"These men are *nothing* like me," he spits vehemently. He raises a hand again. "They deserve to die." My aura flashes brightly, and I wave my hand before either side can speak up; neither side can know how alike they are to each other. Spears of light shoot out in every direction, impaling many of the Lost Boys. Petravin dances backward, flying up out of reach. He whistles, and the few remaining Lost Boys retreat, leaving my soldiers alone. I sigh and drop to my knees, my aura dimming as I hit the ground.

CHAPTER FORTY-SEVEN

I slam my palm on the table and everyone quiets. This war with Evermore has gone on longer than we were prepared for, and it's beginning to take its toll—not only on the troops, but on everyone's moods. Evermore hasn't pulled a successful harvest in two autumns, but we've done even worse. *You ever think there's a reason for that? You're not farmers—you're soldiers, or...at least, as close as you can get with your band of rebels.* I run a hand through my hair, the red strands flowing over my fingers; we haven't had any major victories since spring, and the first frost is imminent. We're losing this war. *Not to mention all those monsters everywhere, attacking everyone, multiplying like rats.* The ghouls appeared at the beginning, nearly two winters ago now, soon after Mister E disappeared; they are true monsters.

I look at the people gathered at the table; Wilhelm, Petravin, Artemis, Benson, and the dog. Wilhelm and Petravin have been able to do a large amount of the recruiting for the cause and are the main reason that our numbers continue to grow. Artemis brings a certain strategic mindset to the board, though her solution is always to kill whatever is in the way; sometimes that's necessary, but most of the time it's just distracting. Benson provides a large amount of information, but I don't fully trust him; I know he's hiding something. *And the dog?* Totomir he...well he...despite his attitude, his money and his labor force make him a valuable ally. *You don't trust him, do you?* The only one I trust here is Wilhelm; all the others are here for their own personal reasons. *You still haven't explained your job in all of this you know.* I just keep them alive, because they tend to act like chickens with their heads cut off. It's all I can do to keep them from turning on each other in an instant. *You're a glorified babysitter.*

"This is a horrible plan!" Artemis says, looking around the table. "We don't have the numbers or the resources to make this plan come to fruition!" I glare at her, my anger seething out of me; keeping them all alive isn't the easiest job in the world. If this war has taught me anything, it has drilled into me the importance of self-control. *Finally, Mister E's lessons have hit you, and all it took was his death.*

"If we don't act now, we won't have another chance," I growl, my hand clenching on the table; I refuse to believe Mister E is dead. I think about him every day—I search every day; these...fools distract me enough from that as it is, without needlessly questioning a perfectly *rational* plan. *Maybe they question it because it's rational.* "Those monsters out there continue to grow in number, getting more powerful every day. Evermore just lost a large portion of her forces in a battle with them; right now, she's weaker than she's ever been. Our numbers may not be high, but they're higher than hers right now; the only ones that outnumber us are those creatures, and that's not something we can change. What we can change," I glare at each of them, my gaze only softening at Wilhelm, "is what we do against Evermore and her forces."

Those ghouls—those monsters—they are a plague, but we don't have the resources to fight them *and* Evermore. The headless dullahan, scythe-wielding teketeke, shape-shifting catsith, and other...horrendous creatures; we can barely fend them off when they attack. I clench my hand into a fist, shuddering; they kill without discretion. Some of the members here believe that Mister E set them loose on the world; I can't believe them, like I can't believe that he's dead. I have to have faith that even if he's not in Legend Land, he's not fully dead, or else I would have forgotten everything. I fight to avenge his memory. I fight for what he stood for, to me, and I fight against Evermore, and everything she is. She's no better than the ghouls, killing nearly indiscriminately; her own actions fill our ranks, but she's too blind or mad to stop.

"I'm with Scarlett on this one," Wilhelm says. Artemis ignores him, as does everyone else, keeping her gaze on me.

"We'll be weak and ill-prepared if this doesn't work. Even if it does, we'll still be too weak to fight if a large number of those monsters attack us!"

"It's not like we can't fight back," Petravin offers. He tried to kill me, I tried to kill him; right now we share a common enemy. Sometimes, for the greater good, you have to commit necessary evils. *You're starting to sound like him.* He was right, about everything; I should have paid closer attention when he was still here. Petravin is right, though. After I found Mister E's underground room, I gathered all the shards of orichalcum and had them smelted into our weapons. They allow us to harm the monsters, which gives us a fighting chance, something that Evermore and her soldiers do not have, fortunately. *Or perhaps unfortunately; if you combined your forces, you might stand a chance.* I will *never* ally myself with that woman! *Maybe she's a necessary evil.* She is a plague, like the ghouls. "If we're in the castle, we can fortify ourselves against the attackers."

"That won't stop the dullahan," Benson says; he's right. Gates and doors always remain open for the dullahan; there's no way to keep them out. "I've been testing something that might help with that though." We all look at Benson and he gives a wolfish grin, eyes twinkling. "Ever since we seized Evermore's mine, with the help of Totomir, we've had a large supply of gold. After some experimentation, I discovered that the dullahan don't particularly care for it," he says, grinning. I smile; Benson has his many uses, though I have to keep an eye on him.

"I've been in the castle; I've attacked it. We're going to need more than this rabble if we want to stand a chance," Artemis looks to Totomir, who sits up straighter. While he's not the most popular with...well, anyone, he's surprisingly useful.

His deep voice rolls out, ears flopping as he shakes his head. "It's a suicide mission."

"Then you'll be coming?" I say, and Totomir looks at me, grinning.

"Yeah I'll be coming," Totomir replies and pulls out his rapier, the thin weapon glinting in the light of the war room. "I have some unfinished business I want to settle."

"It's decided then," I say, ignoring Artemis's glare. "Wilhelm, Petravin, and Totomir will lead the main forces in a siege. Benson, Artemis, and myself will infiltrate the throne room directly and engage Evermore." Everyone except Artemis nods in agreement.

I stop at Wilhelm's door, hand poised to knock, when I detect voices. *Are you really going to eavesdrop on your boyfriend?* I press my ear to the door, closing my eyes to focus. *I guess so.*

"So why are you even fighting?" Totomir's deep voice easily carries through the door.

"Yeah. I mean," Petravin stops, hiccuping; he's been drinking, again. "I get that Scarlett's hot, but are you really fighting, really ready to *die* for her, for some girl?"

"I love Scarlett, and I'd die for her if I had to," Wilhelm's voice is uncharacteristically serious, even before a mission.

"You didn't answer my question boy."

"Petravin is younger than I am," Wilhelm says, dodging the question.

"I'm, *hic*, older than I look!" Petravin protests drunkenly.

There's a moment of silence before Wilhelm sighs, and I can almost see him running a hand through his already messy hair.

"When Evermore went after Benson and didn't find him," he pauses, and I press my ear to the door harder; he's never even mentioned any of this to me, "she took her rage out on a nearby village, *my* birth village. I watched while she killed my parents, my brothers; I couldn't do...I couldn't do a damn thing." Silence echoes out into the hallway; he never mentioned family. Even during the war, he seemed... he seemed so happy; I had no idea. *Maybe he didn't want you to know.*

"Damn," there's the sound of a bottle being dropped, then scrambled for. "That's heavy."

"Do you want to kill Evermore?" Totomir asks quietly, my ear aching from being pressed so hard against the wood.

"Even if I wanted to, I don't think I could," Wilhelm sniffs; is he crying? He's never cried in front of me before; I barely stop myself from barging into the room and taking him into my arms. "I just want her to...to *understand* all the pain she's caused. I think the only reason she can do any of this to us, to her own *people*, is because she doesn't understand their...*our* pain. I don't mean torture." He sucks in a shaky breath that sends twinges of sympathy to my already heavy heart. "I just...I just want her...she should understand." Nobody speaks, and the silence stretches on for what feels like infinity before Totomir speaks up again, chairs scraping against the floor.

"Come Petravin," Totomir orders, footsteps nearing the door. "We should let Wilhelm be for now." I barely make it down the hall and around the corner before the door creaks open, Totomir and Petravin walking out. I lean my head against the wall, wiping tears from my eyes; why did he never tell me?

CHAPTER FORTY-EIGHT

I gasp for breath, sucking in crisp night air as Benson, Artemis and I materialize. I look around, frowning; this is decidedly not the throne room. Everything is still, even the wind; not a sound can be heard except for our breathing. The grass remains absolutely still until Artemis moves, the grass rustling underneath her boots as she steps forward, looking around.

"Where the hell are we?" she growls, turning to glare at Benson.

"Something stopped me from teleporting inside the throne room, teleporting us here instead," he says frowning. The stars seem very faint, and the moon can't be seen in the sky, it merely being a dark, nearly blank canvas. "I can't get us into the castle; something's interfering with my abilities."

The tall grass rustles, swaying behind us. I draw my dagger, and Artemis drops into a fighting stance. *Teketeke.* I whirl around, but see nothing except the barely visible, swaying grass. *Teketeketeketeke.* I spin, Benson growling. Artemis starts to carefully move through the grass; no, you don't move out on your own! Stay with the group; there is safety in numbers. Get back here, Artemis! *Teketeke.* I spin as a teketeke leaps out from the grass, screeching. Its scythe flashes through the air, barely visible in the night, and I roll out of the way, turning and slicing at its neck with my dagger. It disintegrates, and I stand up, eyes searching the grass. All around us the grass is rustling, swarming with teketeke.

Suddenly the clouds move and the moon shines down brightly, illuminating the field. The teketeke screech, moving quickly. Their warped faces are twisted in everlasting anger, their claws clicking on the handle of their scythes. Their entrails and spines trail out from behind them as they crawl on their elbows at a terrifyingly quick pace. Behind us on the hill stands a dark figure, hands raised. Their hands lower, and the teketeke all leap into the air. Benson leaps onto Artemis and me, teleporting us. It feels like I'm being compressed into a small can, then shot out again at high speeds. My ears pop and my jaw cracks as we reappear, air filling my lungs. The teketeke all turn, hissing and shrieking.

"I can't get us out of this field," he growls. Artemis's armblades and claws gleam wickedly in the moonlight, a ferocious snarl on her face.

"Then we fight," she says, her snarl morphing into a sick, combat-eager smile. I internalize the rush of oncoming combat, my hands deadly still on my orichalcum imbued daggers; I must have control over my actions. I can't lose myself in combat; that is when fatal mistakes are made, and when you forfeit your life. The teketeke begin to swarm toward us, and I turn to Benson, my voice low.

"We can't kill all of them," I say, and he nods as the hoard grows closer. "That figure up there seems to be controlling them; if you teleport me up there, I can take him down. I'm going to need you and Artemis to hold off the teketeke until I do though. Can you do that?"

He nods; it's the best option. I can't afford to trust anyone, but I can't afford not to; his life is in my hands, and mine in his. A fellowship born from combat. None of us have a death wish so close to being able to confront Evermore; I have to make it out of this alive. I have to make sure *they* make it out alive. Benson grabs me, and I feel that familiar compressing situation. I appear in front of the dark figure, and he disappears quickly, returning to aid Artemis.

I quickly evaluate my opponent, my eyes taking him all in at once. The figure is a tall man dressed in all black. He towers above me with a long petticoat doing nothing to hide broad shoulders and thick arms. His large boots leave deep imprints behind in the ground as he moves slowly. His arms allow him to easily hold a large, two-handed battle axe; the edges curve upwards wickedly, the centerpiece between the two blades a grinning skull. The skull looks at me with its hollowed, soulless eye sockets, his hands tightening on the battle axe.

"Are you the one that diverted us from the castle?" In such a time filled with chaos and uncertainty, I have to be sure of who my enemies and my allies are; I can't simply assume based upon appearance.

"Yes," his voice comes from somewhere in his chest, the mouth of the skull unmoving. His voice is deep and powerful, reverberating throughout my body; of course, my assumptions are commonly right.

"Why?" If you know an enemy's motivations, you can use them to crush him, *obliterate* him; combat can be its own kind of torture. When Mister E returns, as I am sure he will, maybe *I* will have some things to teach *him*.

"I wish to test you," he rumbles as I begin to circle him; he stops moving, still as a statue. "The end is coming, and she will arrive soon; I am to prepare the way. I must know how strong you are, to decide whether you will be a threat." All this attention on little old me? I'm flattered.

"I assure you I'm a threat." Intimidation. Sabotage. Combat is a mental game, as much as it is a physical battle; I understand what Mister E was teaching. I will honor him by implementing his methods. *So you do care! You two are just a couple of peas in a pod; you're both emotionally broken, and it shows.* It's the way he would want me to honor him.

"We shall see," he says, nodding. I rush toward him, in what would be a blind spot to a human; his lack of actual eyes make it a guessing game. His entire torso turns in my direction, and he blocks my dagger with his battle axe, pushing me back and swinging it at me. I dodge backward, and his legs turn in the same direction as his torso. He takes slow, deliberate steps toward me, trampling the grass in his wake; I suppose a little stiffness is to be expected when you're dead. Fortunately for me, I remain alive and more dexterous; recognize an opponent's weakness and exploit it.

I rush at him again, slicing at his hands now. They slide further apart along the battle axe and he blocks again, his boot hitting my chest. I go flying back and land, skidding in the dirt. I try to stand, but my vision swims with stars; I can't breathe. I clutch at my chest as he takes those deliberate steps toward me, each one another count to my demise. I suck in a rattling breath, my lungs protesting at their sudden expansion but also crying out in relief. I stand up, dodging as he swings his battle axe, then stops mid-motion, smacking down at me. I roll backward, skirting around him. I leap at him from behind, and his entire torso turns again.

He pushes the handle of his battle axe out to block my strike; but instead of hitting it, I grab the outstretched handle, swinging myself at him and planting both of my feet on him. I kick off and he stumbles back only slightly, but it's enough. While he's off balance, I rush forward, slicing at his ankles; he's able to stumble backward, but I still manage to leave a deep gash along his calf. I hear him growl, a deep sound in his chest that makes my skull vibrate and my teeth rattle, despite the complete absence of blood from his wound. He turns to me, moving quicker now, swinging his axe at me constantly. I dance back, dodging and rolling to avoid his swings. I turn my eyes to the field; Benson and Artemis are back to back, fighting off the swarm of teketeke, which seem to never end. More always seem to be crawling from the grass, leaping and screeching; I can't let them keep fighting the swarm, or they'll be overrun—and soon.

Taking advantage of my momentary distraction, my attacker steps closer, his battle axe seeming to slice apart the very air. I duck underneath the swing and step aside, grabbing the axe and tugging. He doesn't budge and jerks the axe hard towards him. I fly through the air and he brings up his knee, but I flip my dagger around, stabbing it deep into his thigh. He roars, smacking me with the handle of his battle axe; he obviously still feels pain. Good—pain I can deal with; pain I can use.

I wipe my bleeding lip as he bends down to rip my dagger out; I rush toward him, leaping at him as he rises back up. I wrench my dagger from his hand and he flings me off him, but I leave a deep gash in his arm in the process. I land, breathing heavily, and he remains still for a moment. Then he slams his battle axe on the ground, and the darkness around him swirls. A smokey dark horse appears, and he leaps onto it. I rush at him, but the horse rears up, snorting out fire, and I'm forced to keep my distance. Of all the things, it *had* to be a fire-breathing horse. I glare at him and he chuckles, the horse neighing, sending chills up my spine.

"It seems you will be a threat after all," he rumbles, sounding amused. You bet your flaming horse I'm a threat.

"Who the hell are you?" I growl, and he sits up straighter, his wounds healing, clothes repairing themselves. My eyes widen; my blade is infused orichalcum, that shouldn't be possible! Orichalcum negates the powers of those it hurts, at least where my dagger is concerned. *Cheater.*

"You may call me Azrael," he says, yanking on the reins. The horse turns and I race toward it, but it disappears, leaving a ring of fire where it was. I turn and Benson and Artemis appear in front of me, breathing heavily, soaked with sweat. I look past them, but the field is empty save for the swaying grass.

"Where did the teketeke go?" I ask, and Artemis shakes her head, out of breath. Benson answers, several cuts bleeding out, staining his fur.

"They just vanished," he says, shaking his head. I sheath my dagger angrily; I sorely miss the days when giants and earth golems were my only problems.

"I suggest we do the same," I say, rubbing my chest, feeling my bones and muscles protest severely. Benson nods wearily, grabbing me and Artemis, that compressed feeling pressing in on me once more.

CHAPTER FORTY-NINE

I wake to the sound of screaming. I sit up then groan, my head throbbing; I've been overdoing it. A soldier bursts into my room, flushed and bloody.

"We're under attack!" he shouts, then falls forward with a cry, an arrow protruding from his back. Several insurrectionists and one or two members of the Lost Boys quickly enter my room; this must be the surprise Petravin was talking about. I remain sitting on my bed, keeping my aura dim; I'm not as weak as before, but I have to play this carefully.

"Keep this room secured; we're supposed to make sure the queen remains alive until they get here," the leader says, pointing her fingers at two soldiers. "You two, restrain her; I don't want her causing any trouble." They walk to me and I stand up, several bolts of light quickly piercing them through their heads. The other fighters barely have time to widen their eyes in surprise before they, too, fall to the ground as corpses. I walk to my closet calmly and get dressed in my slip-on shoes, pants, and shirt with thin scales of armor sewn into it. I am prepared to fight for my throne and my kingdom; they will have to wrench it from my cold, dead hands. The Kingdom is mine, this castle is mine; I will have Legend Land as well. They will not take this away from me; they *can't* take this away from me.

I step into the hall and several insurrectionists turn to me, drawing bows. I throw up a wall of light, and the arrows thud harmlessly against them; I lower the light and several bolts of light leave clean holes through each of their heads. A door to my right bursts open, and two of my soldiers stumble backward, fending off the blows of several rebels. I look behind me and pick up a small sword off one the corpses behind me. I move forward, slicing one along the neck, impaling another through the chest. I move his corpse over so that he blocks the blow from one of his comrades. I wrench the sword out, kicking the corpse onto the other insurrectionist, who collapses under the weight, allowing me to drive my sword deep into her eye and brain. I stand up and look behind me, my soldiers have taken care of the small group. I look down at the sword and nod; maybe there's something to physical weapons after all.

"You men stay here; kill any rebel that you see. I don't want any of these traitors escaping with their lives." The soldiers give me short, terse nods. I quickly make my way down to the throne room, soldiers engaged in battle all around me, but I pay no attention. I blast an attacker, sending their smoking corpse flying against the wall. The doors to the throne room bang open and then slam shut behind me, the dim sound of battle barely penetrating the thick doors. I put my hand on the door, pausing; if I put a barrier over it, nobody will be able to open the doors. That includes my soldiers though, leaving them trapped outside; I take my hand way, shaking my head. They have a duty to their queen, to protect me, even at the cost of their own lives; a shimmer of white glistens over the doors for a moment, then disappears.

I look around the throne room; it is once again long and ornate, fully repaired. I sit on my throne and look at the door; it seems eons ago I was on the other side of those very same doors, forcing my way into this room to take the throne I now sit on. I turn and can make out the faint color difference in the wall marking the whole where Artemis had escaped through. I turn my attention back to the doors; it seems that usurpation is a vicious cycle that never ends, or at least, not until now.

I take a deep breath, forcing my heart rate to slow down, my aura fluctuating slowly in time with each easy breath I draw; come take my throne if you dare, insurrectionist filth. The sounds of battle reach my ears, but they sound distant, far away from the throne room. I detest being so far from battle, unable to destroy the vermin myself. I sigh, flexing my fingers as a pleasant warmth begins to fill my muscles, allowing me to relax as my aura shifts around; soon I will join battle. These traitors must be dealt with, even if I have to end them personally. After I defeat these petty rebels here, I will deal with those blasted ghouls plaguing my kingdom; afterward, I turn my sights to the whole of Legend Land.

I suck in a quick breath, heat flashing over my limbs; there is one thing I must do first though. Scarlett stands in my way; first, she was the source of Eurael's betrayal, and now she is leader of the insurrectionist movement. She stands as a source of opposition that must be taken care of; and when I kill her and send her soul to the Underworld, Eurael will know that he failed. Revenge may seem petty compared to my plans, but it is crucial; I *must* have revenge. Heat flashes across my skin again, and I writhe, then it suddenly cools. My breath mists in the air, my hands going numb. My aura shimmers weakly and I slump back in my chair, eyes rolling back in my head.

"Evermore, you must stop!" Valkyrie shouts. I come to my senses all at once; I'm standing in Valkyrie's room, looking up at her where she sits on her throne of bone. I shake my head, my aura shining weakly.

"What?" I look up at her, confused; I thought she wanted me to secure Legend Land.

"Death is returning to Legend Land," she says, seeming panicked and excited at the same time. "I know you plan to spread your rule to all of Legend Land, but you must not; Legend Land is the property of Death. He will view it as an act of war."

"So what?" I glare at her; she summoned me just to tell me to abandon my plans? I can't, I *won't*; Eurael must know his failure, and I must rule Legend Land. "I don't care; I *should* rule Legend Land.

I took over the Kingdom and I raised it up, better than before; if Death loves Legend Land so much, he shouldn't have abandoned it."

Valkyrie looks at me incredulously, stepping off her throne. "This is *Death*, one of the most powerful entities in the cosmos. He is returning to claim his property; you will not stand in his way," she says urgently.

"I don't care who he is," I snap. "I will not let him take away what should be mine."

"Evermore, do not do this!" she shouts, looking at me coldly. "You cannot afford—"

"Let him come," I cut her off, my aura fluxing out brighter now as I glow. "I will rid the cosmos of him as well. Legend Land is *mine* now. Crawl back to Death and tell him that if you like!" Valkyrie opens her mouth, but I shine brightly, disappearing.

CHAPTER FIFTY

Artemis removes her claws from the chest of a soldier, watching her drop to the ground, blood seeping out of her fatal wounds.

"We don't have to kill them all," I remind her, ducking underneath a slash, elbowing the attacker in his throat, dropping him with a kick between the legs. I yank off his helmet and smack his bare head with the metal, knocking him unconscious.

"Scarlett is right," Benson says from behind, the last of the soldiers falling to his claws despite his words. "We still have the ghouls to deal with afterward; it doesn't make sense to kill them *all*."

"If we don't, they will kill us. It is kill or be killed, and I don't want to die." Totomir looks up at us all, his rapier dripping with blood.

"No, I don't think that these soldiers want to be here either. If Evermore is cruel to her own soldiers, they act out of fear. After this, we should let them surrender; there doesn't need to be any more bloodshed."

Petravin has remained uncharacteristically quiet during this, and everyone turns to him. He shakes his head, twirling his blades restlessly. "There's no reason they should all die," he says, then turns to the doors. "But we don't need to show mercy either. If they attack us, they get what's coming to them." I step in front of them all, my back to the double doors.

"We began this as separate individuals, fighting for the same cause. We came together as allies out of necessity," I tighten my grip on my bloody daggers, desperately trying to control my breathing; give them a speech to rally them. They need to believe we can win this. *Can you?* "But we will finish it as comrades, as friends in arms."

"We're not friends!" Artemis says with a harsh bark of laughter; maybe "friend" was too strong of a word to use.

"Perhaps not," I let my gaze fall on each of theirs, hiding nothing; these could be our last moments in this world. I don't want to go out a liar. "But we're more than just allies now. Maybe we're not friends, but we have a connection stronger than mere ties of necessity; like it or not, we have bonded. We have to rely on each other; our lives are dependent on one another. My life is in your hands," I sheath a dagger, placing my palm on the warm throne room doors. "Once we go through these doors, there's no turning back. I put my life in your hands, and now I must ask you to do the same; you must do what I tell you to do. We must trust each other, but this is not a democracy. Division will only get us killed." Silence follows my words, the distant sound of combat filling it quickly.

Petravin steps forward, putting his palm on the door next to mine, his face nearly touching mine. "I will put my life in your hands," he says, then grins, shrugging his shoulders. "Hell, it's gotta be better than putting it in my own, right?"

Benson steps up next, his large paw dwarfing ours, towering above us. His voice rumbles out from underneath his unarmored fur, muscles rippling with each word. "I will stand by you all, no matter what may await us." He turns his heavy gaze to Artemis, who places her steel-clawed hand next to ours.

"At least until that witch is dead," I grin, despite myself, and she returns it, shaking her hair.

"At least until the witch is dead," Wilhelm steps up, but I shake my head. "No, you and Totomir need to stay out here, make sure we stay uninterrupted while we take care of Evermore."

"But—"

"Relax kid, Totomir says, surprisingly agreeable ever since we entered the capital. I nod my thanks at him, but he turns his back on me, smacking Wilhelm's leg.

I turn to Benson. "Can you get us in there?"

"Please," is his only response, his snout morphing into a wolfish grin, placing his other palm on the door, muscles and fur straining against his skin. A feeling of compression presses in on me, and I suck in a deep breath. *He would be proud.*

My eyes flicker open, and I sit up in my throne. I look around the room, tapping my fingertips against my throne; something is off. The distant sounds of battle still rage on, but near this room it is...quiet. My aura glows brighter when I stand, burning away echoes of pain; something is about to happen, I can feel it in the air.

The door to the throne room glows brightly, and I leap off the dais, rushing to the doors; someone is trying to breach them! The doors gleam blindingly bright, the explosion of energy lifting me off my feet. I roll backward, eyes narrowing at the intruders. Artemis, Scarlett, and Petravin all let go of Benson, turning as one to face me. The queen, the girl, the forest rat, and the glorified dog; they won't leave here alive. I grin, cracking my neck and knuckles, shaking my hands.

"Welcome all," I take a step forward, and they draw their respective weapons in the amount of time it takes for me to blink. "I hope you all said your goodbyes before you began this suicide mission." I chuckle, nodding to myself; that's good, that's good.

"I want my throne back," Artemis growls.

"You shouldn't have lost it in the first place," I say smugly. She snarls, taking a run at me, but a quick flick of my hand stops her in her tracks. The wall of light presses her against the wall harder before it disappears; I can't kill them all yet. What would be the fun in that? "And I know why you're here, Scarlett," her hands clench on her daggers, but she says nothing; boring. "But I must say that you two," I point to Benson and Petravin, tilting my head. "Your being here stumps me."

"I'm just here for the glory," Petravin says with a crooked smile, trying to play it easy; he can't hide the trembling of his upper lip, the sweat trickling down his temple. He's a scared little boy who's not fooling anyone but himself.

"Oh of course; did you get tired of being treated like dirt, little forest rat?" Petravin steps forward, but Benson puts a paw on his shoulder, stopping him; he just saved your life, fly boy.

"And why are you here, Benson? I must say, I'm a little hurt; we had a good thing going." His gaze is serious, but his body remains loose, white light trailing between my fingertips; I don't tolerate betrayal. His usefulness expired when he turned traitor; he will die a traitor's death, like the rest of them.

"You forced me to kill Eurael," he says, his voice low and steady.

"I didn't want you to kill him!" I snap, aura flashing. Benson killed Eurael! He deprived me of revenge! I'll rip him apart!

"No, because you wanted to kill him yourself. You wanted to torture him and make him suffer before you erased him, Godkiller." He glares at me, his voice full of loathing. I stand straighter, heat flushing my skin. They will burn, *Benson* will *burn*.

"You were the one who killed him," I smirk contemptuously.

"I was forced to—to save him! Save him from you!" he shouts. You will be the one that needs saving now Benson; there is nowhere to run.

"Enough of this! Let's just kill her," Artemis snarls, stepping in front of Benson, letting loose several arrows. I duck underneath them, spears of light shooting toward them; you'll go first, Artemis. They all dodge, and Scarlett races toward me, Artemis covering her with a constant stream of arrows. I take cover behind a column, and Benson appears in front of me, swiping at me with one large paw. I block it with a column of light, shooting a bolt at him, but he disappears, reappearing at my side. I grit my teeth as his weight slams into a wall of light; I hold out my other hand, a block of light racing toward Scarlett. Petravin glides over her, scooping her up and tossing her at me. I let the wall of light fade, rolling out of the way. Benson stumbles forward, then his eyes go wide. Scarlett turns so she won't stab him, and he disappears quickly; you don't know how to act as a team. You just get in each other's way; how unfortunate for you.

Scarlett crashes against a wall and I flick my hand, a wall of light smashing her against the wall further, then disappearing. I leap back to avoid Petravin's quick slashes, rolling underneath Benson's claws as they slice past. A spear of light forms in my hand, which I hurl at Artemis. She ducks to the side, rushing forward, eager to join the fray; come hither former queen, to your demise. I will finish what I began so long ago. She leaps at me, talons gleaming; several spears of light protrude from the ground in front of me while I hurl a bolt of light at Petravin. He flies higher, and two walls of light slam closed toward him. The walls only manage to catch his ankle, but he cries out all the same, the walls holding him firmly in place as he tries to escape.

Sweat begins to drip off of me from maintaining the multiple objects, but I let the embankment of spears disappear as soon as Benson rescues Artemis, disappearing several feet away. I smirk, turning and hurling a spear of light at Petravin, catching him in the chest. The walls of light fade away, Petravin falling to the ground. You flew too close to the sun, and like Icarus, were doomed to fall. The shaft disappears from his chest, leaving only a smoking hole behind.

"No!" I throw up a wall of light, stopping Scarlett from tackling me. I drop the wall when Benson flashes near me. A spear of light materializes in my hands to block his claws; I dance backward, side-stepping a savage swipe from Artemis. I keep up a wall of defense against their claws while Scarlett uselessly tries to breathe life into the boy's corpse; he was out of his league. I duck underneath Benson's slash, knocking Artemis's feet out from under her with the shaft of my spear. I plant the head into the ground near Artemis's face, leaping onto the spear and swinging myself around, catching Benson in the chest with my feet just as he reappears; you can't predict me, Benson, but you...you I *can* predict.

I use his chest as a springboard, catapulting myself off, throwing a bolt of white light. It explodes on impact behind me, and I land in a roll, coming up near Scarlett. I grab her wrist before she can slice my throat, slamming my head into her nose. She reels back, a burn mark covering the bride of her nose, a white block lifting up from underneath her unsteady feet, another wall appearing as she falls backwards through the air, crushing her against the wall before disappearing; you don't get to die that easily. I look at Petravin's corpse near my feet and kick it away in disgust.

"Filthy forest rat," I growl.

"Do you not care who you murder? Do you not care about the innocent lives you destroy?" Scarlett tries to pick herself up on trembling arms, but I swing my leg up, my shoe catching her in the chin. I squat next to her, grabbing her by that awful red hair of hers; I'll color her entire body red, to match.

"I care about *revenge*," I hiss, her locks smoking in my hands. "No matter the cost. You and your teacher are responsible for all of this; the lives I destroy, the innocents I murder in my quest. You, and this world, can only blame the two of you." I heave her up, yanking her by her hair in front of me. Benson quickly disappears before he hurts Scarlett, reappearing next to Artemis. Dozens of thin, white hot needles of light appears all around Scarlett's body, pricking her skin. I take quick breaths to cool down the flames licking at me inside, spears of light shining behind the taught forms of Benson and Artemis, from one wall to the other; my victory is assured. They cannot stand against my power; even their combined might is not enough to stop me! With Eurael dead, Legend Land is mine!

My aura flashes, my breath hitching, and I act on instinct, pushing Scarlett away, shielding myself within several walls of light. Moments later, a torrential blast of energy shakes the castle. My walls of light shatter, heat engulfing my body, tossing me about in the room like a rag doll. Slowly, the blinding light dissipates to a level where I can see. Two dark forms begin to gain definition to my blurry vision, breath hissing out between my teeth, several small cuts and scrapes stinging as the hot air hits them. One figure is finally revealed, wielding a scythe, my legs standing firm underneath me as I take a deep breath, my aura fluxing out. A new challenger then, come to try and wrest my throne from me? I turn my attention to his partner and…no! It's not…it can't be possible! He…no…he's dead! He's supposed to be dead!

CHAPTER FIFTY-ONE

I open my eyes slowly, my head filled with a soft buzzing, my entire body feeling lighter than it's ever been. I see I'm in a small room with beige painted walls and soft, easy lighting. A fire gives soothing warmth to the room in a quaint stone hearth to my left, the logs crackling and popping as the fire slowly consumes them. I sit up a little straighter in the comfortable brown leather armchair I'm in, an identical chair resting across a coffee table, an empty glass pitcher and two empty cups sitting on the table. I close my eyes, covering my face with my hand; I wish for the darkness again. Simiel is in that darkness, somewhere, and with my sister is her forgiveness; I have to find her.

"I have to say I didn't expect you here so soon, Eurael," a voice says from behind me. I stiffen, that soft voice making me catch my breath; it has been so long. "Nothing to say to me Eurael?" There's movement behind me and a figure appears in front of me, shrouded in black. "You show up on my doorstep and I bring you here, where you are safe, and you have nothing to say to me? I thought you despised rudeness, yet here you are—a prime example."

I stand up quickly, and the darkness evaporates from the figure. Before me stands a tall lanky man with fiery orange hair pulled back into a ponytail, a black shirt with skull and crossbones covering the pale skin of his chest, and ripped jeans covering his legs; adorning his wrists are spiked bands and on his feet are large faded boots. His attire has changed little since our last meeting, centuries ago. Our dark eyes lock, the short distance between us seeming to span on forever when he steps forward and embraces me; I wrap my arms around him and clench my eyes shut. I feel hot tears stream down my face, landing with barely audible drops on his shirt, though he says nothing. He knows exactly what to say and when, or when not to say anything at all. I shudder against him, his embrace growing tighter around me, his hand running through my dark hair, pressing me into his shoulder. I sob openly into his shoulder, the torrent of emotions spilling out of me, his body becoming my silent confidante for the tears that pour out of my eyes. My eyes sting and my throat burns when he holds me away slightly, tilting my chin up with one thin finger. He looks into my eyes, gingerly wiping away my tears and sorrow, a soft smile on his face.

"I—" I try to begin, but he puts a finger to my lips, taking both my quivering hands in his, shaking his head.

"Wait until you are ready," he says softly, sitting me back down in the leather chair, keeping my hands in his, kneeling in front of me, waiting. I was numb before, the guilt having shut me down; now it wells up, wrenching a torrent of emotion from me that I...I'm not sure I'm prepared for. I can't keep it in anymore though—I can't keep it all to myself. Now he is here with me, *for* me, to share my pain; and while that drags even more unwelcome emotions to the surface, I just feel...grateful.

"I...I just don't know where to begin," I say, and he nods, pouring water from the previously empty pitcher and handing me a glass. I sip at the cool liquid looking down at my hands, covered in their gloves; how much blood is on these hands? How many lives have they taken? "I can see their faces, Z. Everyone that I..." I stop and close my eyes, resting my head back, hot tears streaming down my face again, dripping into my glass. It's not just Simiel who will never forgive me, but everyone I've wronged; in my pursuit for vengeance, for some twisted revenge, I lost sight of my emotions. I knew anger, pain, and anguish, but I knew not sorrow, or this guilt; now they consume me and leave me almost broken inside. The shattered fragments from where my long-forgotten soul used to reside twist and scrape inside of me, new emotions welling up that I never thought...I never thought I'd feel them again.

"I have never seen you like this Eurael," Z confesses, and I can feel his hands on my shoulders through my clothes, his breath on my face. "You have always been strong, resolute; I'm not used to seeing you so vulnerable." I open my eyes, Z's appearance blurred from my tears and bark out a short laugh that chokes me and sends me coughing.

"That's because I've never been like this," I reply, looking down at my glass to avoid his eyes; they are soft and understanding, but I know I'll confess everything if I look into them. As much as I want to tell him, and as much as I know he will understand, these are not his problems. I can't keep them inside, but I can't burden him with anything else. They aren't anyone's problems but my own, and I can't let him deal with them. As soon as I've made this resolution, though, I briefly glance up and see his dark eyes, and, loathing myself for even this weakness, I confess.

It spills out of me, a torrent of emotion; emotion that I didn't know I possessed, or maybe that has only actually recently surfaced, or resurfaced. He listens silently as I tell him everything, everything since I last saw him. My goals, my plans, my downfalls, my minor triumphs, and my sorrows; through it all he listens silently, unblinking, his smooth, pale face not revealing in the slightest what he's thinking. My jaws snap shut, and I breathe heavily through my nose, my throat dry and sore from talking; I have laid myself bare to him. Slowly, an expression begins to form on his face, and it kills the little bit of me that had yet to be broken; he understands. For him to understand my pain, he must have acutely felt it, and I have unwittingly caused him greater pain. I seem to hurt everyone; how can I expect forgiveness from those I have wronged when that list only grows larger with every action and step I take? I put my hands in my hair, tugging; even now I can't deal with my failure and my sorrow in any other way than vehement anger. Anger directed at myself, but anger nonetheless; am I incapable of feeling other emotions? Is this broken feeling inside me what I am? Am I...broken?

"You have endured much Eurael," Z says softly. "You have felt things you believed you were incapable of feeling: betrayal, sorrow, guilt. Though you have felt these things you have yet to confront or deal with them." Z tilts his head until he can look me in the eyes, taking the glass from my hands, removing my gloves. He places his palms on top of mine, squeezing them; his hands are warmer than anything I've ever felt. I take a deep breath, straightening up, feeling the warmth filling me inside. "You're going to have to deal with these things, or they will destroy you from the inside out."

I feel myself sinking back down at the prospect of confrontation; I don't want to confront these things. I don't want to face them; I want forgiveness, and that won't come through confrontation.

"I...I can't," I whisper and he tilts his head.

"Why not?" It's not accusatory, simply curious. I take a deep breath, closing my eyes, doing my best to collect myself, feeling my chest constrict momentarily before I let my breath out, opening my eyes again.

"I want forgiveness Z," I say. I remove my hands from his and stand up, pushing my chair away. "It's even best now that I'm dead; I'm free to find those I have wronged and beg forgiveness." There is one person from whom I truly wish to receive forgiveness from; Simiel. I can't ask her forgiveness until I have received it from others; she wouldn't forgive me any other way, I feel it.

"Why do you want forgiveness Eurael?" he asks; he is always, for as long as I have known him, trying to get to the root of the problem—to the core of things.

"Why does anyone want forgiveness, Z?" I reply with a sigh, running a hand through my hair. "I have done wrong, and I wish to right it."

"How is getting forgiveness going to right your wrongs? It sounds like you're doing this to make yourself feel better," I push down a flicker of indignation; I have no use for an emotion like that right now. I have no right to it, no entitlement to such an emotion that would only wound someone further. He steps closer to me, putting his hands on my shoulders. "From the first moment I met you, you were unconcerned with your own feelings; they simply got in the way. Now they have risen up and got the better of you; the old Eurael would never stand for such a rebellion." I don't shrug him off, but I can no longer look at him; I'm not who I was. I might never be that person again; I'm someone...*something* different. The truth is that I'm not sure if I ever want to be that person again; I'm not sure if I even could.

"I'm not the person I used to be," I reply. "The old Eurael would never have let emotions rise up in the first place."

"My point exactly," Z says, squeezing my shoulders tighter. "You used to stress the importance of ridding yourself of the unnecessary; even if you truly do wish for forgiveness, you won't find it by letting yourself wallow in guilt, drowning yourself in sorrow." I shake my head; I know what I need to find forgiveness, I know it.

"It's because I didn't allow myself to feel those things that I wound up here in the first place," I grab his wrists, removing his grip from me. "I know you're just trying to help Z, but I can do without it; let me leave." Z looks at me sadly, taking a step back, shaking his head.

"You're deluding yourself, Eurael; you're willing to throw away everything you've worked so hard to build; it is natural and good to feel guilt and sorrow, but you cannot let new emotions consume you. You have to face them, or they will eat you alive just like rage or anguish would. You cannot let yourself be taken by these emotions Eurael; you used to preach the necessity of controlling your emotions. From your tale, it sounds like you have let your emotions control you; giving yourself into the feelings of guilt, sorrow, and betrayal will bring you no more forgiveness or happiness than giving into rage or pain. I'm sorry Eurael," I feel the sting of his words acutely, as if each one pierced me to my heart. I move past him, unable to find any words to express myself, though I don't know what I would express if I could.

"But I have to do what is best for you. I know you would do the same if you were in my position. I know you are strong enough to face these new emotions; and if you will not let me help you in this manner, you will have to go to the root of the matter." Suddenly a small black door, smooth like unmarked obsidian, appears before me and silently swings open. I turn and see Z push me backward into the door; I reach my hands out, but the door slams shut, trapping me in inky darkness.

CHAPTER FIFTY-TWO

I am surrounded by darkness on all sides, as if it is a physical force pressing in on me. It threatens to suffocate me, but I do not resist; I wished for darkness, for Simiel is in darkness, lost, like I am now. I will find her—I have to find her; we will find each other. I will blindly stumble through the shadows to find her, and I will beg forgiveness; I will show her that I know, and now feel, guilt and sorrow. In the darkness, a circle of bright white light appears and then she is there, clearly visible. I stand still, in awe or shock I do not know. This is not in my head; she is here, in front of me, pristine and perfect. My legs wobble, and I lurch toward her, my breath hitching as my throat closes up painfully, as if my body itself does not believe this can be real.

"Simiel," I gasp and reach out to her with trembling hands; I quickly rip my gloves off and touch her skin; it's so warm. It's warm and she's here, truly here! "Oh Simiel!" I embrace her and breathe in her scent; wildflowers. I never tire of the scent, wildflowers wafting pleasantly up. I run a hand through her hair, holding her so close to me that for a moment I'm afraid I might crush her. I bury my face into her neck, murmuring in her ear. "I'm so sorry, Simiel; I know I acted out of anger before, in a pursuit for revenge but now...oh Simiel, I am so sorry. This guilt inside of me," I pull back, though a large part of me loathes doing so. I grip at my chest, curling my shirt up over my heart. I shake my head, blinking back tears. "This guilt kills me,

473

this sorrow breaks me; they rip me apart and I—" She stops me by putting her finger to my lips. I look at her, tilting my head back so I can utter a few, broken words. "Please forgive me."

"Eurael," she whispers, her voice softer than the coo of a dove, and I hold her close once again, shutting my eyes tight. "It's—" I feel her body heave against me then stiffen as something warm lands on my shoulder and neck; I put my hand on my neck and bring it away, covered in blood. I pull her back from me as blood gurgles out of her mouth, running down onto my hands, coating them in her hot, sticky blood; no, this can't be happening! No, I found you! Please! Please don't leave me again!

"Simiel!" I shout as her dress rips, cuts and bruises appearing on her form. She bleeds from horrifying, familiar wounds all across her body. No, please, I need you to forgive me; I need you to know I understand now! Please! "Simiel!" I shout shaking her, but she remains still, bloody, and bruised. I sink to my knees, cradling her cold body in my arms, her blood covering my hands; her blood is on my hands. I rock back and forth, squeezing my eyes shut, hot tears flowing down my face. "Simiel," I groan, holding her to me. Her cold weight against me disappears, leaving behind only her warm blood, but it doesn't matter; she's gone now. I had her in my arms, protected, ready to forgive me, and now she's gone, lost...forever.

"Well don't you look like a right mess," the voice shocks me from my numbness, and I look at Verran, grinning, crouched in a pool of her blood; it's just like how it was before. *He* is responsible for this, again?! "You just can't seem to save her, no matter how many times you try, can you? Not in your head, not in here; nowhere is she safe. You want to know why?" He waits for me to respond, but I don't, or can't, my lungs feeling shriveled, dead; I want to disappear. I want to die again; and this time, I don't want to be found. I want to fade into nothingness and just forget. "Because I'm still here; *I'm still inside your head*. Wherever you go, happily trying to find some way to bring our dear, beloved sister back from the Void, I will be trailing right alongside you, thwarting your every attempt, sabotaging your every move. I will stop you from bringing her back with Ragnarok, I will keep you from finding her; you can't succeed. Deep down, you know you can't do it."

"That's not true," I mutter, shaking my head. "I know I can bring her back."

"Awe, do you think you can? Do you think you can, you think you can? I'm sure if you close your eyes and wish hard enough that it'll come true," he laughs harshly, standing up. "Open your eyes, little brother, you're not in a fairytale; you can't just hope for something to happen. You're drowning and wallowing in your guilt and sorrow; you'll never be able to do anything in this condition. I can't believe," he shakes his head, turning his back on me, "I can't believe that you broke this easily. I honestly expected more from you." He takes a few steps into the darkness, leaving me alone once again. I hold myself, screwing my eyes shut as hot tears leak down my face; I want to drown in them, drown in my sorrow. My body trembles as I shake my head; I can still do it.

"No," I mutter, trying to fight off the cold fear of Verran's words, the fear that he might be right, that he's telling me what I already know; the truth. "No no no no no," I squeeze myself tighter; it's not true, I can do it. I can still bring her back! My mind desperately tries to reject any possible truth Verran's words contained; he's a liar, he's just trying to hurt me. But the slight possibility of his words being true leaves me hollow, and I can only slump forward, tears dripping steadily onto the dark floor. I know now I am broken, because she is what made me whole; if I can't bring her back, what is my reason to remain?

"Hey there," a soft voice says from behind me, a hand settling onto my shoulder. "You're not alone here, remember? You can't give up; some of us are still counting on you." I turn and my eyes widen; of all the people, I wasn't expecting—I couldn't have expected this.

"Jack?" I gasp out. He smiles and nods, brushing his thumb against my cheeks, wiping away my tears. He glows with his former youth, stroking my cheeks with the pads of his thumbs. "What...how..."

"This is a part of the Land of the Dead, remember? Last time I checked, I was dead," he says with a light, tinkling laugh.

"Unlike those apparitions of your mind," he says, his voice turning serious.

"Jack I—"

He holds up a hand, looking me in the eyes intensely. "Worry not, my friend; I understand. This place will play tricks on you, I am well aware. But you cannot wallow and wait here; there is nothing left here but pain and sorrow. Pain can drive you, yes, but too much and it will cripple you, as it threatens to do now." I look up at him, my mind latching finally onto something he had said before.

"You said that some of us are still counting on you. What does that mean?"

He smiles and turns toward the swirling, hissing darkness, holding out one small hand. For a few moments nothing happens, then a larger hand grasps his, and his mother steps forward.

"Mrs. Helvare?" I look at her incredulously, my heart beginning to race, guilt crashing down on me once more. "I am so sorry for what I did. For taking your boy, more than once, for letting you live in agony and for...for..."

She smiles, bending down next to me on the opposite side of Jack, putting her hand on my shoulder. "All is forgiven," she says softly, her gentle fingers pushing strands of hair out of my eyes. I turn to look at her and her soft, gentle smile melts me. I collapse into her arms, sobbing.

"I'm sorry," I murmur again and again. "I'm sorry, I'm sorry." Everything I've done will earn me a place of eternal damnation, but the crown jewel of my sin was ripping this beautiful, strong woman from her son. And now she holds me close while I cry my eyes out to her, crooning to me softly, stroking my head; a mother until the end. I feel her push at me gently and, loathe as I am, I pull back, letting go; I still wish to cling to her like a child. She smiles, wiping the tears from my face, then looking me square in the eyes.

"I want you to listen to me—can you do that?" I nod; anything to make up for what I've done. "I want you to stand up, square your shoulders, face the darkness, and walk into it." I blink and shake my head.

"I can't. I won't be able to until I've found forgiveness for—"

A sharp smack resounds out as her hand connects with my cheek, leaving a burning hand print. I gasp, putting my hand to my face, looking at her. She stands up taller, her eyes burning fiercely.

"You want forgiveness, is that it? You took my boy from me, then swallowed with me your shadows."

"I know and I—"

She cuts me off, gripping my head in both her hands as she bends over, her face an inch from mine. "And now I'm together with my baby boy, forever. So you have my thanks, and my forgiveness. Now stand," she commands, gripping me by my forearm and yanking. I rise and she nods, brushing off my coat. "I may have found my boy thanks to you, but you still have to find someone—someone for whom you've been searching for a very long time." I nod, and she pats my chest. "Then turn around and walk, and don't you quit walking. You walk until this darkness turns to light and until you can hold your head up high again. Or I swear to all that is high and mighty I will find you, and I will make you earn my forgiveness. Now go!" She spins me around and gives me a push.

I look back and Jack shoos me on; I take a deep breath and take one step. Then another. Then another. Without realizing it, I begin to walk deeper into the darkness, until I can no longer see a thing, but even then I don't stop. I keep walking.

After walking for mere moments, or perhaps it's been hours...it could be years. Decades. Eons. Time seems to have none of its crushing weight on me any longer. I slowly become aware of a certain light, not bright enough to draw my attention, but still there, at the edge of my peripheral vision. I shake my head and keep walking; all I have to do is walk. The light encroaches on my main line of sight, the darkness around me first turning a dull grey color, then fully becoming white. I stop walking; have I reached my destination?

"Welcome to my prison." My eyes slowly travel around, searching, until they alight upon a black figure with a large red mouth, too big for its head; Mutovinatum. "Welcome to my hell."

In response, I calmly seat myself down on the floor; I knew I would be encountering Mutovinatum sooner or later in this place. I feel nothing toward him now; I do not seek his forgiveness. I have no business with him.

"You do not know hell," I reply, staying seated.

"I have been caged away for centuries, completely bound and imprisoned, unable to do a single thing; is that not hell?" I do not reply, and Mutovinatum walks until he stands over me, the red smile growing even wider. "Where is your fire, Eurael? Where is your determination? Has it been taken away? Have you lost your will?" I look up and Mutovinatum raises a hand, but I do not move. "You are unflinching, unmoving; maybe you have grown stronger; maybe death was what you needed."

I look placidly up at him; another obstacle until I can finally be forgiven. I need not do anything; this will pass, like the others, and I will continue. I won't be manipulated by my head any longer.

Mutovinatum growls, stomping hard. "I know all your secrets, Eurael! I know your deepest darkest fears! Does that bother you?" Mutovinatum appears behind me, leaning close to my ear. "Does it bother you that I was able to manipulate you and terrorize you so easily? That before I tortured you in your own mind, but now I am truly here? How does it feel to have me so close again? Does it bother you that I broke you down, using your innermost secrets against you? You have to face your demons eventually, Eurael, so look at me!" I look down at my hands, studying my nails; this is a waste of my time. "Look at me!" he roars, the air around me rippling with angry energy; I can feel his vehemence, his raging desire. For a moment I feel something deep inside of me flicker, like a kindred spirit calling out; I know those feelings. I know rage, and I know guilt; I know desire, and I know sadness. None of that matters; all I want to know now is forgiveness.

"You will not bring me forgiveness," I state neutrally, looking up at the ghastly red smile plastered on his featureless black face; the object of my nightmares before me at last. In the past, there were many things I wanted to do to this monster, this personification of all my darkest demons; I would have torn him asunder from head to toe, obliterated him from the fabric of the cosmos. Not so long ago, or perhaps very long ago, I would have begged his forgiveness for having thought such things; I received my forgiveness form Mrs. Helvare, and that has eased my conscience. If she, a woman I wronged so horrendously, could forgive me, then the others I had wronged and hurt can forgive me as well. Now all I desire is forgiveness from Simiel; I must hear it in her own words.

"Is that what you want?" he sneers. "Forgiveness?"

"Yes," I say and he chuckles deeply, the sound reverberating around this place that seems to have no boundaries. "But not from you."

He snarls, swooping in close. "You want forgiveness from all those that you hurt? You can never have such a thing! You have hurt and wronged so many that not even I can count them all; you are a true monster, Eurael. You will *never* be forgiven."

"Monsters can be forgiven," I say softly. "The woman that you tortured when I came to the Underworld, she recognized me as a monster, but she not only forgave me, but trusted me as well. I only require forgiveness from one now." Mutovinatum looks at me, seeming confused. His grin grows wider and he draws closer to me, only a few inches away.

"You won't find her here, Eurael," he says; Mutovinatum has always lied to me. There's no reason to believe anything he says. "Her soul is not in the Underworld; you know as well as I what happened to her when that blade was sunk into her heart." I look up at him quickly, my voice sharp.

"You're wrong."

He chuckles, standing up straight, rising taller. "You failed to create Ragnarok; you failed to bring her back. You failed from the very beginning; even if you were able to find her or bring her back, why should she forgive you? She knows the most, perhaps out of anyone,

just how incompetent you are. Why would she forgive such a *failure?*"
I stand up, clenching my fists, my eyes burning themselves deeper
into my skull; that something deep inside of me coos in pleasure,
reaching out.

"I will find her! She can forgive me!" I shout. His laughter rings
out around me, and I turn my back on him, taking a deep breath;
he's simply trying to provoke me. It won't work; I won't let him in.

"You've tried for so long to find a way to bring her back, yet you
had so many shortcomings; it took much longer than necessary for
you to acquire all the necessary pieces. And once you had them all,
your plans were dashed, ruined; your hopes destroyed before your
very eyes." I feel his rank breath on the back of my neck, hissing his
words into my ears. "You don't want her forgiveness for letting her
die, or even for failing to bring her back; you want her forgiveness
because you gave it all you had, and that still wasn't enough. You still
weren't enough."

I whirl around, a low growl in my throat as Mutovinatum takes a
small step backward, that red smile morphing into an amused smirk.
"How do you know that?" I growl, feeling my suppressed anger begin
to rise up, raging inside of me. I know I want Simiel's forgiveness,
but I *need* to know this. "I was the only one inside that room and,
still, some outside force was able to sabotage me and ruin everything.
That force wasn't you though," I close the distance between us, nearly
quivering with my mounting anger. How did he know? "So how did
you know those details?"

Mutovinatum chuckles, first a low, distant-sounding rumble
that quickly shifted into a loud, booming thunder. I grip him by his
inky black shoulders, squeezing tightly, my fingers partially sinking
into his form.

"While you may have trapped me here when you stole my powers,"
he breaks my grip, his voice turning cold. "I still was able to reach
out; not very much, but enough. There are plenty of people who
despise and hate you Eurael, but the key was finding someone who
was strong enough to do something. So I waited, biding my time
until you were close enough to me; when you traveled down to one

of the layers of the Underworld, I gathered myself and reached out. Of course, you easily rebuffed me, but some portion of my power lingered; and then it attached itself to someone. Even after she rid herself of me, and she believed my form was rid from Legend Land, I survived and continued to make suggestions; I whispered in her ear and planted little seeds, leaving a trail of bread crumbs. And it culminated in your ultimate failure."

His low, scraping laugh shreds and tears itself into my bones, grating within me. A low whine fills my ears, my vision blurring; he is responsible for this. He is responsible for the failure of my attempt to create Ragnarok; he is responsible for the destruction of my one chance to bring back Simiel. The need for forgiveness is replaced by the anger that suddenly snaps everything back into focus, the whine suddenly disappearing; my vision clears, my eyes narrow, focusing completely on Mutovinatum. That part deep inside of me where my soul should be, previously drowning in sorrow, roars with flames, licking their way through my bones, through my entire body, threatening to consume me. The pain that ensues is familiar, like an old friend, more welcome than ever before; I reach a hand out towards Mutovinatum. He will be my outlet; he is responsible.

"I came here looking for forgiveness," I take a step forward, and he takes a step back, his sick smile still plastered on. "I found it, and I thought all that was left was to find that final forgiveness I desired from the one person I care most about. Instead, I find you; the being truly responsible for destroying any chance I ever had of achieving that last, great forgiveness. I hold you fully accountable for everything that happened."

"Finally some recognition," Mutovinatum sighs. I lash out without warning, my foot connecting with his torso whilst my fist connects with his head. There is only a small amount of resistance before my limbs passed right through them, throwing me off balance. I feel my feet leave the ground as I am tossed aside like a rag doll. I land heavily on my side and look up to see Mutovinatum stomping his foot down directly towards my head; I roll out of the way, spinning my leg in an attempt to sweep him off balance. My leg passes through him, and he reaches down and hoists me up, his cold dark hand squeezing my throat.

"I was hoping you would be a bit more of a challenge once you got that fire back in you, but I see I was hopeful for naught." He shakes his head, disappointed; I growl, grabbing his forearms and pushing off with my feet. His grip remains strong, and he drops me to the ground, kicking me in the chest. I slide back several feet, my lungs straining against my chest, feeling like it's been caved in. I spit a glob of blood from my mouth, gnashing my teeth, standing and straightening my spine. I thrust my palm out, the fire inside of me swirling like a raging inferno, a sick twisted pleasure filling me, knowing the devastation I am about to unleash upon Mutovinatum will in some way atone for my failure with Simiel. I cannot ask her forgiveness, but the creature for my failure still exists; I could not bring myself to face her if I didn't destroy Mutovinatum. When nothing happens, he begins to laugh, laughing until it shakes me to my very core.

"Enough!" I shout, rushing toward him. Whether the shadows obey me here or not, I will destroy Mutovinatum! I duck underneath his swipe, jabbing him several times in the torso, then circling around to his back, planting a knee in his back, grabbing the back of his neck. Mutovinatum simply steps backward, my attacks passing right through him as he fades through me.

"Did you forget where your power came from? *I* am the source of your power, boy!" he thunders, extending one arm. I leap back as several tendrils erupt from the ground. They spin, hissing as they speed through the air toward me. I roll, dodging them when several more shoot from the ground, wrapping around my limbs. I struggle, trying to wrench my arms and legs free; no, they will not contain me! I grab one tendril by twisting my wrist, squeezing it until my knuckles turn white; you have known me for millenia, you will obey *me!* The shadows simply spit in contempt at me, squeezing me tighter until I'm forced to release my grip.

Mutovinatum slowly walks toward me, his grin spanning the entire width of his otherwise formless, featureless face. He stops barely an inch away while I breathe heavily, glaring at him; I will not be contained here. I will make you pay for everything you've done to me; you cannot contain me here. I will have Simiel grant me forgiveness; you cannot trap me.

"Nothing to say to me? Nothing at all?" He turns his head, cupping the side of his head as if he had an ear.

"Rot in hell," I spit.

"I've been rotting here for centuries! Because of you!" he roars, smacking me in the face. I feel my jaw fracture, pain splintering up the side of my head, but I don't let it show; he will get nothing from me. He has taken enough from me already.

"Now you plan on making me share your fate?" I snarl in contempt. Mutovinatum shakes his head, tapping one of the bleeding scratches he left on my cheek.

"Share my fate? No, you will not be sharing in my fate; in fact, you won't be doing anything at all after this point. Death has so kindly dumped a perfectly suitable vessel on my doorstep, one that can exist outside of the Underworld; I plan on making full use of this opportunity," he chuckles, dissolving into pitch black smoke, curling its way up my legs, around my torso. I keep my mouth closed, trying to twist my head away but the smoke spreads out, trickling up my nostrils, then plunging down my throat. I gag, and the smoke shoots through my mouth, down my throat. My lungs scream for air as the smoke begins to spread out into every part of my body, still blocking my throat. My entire body begins to spasm, and shake as I try and reject Mutovinatum, foam frothing at my mouth around the invading darkness. With a gasp, the smoke clears and I drop to the ground, crumpling in a sweaty mess. I can feel Mutovinatum nestled deep down inside of me where my soul should be, and it fills me with the urge to vomit. I weakly make a fist, swallowing the bile down, panting.

"I...won't let...you control me," I pant, my lungs heaving for each thin breath of air. *You're still here? I thought I forced you out; a situation that can easily be rectified.* I shut my eyes as white hot daggers of pain spear themselves into my mind. Thousands of needles work their way into my nerves, acid coursing through my system. I feel the air against my raw throat, and some part of my mind realizes I'm screaming, curled in a ball. I bang my head against the floor, desperate to get the pain out. This acid, this pain coursing through me has to come out!

"You can overcome this."

I look up, my vision blurry; I can make out the outline of a white dress and black hair. I shake my head, tears rolling down my cheeks, claws tearing up my insides.

"No, I can't," I gasp out, the veins popping in my arms and neck as a new wave of pain crashes down onto me.

"You've beaten worse than this," I feel a cool touch on my feverish skin, and a small wave of relief washes through me, giving me a small moment to think. "I'm still out here, waiting for you, Eurael. I know this won't beat you; I don't think you'll ever give up trying to bring me back. Don't prove me wrong. Please, Eurael, I need you."

I nod as a new wave of pain hits, and I cry out. My senses go numb, my body becoming a crying, twitching mess. It wipes out any coherent thought, any sense besides raw, overwhelming, all-consuming pain. Then, I find a way to push back. I won't be stopped here, Simiel, I will find you; I swear it. Grabbing at the pain, shoving it backward, putting up a wall—bit by bit, centimeter by centimeter, I drive the pain out of my body. I can feel grass underneath my fingertips, I can see the lace of a white dress; I can smell the wildflowers. I slam my palms on the ground, groaning as I push myself up, lances of pain shooting up my spine and down my legs as I stand. I must still have her forgiveness; you shall not win. The world swims around me, and my legs threaten to collapse, but I brace myself against my internal walls, standing up straight.

"You...won't...beat me," I gasp, sweat dripping off my face; I have beaten him. I have won; in my rebellion, I have won. *That was, admittedly, impressive considering you haven't been with me for several centuries. I don't give up a host that easily; you should know that Eurael.* "I know how you are with your hosts," I feel strength returning to me, allowing me to breathe easier; just a few more moments. "I used to be one of them, until I broke free and imprisoned you. You gave me power, but you used it to enslave me; I no longer need your power. You only gave me the power that you stole which was mine to begin with, my birthright. Now, you have nothing to offer me; I have grown stronger. If, in my state when I battled you centuries past, I was able to defeat you, I have no doubts about the outcome of this situation. This power is not yours, Mutovinatum."

I plunge deep down inside myself, grabbing Mutovinatum. Pain spikes through me, but I grit my teeth, holding on, dragging him up out of me. He fights, clawing and scratching, tearing me apart as I wrench him up. *No! No! You won't imprison me again! Not this time!* I snarl, squeezing him tighter, forcing him up. Mutovinatum turns back, biting and swiping at me. I feel him wriggle free, and I plunge down into the layers of darkness, grabbing him again. I know darkness; I live in darkness. The darkness he has lived in has only sheltered him, coddled him, protected him; I live in shadow that has forced me to fight. Every day, every moment, was a moment I could be betrayed, snapped up by my own monsters. There is nowhere in those shadows that he can hide from me; intruders will not be tolerated. I wrench him out of the depths in which he tries to hide, bringing him closer to the surface. *No! Wait, please! Stop!*

"I will stop once you are removed and destroyed like the parasite you are," I growl, digging in deeper, shaking him as I tug out. *No! Please! WAIT!* "Your words will do nothing for you," I am far too committed to allow him any quarter, wrenching him inch by inch out of my body. He will not escape my grasp this time; he will not win. *I can help you! I may have said whisperings, yes, but the one who did the act was Evermore; you know this.* "You drove her to it; she's not here, you are. You are responsible; I will not let you get away with what you've done!" I heave and his grip weakens, sliding nearly to the surface. *After you are done with me, you will go after her! You accuse me of being responsible, but she is equally responsible; we both know this. She bested you in the past, she will do it again.* "I will not be defeated by her," I growl, relishing the scream Mutovinatum makes as the light begins to hit his darkness, weakening him. *You were nearly defeated by me! She defeated me, and I nearly defeated you; you can't possibly defeat her on your own!*

I try to shake his words out of my head, but they echo in my ears; I can't concentrate enough to keep a hold on him, and he presses his advantage. *I can help you; you will have one of those responsible within your grasp, and the other you will be able to crush.* I shake my head, trying to tighten my grip once again on him; no, I won't let this happen. I can take them both without any help. I don't need him; all I need is Simiel's forgiveness. *You defeated me here; if you so wish, after you defeat Evermore, you can destroy me. How will you gain Simiel's forgiveness when you cannot defeat those responsible for your failure?* I will not succumb to an old weakness, an ancient addiction! I do not need Mutovinatum to fight my battles! *You will not be succumbing, you will be using me to further your own goals. You will never be able to receive forgiveness if the woman responsible for your failure is still alive. And she will remain that way unless you use me.* Will Simiel forgive me if I let Evermore live? I can finish Mutovinatum off at any time, but Evermore...Evermore has bested me in the past. I cannot be sure of a victory fighting her alone. *Before, when I inhabited you, you were weak, yet still able to defeat some of the strongest foes you have ever faced. Now you are much stronger; you have grown powerful, more powerful than I could have predicted. I chose Evermore as a host because she rivals your own power; she cannot rival our power combined.* Victory would be assured with the aid of Mutovinatum, but at what cost? Nothing is ever as simple as it seems with Mutovinatum, though I defeated him several times before; I am confident I will be fully able to do it again. *Do we have an agreement?* "I...I accept your terms."

The dark, featureless door closes behind me without a sound, disappearing without a trace. Z looks at me with concern, trying to decipher what exactly happened; some things are shielded from Death, even in his own domain. I walk up to Z, looking him directly in the eyes. Z is my oldest and only true friend; I would, and have, gone through hell for him. I know he would do the same. His eyes implore me to tell him something, anything; I open my mouth, then my fist crashes out of nowhere into his cheek, sending him reeling across the room, spilling over a chair onto the coffee table.

"Thank you," I growl, walking over to him. "You got me back on my feet, and you reignited that fire in me." I offer him my hand, and he looks at me for a moment before taking it, allowing me to hoist him to his feet.

"You're welcome," he says, rubbing his jaw and cheek. I grab him by the shoulder, my fingers digging in.

"I never wanted that fire in me again, and I'm not sure that I'm content with it now. I didn't want anything to do with Mutovinatum ever again, and now he rests inside of me. But now I have the power to enact vengeance on those responsible for the destruction of Ragnarok and my failure to retrieve Simiel."

His eyes show no pain, his thin, long fingers moving to rest gently on my gloved hand.

"I gained forgiveness from those that I wronged, and for that I am thankful. You also put me through something horrid that has changed me forever, and I'm not sure I can ever forgive you for that." Z nods, my hand releasing him.

"I understand," he says, nodding, looking at me with those dark, fathomless eyes of his. "You change constantly, Eurael; I have witnessed several changes in you myself. Many creatures will only undergo a single metamorphosis in life; you have already undergone several, and I'm not sure you're at the end either. There is a type of beauty in your inherent rebellion against the laws of nature."

"You, yourself, are a law of nature."

"Must be why you never listen to me," he says with a small smile; I turn away slightly, clenching and unclenching my fists, grabbing the pommel of my sword and then releasing it.

"Get your scythe; you're taking me to Evermore's throne room." Out of the corner of my eye, I see him begin to do as I say without complaint or hesitation. *You won't beat Evermore if you're worried about him.* I'm not worried about Z; he is Death, he has more than enough power to best Evermore. She tried to take Legend Land from him; he is more than willing to help. *Still, the emotional attachment could be a risk. You need to let go of your humanity; to beat a monster like Evermore, you have to be one.* Becoming a monster is always the end result of my metamorphosis; Evermore will not be an issue for much longer.

"Are you sure you want to do this?" Z asks, scythe in hand. His concerned eyes sweep over me, and I nod; Evermore must pay.

This calm—it is something I have not felt in what feels like decades; for the first time, I have a clear path, with an end in sight. There is no long plan, no complicated undertaking; only the path that lies before me—and at the end, Evermore.

"Alright then; prepare yourself."

CHAPTER FIFTY-THREE

With a blinding flash, I appear in the throne room for the capital of the Kingdom. I keep my eyes locked on Evermore, and she keeps hers on mine. Z steps forward, his eyes narrow, becoming even darker if possible.

"So you are the one who has been trying to steal this world from me," he lowers his scythe, but I put a hand on his shoulder, my voice calm and even.

"I will take care of this. Protect the others; do not let them interfere." I say. He searches my face, his eyes flicking over my features before nodding, walking to the others, and slamming his scythe on the ground. The air shimmers around Z and the others; Scarlett rushes forward, slamming her hand against the barrier, shouting something. I turn and bend backward onto one hand as a bolt of white light flies over, barely missing my face. I flip myself sideways to dodge another one, and a tendril of darkness wraps around my arm then hooks into the ceiling, swinging me out of the way. With Mutovinatum and I on the same side for now, the shadows instantly obey me; I drop, tendrils of shadow spinning and writhing around me as I crash near Evermore. She dances backward, but a small bit of stone strikes her cheek, a thin line of blood trickling down the side of her face. She glowers at me, several bolts of light being thrown in my direction.

You should pull out your sword; get close and finish it. You'd have the advantage. "I do not need you hissing advice in my head," I growl and he laughs. I narrowly avoid another bolt, tendrils of shadow shooting out toward Evermore to spear her. She simply glows brighter and the tendrils shriek, retreating quickly, smoking and spitting. *I told you, but you just don't listen.* I unsheathe my sword, dashing toward Evermore, swiping at her chest. She spins out of the way, raising her hand; several spears of light shoot toward me. I swing my sword and slice them apart before they reach me, but a blast of light smacks me in the chest, sending me backward. I stand up, smoking and I growl, shaking my head. *You need to be more aware of everything around you.* "Quiet," I growl. *I'm trying to help; if you lose, so do I. It's simply self-preservation.* "Then remain silent; you are a distraction." Shadows come at her from her left as I dash toward her; she brings up a wall of light around her, and the shadows turn to smoke on contact. It feels like a hand has suddenly tightened its grip on my heart, but I continue forward nonetheless. As the wall of light lowers, I'm in front of Evermore, thrusting my sword toward her chest. Her eyes widen, and a spear of light quickly materializes in her hands so she can block my strike. My sword glances up, but still scrapes her neck and chin. She hurls a bolt of light at me, several small streams of crimson staining her flesh. I sidestep; but as I set my foot down, a large block of light shoots upward, throwing me off balance. Evermore rushes forward, thrusting her spear at me as I fall. I land heavily on my back and bat her spear to the side, swinging my legs at hers. My legs collide with her ankles, and she falls as I stand. I grab her by the wrist, jerking her to a stop, swinging my sword at her arm; I need not even kill her immediately, just disable her enough so that it becomes easier. She glows brightly searing my hand; I refuse to let go, but my hand releases her without my command, and I stumble backwards. *You can't just resist that light; it will kill you.* "No, it will kill *you.* Do not interfere again." I reply, standing up.

Evermore looks at me, then behind me, hurling several bolts of light. I turn quickly and see them collide with Z's barrier; they do no damage, thought that is not what matters. She tried to attack Scarlett! Rather than face me, she tried to attack my student. Scarlett has no part in this fight.

"You murdered me and tried to do the same to my student; and now that I have come to face you, which is what you desire, you attack my student once more. You have become too large of a thorn in my side."

"I didn't want you to die," she says as we begin to circle each other. *She could be lying.* "Not immediately anyway," she continues, hurling a bolt of light at me, and I duck underneath, tendrils of shadow shooting at her feet, but they stop before they even touch her. "Revenge requires planning, and time."

"Is death not revenge?" I run forward, slicing at her arms, her neck, her chest; anything within reach. I don't believe for a second she wouldn't take any chance she got to kill me, and I will return the favor. A block of light smacks into my side, sending me careening through the air. I quickly roll to avoid another bolt of light, coming to my feet. *I think you may have lost your touch, Eurael.*

"Death is *mercy*," I dance backward as another bolt of light shoots at me; I send tendrils of shadow shooting at her, but, once again, they cannot touch her. How can I beat her if I can't touch her? "Death is not my revenge!" I feel my back touch the wall as Evermore closes in, throwing bolt after bolt of light at me. Once I judge she's close enough, I jump and kick myself off the wall, using the shadows to swing myself over, landing behind her. I swing my sword down at her head as she turns, a spear of light once again materializing in her hand. My blow drives her to her knees, the shaft of the spear stopping my blade from cleaving her head in two. Her arms tremble, and she grits her teeth, aura fluctuating rapidly.

"What then?" I growl, bearing down on with two hands on my sword now. *Why does it matter? Just finish it!* It matters to me! "What is your revenge?"

"I want you to feel sorry for what you did to me!" she shouts, struggling to keep me off of her, even as my clothes begin to smoke. "I want to see the guilt in you as I kill you; I want there to be remorse in your eyes as the life fades out of you. I want you to know you were responsible for the death of everything you held dear, because you were too cold to care." She glares up at me, my clothes smoking, something inside of me screaming, even as blood roars through my head, blinking rapidly to keep my vision from swimming with red. I bear down harder, and a wall of light slams into me, knocking me away from Evermore. I stand at the same time as Evermore, a vacant grin on her face. *She's lost it.* My sword trembles in my hand, my knees barely able to support me; she is like orichalcum, like poison.

"I am sorry," I say, walking toward her, forcing my feet to plant themselves firmly each time, lest I stumble. Her eyes widen, then narrow again, bolts of light crackling. "I wasn't before, but I know the pain of being unforgiven—of wronging someone—of not doing anything and having them hate you for it. I did what I had to do to save Scarlett, but I should have found another way. I can admit that to myself, but I'm not going to stop because of that. I've come to terms with what I did, and I've accepted I can't change it; you have not. You have done so much more to me than what I could ever do to you; it is you who should feel guilt over what you've done." Evermore shakes her head, disbelieving.

"No, you're lying. You're lying! I did nothing except repay the wrong you had done to me!" She shouts, eyes wide, pupils dilated. *Just stop talking and kill this wench already.* I take another step forward, and she blasts a bolt of light at me, but it misses wildly. *Finish her.* I calmly take another step and again she misses, stumbling back. "*You* are guilty! *You* wronged *me!*"

I remain silent, tightening my grip on my blade; she's right, death is mercy. I leap high over her constructs, suddenly bringing my blade down in a vicious chop at her skull. She rolls out of the way, trying to smack me into the wall with a block of light; I manage to clamber over it quickly, dropping down onto her, aiming a swipe at her legs. Tendrils of shadow slam her into the wall as soon as she makes it to her feet, screaming in time with my blade as it rushes toward her. Her aura bursts in a blinding flash, and though the shadows disappear, my sword remains on course; my eyes readjust, to find Evermore stopping my blade with a spear of light, panting and gasping.

"You...you are guilty."

I shake my head, bearing on her with my full strength.

"You cannot possibly understand what you have done," I growl low in my throat, pressing harder on the blade.

"I *understand*," she spits, pushing back against my sword. "I *understand* what you have done to me, and that is why I hate you."

"You do not know hate," I hiss, and a bolt of light explodes near my feet, sending me flying backward. I roll and collide with the hall, my head banging against the stone. *You are losing, Eurael. I think it'd be best if I took over.* I try to push myself up, but I feel my will quashed down, forced out of my limbs. "No," I gasp. *Let me take over; I will defeat her. You're restricting yourself by limiting your powers.* "You can't even get close to her."

Evermore stalks closer, glee written on every inch of her face, even as I feel myself restricted to stillness. *Your body is the only shield I need; let me take over.* "No," I insist, even as my limbs grow cold, my vision turning black as the shadows slithering up my neck. *Let me take over!* "Never!"

"You cannot defeat her on your own; you *need* me." Mutovinatum's voice hisses around me, his breath hot on my ear.

"I can do this, I don't need your help." I growl, whipping around. I fly through the air, sliding on the ground, pressure keeping me still before I can move. A red mouth hovers over me, sharp teeth gleaming in a twisted grin, the only thing visible in the darkness.

"I was hoping to do this with your consent," he says, his grip tightening on my wrists as I struggle and twist against him. "I suppose I'll just have to take what I want by force."

He lays over me, his mouth widening. I tug at my bonds, Mutovinatum's dripping maw drawing closer, his rancid breath heavy on my face. His grip is firm, solid, unyielding; if I don't escape, he will be the destruction of us both. I kick my legs up, my knees knocking his head forward. I use the small amount of momentum to toss him over me, scrambling to my feet, plunging my hands into the darkness around me. I hear Mutovinatum howl, my hands clawing at the shadows until a point of light appears, slowly widening as I rip and tear until it becomes a hole, an escape. "No!" He roars as I slip through the hole.

Eurael goes flying, landing against the wall. He struggles to stand for a moment, and I raise my hand; he must not win here. After I defeat him, the others will be next, even Death; my body trembles at the thought of taking on Death itself. I allow myself a small smile; with my increase in power, this has been easier than I expected. Still, I was expecting something more…satisfying from Eurael. His disappointing performance means it will all be over. My vision swims, and the light in my hand dies for a moment, my chest feeling constricted; I suddenly can't breathe. I gasp out for air, darkness enveloping my mind, my knees colliding with the cold floor.

"Your task is not to kill Eurael!" I look up at *her*, the mist swirling around me, the pressure constricting my chest, keeping me on my knees.

"I…have to." I gasp out, tugging at my shirt, trying to relieve the vacuum surrounding me. I can feel her cold gaze even if I can't see it, the mist swirling faster as the pressure mounts. My skull feels like it will crack, my lungs screaming for air.

"You will not disobey me!" I look up at her, and I collapse on my stomach, clawing weakly at the mist. "If you will not complete your task, then you are of no use to me."

I'm close, I'm so close this time; he's here, right in front of me, and I'm about to kill him, to *finish* this. Finally I will have my revenge—finally—and now I am to be denied? I bite the inside of my cheek, my aura rebelling against the pressure. It fluxes, straining, then with a loud crack it shines forth brightly. I stand up, gulping in a breath. The room fills with light as I close my eyes, drawing away.

"You will not get away with this!" she screeches as she disappears. When I open my eyes, Eurael is making his way to his feet; several spears of light appear, shooting toward him as I glow brightly. I need to finish this.

I return, barely dodging several spears of light that try to impale me. I feel a sudden pressure on my head and I stumble, narrowly avoiding being impaled by another spear of light. *Let me in, Eurael!* I grit my teeth, slicing another spear in half as a bolt comes at me from the other direction. I duck underneath and a block slams into me, holding me down. I stab into it, shoving it off of me. *Eurael, you can't fight us both.* I roll out of the way, rushing toward her. A wall of light comes up suddenly catching me in the chin, sending me tumbling back. *I'm trying to help you!* I wipe blood from my mouth, renewing my assault. She ducks underneath my blade, a blast of energy erupting from her hand. I slam against the far wall, and dozens of spears of light thud into the wall around me, tight enough together that they hold my limbs in place. I struggle, beginning to smoke and blister, but I cannot move.

I growl, tendrils of shadow trying to wrench them free, but they hiss, moving away; I cannot be defeated now! I have finally found her; I came back from the dead to destroy this woman! I try and reach for my sword, but Evermore kicks it out of the way, a twisted smirk on her face. Her hands crackle with energy, and she looks down at me with a mixture of hate and satisfaction.

"Looks like you're a little stuck," she says, her smirk morphing in a sadistic grin. "You won't have to worry about that for long," she says, bending down, grabbing my face, and turning it to look at Scarlett, my skin sizzling and burning. "You see that girl? The one that you went to the Underworld to save? The one you died for?" she smiles, patting my cheek. "I'm going to kill her. I will take them all from you, every last one; *then* you will die." She twists my head to look me directly in the eyes, the scent of burning flesh curling up between us, not even an inch away. She moves next to my ear, her lips parting with the softest audible sound, her voice slithering out in the most familiar way. "That is my revenge."

I look past her, over her shoulder, through the haze of pain filling my vision to my student. Scarlett's hair turns from red to black, her eyes slowly shifting from green to orange, her armor turning into a thin white dress, the scent of wildflowers tickling my nostrils, replacing the stench of combat and death.

"Simiel," I whisper.

"Your sister? Ah yes," I feel her smile next to me, her aura shining brighter as I jerk against the spears. *Quickly, let me take control; I'll get us out of this!* The pressure on my skull mounts, but I clamp my mouth shut, my vision flickering between red and black. "You should know," her breath on my ear halts my movements, my eyes slowly travelling to look at her. "You're not the only Godkiller here, Eurael; you're not the only one who's looking for your sister." She leans back and I begin struggling again; no, this can't happen! I cannot be erased! I must find Simiel; if what she says is true, it is even more important than before. I won't let her erase me!

"No, no!" I roar, shaking. Tendrils of shadow shoot out to Evermore, but she simply turns them to smoke, her hands crackling with white light.

"Goodbye, Eurael," she says with a smile, white light blinding me.

"I will not die!" Mutovinatum shouts, racing through the darkness. I tackle him, the entirety of the darkness rebelling against me underneath my fingers.

"If I am to be erased, I will not allow you to escape. You will share my fate," I growl, holding him down. Tendrils of shadow smack me off him, and he scrambles up, racing away. I hold out my hand and shadows come up, wrapping around his legs, holding him in place; this is my mind. He breaks through them in an instant, but that was all the time I needed to get to him, pulling him backward, my arm wrapped around his throat. "You will not escape this time!" I growl, holding onto him as he claws at my skin, squirming in my hold.

"No! I will not die! I cannot die!" he screams, twisting and turning. "Release me!" I hold him tighter, blood dripping down my arms and body as he claws at me further.

"You wanted to reside in me once again," I growl, my lips right next to his head. "I have only granted your wish."

"No!" he roars, slamming his elbows into my ribs, tendrils of shadow ripping me off him. He scrambles away and I race after him, my body protesting severely with each step I take, each pump of my arms. I will not let him escape this time! He tears a hole in the darkness, and I lunge out toward him.

"No!" I roar, hand outstretched to the light that draws ever closer.

My hand does not move, the spears holding me in place resolutely. I blink sweat and blood out of my eyes, looking up. Mutovinatum stands before me, a solid shadowy figure, his red mouth turned into a grimace, a bolt of white light stuck through him. He swears pro-fusely, groaning.

"You're welcome," Evermore says, as Mutovinatum disappears into smoke. "It seems—"

She stops, her mouth open. She screams out, her light flickering and shimmering; the spears around me disappear, and I stand up quickly. I move forward once the spears disappear, but a wave of energy knocks me back. Her light begins to fill the room, fluctuating as she glows brighter. "No! You can't do this to me!" She screams, her veins turning black, popping out against her skin, nearly wriggling like living things.

"Stop resisting," Mutovinatum growls from her mouth. Her expression is twisted in pain and anguish as she claws at her skin, shaking her head, dark smoke pouring off and sinking into her skin at a rapid rate as she fights off Mutovinatum. Her light fluctuates faster and I run to Z, the barrier lowering.

"When Mutovinatum possesses, her there's going to be a tremen-dous amount of energy released," he says, looking past me warily. "We won't be able to get away in time, and I'm not sure I can protect them," he says, looking at the others, who seem frozen, all their eyes locked on Evermore, stumbling and screaming. I nod, stepping back and the barrier goes up again. I look at Scarlett and see her dark hair, her orange eyes. Simiel. I will not allow you to die again; I protected you in the past, and I will do so again. I keep her firmly in my head as I walk to Evermore; I was unable to save you once, but I will not make that mistake—not here, not now. I spread my arms out, shadows swirling around my feet, expanding around Evermore; I do this for you, sister.

"What are you doing?" Mutovinatum growls.

"Stop!" Evermore cries out, dropping to her hands and knees, tears running down her face as she glows brighter. She screams out, shrieking.

"Eurael!" Mutovinatum shouts. The shadows swirl faster, slowly rising; I keep my breathing steady and calm. I must do this, I have to do this; no other option remains. The shadows rise quicker, covering us now. Evermore shrieks and moans, curling in a ball as her light fluctuates quicker; she's going to give in. Shards of light shoot out, trying to escape from the darkness, but I grit my teeth, forcing the shadows in closer. The light rebels, trying to pierce the darkness; I clench my fists, bringing the shadows in closer. They lay over Evermore, smoking and hissing, blocking out her light. They swirl around, darkness everywhere. Her screams can no longer be heard, wind whipping my hair. I have to do this; it must be done. My breath comes in ragged gasps until the wind steals it away, leaving us in a vacuum. They swirl faster and I close my eyes, sitting down and letting my arms fall; it is out of my control now. They press tighter, trying to crush us into the smallest space possible. I keep my breathing steady as they cover me, pulling me into them, filling me. I did this for you sister; I love you Simiel.

The last thing I can sense before the shadows envelop and swallow me completely is the faint scent of wildflowers, curling pleasantly in my nostrils and resting in my core, where my soul should be.

ACKNOWLEDGMENTS

Great projects are rarely accomplished by a single individual, and *Legend Land* is no different; there were many who contributed to having this novel actually *happen*, and to making my lifelong dream of becoming a published author come true.

This novel would have had a much more difficult time making it out into the wide, scary world if it hadn't been for the support of all those on Kickstarter who backed this behemoth of a book. Specifically I would like to thank the Zolkowski family and my grandparents: Randall and Beth Barfield, and Donnie and Lena Lipe for their significant contributions to my Kickstarter, and helping give this book the boost it needed.

In addition, there are an innumerable amount of family and friends who continued to believe in me every step of the way, and show their support. The road that *Legend Land* took me on was not always an easy one, but it would never have been possible without my mother, Mandy Barfield, constantly encouraging me and my father, Chase Barfield, always being my rock and stability in times of stress, moments where I questioned the point of everything, and other assorted common writer problems. I always want to thank my younger brothers for keeping spice in my life, and making it all very…interesting. A big thanks to everyone at Indigo River Publishing for everything they have done for me; all the guidance they have given and the *incredible* amount of belief they have shown in me. Finally, thank you, dear readers, for purchasing this novel; by doing so you help me continue to do what I love: write. This would never have been possible on my own, and I dedicate this to everyone involved. Everyone, I give a *huge* "thank you" for just…everything. This is for you; enjoy.

www.ingramcontent.com/pod-product-compliance
Lightning Source LLC
Chambersburg PA
CBHW020323140726
47905CB00012B/37